Emperor Norton's Ghost

*Norton I, Emperor of the United States
and Defender of Mexico*

Emperor Norton's Ghost

DIANNE DAY

A Fremont Jones Mystery

DOUBLEDAY

New York London Toronto Sydney Auckland

PUBLISHED BY DOUBLEDAY
a division of Bantam Doubleday Dell Publishing Group, Inc.
1540 Broadway, New York, New York 10036

DOUBLEDAY and the portrayal of an anchor with a dolphin are
trademarks of Doubleday, a division of Bantam Doubleday Dell
Publishing Group, Inc.

Book design by Paul Randall Mize

Library of Congress Cataloging-in-Publication Data
Day, Dianne.
Emperor Norton's ghost: a Fremont Jones mystery / Dianne Day. —
1st ed.
p.   cm.
1. Women detectives—California—San Francisco—Fiction.
2. Feminists—California—San Francisco—Fiction.   3. San Francisco
(Calif.)—Fiction.   4. Carmel (Calif.)—Fiction.   I. Title.
PS3554.A9595E4   1998
813'.54—dc21   98-2809
CIP

ISBN 0-385-48608-1
September 1998
First Edition

1   3   5   7   9   10   8   6   4   2

To Ava Wilson, my dear aunt,
now in the realm of the spirits,

AND TO

Emperor Norton, whose spirit,
both before and after death,
made the people of San Francisco smile

CONTENTS

Emperor Norton's Ghost

ONE

Spirit Shock

AS RECENTLY as a week ago I would not have thought that I, Fremont Jones, should ever find myself in a place such as this. I peered surreptitiously through the dim light in an effort to see if the others present were handling the eerie atmosphere with more equanimity than I. I was, in point of fact, decidedly uncomfortable. Even apprehensive. Only loyalty to my new friend—whose risk was, after all, far greater than mine—kept me in my seat; otherwise I should have bolted. Facing resolutely forward, I sneaked a look at her from the corner of my eye.

My friend, Frances McFadden, waited alertly, eagerly, for the séance to begin. Her eyes glinted, picking up light from the candles that burned in sconces on the wall; her lips were parted and her breath came light and fast. In truth I could not comprehend her attraction to Spiritualism—so great an attraction that she would deceive her husband and come on the sly. I was helping her, of course, out of my own curiosity, as well as a profound belief that one owes it to one's gender to thwart the sort of husband who is forever telling his wife where she may go and what she may do.

We were eight around the table; when the medium entered, she would make nine. Whether there was significance to that number or not, I did not know. The medium's empty chair was to the right of Frances, and Frances at my own right. On my left sat a man who smelled unpleasantly of cheap cigars, a bulky fellow whose scratchy tweed sleeve kept rudely impinging upon my more lightly clad arm. The woman beside him I could not readily see, though with the curve of the round table one would have thought she should fall in my line of vision. I mentally pictured a wife shrinking in her husband's shadow—though I knew neither of them from Adam or Eve.

Continuing clockwise around the table, in the place of honor as it were, directly across from the medium's thronelike chair, sat a handsome man with a hawkish profile. He was clean-shaven but had a good deal of dark, wavy hair on his head—in color either black or brown or dark red; it was impossible to tell without staring rudely in the dim light. Diagonally across from me, next to Mr. Hawk, sat a blob of a pasty-faced woman, whose several chins spilled over the high neck of her fancy black dress and thus obscured most of a very large cameo. She breathed with a wheeze. Two more women made up the balance of the table, both middle-aged and unremarkable in bearing and dress, but I thought a great deal of sadness seemed to emanate from them.

Emanate, indeed! I gave an inward snort. This séance and its oppressive atmosphere must be poisoning my mind—ordinarily I'd have no truck with anything such as emanations, not even in my vocabulary! I should have to watch myself, or I'd become as enamored of the spirit world as Frances.

The room was stifling, all the windows closed and hung with heavy velvet drapes. I squinted and judged the drapes to be dark green, matching the embossed, brocaded wallpaper whose color was just discernible in the candleglow. The silence was thick, disturbed only by the wheezing of Madame Blob. I heard Frances catch a breath in her throat, a little gasp, and at the same moment the candles began to waver and cast weird shadows as if in a draft, although I had neither seen nor heard a door open. From my friend's palpable sense of anticipation, as well as by these slight signs of movement, I guessed the marvelous medium's advent was at hand.

The hawkish man stood up suddenly, raising his eyebrows in an expectant manner. When I moved as if to stand up too, Frances tugged on my skirt and I subsided. The others sat riveted in place. I thought: It is embarrassingly obvious who is the neophyte here. And I concluded that Mr. Hawk, the only man of passable good looks in the room, must be the medium's confederate—which showed she had some taste in men at least, though one had to wonder at her choice of vocation.

"Mrs. Locke!" Mr. Hawk announced, in a voice like a gong. He might as well have prefaced his announcement with "Behold!" for such was clearly his intent.

I made a swift survey of the table to determine which way I should direct my gaze in order to behold, because for the life of me I had seen no door other than the one by which we'd all entered. She would not come in that way, surely? For that door led only to a large, bare entrance hall, which offered no possibility for concealment of the various engines necessary to work the medium's chicanery and deception. Everyone knows that these people are fakes; though I must admit that Frances was convinced quite otherwise.

Suddenly I realized the others were all looking at me! In that same instant I felt a *frisson*, a sort of premonitory rush, and *then*—but curiously not before—directly behind me I heard that door, the *only* door, open. They had been looking not *at* but rather *beyond* me, and I turned around slowly and did the same.

Mrs. Locke, the marvelous medium, was a tiny woman dressed all in lace that may have been white but looked ivory in the candlelight. She moved with dainty steps, and absolutely no facial expression whatsoever, to her chair at the head of the table. She did not acknowledge our presence. Her age was impossible to determine; she was neither pretty nor plain, nor had she any character in her face. She was as near to a mask, or a cipher, as a human being may become. Her male confederate first closed the door and then came with long, efficient strides to assist her into the huge chair, pulling it out, tucking it in, then placing beneath the table a stool for her feet. Despite the fact that her feet could not possibly reach the floor, and that she did need the height of the chair to make her our equal at the table, I nevertheless immediately thought: Aha! The means by which she does her tricks are somehow hidden in the overlarge chair and in that footstool.

I, of course, do not believe in spirits. I believe that when we are dead we go to make dirt, and there's the end to it; but Frances had declared that one session with Mrs. Locke would persuade me otherwise. That was not very likely—yet I had to allow that I could neither deny nor ignore the eerie feeling that pervaded this room. What, I wondered, was its source?

I had previously asked Frances what we might expect at this séance. She had replied: "It is always the same yet different, depending on which spirits come through. They come through her, Mrs. Locke. She doesn't do manifestations—you know, ectoplasmic extrusions and ringing bells and blowing trumpets and all that—she just talks. But not in her own voice; in the voice of the spirits. Oh, and she has a control." Of course she does, I'd thought, and her control will be a Red Indian or an Arab or some two-thousand-year-old man. But Frances had said, "He's a little boy named Toby."

Now Frances seized my right hand and squeezed the life out of it. She shot me a quick, bright-eyed glance, as if to say, *Isn't this the most exciting thing!* And because I myself was so pleased to have a woman friend of about my own age and background, I squeezed her hand back and smiled, although that room was hardly conducive to smiling. A little riffle of nervous anticipation passed through our circle around the table. Mr. Hawk placed a green pillar candle in front of Mrs. Locke and lit it; as he did so, Frances leaned to me and whispered, "Green is Toby's favorite color."

Mrs. Locke said, in a voice like a clear bell, "Thank you, Patrick." So that was Hawk's name; it was the only one I was likely to learn here tonight. Part of the appeal of séances must be, I suppose, the anonymity in which one participates. It makes for more of a thrill. Patrick did not acknowledge her thanks, but went about extinguishing the candles in the wall sconces, then took his seat opposite the medium at the table. The room smelled of burnt candles and something else, something sweetish that I did not like, perhaps incense from the pillar candle into which Mrs. Locke now gazed.

For a moment I studied the medium's perfectly blank face. Her eyes, I noted, were wide and staring.

And after what seemed an unbearable length of time she said, "Let us join hands. By the joining of our hands we declare that we are all pure, honest, and determined in our intent to contact the World of the Spirits." Her voice was high, virginal, of the most convincing sincerity.

I closed my eyes because the others did; I was unconvinced but wavering. I thought: What harm can it do? Why should I not, for Frances's sake, let go my disbelief for the next hour or so, and participate with an open mind? I decided that I would.

The man on my left gripped my hand in a tentative fashion, as if he were afraid of contagion; or perhaps he wanted to bolt and run, as I had earlier. His palm was hard as horn. A laborer, I guessed, perhaps one who works the docks. I wondered what had brought him here. On my other side, Frances's hand felt hot—my own were cold by comparison. Yet, having given up my disbelief, I was now eager to get on with the séance. Burning with curiosity, I opened my eyes.

The flame on the pillar candle seemed hypnotic. For a single light it gave a good deal of illumination. Faces were easily read. The two unremarkable middle-aged women now seemed starkly terrified, with almost identical facial expressions; Madame Blob looked pettish, with her eyes closed; Patrick stared abstractly ahead, nobly serene. Frances, her eyes shut tight, was frowning; she began to rock slightly back and forth. And the medium appeared all of a sudden to be in pain.

"A-a-agh!" she gasped. She twisted about while clinging with great force to the hands of the people on either side of her, one of them being Frances. I fancied—or maybe it really did happen—that a current like electricity shot through all our linked hands. Mrs. Locke slumped forward, then threw her head back. Her neck popped, I heard it, and my own shoulders hiked up to my ears in sympathy.

"Who is here?" That was Patrick's orotund tone, with an edge of urgency added.

Not Toby, I thought, that's no little kid—though precisely why I had that thought, I did not know. A moment later I was proved right.

Mrs. Locke groaned. A sheen of perspiration covered her face, now wreathed about with pain. Frances rocked harder; her hand trembled in mine and I gripped it more tightly.

"Speak to us!" Patrick commanded, "Tell us your name."

The medium started to laugh, but this laughter had no merriment in it. Her clear, high voice had gone all low and harsh. And over to my left a small, hesitant female voice said, "Why, he laughs just like my papa!"

I would not have liked to have someone who sounded like that for *my* father!

The hesitant voice acquired more vigor. "Papa," she said, "we didn't come to talk to you, we came to talk to Mother. To make sure she's all right, and to see if she had something to say to us, since she died all sudden-like."

Somehow I got the feeling this was not how séances were supposed to go. Patrick apparently agreed with me, for he said, "Leave us, Laughing Spirit! You are not wanted here. Mrs. Locke wishes to speak to her control, the boy named Toby." In an aside to the woman I still could not see beyond the man next to me, Patrick added, "Don't worry. Toby will come through and take control. He died when he was just a boy, you see, but he's a good, strong soul and he's devoted to our Mrs. Locke."

I did not find Patrick's words particularly reassuring. The older I grow, the more experience has caused me to question the commonly held belief that good in the end triumphs over bad, or evil. I watched the medium—she was having a time of it, as if to prove my point. No more of that harsh laughter came from her throat, but she had begun to growl. Yes, growl, and snarl, like a dog. Her mouth simply hung open and the sounds poured out of it. The extreme oddity of this gave me the shivers. Her eyes were open too, fixed on nothing. Her head slumped in an unnatural posture against one shoulder, as if her neck had been broken, and a shudder passed through me as I remembered that awful pop.

I closed my eyes, concentrating, willing the boy ghost Toby to come through. But it was no use; Frances distracted me with her rocking and, besides, the medium began to bark! A fierce, raucous barking that might have been funny but wasn't. My eyes flew open. The barks apparently had jerked Mrs. Locke out of her slump; at least her neck wasn't broken. But now she was being tossed about like a rag doll, held in her place at the table only by her hands still linked to Frances and one of the terrified middle-aged women. This was most bizarre!

Madame Blob wheezed uncontrollably—I was becoming alarmed for her. The middle-aged sisters gawked at the medium's antics less with terror now than consternation, and Patrick called out: "Break the circle! Drop hands immediately! Our dear Mrs. Locke is in trouble!"

There was a good deal of gasping, plus a terminal-sounding wheeze from Madame Blob, while hands were dropped all around the table like hot potatoes. The medium continued to bark, sporadically now, and with less ferocity. But Frances would not let go my hand, nor Mrs. Locke's. Frances still was rocking, and I whipped my head around to regard her in alarm.

Her eyes were screwed shut, and the strain I felt in her iron grip was written on her features. Above the lace of her collar, the cords of her neck stood out. Her lips were drawn back from her teeth in a grimace, and her chin thrust forward. Suddenly, on the forward apex of her rock, she went rigid.

I thought: She is in trance!

The candle flame trembled and came dangerously close to extinguishing itself—although there was not a breath, not a whisper of moving air in the room.

The medium let loose another flurry of barks.

Patrick came hurrying around the table to plant himself between the medium and Frances, urging *sotto voce*, "Let go! Something has gone terribly wrong, you must let go!" He attempted to pry my friend's fingers from Mrs. Locke's hand, and I did not know what to do. I worried that somehow his interference might injure them in some way, as they now seemed both to be in the same unnatural state, but what did I know of these things? The very air was charged, and my skin all over little prickles. I hadn't the slightest idea what was going on.

As I fretted over what to do, Frances opened both her eyes and her mouth, and a deep, rough voice, not at all like her own, came from her throat: "Lazarus, come away from there!"

This caused more gasping all around. The medium whined once and fell back in her chair, Frances fell forward onto the table, all of a sudden limp as a wet noodle, and I had my hand back. So, one assumed, must Mrs. Locke.

Sounding the paragon of reason, at least to my own ears, I remarked, "We need more light to help us ascertain what has happened here."

"A moment, a moment." Patrick hovered over Mrs. Locke, but I could not see what he was doing because his back was to me. As no one else volunteered to light the wall sconces, we still had no illumination but the one candle. I did not want to leave my friend's side. With Patrick so solicitous of his own friend, employer, mistress—perhaps she was to him all three—I turned my attention to Frances as best I could in the near dark.

I placed my hand on the center of her back below the shoulder blades and found that she was breathing slowly and regularly. Somebody said, "Oh dear," and someone else said, "Well I never!" and the man next to me rumbled, "We oughter get our money back if that's all there's gonna be to it." I put my head near hers and called softly, "Frances, can you hear me?" I repeated this several times, with no result whatever.

Mrs. Locke, however, had recovered and was holding a whispered conference with her solicitous confederate. He straightened up and said, "Mrs. Locke requests that you all keep your seats." Then he went about relighting the candles in the wall sconces. I reflected, as I rubbed Frances's back, how much simpler it would be if they had electric lighting in this place. Or even gas, though now that I have been away from it for a while, I daresay gaslight smells rather unpleasant.

The sense of disturbance around the table subsided somewhat, and I became gradually uncomfortable from everyone's staring at me and Frances. Everyone except Mrs. Locke, who had her hand to her head, obscuring her eyes, in a pose I thought overdramatic. My skepticism had returned; I wondered if some piece of elaborate chicanery had gone wrong, injuring an innocent in the process—for Frances was still out cold. My suspicions made me bold, and I addressed the medium directly, for surely if anyone were in charge it was she!

"Mrs. Locke," I said, then waited until her hand descended from its pose. Except for the fact that some of her hair had escaped its pins, she seemed none the worse for her recent experience. The blank expression had reclaimed her face; she looked like a life-sized doll. She did not look at me or in any way acknowledge my address, but I went on nevertheless: "Perhaps you can tell me what to do for my friend? She seemed to go into trance along with you. Surely we must bring her around!"

Slowly, and a little jerkily, like one of the automatons in Mr. Sutro's Palace, the medium turned her head upon her neck—just her head, the rest of her body did not move a jot—until her face met mine. I watched anger build up in her dark eyes, which she then proceeded to unleash on me and poor unconscious Frances.

"Get out!" Mrs. Locke shrilled. "Get out of here, both of you! How dare you come to one of my séances under false pretenses! You have created a disruption on the etheric plane, disturbed the vibrations, and caused a breach with my contact in the spirit world. You must go. Now!"

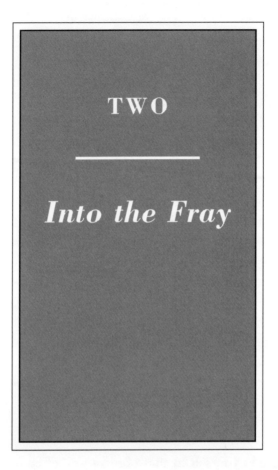

TWO

Into the Fray

BUT HOW," asked my friend Michael Kossoff, who used to call himself by the pseudonymous surname Archer, "could you leave there with Mrs. McFadden unconscious, or in a trance, or whatever it was?"

I stretched my stocking-clad feet toward the fire luxuriously, rotating my ankles. Now that the experience was all behind me, it made a good story, and from the other end of the couch Michael listened intently while I continued: "Patrick, the man with the face like a hawk, carried her to the auto. Frances was in a trance, that is for certain. It was no ordinary faint. And besides"—having toasted them sufficiently, I tucked my feet beneath me, Indian

11

style, and leaned back in the cushions—"I heard her myself speaking in that strange voice. It really was the most peculiar thing!"

"Hmm," said Michael, frowning and drawing his black eyebrows together in an ominous fashion.

"Oh dear," I said, "I hate it when you do that."

"My dear Fremont," he said, still frowning, "I am not *doing* anything."

"Well of course you are!" I reached over, stretching my arm until my fingertips touched his forehead, and then I rubbed away the puckers between his shapely brows. "You are frowning and saying *Hmm* in a way that means, *I shall have to look into this matter.* I will not have you investigating my friends, Michael! It won't do."

He seized my hand and kissed my fingers. A quite delicious thrill went through me and I grew much warmer than could be accounted for by the fire alone. Then he began, by tugging on the hand he'd trapped, to pull me toward him. His frown was gone but one of those expressive eyebrows arched sharply up and he said, "With your record for making peculiar friends, the bestowing of your friendship should, in itself, be sufficient to warrant an investigation."

"You include yourself in that observation, of course."

"Not really." He tucked me under his arm, and I rested my cheek upon his chest. He was wearing a smoking jacket over pajamas, having bathed while I was out at the séance with Frances, and he smelled of Pears soap.

"Oh?" I angled my head the better to look up at his face. It is quite a distinguished face—especially since he has grown his beard back—but sometimes I miss that surprising little dent in his chin. "I suppose you think you are not peculiar?"

He chuckled and his eyes danced. "I think, rather, that I am not about to investigate myself, and your own as yet rudimentary investigatory skills would not get you very far if you were to turn them on me."

12

"Is that so?" I reached stealthily behind me, seized upon a small needlepoint pillow, and then in one fluid motion sat up and bashed him with it. This aggressive act brought on a flurry of physical contact that ended with us both naked, sated, on the hearthrug in front of the fire.

After that, spirits and séances did not seem at all important.

I awoke in my own bed, with that distressing feeling of having slept too late—though how one knows one has slept too late before even being awake enough to see the clock, I have no idea. It is one of life's little mysteries that has yet to yield itself to my assiduous probing. A glance at the clock provided confirmation; nevertheless I took the time to gaze fondly at the tousled, dark head on the pillow beside me before I nudged its owner with my elbow.

"Michael, wake up. We've slept too long!"

He growled and groused, but as he was making little noises I knew he was awake. Regretfully—I do so hate getting up in the morning—I slipped from under the covers before he could reach for me, for if I did not, we would soon make ourselves even later. I thrust my feet into my slippers and grabbed my robe from the bedpost, belting it around me as I went to the window and looked out.

Fog still shrouded the hills, but from this north-facing window I glimpsed a glow through the mist, proof that the sun would soon break through. Every morning when I got up, the first thing I did was to come to this window and give thanks for being back in San Francisco. While the Monterey Peninsula had been an interesting and beautiful place to spend most of the previous year, this was better. This was my true home. Even if our big, Italianate double house at the north end of Divisadero Street did belong mostly to Michael.

Michael shuffled over to me, wrapped his arms around my rib cage just below my breasts, and dropped his head into the curve between my neck and shoulder. His lips fastened on my skin and he rumbled like a rusty old cat: "If you would marry me, Fremont, I wouldn't have to spend so many blasted mornings going clear back to my side of the house to get dressed."

"Hush!" I replied affectionately, giving him a peck on the head and a little shove toward the door. "If you were at all serious, you'd never mention marriage at this time of day, when I'm most likely to refuse whatever's on offer. I'll make our coffee downstairs in the office this morning. We don't want to miss any clients."

"God forbid!" Michael yawned and stretched and rubbed his eyes, but I did not feel in the least sorry for him. I knew once he'd washed his face and brushed his teeth he would be wide awake and bursting with energy much sooner than I. In the doorway he turned and said, "I suppose I'm elected to go to the bakery for muffins, then? No chance of a real cooked breakfast?"

"There isn't time."

Michael went off into the hallway muttering something about changing the hour of opening to ten o'clock, but I knew he would never do it. A certain percentage of the (admittedly few) clients we have already had find it necessary to stop by our office before going to their own work. Therefore we open every day, except Sunday, at eight-thirty. I myself would prefer a later hour, but it is not practical.

Our business, which has been in existence for roughly six months, is called the J&K Agency: J and K standing for Jones and Kossoff, of course. Our card, and the brass oval on the front door at my side—the north side—of our double house provide slightly more information about the nature of our business:

THE J&K AGENCY

DISCREET INQUIRIES

J&K was Michael's idea: He claims that with the agency we can capitalize on my natural talent and his own acquired skills. (For complex reasons having to do with family and circumstance, Michael has been a spy for most of his life; but for the past couple of years he has been trying, with some success, to extricate himself from spying.) I cannot argue with his reasoning, and have been happy that he is teaching me the rudiments of the investigatory process—though I daresay I could learn quite a lot faster than Michael is willing to teach. It is only the discreet part of this inquiry business that consistently gives me trouble.

Fortunately we have one already well-trained employee, a young man (well, I suppose he is about my own age, but somehow he seems younger) named Aloysius Stephenson. He prefers, for obvious reasons, to be called Wish. Wish is one of those rare individuals who are too honest for their own good, and therefore it was not difficult for Michael and me to lure him away from his job with the San Francisco Police Department, where he was forever getting himself into hot water.

The three of us do well together. Michael is, as it were, the head honcho of our little outfit, being both chief adviser and principal investor. I am more or less an indentured servant, having signed a promissory note to Michael for one third of the house (corresponding to the part I live in) and one half the cost of starting up the business. This was necessary if we were to be partners, for I have no means of my own until I come into my inheritance—a thought not to be borne as in itself it implies my father's death. Sometimes the one-sidedness of our supposed partnership does bother me.

It was bothering me now, as I twisted my reddish-brown hair into a coil and pinned it into a figure eight at the nape of my neck. I frowned at myself in the mirror, feeling suddenly giddy and disoriented by the riskiness of my refusal to marry. For Michael could change his mind, withdraw his support, dissolve our partnership at any time, without damage to himself; whereas I . . .

"No," I said aloud, "this train of thought will not do!" I finished dressing, took a last look in the mirror, pinched my cheeks to give them color, and headed downstairs. As I went, I reminded myself that, even should the worst happen and Michael grow tired of me, I would be no worse off than I had been before accepting his proposal that we make a partnership of our lives and our work. Actually, I should be better off for the excellent training Michael was giving me—soon I should be able to snoop and spy and detect along with the best of the professionals. And of course I still had my typewriter.

I trailed my hand over that dear machine as I passed the desk where I kept the records and typed up the reports. When my training period was over, and we had sufficient business to warrant it, we would hire a secretary. But for the moment I served in that capacity as well as junior investigator. Wish was senior investigator. Michael preferred to remain behind the scenes, in his advisory capacity.

The downstairs of my side of the double house constituted J&K's office suite. The front parlor was for reception and initial interviews, the dining room provided a conference room, the morning or breakfast room had become Michael's private sanctum; but the kitchen was still a kitchen and that was where all three of us—Michael, Wish, and I—spent most of our time. The hands of the big Regulator clock on the kitchen wall clicked into the eight o'clock position as I spooned ground coffee into the percolator, and I thought, *In half an hour Wish will be along, and I will ask him what he knows about Mr. McFadden, Frances's husband.*

"Jeremy McFadden," Wish Stephenson said, then paused to blow across the top of his coffee cup, "lives in one of those big houses over thataway a few blocks." He waved his long, lanky arm vaguely in the direction of Van Ness Avenue.

"I know where they live, Wish," I said impatiently. "I want to know more about the man himself. What he's like. What he does for a living, who his friends are, that kind of thing." *And why his wife is so afraid of him*, I added silently.

There was a part of the séance story that I had not told Michael the previous night. With some help from the redoubtable Patrick, Frances had come out of her trance shortly after we had arranged her, sitting upright, in the passenger seat of Michael's Maxwell automobile. She had seemed fine, yet I'd insisted on accompanying her into her house for a restorative cup of tea. I wanted to be sure she was completely well before going on my way. And she had seemed to be, aside from the curious fact that she could not remember anything about the medium's barking, or her own odd utterance of "Lazarus, come away from there!" I was, of course, dying to know more about this Lazarus. In my imagination I saw him shrouded, emerging from the grave; but the words associated with that vision were "Come forth!" not "Come away."

At any rate, Frances became quite animated as we drank our tea. Her cheeks regained their color and her eyes their usual spark. I was reassured, until we heard the sound of a door—a heavy one, probably the front—opening, followed by ponderous footsteps in the hall, at which point all color drained from my friend's face. She said, "Oh no!" in a strangled voice, shoved her tea—the cup rattling in its saucer—onto the table, grabbed my arm in a hard grip, and pulled me close.

"He wasn't supposed to be back for hours! You mustn't tell him where we've been," she said in a terrified whisper. "He can't know, he must never know I left the house after dark!"

Frances stood up just as those heavy steps reached the arched entry to the parlor where we sat. Before my very eyes I watched a remarkable transformation in her countenance as she composed herself. Though her skin remained pale, her face smoothed out into placidity, she lifted her chin and turned as she clasped her hands together in front of her to stop their trembling. "Mr. Mc-Fadden," she said formally to her husband, and as I rose I wondered if she always called him thus, "this is my friend Mrs. Jones, who has stopped by on an errand of mercy."

"How do," Mr. McFadden replied abruptly, snapping his head up and down in a nod. He wore full whiskers that covered heavy jowls, in a now outmoded style once made popular by the younger Vanderbilts. He was an enormous figure, large without being fat; I thought him extremely unattractive. He looked, very simply, like a mean man. And he was clearly skeptical of me. His eyes roamed rudely over my body and he said, "A little late, isn't it, to be doing errands of any kind." It was a pronouncement, not a question, and he went on: "I assume your husband knows your whereabouts, madam."

"Of course," I replied, taking a kind of prickly pleasure in the opportunity for mendacity. "My husband is fully supportive of all my charitable endeavors."

"The vehicle at the curb would be yours, then." He said "vehicle" with disdain, as if poor Max were not at all good enough for a McFadden's high standards.

"If you mean the Maxwell, then yes, it is ours. My husband's and mine." I could imagine how droll Michael would find this conversation, with me repeatedly referring to him as my husband. I was rather enjoying it myself.

"And the charity you support, which requires you to be out so late of an evening, what would that be?"

"Why, the Widows and Orphans of Deceased Seafarers, of course," I said, making one up on the spot. "Surely you've heard of our campaign?"

"Can't say as I have, no." The enormous man rocked forward onto the balls of his feet, leaning toward me in a manner I found rather threatening, although I was separated from him by a distance of several feet.

Frances was suddenly at my side, tugging my arm. "Mrs. Jones was just leaving. I've told her I'm overcommitted to my own charities at the moment. If you'll excuse me, Mr. McFadden, while I accompany her to the door?''

And with that, Frances had guided me deftly around her husband and into the hall. Once there, she'd kept grimly on toward the door and had refused to answer any of my whispered questions, only shaking her head. In nothing flat, I had found myself outside.

Now Wish Stephenson said, "I can look up his club membership if you want me to. Living in a house like that, he must have a club. Then I'd go round and talk to the club help, find out all about him that way.''

From behind the pages of *The Chronicle*, Michael said, "No need for that, Wish. Jeremy McFadden belongs to the Parnassus Club, like his daddy before him. Daddy was a land speculator. Jeremy does his speculating in the stock market. He's seldom at his club, so it would do you no good to inquire there. Fremont''— he lowered the paper so that he could peer over it—''why do you want to know?''

"Because," I said, "his wife is afraid of him."

"Ah," said Michael, nodding his head, as if that explained everything, and then he retreated behind the newspaper again.

I turned to Wish. "It wouldn't do any harm, I suppose—that is, if you just happened to be passing by the Parnassus Club—if you were to slip in the back door and ask a question or two? Even if he's seldom there, someone might know something. Who knows, the cook could be his old nursemaid.''

Michael snorted.

I pretended I hadn't heard, going on: "You'll never know if you don't ask. But don't go out of your way, Wish. This isn't a real investigation, not a paid inquiry or anything. Just my own curiosity, that's all.''

Wish grinned. He has an open, bony yet sensitive face and a wide mouth that seems even wider when he smiles. "I'd sooner go out of my way for you, Fremont, than for anybody rich enough to hire us, and that's a fact! Sure I'll see what I can do for you.''

Michael snorted again.

I buttered another muffin and winked at Wish, who blushed a bit and gulped down the rest of his coffee. With Michael, the two of us were often like a couple of kids plotting mischief against a favorite teacher. Not that we'd ever actually *do* anything . . .

''Well,'' Wish said, pushing back from the table, ''I'm off.''

''You still working that same case?'' Michael lowered the paper to his lap.

''Yeah. Checking the cemeteries now. I don't think we'll ever find that poor man's daughter. I don't feel good about continuing to take his money, and that's a fact, but he says leave no stone unturned. Gotten down to the tombstones now.'' Wish shook his head dolefully.

''If that's what he wants,'' I said softly. The client had come to San Francisco from up in the northern part of the state, around Eureka, in search of his married daughter who had just stopped writing home about a year ago. He claimed he'd had one letter from her after the earthquake, saying she and her husband had survived, but nothing since. Missing people were still very hard to trace, because so many had simply left; and though no one talked openly about it, there had been bones recovered from the ashes of the great fire that would likely remain forever unidentified.

''Yeah, well,'' Wish said, ''I'm planning to finish up today. I can't stand much more of it myself. Stopping by the Parnassus will make a nice diversion, Fremont. See you later, Michael.''

''Right,'' Michael said, returning to his paper.

''You're unusually taciturn this morning,'' I commented, licking butter from my fingers.

Michael said nothing until we heard the front door close behind Wish; there is a little bell on that door, so it is easy to tell when someone goes in or out. I affixed the bell myself and am most fond of it, because it reminds me of one I had on the door of my first office, on Sacramento Street, some three years ago. As the bell's silvery tone subsided, Michael carefully folded the newspaper in half, and then by half again, and set it precisely on the table beside his plate.

"What?" I asked, already suspicious. I knew that look in his eye. It was a superior, I-Know-More-About-This-Than-You-Could-Ever-Hope-To sort of look.

"You think your friend is afraid of her husband."

"I *know* she is!"

"She confided this to you?"

"She didn't have to. I could tell!" I said hotly. "So would you have been able to tell, if you'd been there. And besides, she did say that he mustn't ever know that she'd gone out of their house after dark. Imagine that! Even though we were together, properly chaperoning each other, and it was early in the evening."

"But you did go to a séance. Not, for example, to the opera."

My cheeks were burning. I knew he had a point there, but still my chin went up and I said: "So?"

Michael wore his most serious face. He is of Russian descent, with almost black, silver-shot hair and beard, high cheekbones, a straight nose, eyes that are sometimes blue and sometimes gray, depending, I think, on his inner weather, and a most expressive mouth. His eyes at the moment were slate gray and his lips formed an uncompromising line. Yet, to my surprise, he did not meet me head on, but rather asked a sidewise question. "Where, again, did you first meet Frances McFadden?"

"At the little library on Green Street. We are both frequent patrons. We grew to recognize one another, and so one day last week, as we were leaving the library at the same time, I invited her to accompany me to that new tea shop over on Van Ness. Frances and I are most compatible, Michael."

Indeed, Frances and I had talked in a way that a woman may

only talk to another woman, deeply and confidingly. Therefore I knew she had come from modest circumstances to marry a wealthy man; and she knew about my flight from respectability in Boston to freedom in San Francisco, and that I did not intend to compromise my freedom by marrying anyone. And then I'd mentioned my arrangement with Michael. Of course I'd feared rejection all the while I was telling her the truth, but she had not rejected me. Rather the opposite: Frances had been full of understanding and admiration. For such a friend I would do much, whether Michael liked it or not.

"Your father must be an unusual man," Michael said, still moving sideways.

"I don't quite take your point," I said, though he hadn't made one yet.

"My point is this: It is not unusual for a man to be unhappy if his wife goes out without him, particularly after dark. And most men would be unhappy in the extreme to find out that their wives were becoming involved in Spiritualist practices."

"Why is that, why 'in the extreme,' Michael?"

"Because the vast predominance of mediums are female. They seem to have certain, ah, powers. It smacks, my dear Fremont, of witchcraft. And anything that smacks of witchcraft makes us men uncomfortable. Most women too, I daresay."

"I thought that was what you'd say." I nodded impatiently. "But I still don't understand. Surely you don't expect me to pay attention to something just because it's the opinion of most people?"

Michael chuckled; for just a moment his eyes flashed, but then he sobered again. And perhaps by contrast to the moment of jocularity, he seemed even more somber than before. "Fremont, I do not think it's a good idea for you to come between a man and his wife," he said, "and I am deeply concerned. Jeremy McFadden's father was a rough character, and I have no reason to believe

Jeremy is not equally rough himself. If you continue to befriend Frances, it had better be on terms that are acceptable to her husband."

I arched my brows and wriggled my toes, just itching to tap my foot under the table, but I did not. I said: "Or else . . . what?"

THREE

Father, Dear Father

I DID NOT GET my question answered—which was just as well, since probably I should not have liked the answer—because at that moment the little bell on the front door jingled and someone called out, in a rather timid voice, "Hello?"

"I'll go," I said quickly, and sped away.

I arrived in the front office (the former parlor) just as a young man in a Western Union uniform came to a halt in the doorway, with a confused look on his face.

"Come in," I said in a manner I hoped would encourage him to overcome his hesitation.

He looked down at the envelope in his hand, then at me, and took two steps forward. He was a pale fellow, and from beneath the uniform's cap his yellow hair stuck out like straw, suggesting a truly dreadful haircut. He had a lost air, and my heart went out to him.

"I'm looking for somebody named Fremont Jones," he said. "This is the right address. But is it a house or a business? I got a residence address."

"It is both, my residence being upstairs and my business being right here. I am Fremont Jones." I smiled warmly and moved forward. "You are in the right place. I take it that you have a telegram for me?"

"Yes, ma'am." He made as if to hand me the envelope with one hand, while getting a notebook from an inner pocket with the other. For a less awkward person this would have been easy, but this poor fellow became all elbows and angles, as the notebook stuck in his pocket and he let go of the envelope before it was quite in my hand.

I restrained my impulse to retrieve the telegram, else we should have bumped heads; I had to restrain my impulse to laugh, too. He would have thought I was laughing at him, although I would have been laughing at the situation, and at the awkwardness of boys in adolescence. He could not be long out of school. Or perhaps circumstances had forced him to work when he would have preferred to be at his lessons.

"Sorry, ma'am," he muttered, handing over the envelope a second time.

"That is perfectly all right," I replied, moving to my desk and opening the top drawer, while glancing curiously at the telegram. I would have loved to rip it open right on the spot but a desire to be kind to its deliverer took precedence.

"You have to sign for it!" he cried, as if afraid I would disappear, although I had moved only a few feet.

"Of course," I said, rummaging in the drawer and coming up with a half dollar, "and so I shall, if you will be so good as to come over to the desk."

He came like a cautious cat investigating new territory, shoulders hunched and eyes wide. "I don't get asked in much. I mean, mostly people just keep me standing at the door."

He fumbled his notebook open and offered it to me, indicating with a callused finger the line for me to sign. This boy had until recently done some heavy physical work, judging by the condition of his hands.

I signed with a bit of a flourish and returned the notebook. "And this is for your trouble," I said, slipping the large coin into his hand.

"Oh," he said, shaking his head, "I got no troubles now. I got a fine job, soon's I learn how to do it some faster, learn my way around the big city and all."

Now I did laugh, lightly; and I sensed that Michael had arrived somewhere behind me, but he was hanging back. I cannot tell how I am able to do it, but I usually know when Michael is anywhere about, whether I can see him or not. To the Western Union boy I said, "You must keep the money anyway—it's a gratuity for services rendered. A tip."

His face shone as if the sun had come up behind his light brown eyes. "Oh, a tip! Yes, ma'am, thank you, ma'am. It's my first one of those."

"How many days have you been on the job, then?"

"This is my second, and I best be moving on. Thanks again."

"You are entirely welcome."

Michael came forward as the bell jingled behind the delivery boy letting himself out.

"You were lurking at the other side of the arch, I take it," I commented without turning around. There is a deep archway between the office and the conference room—it is, in effect, a little tunnel about three feet in depth. It is an architectural anomaly that neither Michael nor I have accounted for, as the space between the walls of what used to be parlor and dining room is not occupied by any cabinet or closet.

"I was listening to you flirt with the delivery boy."

"Eavesdropping." I slit the envelope with a letter opener.

"Spying," said Michael with his version of an evil chuckle.

"Michael!" I exclaimed. "This is astonishing! I do believe I had better sit down." I sat in the chair at the desk and read the telegram again.

"May I inquire who it is that has so astonished you?" Michael leaned against a corner of the desk, crossing his ankles.

"My father! First of all, he has addressed the telegram not to Caroline but to Fremont, and he's *never* done that before!" In fact, my use of my middle name rather than my first name had been a sore spot between us ever since I began the practice on my move to California three, going on four, years ago. "Let me read it to you:

" 'DEAREST DAUGHTER STOP AM COMING TO SAN FRANCISCO TO CELEBRATE YOUR BIRTHDAY WITH YOU STOP HAVE MADE RESERVATIONS AT HOTEL SAINT FRANCIS STOP ARRIVING NEXT MONTH ON THE NINTH AT FOUR PM STOP COMING ALONE STOP YOUR LOVING FATHER.'

"I must say, I'm stunned."

"So I gather. But why? Other than speaking of the devil, of course."

I frowned up at my partner, my friend, my lover, about whom my father knew absolutely nothing. Yet. "I beg your pardon?"

"Speak of the devil and he sends you a telegram. I mentioned your father not long ago, when we were in the kitchen. I said he must be an unusual man. Surely, Fremont, you will be glad to see him. Especially as he says he's coming alone. As I recall, it is your stepmother you're not too fond of."

"Don't call her that! Eeuw! I prefer not to hear the word 'mother,' in any form, in the same sentence with that woman. Just call her by her name, which is Augusta. Anyway, you are quite right, I'm not at all fond of her, but Father is besotted. He positively adores Augusta. How odd that he would come alone!" I jiggled my foot and tapped the telegram against my lip, thinking.

"If he's coming to celebrate your birthday, and he knows how you feel about Augusta, then I should say he's being considerate of your feelings."

"Yes, I suppose so, but still, it's most peculiar."

"You don't look very happy about it. You haven't seen your father in, let's see, how long?"

"Since January of 1905. As it is now mid-March of 1908, it has been three years and three months." As I toted up the months and years in my head, I felt a pang, a deepening ache that told me I had indeed missed my father more than I wanted to allow myself to know, or to feel.

"And how old will you be on this birthday, which, as well as I remember, will take place on the tenth of next month?"

"I will be twenty-five." I looked up at my lover. "So old."

"No, my darling," he said, bending to kiss my lips, "so young."

I had a job to do, I could not hang around the office fretting over Father—or rather, fretting over what I suspected Father would think about my chosen style of life when he saw it with his own eyes. It was one thing to persuade myself I did not care, with Father a whole continent away; quite another thing entirely, now I knew he was coming. But I mustn't think about that now.

I went upstairs to my abode, which was quite spacious, lacking only a kitchen; this was not inconvenient in the least because I generally joined Michael for meals, in his side of the house. If for some strange reason I felt inclined to prepare a meal, I could always do it in the kitchen downstairs on the first floor. I had turned my second-floor rooms into a parlor, a bedroom, and the beginnings of a library. As I was furnishing them myself out of my meager means, everything looked rather sparse still.

Father will be shocked, I thought as I opened my shabby little wardrobe cabinet and retrieved the garment that constitutes my disguise.

I was dismayed by my inability to put his visit out of my head, and to stop caring what he would think. It is so hard to bear the disapproval of a parent, especially so for me with Father. I was only fourteen when my mother died, and he did not marry again until after my twenty-first birthday, so the bond between us had grown especially strong.

When I looked at myself in the long mirror, to be sure I'd done up all my buttons properly, there was a film of tears in my eyes. I swiped at them once with the back of my hand, pressed my lips together firmly, and stood tall with shoulders square. That would do, but my disguise was not yet complete. It lacked the hat, which I was loath to put on because I hate hats.

To tell the truth I was none too fond, either, of the long gray coat that covered me from neck to toe. It was absolutely plain yet tolerably well cut, buttoned all down the front with cheap but matching mother-of-pearl buttons. A more boring garment can scarcely be imagined, but that was the point: to render me unremarkable. Michael said it was quite a chore to render me unremarkable, due to my height—five feet eight inches, which is tall for a woman—and a number of other factors he declined to mention. Nor did I insist upon enlightenment, being somewhat wary of what he might say.

It was the loathsome hat that made my disguise most effective. In a style that had been popular a couple of decades earlier, this hat came down low in the back to cover my hair, almost like a bonnet; it had a little peaked brim, trimmed in ruching, from which hung a half veil. That is to say, the veil covered half my face: forehead, eyes, nose. Altogether this did not leave much of me to be recognized.

A few moments later I tapped on the door of Michael's little private room downstairs and said in a slightly raised voice, "I'm off. Wish should be back here shortly but in the meantime—"

The door opened so abruptly it startled me, and Michael was standing there with a gleam in his eyes, finishing the sentence: "I know, I'll answer the telephone and listen for the door. You look so demure in that outfit, Fremont; it makes me want to ravish you."

I took a couple of steps backward. "Don't you dare! I haven't time to do up all these buttons again."

"A kiss then," said Michael, aiming his lips toward the one section of my anatomy that remained uncovered. And a fine kiss it was, too.

With a deep, abiding surge of affection I touched his cheek, replied, "I will," to his counsel that I be careful, and sailed out of the house.

When Michael proposed, several months ago, that he and I start up a business of private investigation, I had felt in one way excited by the prospect, and in another resigned to it—the latter due to something very bad, indeed irrevocable, that had happened to me the previous year. I didn't like to think of it, and never spoke of it, not even to Michael; yet this bad thing had changed me. Even more than the Great Earthquake did—and that event had changed all of us who went through it.

I parked the Maxwell a few blocks from my destination and walked the rest of the way, into a part of the City called North Beach. As I walked, I thought of the days when I'd first come to San Francisco, with nothing but a typewriter and a lot of hope. The memory seemed to shine with a kind of innocence, now gone forever.

If Father ever finds out what I did last year, it will kill him.

A shudder passed through me, but I raised my chin higher and quickened my steps, and the moment of unpleasantness was soon behind me. I walked briskly until Columbus Avenue came in sight, then I slowed to a sedate pace, relaxed my shoulders into a kind of Victorian slope, and directed my gaze downward. Or so it should appear. In reality, though the angle of my head suggested demurely downcast eyes, I was making the fullest use of my peripheral vision—albeit through a haze of gray veil.

The J&K Agency had been hired to identify a petty thief whose crime sounded negligible until one realized that when small items are stolen day after day, month after month, the cost does mount. The police, when told of missing cabbages and spools of thread and suchlike, had not been particularly zealous in their attention to the problem. So the victims, Mr. and Mrs. Garofalo, had asked us to find out who was repeatedly robbing their corner grocery and dry goods store in broad daylight. This was my third day on the job. I suppose I needn't say I had not yet had any results. As the Garofalos had been none too keen to have a woman investigator to begin with, I hoped to come through for them soon.

I felt my pulse quicken, and a pleasant little tingle of alertness that comes when I arrive on the scene. Surveillance does not bore me as it does our more experienced investigator, Wish Stephenson. He says that's because I'm new at it, and he may be right; but I think this business excites me because I know I have a talent for it. From the time when Michael first took me in hand (professionally, that is) and began to train me, I had excelled—for example, at being taken into a room, left there for five minutes, and then removed and asked to name the objects I had seen. Right away I'd been able to recite almost all. When it comes to remembering what I have heard, as opposed or in addition to what I have seen, I possess the curious ability of total recall. Entire conversations implant themselves in my brain word for word—yet if I were to read the same on a printed page, from memory I should only be able to paraphrase it. This total recall is not something I ever had to learn; I seem to have been born that way.

Being able to acutely observe with one's peripheral vision is definitely a learned skill, however, and it can give one a headache after a while. My head had started to ache, and I had been thinking that if I didn't spot this thief soon Mama and Papa Garofalo would be sure to attribute my failure to my gender, when a blur of rapid movement off to my left caught my eye.

Aha! I thought. *I am about to be vindicated.* I had proposed to the Garofalos a theory that their thief might likely be a woman, who could more easily hide upon her person the wide variety of objects that were disappearing; in fact, it was this argument that had finally persuaded them to accept me as their investigator. And now the only figure in the region where I'd seen the blur proved to be female. On closer inspection, she was not a woman so much as a girl who looked scarcely out of childhood, despite the fact that she appeared to be *enceinte* (as one says to be polite) herself.

I watched this fallen angel for half an hour, and then I followed her home. She was clever. Like the deceitful child who shares by counting out "one for you and two for me," she shopped by pocketing two items for each one she put in her basket, so that she appeared to be a paying customer. She lived in the neighborhood, and in fact, when I went back to the Garofalos' store and told them to call the police to that address, they were shocked. They did not want to believe their thief could be their neighbor, a daily customer.

"Nevertheless," I said, "I observed her in the act of stealing. I expect the police will find that she has been doing a nice little business in selling and trading stolen goods out of her home; and further, that they will find this clever but bent girl is no more expecting a child than I am."

"Oh!" said Mama Garofalo, shocked that I would mention the girl's condition. Her hand flew up to cover her mouth as if it had been she, not I, who'd said the indelicate words.

I proceeded to be more indelicate still: "People naturally avert their eyes. Just think how many things could be hidden beneath her clothes, in a pouch that size!"

Papa Garofalo bit his lip, narrowed his eyes at me shrewdly, and with one nod of his head, reached for the telephone. "Hello, Central," he said, "get me the police."

With a great deal of satisfaction I said, "I won't stay to see her arrested. I know they will find the evidence on her premises. And you will receive the bill for my services in tomorrow's mail."

Then I sailed out of the door in fine fettle. The hat was off before I'd walked half a block.

I stopped the Maxwell on Broadway in front of the McFadden house, which I supposed someone like Mr. Jeremy McFadden might call the McFadden mansion; it was certainly big enough. Being west of Van Ness, it had received very little damage in the quake and fire two years before. And while the formerly great neighborhoods like Nob Hill were still disrupted by the noise and clutter of rebuilding, this area had come into its own as a desirable place to live. The view, similar to that from my bedroom window on Divisadero, was rather spectacular and compensated for the precipitousness of the house's hillside site.

After carefully setting the handbrake, for I certainly did not want the Maxwell to roll away, I climbed the sidewalk and far too many steps up to the front door. It would have been much easier if I had driven up their driveway and parked beneath the *porte cochère*, as I'd done when Frances was with me, but on this occasion I thought it wise not to advertise my presence.

I hadn't thought about the extreme plainness of my dress until the maid who opened the door to my knock gave me the severest sort of scrutiny up and down. "I'm Mrs. McFadden's friend, Fremont Jones," I explained, "and I'd like to see her if she's in."

"You're not expected." The maid, who was neither young nor pretty, but rather the opposite, stated this flatly.

I did not like her tone at all, so I put on my best Wellesley-educated persona and declared, "Mrs. McFadden is always at home to me, and I'm sure she would like to be acquainted with the fact that I am here inquiring after her health. I know she had a bit of a turn last evening. It was I, in fact, who brought her home."

The maid, who was looking to me more like a prison matron every minute, planted herself quite solidly in the middle of the entry and said, "No one is expected today. The Missus is not up to seeing anyone, and Mister said she's not to be disturbed. Not by no one, all day. So good afternoon." And she started to close the big door.

"Just a moment!" I stuck my hand out, risking a sore wrist if she closed it in my face. But she didn't; she held the door with her fingers curled around its edge and simply glared at me.

I reached into the pocket of my long coat. I had no calling cards—I hadn't thought about needing any, what with everything else that had gone on since I'd lost my former home on Vallejo Street—but I did have some of our J&K business cards with my name at the bottom, and our address and telephone number. I never went anywhere without them; in business, one should always be prepared to advertise. "My card," I said, thrusting it in the woman's face so that she was forced to take it or risk being blinded, "which I trust you will give to Mrs. McFadden, along with my most sincere wish that she will be feeling better soon."

Was it only my imagination, or was there a momentary softening of the eyes in that hard face? I took advantage by urging quietly, as if the maid and I had just become confidantes, "Please? Everyone needs a friend."

"Huh!" she snorted, and this time she did close the door in my face.

FOUR

Pure Evil

WISH STEPHENSON was sitting at his desk when I returned to Divisadero Street. Owing to his seniority in the investigation business, he has the desk with the most privacy—that is to say, it is farthest from the door. I do not begrudge him this in the least, but I did wonder why he took so long before looking up when I entered. Surely he'd heard the bell?

"Wish?" I inquired, setting my hat down on my own desk and moving toward him as I began the long unbuttoning. "Are you all right?"

"Oh, Fremont, I—" His head jerked up and he regarded me with a slightly dazed expression, as if I'd brought him out of a deep reverie. Or as if he'd recently been hit upon the head and lost some of his wits. He rubbed at his forehead with unusually long, big-knuckled fingers. "I'm sorry, I forgot to go by that club for you."

"It doesn't matter, and was not what I inquired about anyway. I merely asked if you were all right, because you appeared so, shall we say, distracted."

"Oh, yes, I'm okay. I guess, somewhere in the back of my mind I heard the bell on the door, but this cemetery thing . . . It's really getting to me."

"I'm sorry," I sympathized. I turned a ladies' chair—so called because it was made without arms, to accommodate the huge skirts of the previous century—to face him and sat down. As I carried on undoing all those buttons on my gray coat, I asked, "Do you want to tell me about it?"

"You first," he said, brightening; he had a wonderful facility for letting go of his own woes. "How did your surveillance go today?"

I smiled with genuine pride and pleasure. "I identified the thief! As I had suspected, it was a woman." My smile faded. "Unfortunately she was more of a girl, not long out of childhood. I'm glad my part was only to identify her, not to place her under arrest. I fear I would have been tempted to give her a good tongue lashing and then let her go. I wouldn't make a very good police officer, Wish. How did you bear it? Didn't you ever feel sorry for the criminals?"

"Um-hm, some of them," he nodded, his long face serious. Everything about Wish is long, or big, or bony. But he had been growing into himself, as it were, during the past couple of years, so that he no longer looked like a gangly youth. Nor was he so awkward physically as he once had been. Now he moved with the kind of gentle gravity that many big men have, as if they must be careful of all creatures smaller than themselves—in other words, of most of the rest of us. With that same gravity he said: "But I concentrate on the victims, and that gets me through. When laws are broken, Fremont, somebody always gets hurt."

"That's true," I agreed, chewing on my lower lip as I thought about Mama and Papa Garofalo. They were honest and kind-hearted; from the hours I had spent in their store I knew there were people in the neighborhood for whom the Garofalos kept a tab. In some cases, I suspected, a very long tab. If that girl had only asked for their help instead of stealing from them, what might they have been willing to do for her?

"And what's more," Wish continued, "there's people who're always wanting something for nothing, or wanting to get away with all sorts of lawbreaking just to prove they can do it. They're your run-of-the-mill sort of criminal. But the really big ones . . ." He shook his head from side to side, letting his words trail off. Then suddenly he finished, in a voice so low I had to listen hard to hear him: "The really big ones are pure evil."

Pure evil! That gave me the chills, and I shivered in the small silence that fell. Gathering myself together, I shrugged out of the gray coat and let it drape over the back of the chair. "Well," I said briskly, to break the pall, "at any rate, I told Mr. and Mrs. Garofalo who their thief is, where she can be found, and instructed them to call the police. Now all I have to do is send them the bill: case successfully concluded. Your turn, Wish. What was that you said, about the cemetery thing getting to you?"

"Yeah, but I don't quite know what precisely is bothering me. That's the hell of it. Probably best not to talk about it." He turned away and began to fiddle with some papers on his desk.

Ordinarily Wish would have said *heck of it*, so I knew this was serious. I couldn't stand not knowing, so I somehow had to persuade him to say more. I tentatively ventured: "I gather this is something to do with Mr. Fennelly's daughter?"

No response. I tried again: "Oh dear, I've forgotten her name. Poor girl. And poor you, to have to go poking about in the cemetery looking for her."

"Cemeteries, plural." My young colleague turned back to me. He was wavering, but he was also a little cross. "And her name is

Tara, but I've given up on her. I'm not going to find her. This thing . . . it's something else."

I leaned forward. "Michael is out, isn't he?" He usually was at this time of day.

Wish nodded, frowning in most un-Wishlike manner. "So?"

I urged, "So tell me. If it's tricky, I'll keep it to myself."

"We-e-ell . . ."

"Come on, Wish! You know I'm not as conservative as Michael, and I can keep my mouth shut if need be. Surely you need someone to talk things over with; who better than me? I mean, I?"

A look of relief flooded Wish Stephenson's open countenance, for which I was glad, because I would hate to have caused him further discomfort. Almost as much as I would have hated not knowing what was bothering him so. He leaned back in his chair, placed one ankle on the other knee, and said: "Okay, but I do want you to keep it to yourself until I've decided what to do."

I nodded encouragement. "I promise."

"I s'pose you know most of the cemeteries in this city are up on Lone Mountain."

I nodded again, for I did know: that hilltop, to the west and south of the Presidio, was called San Francisco's necropolis. There were a few architectural monuments in the area that were said to be rather grand, but I had not seen them myself, having no reason and less inclination to go there.

"So that's where I was for most of the day," Wish said.

"It cannot have been pleasant."

"While I didn't find Tara Fennelly Roberts, I did come across something else. Nobody would have wanted me to find it; and as a matter of fact, maybe it's not what I thought it was. Most people wouldn't have noticed, and if I hadn't been investigating, I probably wouldn't have noticed either."

I gave him a look such as I imagine a big sister might give a little brother, and said softly but sternly, "If you do not tell me *right now*, Wish Stephenson, what it was you found, I swear I will take you back up to that cemetery and tie you to a tombstone!"

His face turned a shade whiter. "Fremont, it's not so much what I found as what I didn't find. I swear to the Almighty, there's empty graves up there!"

His eyes got wider, and so did mine; but we had no chance to speak of it further because at that moment the door opened, jingling its bell.

Michael came in, removing his hat and pulling a white scarf from about his neck. "Well," he said, "what are you two hatching, all huddled up together like a couple of conspirators?"

And Wish and I popped up straight in our respective chairs, pulled our lips into similar grins and said brightly, almost simultaneously: "Nothing!"

Michael and I do not spend every night together. There are good reasons for our not living precisely as man and wife. I admit most of them are mine. Such as: I do not wish to be regarded as chattel, which is how many men view their wives. Indeed the history of the Western world, at least—I cannot answer for the history of the Eastern half of it, as not much of that was taught at Wellesley—is full of examples. For illustration one need go no further than the Bible itself, to the Ten Commandments, where one finds written: *Thou shalt not covet thy neighbor's wife, nor his ox, nor his ass, nor anything else that is his.*

Oh really! I swear it makes my teeth curl.

Generally speaking, even leaving aside the more outrageous of my ideas, I believe it is a good thing for a couple not to become entirely dependent on one another's company. So it was that this particular night I told Michael I preferred to be alone. I fixed myself a simple supper of omelet, bread, and fruit in the office kitchen and took it upstairs to my apartment. When I was done eating I called Wish Stephenson on the telephone, praying that he—not his mother—would answer. His mother loves to talk on the telephone above all things, and she will keep you at it for so long you'll forget why you called him in the first place.

The instrument rang hollowly, over and over, in my ear. "Oh, botheration!" I said. No one was home. And I had so wanted to find out more about those empty graves!

I felt all at loose ends. I sucked on a lemon pastille. I walked from room to room, looking out the windows but paying no attention to the view. I tried calling again, and still there was no answer. Good son that he was, Wish had probably taken his mother out for the evening. If they'd merely gone out for supper, I fancied they would have returned by now. If they did not come home soon, it would be too late to call, for politeness' sake. And what I was really doing with all this aimless activity was trying to push Frances McFadden out of my mind.

I leaned against the window frame and looked east toward Russian Hill, where I used to live in Mrs. O'Leary's house. She has a fine, wealthy husband now and lives in Los Angeles. She has not seen the new houses that are springing up like mushrooms there, where we used to live—in that part of the City where everything burned after the earthquake not so long ago. I watched the contours of houses and buildings go fuzzy and gray with twilight, no fog tonight; watched the gray grow a blue tinge, like spreading ink; and then the electric lights started to come on. Pop! pop! pop! they came on one by one, or a whole handful at a time, like diamonds scattered over a dark counterpane by the Hand of Night. I shoved the window open an inch, drew in a deep breath of air that tasted of evening, and was suddenly seized by a fit of melancholy without cause.

Divisadero Street was empty, uphill and down, everyone tucked up safely at home. By listening hard I was able to discern the whine of an electric trolley on Van Ness Avenue, and somewhere someone tootled a car horn, but on the whole, all was still. *Too* still.

It was a strange moment. I should not have been surprised to see a spectre materialize in a blank window of the house across the street, whose inhabitants appeared to be perpetually away. Surely in this sad, foreboding stillness something would happen?

But nothing did. I tried calling Wish one last time, and he was still not at home.

At last, knowing it was a mistake, I called Frances McFadden— even though I was well aware her husband kept their one and only telephone in his study, practically under lock and key. I had the oddest feeling Frances had been thinking of me all this time, trying to communicate with me somehow, and perhaps if I telephoned she might answer. She did not, but Jeremy McFadden did, and I broke the connection without saying a word. My cheeks burned as if he could see me, in my cowardly silence, through the wires.

After a perfectly horrid, restless night, I got up early. Dressed in a dark green skirt, a wide brown leather belt, and a lace-trimmed ecru blouse, I had already made the coffee when I sensed Michael's presence in the office kitchen. I turned around and there he was, though he hadn't made a sound.

I frowned. "I don't know how you do that," I said.

"Good morning to you, too. Do what?" He reached around me to remove the coffeepot from the burner, but stopped short of kissing my cheek.

"Sneak up on me sometimes." I frowned harder. "Generally, I know when you are there; and besides, I should have heard the door."

"Poor Fremont." Now he kissed my cheek. His eyes twinkled with mischief. "Even those famous ears cannot be expected to hear everything."

"So far as I know, my ears are not in the least famous."

"They are with me."

"I shall not make such a good detective after all," I groused, pouring coffee for myself and plopping down into a chair at the table, "if I can't even hear my own front door open—and with a bell on it, at that!"

Michael chuckled. "If you were more yourself, you would realize I came in the back."

"Oh. That explains it, then." But it didn't, not entirely. Michael is very, very good at sneaking around. Or at surveillance. I shall most likely never be as good at all these clandestine activities as he is. It rankles that I have never yet followed him on one of our training exercises without his knowing I am there. He has doubled around and come up behind me more than once, and it makes me furious—with myself, of course, not him. Well, maybe just a little bit with him.

I sat glowering over my coffee and worrying about Frances, which did make me cross with Michael, because I couldn't very well turn to him for support. Not after he'd practically forbidden me to pursue a friendship with her. Indeed! Well, he knew that wouldn't work, but I still could not expect him to allay my anxieties, which had no foundation in any case. None that I knew of.

My partner, wisely leaving me alone in my grumpiness, had begun to fry bacon and was beating up some eggs in a bowl. Michael is a more passable cook than I, if the truth be told. "No eggs for me," I said, as I realized what he was doing.

"You have to eat, Fremont. A good breakfast might even make you less disagreeable in the mornings."

It stung. I protested: "That wasn't very nice."

"But true." He picked up another egg.

"Really," I said sharply, before he could break the shell, "I had eggs for supper last night. Toast and bacon will do me quite well, thank you."

"You're welcome."

After a few moments, out of the corner of my eye I saw one of Michael's black eyebrows arch up as he flashed a look at me over his shoulder. I knew what he was thinking: *Is she approachable yet?*

I should be ashamed of myself, but I wasn't. I *was* still irritated with him for bossing me around about Frances. More than that, I wanted and needed to talk with him about my concerns for her, which for no reason at all had intensified overnight. Perhaps, indirectly, there was a way . . .

I joined Michael at the chopping block, next to the stove, and busied myself with cutting bread for toast. "Michael," I said casually as I fastened the slices into the rack, "do you believe in mental telepathy?"

Both black brows shot up. "I beg your pardon?"

"You know, the ability some people claim to have, to be able to communicate across a distance, without spoken words."

"Mind to mind," he said gravely.

"Yes."

"Why do you ask?" Suddenly my partner was as tense as a bow, before the arrow is let fly.

"It's no big thing," I said, bending down and shoving the racked toast into the oven, "just that I've had the oddest feeling someone may be trying to communicate with me in that manner."

I could not fail to notice that Michael's tension immediately lessened. "Oh," he said, sounding amused, "and what is this someone saying? Are the two of you engaged in a dialogue?"

"Not exactly. I do not seem to be very good at it, but the feeling is certainly very strong. So what do you think, is it possible?" I retrieved the toast from the oven just in time to prevent its burning, observing in passing that the two of us had become rather good at this business of preparing meals together. So long as the meals were simple enough.

"There is a great deal of interest in such matters right now in the land of my ancestors," Michael acknowledged—reluctantly, I thought.

"Russia, you mean."

"Yes, because of this man Grigori Efimovich, whom most are calling by the disgusting name Rasputin."

"I've heard of him," I said. "He is a mesmerist, is he not? And why is the name so disgusting?"

"I don't know what he is, Fremont, and neither do some people who happen to be among the few in Russia I still care about. I only know he is already close to the heart of the Tsarina, and I cannot believe that a person of such low birth and no education as this Grigori—"

"Whoa, Misha! And I thought you such an egalitarian."

"Let me finish, if you please." Michael's eyes were flashing. He looked like a candidate for tsarhood himself, or at least a prince; a leader, a ruler, and an angry one at that. "The name Rasputin means 'debaucher,' and he *is* debauched, though he presents himself as a holy man. Like Jesus Christ, may the saints forgive the comparison—"

"I didn't know you were religious." I popped a piece of toast in my mouth. I was enjoying this; it was highly interesting, even if it wasn't helping me much with my own problem.

"You might say Russian Orthodoxy is in my blood, or call it superstition. As I was saying: Like Jesus Christ, this Grigori Efimovich claims that physical contact with him can heal. Jesus healed with a touch of his hand. Rasputin takes it rather further than that."

"What do you mean?"

Michael ran his hand through his hair, messing it up, which he does only when he's deeply distressed. "I should never have gotten into this with you. I'd managed to put it out of my own mind until you became involved with that damn woman!"

I felt the blood flash into my cheeks. "Really, Michael, you had better explain yourself, because I cannot for the life of me imagine what connection there can be between my friend Frances and this—this debauched Russian!"

"All right!" he said hotly, then quickly calmed. "But you must bear with me because it won't be easy. I have heard on good authority that before he went to St. Petersburg, which by the way was only a year or so before I met you, Grigori Efimovich was healing people, especially females, through having carnal knowledge of them."

"You mean intercourse," I said, my cheeks doubly hot now, "on the theory, no doubt, that if a mere touch is healing . . ."

"Precisely," said Michael. "Now that he's at the imperial court, there are those who say he has cast his spell on the Tsarina in the same way, that this is what binds her to him, not just his ability to calm the Tsarevich."

"Begging your pardon, but you've lost me. What or who is a Tsarevich?"

"The boy, the heir, Alexei, whose health is so frail. That is not general knowledge, by the way."

I frowned, perplexed. "But I still don't see what any of this has to do with Frances. And you certainly should not have called my friend 'that damned woman.' Really, Michael!"

"All right. I apologize, I was angry. You see, Fremont, mysticism is still all the rage in Russia, though the craze has passed its peak here in the United States and in England. The Russians are a sort of brooding, mysterious people by nature anyhow—mysticism, mentalism, mesmerism, all those things naturally appeal to them. I think Rasputin is dangerous, and the last thing in the world I want right now is to have to go back to Russia and be part of some plot to expose him."

I reached out and put my hand over Michael's. "Is there such a plot?"

"Not yet. But there are rumblings."

I thought about what I'd seen—and heard—at the séance. "Could he be legitimate, this Rasputin? Could he really have some otherworldly power?"

Michael searched me, through my eyes. He said, "I'm beginning to understand. You think that medium at the séance the other night was the real thing. Don't you?"

"I don't know. But I do know Frances, and something strange—

and I believe otherworldly—happened to her, Michael. Something that has no logical explanation."

Michael inhaled deeply, and his love for me, mingled with a fierce caring, poured from his eyes into mine. "One thing I can tell you for certain, Fremont. Power is only power, but people can be good or evil. Rasputin is evil. Now I have to ask you: How much do you really know about your new friend?"

FIVE

Threshold

I TOLD MICHAEL I knew her well enough, and I would be careful. When he looked at me like that, how could I argue, or any longer be cross? It is not as if I've been the world's best judge of people in the past. So I smiled and caressed his cheek and went on with my day, but all the while I felt as if I were waiting for the other shoe to drop.

I have observed that oftentimes when things are not going very well to begin with, as the day goes on they only get worse. One wishes one had stayed in bed with the covers over one's head; or at most, one might feel safe curled up in a chair with a book. But for those of us who must earn a living, such luxuries are not possible, and so I blundered on, with the kind of results one might expect on such a day. I dropped a whole box of paper clips all over my desk, including into the typewriter; forgot that I was supposed to be interested in Wish's cemeteries until after he'd gone off alone, shaking his head; and I'd been writing and rewriting the same letter to my father for more than an hour when suddenly it happened. The other shoe dropped: Frances McFadden came to my door.

The little bell jingled, a somewhat tousled head and narrow shoulders leaned in, and a tremulous voice inquired, "Fremont? Is this the right place?"

"Yes!" I rushed into the foyer to assist her. "Come in, by all means, Frances. I'm so glad to see you. I've been quite concerned." She was rather oddly dressed, in a black rain slicker several sizes too large for her. Beneath the gaping neck of the garment her throat was bare, with delicate collarbones protruding. Below the slicker's hem I could see an inch or so of thick, smoky blue satin. Need I add that it was not raining?

"Oh dear," I said softly, "you look as if you've run away from home."

"In a manner of speaking, yes, I have." She hunched her shoulders and cocked her head to one side. She appeared neither frightened nor repentant, so I relaxed a bit.

"Come back to the kitchen," I said, leading the way, "where it's a bit warmer, and we'll have more privacy to talk."

Frances was looking around with interest. "This is where you work? Cora—she's the maid who answered the door to you yesterday—gave me your card, but she could not do so until this morning."

"I wasn't sure she would do it at all." We were passing through the dining room so I said, "This is our conference room." I resisted the impulse to tiptoe as we passed the closed door to Michael's study; he was certain to hear us talking in the kitchen anyway, it could not be helped.

"She's not so bad, really," Frances said. "It's just that Jeremy is

48

not the sort of man one can disobey. Not without consequences. And he'd said I should not be disturbed, you see." She shot a keen glance at the closed door, but said nothing about it.

I put on a fresh pot of coffee to perk, then excused myself, explaining: "I'm going to run upstairs and get a warm shawl for you to wear, at least for now. As for later—well, we'll take that as it comes."

"Oh, that's not necessary, really!"

"Yes, it is. Don't argue."

"Fremont, wait. Stop. I can't stay long. I have to go back."

"Go back? But you said you'd run away!"

"Only because I needed to see you. I'll be perfectly fine for some time yet, because I overheard my husband making an appointment for lunch at his club. He can't possibly return before midafternoon at the earliest."

"Nevertheless, I'm going to get you a shawl so that you can take off that dreadful garment. You're wearing your nightclothes under it, aren't you? And you expect me not to be concerned?"

Frances sighed, and made a wave of her hand with a shapely, graceful wrist. "Oh, all right, thank you. I'll explain everything when you return."

"Good. And, Frances, do keep an eye on the coffee while I run upstairs. If a man comes out of that closed door we passed, don't be alarmed. It will be Michael Kossoff, my partner, and he's harmless." Ha! That was a lie if ever I told one—Michael, harmless. But to Frances he would be, as long as I was here . . . or he'd have me to answer to.

I was back in a trice, with my largest shawl. Crocheted of soft wool in an amethyst shade, it was given to me by Maureen O'Leary (as was—her new married name is Sullivan) last Christmas. The color is divine, but it has a deep fringe that can be annoying for things catching in it. I love it anyway, because it reminds me of her: Mrs. O. was always fond of fringes.

"Here you are," I said, placing the shawl on the table in front of

Frances. "If you will allow me to help you out of that thing, I'm sure you'll be both warmer and more comfortable."

"Thank you, Fremont." The slicker fastened with toggles, which she fumbled a bit as she undid them. I went around behind her chair, ready to take the stiff coat from her shoulders. Her red-gold hair had been haphazardly pinned up, and as she shrugged out of the slicker, a curling strand of it came tumbling down. Frances automatically reached up to tuck it back in, and, as she did so, the satin sleeve of her dressing gown slipped above her elbow.

I drew in my breath sharply, audibly, and almost dropped the slicker: her upper arm bore one of the most dreadful bruises I had ever seen.

Frances looked at me over her shoulder. "Well, now you know," she said.

The stiff slicker crackled in my hands. It gave off a damp, fetid smell like an old drain. For distraction I said, wrinkling my nose, "Wherever did you get this thing? It's worse than old fish!" And then I briskly carried it right out to the enclosed back porch, where such a smelly thing rightfully belonged.

By the time I returned, as I'd intended, Frances had wrapped the purple shawl decorously around herself. Leaving aside the fact that her satin skirt was inappropriate for the hour of the day—and I did wonder what she had on her feet—she looked quite decent. I brought the coffee to the table, along with my mug and a cup and saucer. Of course, I was shocked by the bruise and what her words implied, but I would not be ill-mannered enough to comment unless she chose to bring it up herself. So as I poured out, I merely asked, "Now, how may I help you, Frances?"

She slipped one hand into the V of the wrapped shawl, and I steeled myself, thinking she was about to show me another, probably worse bruise upon her bosom, but instead she withdrew an envelope that had been hidden there. A heavy, squarish envelope of creamy paper, such as was used for invitations or correspon-

dence from important personages. Her eyes, I noted, were very
bright.

"When Jeremy left this morning," Frances said, "Cora brought
me this, as well as your card. The note was hand-delivered to the
house before breakfast today."

I held out my hand. "Shall I read it?"

Frances nodded. "Please."

Inside the envelope was a note folded in half, in the informal
style. The top of it was centrally embossed with a circular seal,
after the manner of a notary's seal, but I gathered this was someone's personal mark. In the center appeared an L, wrought in
exceedingly loopy fashion; what exactly the doodads were around
the edges I could not readily discern. I opened the note and read:
*Mrs. McFadden, Kindly come to me at Octavia Street tomorrow
morning at ten o'clock. There is a matter we must discuss.* It was
signed *A.L.*

"A.L.?" I inquired.

"Abigail Locke!" said Frances excitedly. "It must be she, she's
the only person I know on Octavia Street with those initials."

"But that is not where we went for the séance," I observed.

"No. She lives on Octavia. Of course she doesn't do the séances
in her own house. Would you?"

"No," I agreed, refolding the note and passing it back to Frances, "I don't suppose I would, now that you mention it. How
curious that she should send for you. I could have sworn Mrs.
Locke never wanted to see either of us again after what happened.
In fact, she said to get out and never come back."

Frances grimaced. "I can't believe she would treat me like that.
I still haven't remembered any of what happened. Could you be
wrong, Fremont? Could she have been speaking not to us but to
some unwanted spirit presence?"

"I honestly don't think so." I propped my elbow on the table
and leaned my chin against my hand in thought. An idea was
forming, but I—lifelong skeptic that I am—was having a hard time

accepting it. Finally, reluctantly, I said, "I suppose she could have been more upset with whatever, or whoever, it was that spoke from your mouth than she was with you or me personally. Perhaps she has had second thoughts about sending you away. Surely anyone in her line of work, anyone honest that is, would want to look into your experience further. And to encourage the natural talent you appear to have."

Frances nodded vigorously; many curls came tumbling down. "Oh, Fremont, I do need help! And I certainly could use some encouragement. I really don't know what's happening to me. I don't dare tell Jeremy, and I live in fear that one of these—these trances or whatever they are will come upon me when he's in the room. He doesn't usually sleep in the bed with me, he has his own room, but sometimes he falls asleep right after, you know . . ."

Her voice trailed off and she looked very distressed indeed. She seemed to shrink within her own skin, and her eyes lost their verve.

I knew, of course, that many men beat their wives. Even the most respectable men. They can get away with it because who is there to stop them? It was none of my business. Michael was right, of course—I should stay out of these husband-and-wife things. "Frances," I asked nevertheless, "why was it that you were unable to get dressed before coming here this morning? And whose slicker did you wear to cover your dressing gown?"

She blushed, something I'd never seen her do before. "The slicker is so old, I don't know to whom it belongs. It hangs on a peg in the room where I arrange flowers, and anyone who has to go out in bad weather can wear it. The gardener wears it rather routinely, I believe, but then he always leaves it on the peg for the next person." Her eyes beseeched me; she did not want to have to answer my other question.

"You must tell someone," I urged, just above a whisper.

Frances bowed her head. Her words came out hard, and broken, as if torn from her in chunks: "When I do something that displeases Jeremy, he hurts me. In the beginning—I mean when we were first married—I didn't think he really meant to do it, I thought he just lost control momentarily, and because he's so big . . . and I do bruise easily . . .'' She raised her head, and I was glad to see some defiant spirit in her eyes. "But now I know he means to have me utterly at his bidding. If I do anything at all, the least tiny thing, that he doesn't wholeheartedly approve, he hurts me. Not on the face and neck, not where Cora and the other servants can see, but on my body.

"What is almost worse, lately he has taken to locking up all my clothes so that I cannot go out anywhere without his approval. There are new locks on the wardrobes and on the chests of drawers, and only Jeremy has the keys. In the morning and again in the evening, he unlocks them and stands over me while I choose what to wear. Sometimes he will not even let me choose, but insists on making the choice himself. Yesterday and today he said I did not need any clothes at all because I was not to go out. You see, Fremont, he knew I'd lied to him that night I was with you."

"How could he?" My voice quivered a bit with more outrage than I could conceal.

Frances shrugged, and sipped her coffee before replying. "He suspected. And then he made me tell him."

I didn't have to ask how he'd *made* her; I'd seen the evidence on her arm, and I didn't doubt there was more still on other hidden parts of her body. "So you told him we were out—did you also say where we went?"

Frances's golden-hazel eyes seemed unusually large and forlorn as she admitted, "Yes, I told him about the séance. I told him everything. I really believe, if I had not, he would have killed me."

"And yet, in spite of all that, you want to accept this invitation." I gave the note back to her. Suddenly there was a dangerous feel to that rich paper. "You want to go to Octavia Street to see Mrs. Locke."

Frances leaned toward me and her eyes glowed again. With

hope, I thought. She said, "Yes, oh yes, I do! Fremont, what if I do have some sort of natural talent for talking to the spirits? What if that's what's really happening to me? Can't you see—I'd so much prefer that to worrying that I might be losing my mind!"

"Frances," I said in my most no-nonsense tone, "of course you're not losing your mind. What, precisely, are you talking about?"

She shivered, pulled the shawl up closer around her neck, bit her lip, and darted her eyes nervously around the room, as if to satisfy herself that we were alone. "Well, I'm not sure, and that's the worst of it. I feel—not all the time, but just sometimes—I feel as if I'm not alone. There's a sort of, I don't know, a *presence* with me. Like when you're in a room and someone comes in behind your back, and you know they're there before you can see them. Know what I mean?"

I nodded.

Now Frances gazed over my shoulder with a faraway expression, as if she were looking into infinity. "It's not an evil presence I feel, it's good. I don't know how I know that, I just do. And it's trying to say something, to communicate with me."

"I suspect this presence is trying to communicate *through* you rather than *with* you, if what happened at the séance is any indication. I'm certainly not much help in this matter. I wish I could be, but I don't know the first thing about it."

"You believe me, don't you? I mean, you said you heard the . . . the voice that came out of me. Surely that must be why Mrs. Locke has summoned me, don't you think so, Fremont? How can I not go?"

"Yes . . ." I said slowly, "it's very tempting. But are you sure you can get away? What makes you think tomorrow will be any different from today? Or did you think to run away again in dressing gown and slicker?"

"No. I will be very, very good and contrite tonight. I'll promise anything. And then Jeremy will go to work as usual tomorrow morning and all will be well. That is, if you can come for me in your car? Will you, Fremont? Oh, say that you will!''

I confess I did not like it. I was uncomfortable, and not because Michael had told me to be wary of Frances, and not to get between her and her husband. It was something else I could not quite define, some nascent sense that warned of something wrong. But it was all rather vague. In the end I could not deny help to a friend, and a repressed friend, at that.

''I will come for you,'' I said. ''I'll manage it somehow.''

''Oh, thank you!'' Frances gushed.

I frowned at her effusiveness and raised a finger to my lips in that universal gesture for silence. ''It will be easier for me if Michael knows nothing of this,'' I said quietly. ''Now, can you get back to your house on your own? If I drive you, I'll have to tell him I'm going out, and I'd rather not.''

''I don't want to cause trouble for you, too, Fremont. I never thought he might object,'' Frances whispered, reaching for my hand and squeezing it tightly.

''It's all right,'' I hastened to assure her, ''my life is very much my own, but the car belongs to him. That's all.''

''Oh, I see.'' She giggled, then covered her mouth. I smiled in return—she was irrepressible. ''Well, then,'' she said, ''we shall do fine, I'm sure. Until tomorrow then?''

I nodded. ''Until tomorrow.''

I stayed on my own again that night, which caused Michael to raise a dark eyebrow, but no more than that. If he had heard me and Frances talking in the kitchen, he said nothing of it, for which I was grateful, because I really did not want to discuss it. We were not in agreement, and that was that.

By morning I had invented a dental appointment for myself, which necessitated my taking the Maxwell and Michael's watching the office for an hour or so. While I was not entirely happy with this subterfuge, on the other hand I did not want him to be concerned about me either. What harm could possibly come of my driving a friend a few blocks in broad daylight, at ten o'clock in the morning, in a perfectly respectable part of town? Though to be honest, it was a gloomy, gray sort of day, so "broad daylight" did not precisely apply.

I drove right up under the *porte cochère*, as Frances had suggested. She was waiting just inside the door, and in only a matter of seconds she had seated herself beside me in the auto and we were off for Octavia Street.

"You're quite nicely dressed this morning," I observed, "so may I assume you had no further problem with your husband?" She did look lovely, like a whiff of spring in a pale green suit of fine wool with a fitted, waist-length jacket; the sleeves, the collar, and the skirt were trimmed with narrow grosgrain ribbon in a darker green. Wider ribbon of the same type made a flat bow at the back of her upswept hair.

"You are looking well yourself, Fremont," she said in return, but she lied. I wore my usual blue skirt and white blouse, beneath a long knitted coat-sweater in a rather repulsive shade of garnet— another remnant of my refugee status after the earthquake. The sweater was warm, and the morning was cold, that was what mattered.

"Jeremy is in a contrite phase," Frances continued, "he brought home flowers last night. For a few days now I will be able to do no wrong. I must enjoy it while it lasts. Oh, Fremont, I'm so excited about this invitation!"

"Perhaps it would be wise not to get one's hopes up," I suggested, though I was somewhat excited myself. This Spiritualist stuff intrigued me mightily. "After all, you don't know the purpose of the meeting yet. You don't want to be disappointed."

"But even to be invited is an honor. To her *home*, Fremont! By her invitation! Abigail Locke may not be the most sensational medium in San Francisco, but she is the most respected by—well, by people like you and me."

"And who is the most sensational?" I asked, curious. Having successfully negotiated a long downhill section of street, I glanced at Frances as I stopped at the corner for a tattered-looking fellow to cross. Frances had that same bright-eyed, feverish look I recalled only too well from the séance.

"Ingrid Swann, but she's a fake. Or so I believe. She attracts the largest crowds because she's very beautiful. Even the men adore her. She works with a cabinet in a dark room and excels at extruding ectoplasm."

Ugh! I thought. Out loud I wondered, "What good does it do her to be beautiful if she's going to do her act in a dark room? And how does that attract the men? It sounds remarkably unattractive to me."

"I don't know, I'm sure, but it does. I even saw Patrick there once. I suppose he was spying for Abigail—to find out how Ingrid does it, you know. Extrudes the ectoplasm, I mean. It really is most odd. The ectoplasm comes out of her mouth—"

I interrupted: "Excuse me, but here's Octavia Street. You will have to watch the house numbers, if you don't mind." Ectoplasm from the mouth, indeed! There had to be easier ways this Ingrid Swann could have earned her living.

Abigail Locke's house on Octavia Street was an unimposing buff-colored carpenter-gothic-style structure, whose finest attribute was a bay window at one corner. Invitation in hand, Frances stood on the stoop and rang the bell while I waited one step below. I had offered to remain in the Maxwell, but Frances wouldn't have it.

"Why isn't she answering?" Frances fretted, pushing the doorbell again.

"Perhaps she's in the back." I turned my head and looked over at the bay window, through which I could see a round table with a lamp on it. In spite of the overall gloom, the lamp was not lit, which surprised me.

"Oh, bother," said Frances, when still no one came. She stood on tiptoes, shielded her eyes with her hand, and leaned against the door, peering through a little oval of fancy pressed glass that had been set into the wood. Then she lost her balance as the door began to move, swinging inward of its own accord.

SIX

Cross on Crimson

"WAIT, FRANCES! Don't—" But my protest came too late. She had already stumbled through the door and her voice, calling out, cut off my own words.

"Mrs. Locke?" she called. "Abigail, are you there?"

Silence.

We looked to the right, into the parlor: no one there. To the left, into a small sitting room: no one there either.

Frances took a few steps forward. "Mrs. Locke? It is I, Frances McFadden, come to keep our appointment."

I snatched at her elbow, intending to restrain her, but just as I did so she moved another few steps and I missed. So I let her go and stood stock-still to assess the situation. This house was entirely too dark. It would have been dark in any case, since the woodwork was all walnut or mahogany, or stained in imitation of those fine woods; but it was midmorning on a gray day—there should have been a light burning somewhere. On the stairs, or here in the hall, or shining forth from the kitchen door.

Furthermore, it was too silent. I would have guessed its occupants were sleeping, except that the door had been unlocked, and in this city, even in a good neighborhood, one does not go to bed—or remain there—without first locking the front door.

Nor does one sleep to midmorning when one has sent out an invitation. My mind was all full of alarms. I broke my own silence, and stillness, and strode after Frances, who by now had advanced almost to the end of the hall. She was peering curiously into the dining room when I caught up with her. I said in a harsh whisper: "We should leave. We should not even have come in. Something is not right here!"

In an odd, flat tone of voice, not matching my whisper at all, Frances pronounced one word: "No."

My mind worked fast and clean as a lightning strike. I grabbed my friend's hand and pulled her after me, back up the hall. Speaking low and fast, I said, "We've seen enough. If Mrs. Locke is in this house, she will be upstairs. No one has been down here this morning."

"Then we will go up," Frances declared loudly, wrenching her hand from mine with a vicious twist of her wrist. "I must see her!"

Oh, help! I thought, and warned, "This feels like a trap to me."

"Don't be silly, Fremont," said Frances, sounding more like herself as she rustled up the stairs. "Who would want to trap us?"

"Any number of people I can think of," I grumbled under my breath. But I followed her.

"Mrs. Locke, are you here? Mrs. Locke, it's Frances, I'm concerned about you!"

The stairs went straight up without a turning, and so deposited us at the rear of the house on the second floor. It was slightly brighter up here, as the dark wood stopped at chair-rail height and the walls had been covered with a cream damask wallpaper. Thinking that if we must do this it had best be done quickly, I took charge.

"Her bedroom will be at the front, no doubt," I said, moving ahead of Frances and marching purposefully onward.

"I wonder where everyone is," Frances fretted. "I would have thought she'd have a maid."

I myself would have thought the hawk-faced Patrick would be somewhere about; I rather doubted mediums could afford maids. I reached the front bedroom a few steps ahead of my friend. The door was open. The medium slept in a monstrous great bed with an ivory canopy . . . but I did not think she was sleeping. In the doorway I turned. "Don't touch anything," I said, for I knew with a certainty what we would find, and that Frances would not be satisfied until we'd found it.

Until we'd found *her*.

Yes, the shape in the bed was indeed Abigail Locke. And she was indeed dead.

Frances said, "Oh—" ending in a strangled sound, deep in her throat.

"Stabbed while she was sleeping, I should guess," I murmured. Stabbed through the heart—or, at least, in the chest. There was a lot of blood, which had pooled around her; the smell of it was not noticeable until one had approached close to the bed.

For a moment I forgot Frances as Michael's lessons took over my mind: Observe, observe! What do you see? I saw Abigail Locke's eyes were closed, which meant either she had been dispatched without awakening, which seemed hardly likely unless she'd been drugged, or the killer had closed her eyes for her; I saw there had not been much of a struggle. It was a relatively neat, clean kill by someone who knew enough, and had strength enough, to strike the fatal blow straight off. By the color of the blood, I saw she had been killed not long before our arrival, which set off yet another alarm in my mind. And of course I also saw the knife, which had the look of a ritual dagger. It had been withdrawn from the wound and laid carefully between the medium's breasts. The dagger's hilt lay in her blood like a cross on a crimson field.

Frances had begun to breathe convulsively, with her hand over her mouth and nose. Her eyes were unnaturally wide. She swayed, as if she might fall, and her other hand reached out for the bedpost to steady herself. But I stepped in and caught hold of her before she'd touched it.

"We must leave," I whispered fiercely, "now! This very minute!"

Frances rolled her eyes, but she shook her head and wouldn't budge. "How can you say such a thing? We can't leave her like . . . like that! She must have a telephone. We'll call the police."

Shaking my head, I took Frances's shoulders in my hands and forced her back from the bed. "Trust me. We must go. I'll explain when we're away from here."

I was so anxious I felt as if ants were crawling all over my body. Every element in my sensorium—hearing, sight, smell, touch, even taste, for I could taste the blood in my mouth—had been sharpened to an excruciating pitch. Frances didn't move fast enough for me, so I dragged her, mercilessly. Down the hall, down the stairs, out the front door.

"Go on to the Maxwell," I commanded, "there's something I must do so that no one will ever know we were here."

"Fremont!" Tears brimmed in her eyes, but she went.

Michael had taught me about fingerprinting, a technique of criminal detection developed in England, which had been in use by Scotland Yard for some years and is now sometimes done here. Taking my handkerchief from my skirt pocket, I wiped the front door and the doorknob. Then I went back into that dreadful house and wiped the stair rail from top to bottom, on the chance that one of us had touched it, for I really could not remember. While on the stairs I strained my ears so hard I felt my head would break, but I heard nothing. My heart leapt with gratitude for that, and I turned and ran.

Out on the street I cranked Max with a vengeance, and then we took off. "Pull yourself together," I ordered Frances grimly. "Stop crying or your eyes will be red."

"But she's *dead*, Fremont! Abigail Locke was—was *murdered* by somebody!"

"Murdered by somebody who arranged for *you* to find her body! Don't you see, Frances? Somebody wanted you to find her, and to call the police. Wanted you involved." I turned a corner rather viciously, and Max's wheels screeched a protest.

"Why do you say that? That's a terrible thing to say!"

"Never mind. Get out your handkerchief and wipe your face. We're going straight back to your house. Who saw you leave?"

"Well, Cora, I suppose."

"Did she know where you were going? Did you tell her?" I wondered how I could ever have thought this auto climbed hills like a goat. We were moving upward with agonizing slowness.

"I . . . don't remember. I don't think so. But it doesn't matter, she won't tell."

From the corner of my eye I saw Frances daintily wiping beneath her eyes with a corner of her handkerchief, and she sat straighter. Good. "This is what we're going to do. You, Frances, are going to remember that your husband must never, ever know where you went this morning. Truly, I fear for your safety if he finds out."

I had to, quite literally, bite my lip to keep from telling her outright that I thought she should get herself away from him. It was too early, much too early, for me to make a decision in the direction I was already leaning: That Jeremy McFadden had killed the medium, or arranged to have her killed, in order to teach his wife a lesson.

I took my eyes from the road for a moment to fix Frances with what I hoped was a steely stare. "You must never tell *anyone!* Do you understand that?"

"No. Frankly, I don't." She sounded petulant, which was better than teary or terrified. "I think you're being irresponsible, Fremont. I would have expected more of you."

"I'm going to call the police, but not until I've seen you safely inside your own front door. I'll use a callbox and report Mrs. Locke's death anonymously. The police will take over the investigation, don't worry, and her murderer will not go unpunished. Think, Frances, think! What good would it do anyone to know that we were there?"

"We had every right to be there. I was invited!"

"So you were," I said grimly. I lurched the Maxwell up the McFaddens' steep driveway and screeched to a halt in the *porte cochère.* "If you can get to the telephone and be sure we're not overheard, call me and we can talk about this later. Meanwhile, think on this. I haven't been in the private investigation business very long, but I have an excellent teacher, and I can tell you this: Abigail Locke had not intended to get up for any appointment this morning. She was sleeping late, probably because she had a late séance last night. She was killed not long before we arrived, because the blood was still fresh. I could tell by its color, and by the fact that its smell had not yet settled in to permeate the room. You were supposed to find Abigail Locke dead, Frances—that is why you were sent that invitation."

"Oh." She turned very pale. But in her spirited way, still she protested: "How can that be? My invitation was on her own personal notepaper!"

I gave her a little push. "Think about it. And believe I have only your best interests at heart! Now go, and find a way to persuade your maid to keep silent about your having been out at all this morning. I must get to a public telephone and report this murder without further delay."

* * *

"Where is Michael?" I asked Wish Stephenson, who was sitting at my desk when I got back to the office.

Wish looked up and smiled. "He went out somewhere, didn't say. I told him I'd watch the office since I had to write up my report for you to type anyhow." He tapped the eraser end of a pencil on the lined paper he was using, then shook his head from side to side as a mournful expression claimed his face. "I wish I could've done more for Mr. Fennelly. He's not satisfied, you know, Fremont. Don't be surprised if he refuses to pay."

"Nothing would have satisfied that man except our finding his daughter, Wish. It was an impossible task, and you did the best you could."

"Uhm." He bent over the desk and went back to his writing.

I took off the heavy garnet sweater and draped it over a brass clothes tree near the door. Michael's being out was a considerable relief, as he is altogether too good at "reading" me. I had kept my emotions in order for Frances's sake, and for her sake I had decided—though with some difficulty—not to call the police after all. Then, on the way back home to Divisadero Street, I had begun to fall apart.

"How was the dentist?" Wish asked, without looking up. "Not too painful, I hope."

"What? Oh!" The dentist—I'd forgotten. I put a hand up to my cheek. "Thank you for asking. In truth, the dentist does not provide one with an enjoyable experience. I'm somewhat shaken. If you don't mind sitting there a little longer, I'll go back to the kitchen and make us a cup of . . . of, well, something soothing." Coffee didn't seem like quite the thing for nerves already jangled.

"Cocoa?" Wish suggested hopefully. "My mother makes hot chocolate for a treat. Maybe you could use some, Fremont. And I love hot chocolate!"

"Yes." I tried to smile. "That will be the very thing."

* * *

Michael was out all day. Frances did not call. Both these things worried me. So when, in late afternoon, Wish began dithering over the puzzle of those empty graves on Lone Mountain, I said I'd go with him to check them out again. Anything, I thought, for distraction. Even a visit to a cemetery.

We left a note and waited for the streetcar, in case Michael should return and have need of his auto.

"What's on your mind, Fremont?" Wish asked, looking down at me. "You've been off somewhere in your head all day."

"Nothing, really. I was just thinking how much I wish—" I smiled, as one usually did at the intrusion of his nickname into conversation, only in this case I did it to buy myself time to make something up—and then I had it: "I wish we could afford to pay a receptionist. I could still do the typing, we could hire someone without clerical skills, just to answer the telephone and make appointments. I hate being tied to the office."

"I feel the same. There are times when it would be good for us to work in the field together, Fremont. And Michael isn't really interested in the day-to-day activities of the J&K Agency, in spite of his name being on it. He seems . . . well, at times he does seem remote."

I nodded. It was true, but no different from what I had expected from my partner.

"Just as you've been today, in fact." Wish's eyes twinkled. "You and he are very much alike, you know."

"We are not! He has all these skills that I am only struggling to acquire, and he's older, and he's secretive—you can hardly say any of that about me."

Wish grinned openly. "Still, there's some quality in both of you that's the same. Maybe I can't put a name to it, but it's there."

This pleased me inordinately, so I smiled back, but said nothing.

"So-o-o . . . what's been on your mind today, are you going to tell me?"

I clung to my former story. "As I said, I've been thinking how to get some more help in the office. I want to be out working on cases more. I want someone to look after things when we leave early, as we did today, for example. That's all."

"Do we have any new cases?"

"No." I shifted uncomfortably and looked down the street for the streetcar. "But we could have more if we advertised. And another thing," I went on, warming to this diversion. "I feel I've been in training long enough, I want Michael to cut me loose, stop this infernal choosing of what cases I may work, but he says I'm not ready yet."

Wish's eyes narrowed, but the look in them was kind. "Then you must let him teach you how to shoot. He's not going to cut you loose, as you put it, until you can defend yourself more effectively than you can with that blade of yours."

I nodded again, miserably this time, and stared down at my feet. The truth was, I had more familiarity with guns than either Wish or Michael knew, and I did not want to hold one of the things in my hand ever again. Much less pull the trigger. I forced myself to continue: "He also says I have to be able to follow his trail without detection, at least once. I'm beginning to think I'll never accomplish that."

Yet even as I uttered those words, and Wish commiserated with me on Michael's uncanny ability to elude pursuit, I had an idea. An absolutely splendid idea, which I filed away for future reference, for at that moment the streetcar came.

We had a brief ride to California Street, where we changed cars and went on, climbing slowly but steadily. I commented about the amount of construction going on, because I'd thought this part of San Francisco to be relatively undeveloped. Wish said something about a lot of this land belonging to the Church—by which I knew he meant the Roman Catholics. His family of course is of that religious persuasion; they would hardly have given him a name like Aloysius otherwise.

I let that go by, as the Catholic Church is a mystery to me, and I already had another mystery on my mind. The excuse I'd made up for Wish, and my real preoccupation, had come together in my mind, and I was trying to figure out how I could get away from the office to do whatever must be done to help Frances McFadden. She was going to need help, in some form or other, I was sure of that.

I was equally sure I didn't want to hear whatever Michael would have to say about my helping. But how—

"This is it, I think," Wish said, tapping me on the shoulder and interrupting my thoughts. "We get off at the next corner."

I swung down off the high streetcar step with a little hop and looked around. I had never been here before, that much was certain. There was a hint of sea smell in the air, and a stiff breeze that skimmed the top of our hill without a hint of movement in the huge gray clouds massed above. I took a couple of steps away from the curb and then stopped, for Wish was looking about and rubbing his chin. A scraggly line of houses ran along a sidewalk that was mostly dirt. Gritty dirt, with a lot of sand in it, that made a scrunching sound as I walked over to where Wish stood indecisively.

"What is this place?" I asked. "Is this where we're going?"

"No, we have to walk a couple of blocks. But it seems different somehow."

I turned and looked at the intersection just behind us, squinted and stared harder, as if I could somehow bring into existence a street sign that was not there. I knew the streetcar we'd been on ran out all the way to the Cliff House at the beach, but . . . "Why is there no sign at the cross street?" I asked. The founders of San Francisco had been such sticklers for planning their city in a strict grid pattern that streets marched straight up and down hills with no consideration for topography. And they were always named, always.

"I don't know," said Wish, beginning to walk south along the unnamed cross street.

"Where is the cemetery?" I did not see tombstones, only a few houses and some of the construction that was going on everywhere. Reconstruction, new construction—most of the time it was impossible to tell one from the other.

"In this direction we're walking," Wish said. He was moving along so slowly, quite unlike his habitual lope, that I could easily keep up with him. He continued, "On the day I saw, um, what I thought I saw, I'd already talked to the caretakers and examined the books of the major burial grounds. I hadn't found Fennelly's daughter that way, so I was just wandering around, reading the tombstones, the way you do in cemeteries. It was pretty interesting, Fremont."

"I'm sure." As we crossed another unmarked street I looked back toward the east—or at least so I thought, I was beginning to feel quite turned around—and had one of those unexpected glimpses of San Francisco that take your breath away. Even on such a gloomy day, the sweep of the vista down the hills to a dark gray blur of Bay was spectacular.

"No, really," Wish insisted, "it was. From the names on the tombstones I could tell I'd come across a section of family graveyards, and they were old. In one part, the names were all Chinese, written in Chinese characters and English, both."

"Fascinating," I remarked.

"You sound annoyed with me," Wish said, stopping. He had a single frown line creasing his clear young brow, just to the right of his nose. "You think I've brought you on a wild goose chase."

"Not exactly. Forgive me, Wish, I've been short-tempered all day today. It has nothing at all to do with you, I promise. Let's just go and find what it is you want to show me, because it will be getting dark soon."

So we went on. We walked another block, and then another, which brought us right up to the iron-spiked precincts of a cemetery. "Well?" I inquired.

"I'm looking for the gate."

I did not want to find a gate. I didn't want to go in there one bit. Certain places of the dead are peaceful and dignified; one may stroll about them with some serenity, particularly if the day happens to be sunny. But this was not such a place. This place definitely did not invite strolling. It had a doleful, dark atmosphere, enhanced by tall cypress trees bearing an uncanny resemblance to ancient, desiccated, gray-bearded men.

"Here it is, I thought so!" Wish said in a satisfied tone. He opened the iron gate. It creaked, of course.

I shivered. "I don't want to go in there. Must we?"

"No, the gate is more of a landmark. I'm using it to confirm that I am where I thought I was. Where I was that day. Now come, Fremont." He closed the gate without passing through it, then took me by the hand. Wish had never really touched me before, only the merest brush of fingers or a shoulder in passing, and I felt as if, by having my smaller hand engulfed in his, we were doing something wrong. Yet I did not pull away. I felt I needed the warm-blooded human contact.

He counted steps under his breath. We had moved away from the street, which in any case had deteriorated within the last couple of blocks to a dirt road. Being outside the cemetery proper, with its delineating spiked fence, we traversed an irregular terrain of sandy, loose soil, most unattractively spotted with scrub.

Suddenly I felt cold all over, and dreadfully afraid. I cast anxious glances back over my left shoulder toward the dark graveyard. I felt certain something was moving in there, watching us with a malevolent eye, but all I saw were pale crosses—crosses that reminded me of a dagger's hilt on the bloody breast of Abigail Locke. I gripped Wish Stephenson's hand more tightly. The events of the morning were belatedly catching up with me, that was all. Or so I told myself.

Wish returned the pressure of my fingers but then let go of my hand, and I realized we had come to a standstill. He went to rubbing his chin again.

"What?" I asked, hugging my elbows to me, for I was freezing cold. "What am I supposed to be seeing? There's nothing here, Wish, it's just an empty lot."

"No," he said, "I don't think so." He stood close to me and raised his finger to his lips for silence—just as I had done earlier, with Frances. The parallel seemed eerie to me, and frightened me all the more. In a near whisper, bringing his face down close to mine, Wish Stephenson said: "This is where the graves were before, Fremont. I swear it. The last time I was here, they were yawning empty. Today they are gone. We are standing on desecrated ground."

SEVEN

A Far and Lonely Place

I WAS IN AN AGONY of conscience for the three days that passed before the newspapers reported Abigail Locke's murder. I had not thought it would take that long for someone else to find her body. In the interim, I had plenty of time to reflect upon Michael's question, *How well do you really know Frances McFadden?* For she did not call me, nor did she come by, and I dared not call or go to her. They were a very long three days indeed.

I was not idle, however. Since I was so badly in need of distraction I actually accomplished a great deal. To be fair, so did Michael and Wish Stephenson. The former, during one of his quiet forays out of the house, obtained for J&K a contract with a shipping company, which would be enough all by itself to keep Wish busy for several weeks to come. The job consisted of working as a clerk in the shipping company office under a false identity, in order to catch out a clever embezzler of both money and goods.

I knew Wish would not like being confined indoors, but frankly, as I thought he had gone somewhat off his head over poor Tara Fennelly and the cemeteries, I was glad he would be kept busy in one spot for a while. Wish's own great accomplishment, before starting work at the shipping company, had been to impart the results of his investigation to Papa Fennelly in such a way that the poor man was able to acknowledge the futility of any continued search for his daughter. He also paid his bill. I did not think he would ever quite stop looking for her, though.

As for myself, during those three days I went at last with Michael to choose a suitable firearm; then submitted—with disgusting docility—to his lessons on how to shoot it properly. As I did not want a pistol or a revolver, and a rifle would hardly have been practical, I obtained a gun that falls somewhere in between, in both appearance and power. It is called a Marlin 44–40 carbine, with lever action, and it holds seven rounds of ammunition. It looks like a short shotgun, with a barrel fourteen inches long, and just jacking the shot into the chamber in itself sounds a formidable warning.

My hope is that the very sight of this weapon in my hands will prove a deterrent, because I am not yet a very good shot. It has an adjustable sight, as Michael showed me, but how I am to make much use of an adjustable sight in the heat of the moment—one assumes one would primarily need a gun only in the heat of the moment—I'm sure I cannot imagine. Wish teased me for choosing a weapon that is not the latest, as these carbines have been around since the nineties; but Michael is pleased, and that is what really matters.

Michael would probably not be nearly so pleased with me when he discovered the other thing I'd done during those tense days of waiting. I had put together a daring new disguise, with which I planned to deceive him successfully at last. Not—I hasten to say—for the same purpose that a woman usually (or so one has heard) deceives a man, but for the purpose of following him undetected. Once I'd achieved that, Michael could have no further objection to considering me a full-fledged investigator on my own.

On the morning of the third day after Frances and I made our grim discovery, I was sitting in the breakfast room on Michael's side of the house, sipping coffee and thinking how to set up a tail, to use investigator's jargon, on my lover later in the day. He had gone out to a certain bakery he favors to bring back breakfast pastries—Michael has a notorious sweet tooth, and he has been converting me to his wicked ways. The problem I wrestled with was, how to keep him from knowing about my new disguise ahead of time. In the past we had planned these forays well ahead, when he would deviously dart about town and I would tail him, or attempt to. He would tell me he expected to come out of thus and such a place at this particular time, and I was to pick up the tail there. . . .

It will work, I thought, *I can still do it that way, provided—*

The sound of Michael coming in the front door interrupted my stream of thought. "I'm back!" he called out when he was yet in the hallway, in an eager-sounding voice that made me smile. "Wait till you see what I have, Fremont!"

"I shall grow fat just by looking at it, no doubt! Well, let's have it."

Grinning, Michael tossed the bag to me, then settled back in his own chair and opened the newspaper he'd also bought when he was out. I opened the bag and nearly passed out from the delicious smells that rushed forth. I hadn't realized I was so hungry! Greedily licking my fingers in the process, I arranged the pastries on a plate I had previously set in the center of the table for that purpose. They were still warm from the bakery's ovens, drenched in a sugar glaze, sticky with pineapple and cherries and custard.

Perhaps saying that Michael has a sweet tooth is an understatement.

"Good Lord!" he exclaimed from behind the newspaper.

"I presume you do not expect me to answer to that expostulation," I said calmly, pouring more coffee, for the moment focused only on which pastry to choose first. Should it be the pineapple? No, the cherry. I reached for it, and slid it onto a smaller plate.

"This will be of some interest to you, I think," Michael said. "I'll read aloud: 'Mrs. Abigail Locke, a Spiritualist medium who commanded some local respect, has been found dead in her residence on Octavia Street. Mrs. Locke, forty-three years old, had apparently met with foul play. Her body was discovered by Mr. Patrick Rule yesterday afternoon. Mr. Rule, while not a medium himself, has provided professional assistance to Mrs. Locke from time to time, and he had become concerned when he did not hear from her regarding preparations for a séance at which Mrs. Locke was to officiate this evening. Due to the condition of the body, it is assumed that the medium had been dead for some time prior to the discovery. Persons with any knowledge that may shed light on this tragic event are asked to come forward to the Fillmore Police Station.' "

Michael lowered the paper a couple of inches and stared at me over the top of it. "What do you think of that, Fremont?"

My mouth had gone so dry that the delicious pastry became impossible to chew. I had to force it down with a gulp of orange juice before I could reply. I had expected this of course, and had planned what I should say, so I said it: "How ghastly!"

"That is the same medium who presided over the séance you went to with your friend, is it not?"

"The same," I nodded. After the initial shock, I was now experiencing an odd sensation of relief, like a tingling that flowed through my veins, down my arms, into my toes. There would be no more waiting. Let the games begin.

"And you haven't seen her since that night, I assume."

"Mmuf," I said noncommittally, having stuffed a large bite of pastry into my mouth just in time. *I haven't seen her alive anyway,* I thought. When is a person not a person? When he or she is dead. The personhood is gone. Perhaps that was proof of the existence of an immortal soul?

"What about your friend?"

"Frances?" I swallowed and reached for my coffee. "What about her?"

The black eyebrows drew toward each other. "One assumes she may be upset by this news. To me it is an upsetting coincidence—"

"I expect she will be," I said quickly, treading upon Michael's words before he could produce any that proved harder for me to handle. "In fact, if it's all the same to you, I think I'll call around to her house later on this morning. That is, if you would not greatly mind answering the telephone for an hour or so."

"Perhaps," Michael said gravely, putting the paper down beside his plate, "I should come with you."

"No, I really don't think that's necessary. You don't even know Frances; she's my friend, not yours. She would feel awkward and so would I."

"I see. I hadn't thought of it that way."

I reached for the paper and removed a section to read. We finished our breakfast that way, both of us focused on our respective parts of the newspaper like an old married couple. And like many an old married couple, the silence between us was more strained than intimate.

After a while Michael consulted his pocket watch, cleared his throat, and said, "I'll go on and open the office. I have nothing in particular planned for this morning." He paused. "Fremont, kindly look at me."

I complied. "Yes?"

"If anything the least untoward happens when you are at the

McFadden house, I want you to telephone me. Surely they do have a telephone?"

"Yes, of course they do. However, my understanding is that the instrument is kept in Mr. McFadden's study and Frances does not have ready access to it. Therefore, I cannot promise to do as you ask."

Michael blew out a long, disgruntled breath, rubbed his hair the wrong way upon his head, got up from the table, and stamped to the breakfast-room doorway. There he stopped. My heart had begun to beat too fast. It was not like him to be this upset over my independent streak, and so I wondered what he knew that I didn't. However, I pretended to continue to read my newspaper while peering around the edge of it from time to time. He was standing there rubbing at the back of his head in a way that already had his hair looking like a brush. He does this only when he is upset.

Finally he turned back around. "See here, Fremont, I'm coming with you to McFadden's. If you wish to meet with your friend privately in her own part of the house, that is fine with me. I'll sit in the drawing room or wherever I'm put, and wait for you. I will not intrude, but I'm going to be there."

"Why?" Now I folded the paper and put it aside. "What have you learned about Jeremy McFadden that you haven't chosen to tell me, Michael? You're afraid he may be there, aren't you?"

Michael came back and sat down. He leaned across the table toward me, and his changeable eyes were like blue electricity. "He is a rough man, a jealous man, and a powerful one. In business he is said to play fair; he is not dishonest, which is more than can be said of many of San Francisco's most wealthy men. But the women in his life have not always fared well."

"I am not surprised," I said. Although I was, a bit—surprised by the good parts. I cannot see how a man who is fair to his workers can turn around and beat his wife.

Michael put his hand over mine at the table and grasped it

fiercely. "You won't marry me, I accept that, but your decision has certain consequences. One of them is that you appear to be without protection."

"Another is that I am not accepted socially, yet Frances accepts me," I said dryly, "that's why her friendship is so important to me. I don't wish to offend her husband, Michael, you may be sure of that. At least, not as long as she remains under his roof. I will be careful. I won't anger him."

"No," Michael said, shaking his head. With the merest twitch of a muscle, his jaw set in an implacable line. I had seldom seen him thus, and never since we'd begun, in our own fashion, to live together. "That's not enough. You know I seldom refuse you anything, Fremont, but this I cannot do. I have my limits. I will not let you go to McFadden's alone today, of all days. The medium who was murdered has been a bone of contention in that house. Your friend Frances may be involved in this somehow, which makes it dangerous. You must allow me to accompany you."

Now, although I am hardly the damsel-in-distress type, I found myself warmed and touched by Michael's concern. So I put my other hand on top of his, smiled . . . and then I remembered something. A mischievous twinkle came into my eye as I said, "Oh dear, you've caught me out. I'd hoped you would never have to know."

"Know what?" Michael withdrew his hand slowly from between mine, with a suspicious glint to his gaze.

"We-e-ell, the other night when I went out with Frances, and her husband came home while I was still there, I . . . well, I allowed him to believe I had a husband. I said you were very generous and did not mind in the least if I went about town doing good deeds after dark. So if he's there this morning . . ."

"Ah. I see. I'm to be caught in your lie. That's hardly fair." He complained, but he seemed amused. "Especially considering that I would be glad to swiftly make you an honest woman—at least on that particular point."

* * *

Cora, the McFaddens' maid, opened the door to us.

"Good morning, Cora," I said, extending my hand with a business card. "You may remember me, I'm Fremont Jones, a friend of Mrs. McFadden, and this is my partner at J&K, Michael Kossoff. May we come in?"

First she read the card, then she scrutinized us one by one, and only then did she bid us a good morning. "This way," she said, and led off down the hall without having invited us to come in. She took us to a room that reminded me of the morning room in my father's Boston house, which had been my mother's favorite room. Neither breakfast room nor parlor, it served the functions of both; and in my mother's case had held her desk, thus serving as her study.

Frances was there, seated by the window, the light all around her like an aureole and a dispirited droop to her shoulders. She looked like one of those paintings of dejected ladies that are so fashionable nowadays.

"Your friends are here," was Cora's way of announcing us.

Frances turned her head and gazed at us across the room, as if we'd called her back from someplace far, far away.

And I—curse me—suddenly became all too aware of Michael at my back, and his eye for a beautiful woman, and that Frances fitted the bill. Her dress was a glowing shade of amber, with an ivory lace insert covering her throat and neck. She had not yet done up her hair, only pulled it back, where it fell in a cascade of curls to below her shoulders. I thought, *Her husband must like her hair that way,* and in my mind's eye I could see the two of them seated at the breakfast table, she having left her hair down just for him.

Jeremy McFadden was not there now, though the room still smelled of toast. With all my heart I hoped he was gone from the house.

"Frances," I said, pulling myself together, "may I present my

friend and partner, Michael Kossoff? Michael, this is Frances Mc-
Fadden, who is married to Mr. Jeremy McFadden."

Michael murmured, "Charmed," or some such, coming around
me and taking her hand in this particular way he has, that I think
of as European, though I suppose it is merely Russian—he man-
ages to make a woman feel as if her hand has been kissed when it
has only been held for an instant. It is really quite extraordinary.

And while they performed this little ritual I visually searched
every nook and cranny of the room, ending by asking: "Has Mr.
McFadden left for work already? I realize it's rather early to come
calling, but we have good reason."

"Yes, he left a few minutes ago," Frances said, rising from her
seat by the window. "I believe we should still have some hot
coffee. Would you like some? And shall we all sit at the table?"

I glanced at Michael, eager to have him gone. My motives were
perhaps not as pure as one might have wished; whether he knew
that or not, he did take the hint.

"I've heard," Michael said in his most suave manner, which is
suave indeed, "that your husband has one of the finest libraries in
the City. I am a connoisseur of books. If I might examine the
library, while you ladies talk . . . ?"

"Of course!" Frances agreed with alacrity, "Though where you
can have heard such a thing I cannot imagine. Jeremy is far from a
scholar. I believe he purchased the books from someone's dis-
carded library, merely to fill his shelves."

"Precisely," said Michael, "from a great manor house in Ireland
that was torn down, or so I've heard. And I would dearly love to
examine these books."

I wondered if this was true, as Michael is perfectly capable of
making such a thing up on the spur of the moment. In any event,
Cora was summoned—and appeared so quickly that she must
have been listening right outside the door—and was dispatched to
show Michael to the library and to bring coffee to us all.

Frances resumed her seat by the window, and I took the one

nearest, perching on the edge of the seat. I was too excited to relax; anyway the chair was rather farther away than I would have preferred, but too heavy to move. After taking a moment to compose myself I inquired: "Did you see this morning's paper?"

She shook her head. "Of course not. Mr. McFadden belongs to the old school and doesn't want his wife reading newspapers. But I can guess why you're here. She's been found, hasn't she?"

I nodded wordlessly while watching my friend with care and some amazement. She, who had been so upset three days previously, was now far calmer than I. She made no query or comment about my not having called the police that fateful day. She seemed almost . . . illuminated. Transfixed. As if she were the one who had died and was on her way to heaven.

"Who was it?" she asked.

"I'm sure they don't know yet; there has scarcely been time!"

"No, I mean who was it that found her?"

"Oh. It was Patrick. His last name, I learned from the newspaper, is Rule."

Now it was Frances's turn to nod without saying anything.

"Thank goodness," I said fervently, "Mrs. Locke had a séance scheduled for yesterday evening, or she might be lying in that bedroom yet. Frances, I simply could not bring myself to report it. I hope you understand."

She gave a barely perceptible nod.

I went on: "Three days for the body to be found—I thought I should go mad with the waiting!"

Frances darted her eyes to the doorway and visibly stiffened her spine, which I took for a warning, and sure enough Cora came through with a tray of coffee. "We'll serve ourselves," Frances told the maid. "Just leave the tray on the table."

Cora raised her eyebrows and nodded her head once in a skeptical manner, as if to say, *I know what you're about.* But she left the room. And a few moments later, when I wandered over with a steaming cup of coffee in my hand, on the pretense of looking at a picture by the door, I found that she had taken the hint and disappeared entirely.

"Now, Fremont," Frances prompted as we resumed our seats with cups and saucers balanced on our knees, like ladies at a tea party, "you were saying?"

"I was saying that I found the waiting difficult, considering what we knew. I must say, you appear remarkably serene in the circumstances, Frances."

"I am receiving help," she said, and two spots of pink bloomed beneath her cheekbones. "It is a great comfort to me, though it comes from a . . . you might say, a far and lonely place."

"I beg your pardon?" I paused with the cup partway to my lips.

With a dreamy expression on her face, Frances said: "From beyond the grave."

EIGHT

A Ghostly Advent

A N UNPLEASANT CHILL settled in my bones. "You must tell me more," I said.

Frances seemed calm to the point of serenity. Her hand on the coffee cup was as steady as a rock. "I have a new ally," she said, "if you can make an ally of a ghost."

"A ghost."

"A disembodied spirit, a ghost, it is all the same."

"You have seen this ghost?"

Now, for the first time, Frances wavered. "I'm not sure. I think I did, in the middle of the night. He was trying to talk to me. I was in bed asleep . . . You understand, I presume, that like most decent couples my husband and I do not sleep in the same room?"

I nodded. I did understand, though my mother and father—at least until she took so very ill—had slept not only in the same room but in the same bed, and I considered them to be a decent couple.

With that cleared up, Frances resumed: "Well, as I was saying, I was in bed asleep, but I kept hearing this voice. A sort of hearty, masculine, good-natured voice. I assumed I was dreaming that some good, decent man had come to rescue me."

"Oh really?"

Frances went on: "And then I woke up. When I first opened my eyes—of course it was dark in the room—I thought I saw a figure standing not far from my bed. It frightened the dickens out of me, of course, but only until I'd realized it could be the good man from my dream. By then the figure had started to just . . . fade away. I called for him to come back but it was too late. He was gone."

I deduced from the way the pink spots on her cheeks burned so brightly that this ghost had not stayed gone, and said as much.

"That's true." She nodded vigorously, setting her now empty cup aside. She lowered her voice, leaning toward me, and I leaned too. Frances's eyes were sparkling. "Fremont, have you heard of automatic writing?"

With my face only inches from hers, it was all I could do not to roll my eyes. "You mean where the spirit takes over your hand? Supposedly? Yes, I've heard of it."

She nodded again, the curls bouncing prettily on her shoulders. "I tried it, and it works!"

This was too much for me. I could restrain myself no longer. "Of all the—the—what shall I say—*methods* for contacting the spirit world, Frances, that one seems to me to be the most open to self-delusion."

"Not if one's heart and mind are in the right place, Fremont! Really, he has saved my sanity. When Mrs. Locke was, um"—she bit her lip, not wanting to say any of the obvious words, until she settled upon—"rendered unable to help me, I was almost in de-spair. You remember."

I nodded. Yes, I remembered how desperate she'd seemed, and how she'd almost fallen apart when we discovered the body.

"I needed someone so badly."

"Frances, what exactly was it that you needed help with? You never said."

"I was having these experiences. I didn't understand them my-self. Hearing things right on the threshold of audibleness, but not able to quite make them out—it was truly maddening. Then I started losing time."

"Losing time?"

She nodded. "Whole chunks of it. No warning, not even any memory after."

"Hm," I mused. "As if you'd been in a trance, the way you were that night we went to the séance together?"

"Yes, precisely, and I was dreadfully afraid of what would hap-pen if I went into one of those trances when my husband was with me."

"Yes, you did say that. The automatic writing has helped? How?"

"Oh yes. He's explaining everything."

"He, who?"

"The Emperor," said Frances, glowing. "His name is Norton."

"Emperor," I said. "Norton." I managed not to hoot, but only with the greatest difficulty. Really, this was much too much!

She nodded vigorously and smiled an absolutely dazzling smile, while I feared she had lost her mind.

"Frances, what country—er, empire—was this Norton the Em-peror of?"

My question got rid of her smile, at least; I considered that a kind of progress.

"He hasn't said," she replied, "but then, I haven't asked him. We've been conversing about other things."

I placed my cup and saucer carefully on the floor by my feet. This was no time to be juggling crockery. "I'm very interested in this. Tell me, Frances, how does one converse through automatic writing? Doesn't the spirit have to—as it were—take over your hand? Yet words have their origin in the mind; does that mean this Norton is taking over your mind too? That hardly would seem to facilitate two-way communication."

Frances had not been highly educated, but she was shrewd, and she did not appreciate my skepticism. Her posture before had been alert, lively, and yearning; but now her backbone turned to steel, she seemed an inch or so taller, and her voice grew a frosty edge. She said: "You don't believe me."

"No," I shook my head, "that's not it. I do believe you. I just am not so sure as you are that this Norton—"

She interrupted me. "That's the second time you've called him 'this Norton' in that tone of voice. He's an emperor, he deserves more respect, Fremont. He's a good spirit, but I don't think it would do to make him angry. Emperors are powerful personages. You never know what he might be capable of."

"All right." I felt as if I were in one of Sutro's deepest baths, treading water as fast as I could, yet barely able to keep my nose clear of it. "I apologize to you and to Emperor Norton. I meant no disrespect. I was about to say, I'm not as sure as you seem to be that he has come to help you."

She arched her neck and turned her head slightly so that she regarded me out of the corners of her eyes. "What would convince you?"

"A demonstration," I said suddenly, with conviction. "I should like to observe the automatic writing. Also I think it would be a good idea for us to find another authority in the field, now that Mrs. Locke is no longer available. You mentioned Ingrid Swann—"

"Yes, but she's a charlatan, or so they say. She's a celebrity, and charges quite a lot of money for anything she does. Mrs. Locke was supposed to be the most honest and reliable. But really, I don't think I need an intermediary any longer, Fremont. I'm sure the Emperor himself will teach me, through the messages in the automatic writing. We have made a bargain, you see."

Oh Lord, this was getting worse and worse. Dr. Faustus bargaining with the Devil could not have worried me more.

Frances continued: "He is to teach me about the spirit world, and I am to do something he was unable to do when he left the land of the living."

"Which is . . . ?" It gave me chills to ask.

"I don't know yet, he hasn't said. The Emperor has very graciously decided to teach me first what I need to know, to perfect our communication. Then he will tell me what it is that I'm to do."

"Very gracious indeed," I said, and if Frances heard the irony in my voice she gave no sign of it. Talking about the Emperor had restored her serenity. "So, Frances," I asked, "may I be allowed to observe when you next attempt the automatic writing?"

She smiled again, very sunny. "Well of course, Fremont. You're my friend, I'm sure you can be his friend too."

"And when might we do this?"

"Tomorrow after luncheon, I should think. Jeremy is seldom at home at that time, and I can say to Cook and Cora that I've gone to my room for a rest. There's just one problem . . ." Her voice trailed off.

I waited impatiently, thinking there were far more problems than just one, and how I could solve any of them I had no idea whatever.

Frances rose from her chair. "Come and stand by me at the window, Fremont. There is something I want to show you." Beckoning, she went to a long casement window that looked out over a narrow strip of grass between her house and the one next door. Though the houses along this section of Broadway are rather grand, they have no yards to speak of.

When I was standing next to her, she put her hand on my shoulder and her face near mine. "I don't really have anything to show you," she said softly, "but I want to tell you something that absolutely no one else must hear."

I nodded, my eyes fixed on a leafy bush clipped into a round shape just outside the window. A tiny bird, a finch with gray and yellow markings, landed in the bush and began to sing, but I could scarcely hear him through the glass.

"I have my own key to a side door," Frances said, "the one the gardener uses. No one else comes or goes that way. It's how I was able to get out the day I came to you."

I nodded again. I could hear the bird better now, but still faintly. It stopped in mid-trill, hopped a bit, and cocked its head, fixing me—or so I fancied—with its beady black eye.

"I carry the key to that door with me always." Turning slightly, she darted a glance over our shoulders toward the door, then plunged her hand deep into the pocket of her skirt. She whispered, "Give me your hand!"

I did as she asked, and felt the cool slickness of metal in my palm. My fingers closed over the key, and I looked into Frances's hazel eyes, so close to mine.

She continued swiftly, "You can have a copy made, and return the key to me when you come tomorrow. I want you to come in secret, through that side door."

"If you are completely certain it's necessary," I agreed, also whispering. "Where, precisely, is the door? And when I am through it, where do I go?"

"You will enter the small room I told you about, with a sink and storage for outdoor equipment and so on, where I arrange flowers. That room is at the end of the backstairs hall, at right angles to the kitchen. If you're careful, you can go quickly to the stairs without being seen. As for how to find the door from the outside—"

Frances stopped abruptly. For a moment I thought I was again hearing the little bird, but much more clearly; then I realized it was Michael, whistling as he came down the hall . . . and very considerate it was of him to warn us, too.

"Come tomorrow at two o'clock!" Frances quickly concluded. "Now, I'll draw you a diagram for finding the outside door."

She could be quite an actress when the occasion required. I watched with an odd mix of concern and admiration as Frances became the considerate hostess, warmly welcoming Michael again to the room, inquiring as to how he had enjoyed the library and listening to his reply with a rapt expression on her face. Then with a graceful gesture toward the little lady's desk beside that same window where we'd just stood, she said, "If you will excuse me, Mr. Kossoff, there is a recipe I've promised Fremont. I'll just take a moment to write it down and then you can be on your way."

At the word "recipe," Michael flashed me a skeptical look, with one side of his mouth curving and one eyebrow arching upward. I merely smiled enigmatically and shrugged, as if to say, "Who knows? Maybe I've suddenly become interested in cooking."

I decided, on the way home, that I should have to confide in Michael. Selectively, of course. I said, "I'm concerned about Frances. I fear we were on firmer ground when she was going to séances at night, even if that did mean leaving the house against her husband's wishes."

"What do you mean, Fremont?" Though his attention had to be primarily upon his driving, as the Maxwell had a steep section of hill to climb, he turned his head toward me for a moment.

"She is making contact without the medium now," I said, stressing the "without." "Frances has taken up automatic writing."

"Well, I can't see the harm in that."

"She believes she is being visited by a spirit, who calls himself Emperor Norton."

"Did I hear you right? Did you say Emperor Norton?"

"Yes, as odd as that may seem, it is what I said."

To my great surprise, Michael burst out laughing. He laughed so hard that, at the top of the hill, he did not keep enough pressure on the brake and we began to slide backward.

"Michael!" I said sharply. "I cannot imagine what's so funny, but if you don't pay attention to your driving we shall crash."

He rolled his eyes, still laughing, and performed some maneuvers with hands and feet that had poor Max bucking back up and over the top of the hill. As we proceeded down the long slope at the other side, Michael's laughter subsided to snorts and burbles. By the time he had turned left, to take us up to Divisadero and home, I was wanting to laugh too—laughter being catching, like a disease—if only he would let me in on the joke.

"Well," I urged, "are you going to tell me?"

"I'm sorry." He wiped his eyes with the back of his hand. "It's just that the idea of that old reprobate coming in spirit to visit your fair friend Frances . . ." Michael gave one last whoop and then sobered. "You know, if she's making it up, she's made an exceedingly odd choice."

"I haven't the slightest idea what you're talking about."

"Emperor Norton was a real person, though not, of course, a real emperor. He lived here in San Francisco during the previous century; arriving, I think, during the second wave of Gold Rushers. He made a lot of money somehow. I'm not up on all the details. He got in over his head, though, on some speculation—having to do with rice. And he lost all his money, after which he disappeared for two years. When he reappeared, he was wearing an outlandish sort of military costume with epaulets and gold braid and a crosswise sash, a high hat with ostrich plumes in it, and a sword in his belt. He said he was Norton I, Emperor of the United States and Protector of Mexico. He'd lost his mind, poor fellow."

I began to smile. Though of course there is not much to smile about in a man's losing all his money and then his mind, still there was something amusing in the story.

Michael continued: "The whole city adopted Norton. He printed his own currency, and merchants and restaurateurs accepted it as if it were legal tender. He used to write proclamations, and would stand in Union Square and read them to all passersby. He kept up a correspondence with various politicians and heads of state, including Tsar Nicholas, as I have good reason to know." At this point, we pulled up alongside our double house on Divisadero and Michael tugged at the hand brake and cut the motor.

I did not inquire how Michael would have known that this Norton fellow had written to the Tsar, as I have not at all made my peace with his continuing Russian connections. I simply sat where I was and waited for Michael to finish the story.

Which he did: "Norton even traveled by train regularly to Sacramento, and had a seat reserved for him in the gallery in the state senate."

"Perhaps he was not so crazy after all," I said.

"Some people said the same," Michael acknowledged, "and after his death there were those who insisted he had not lost all his money but merely, in his madness, misplaced it. But I'm getting ahead of myself. I wanted to say that he was, by all accounts, a good fellow. One of his proclamations was that the children of San Francisco should have a Christmas tree in Union Square every year—it was Norton who began that custom, which of course we still follow. And he was devoted to his two dogs, Lazarus and Bummer—"

"Lazarus!" I exclaimed. "Did you say Lazarus?"

"Why yes," said Michael, looking puzzled, "that was the name of one of Norton's two dogs. They went with him everywhere."

"Even in death, they are still with him, apparently," I said. And then I told Michael about the medium's barking, and how the voice had come out of Frances's mouth at the séance, saying, *Lazarus, come away from there!*

I went chilly all over as I said it. Perhaps Michael did too, for the depths of his eyes seemed to swirl and became unfathomable, as they do when he does not want anyone to know what he is thinking. And then he said, "That is very, very strange."

These odd developments with Frances gave me an added incentive, as an investigator with the J&K Agency, to carry through on my plan to free myself of Michael's supervision. I needed freedom to do investigations on my own. To invent a case even, if necessary, to give me time away from the office.

An opportunity presented itself much sooner than I could have hoped. That very afternoon, in fact. Over our lunch at home of soup and bread, Michael casually mentioned that he had made an appointment, under an assumed name, to meet with Wish Stephenson at the shipping company at 3 P.M. Wish had managed to get hold of some papers he wanted Michael to see, but did not dare to bring them out of the building.

"That's nice," I said idly, as if my mind were elsewhere. Which in fact it was—I was already mentally running through the various pieces of my new disguise, making sure I had forgotten nothing.

Michael left in due course, and at two-thirty I went upstairs to my own part of the house. I began to get ready, while keeping my ears, as it were, cocked for the sound of either telephone or doorbell. I did have to go down and answer the telephone once, but otherwise I was not interrupted. When I had finished, the transformation was astounding.

"Fremont," I said to myself in the mirror, chuckling, "you are a rascal!"

Fremont Jones had become a young man.

I had bought the clothes at one of the better secondhand shops, telling the sales clerk I was shopping for my twin brother, who was exactly like me in height, weight, and bone structure. The clerk, a mousy older woman with a distracted, weary air, had left me to browse on my own—exactly as I'd wanted. I had chosen well, if I did say so myself.

My suit was a three-piece of dark gray wool, the trousers of the right length, as were the sleeves; its vest came in handy for further hiding bound-up breasts. The stiff shirt collar was a bit too large—and entirely too scratchy—but its looseness was remedied somewhat by tightly knotting the four-in-hand tie. The tie itself was a silk print with a tiny black figure on a maroon ground; completely unmemorable, it would attract no attention. The plain white shirt had seen better days but was still serviceable. My biggest problem had been finding proper shoes, as my feet are rather narrow; I'd had to settle for women's shoes, black leather, in a clodhopperish style with wide low heels. I thought they looked enough like men's shoes to get away with it.

I had practiced applying the false mustache, which I'd obtained in a costume shop, but even so it seemed to take forever—not to mention that I hated the acrid smell of the spirit gum one had to use to glue it to the upper lip. The spirit vapors brought tears to my eyes and made me sneeze. But when I'd done, the effect was worth it: I looked quite the man. I turned my head from side to side and speculated how I would look in a full beard. Maybe next time . . .

The *pièce de résistance* was the fedora, which I had bought new and to fit, again using the ruse of the twin brother. The hat salesman had not been quite so credulous as the clerk in the secondhand shop, but he'd said nothing and had been quite ready to take my money, so all was well. My fedora was a lovely soft felt, black, with a deep crown (useful for accommodating the hair piled on top of my head) and a brim just wide enough to throw my eyes into shadow. I gave the brim a final tug to get the angle just right, then stood back to admire myself.

From the distance of a few feet, if I had not known it was I in the mirror, I swear I would have wondered, *Who is that handsome young fellow?* I swaggered a bit. I had not realized my legs were so long. Taking up my walking stick, which fortunately is an item that can be used by either sex, I strolled out of my apartments to the stairs, which I descended with a deliberately long, loose gait, somewhat (I hoped) like Wish Stephenson's.

The J&K Agency, behind its handsome facade on upper Divisadero, is hardly the kind of place where one can post a handwritten note on the door—which I have been wont to do in my past places of business. Therefore, I simply locked the door behind me and trusted that anyone who could find our discreetly advertised business would also have the sense to figure out that, if we were closed, the thing to do would be to come back later. Then I strolled off, deliberately punctuating my long strides with a downward stroke of the walking stick. I was having a fine time.

The hands of the clock on the tower of the Ferry Building pointed to three-fifteen as I swung down off the streetcar. The offices of the Red Line—that was the name of the shipping company J&K had been hired to investigate—were here along the Embarcadero. I consulted the slip of paper on which I'd written the address, and saw by the numbers that the building I sought was not by the water, but rather on the other side of the street.

All to the good, I thought. Once I'd found the Red Line's building, which could not be far away, I could watch from across the street. I bought a newspaper from a vendor in a kiosk near the corner of the Ferry Building and moved on. Michael had taught me that it is best, when on surveillance, not to make eye contact with passersby. They are less likely to pay attention to you, or to remember you, if you do not look them directly in the eye.

The street was noisy and disorderly; the air smelled of salt water, and of fish.

Suddenly I felt frightened for no reason. I could not breathe, as if I were a fish out of water myself. The fear had come over me so fast that I was taken completely by surprise. For long moments I stood paralyzed, very much in danger of calling attention to myself. My head was swimming, and I thought I might fall.

I'm in no danger, I told myself, tilting my head down, hiding beneath the brim of the fedora, *it's only Michael I am following, it's only a training exercise, little more than a game.* Groping toward the nearest doorway, where I might lean against something solid, I felt myself losing hold, drowning . . . in fear and shame.

NINE

Mesmer Eyes

IT WAS MY UNWILLINGNESS to bear the shame that saved me. I simply would not, could not, disgrace myself by doing something stupid, like fainting, right out here on the Embarcadero! Leaning against the building behind me, my head still bowed to obscure my face, I reached into my vest pocket as if to consult a pocket watch. I did not own a watch of any sort—I had lost mine in the earthquake and so far had not been able to afford a replacement—but this little pantomime of time-telling gave me a momentary focus.

As I studied my empty, cupped hand, a visual memory flashed through my mind. It was visceral, as well: shockingly cold, utterly airless, wet, and fishy-smelling. It was a vivid memory of the time

I had been kept prisoner on these docks, and subsequently had come all too close to drowning.

Well, I thought, straightening up and returning my invisible watch to its pocket, *no wonder!* I had read somewhere that the olfactory sense is a great trigger of memory—well, just now I had received firsthand confirmation. As soon as I realized that my fear belonged in the past, it disappeared. My breathing returned to normal, and I no longer felt as if I were drowning. With the kind of shrug that I have often seen men do, to settle their jackets on their shoulders, I struck out again down the street.

In a few moments I had located the Red Line's suite of offices, which had a row of windows facing front, with a band of red painted smartly along the top, and RED LINE picked out in gold upon a red background over the door. I merely glanced that way, continuing on a few feet down the street where, on my side, a wide wooden railing between two docks overlooked the water. A fine place for a young man to rest with his weight upon his elbows and his newspaper spread out before him. So I did.

By the clock on the Ferry Building it was almost four when Michael came out of the Red Line door. I had gazed upon that newspaper for so long, I'd fair memorized the thing. Michael was walking fast. He usually did; that was one of the reasons he was difficult to tail, one could not hang back too far. At least I could be grateful he had left the Maxwell at home, otherwise I'd have been in quite a pickle. Michael did not appear to be returning home just yet. He headed not for the streetcar stop that would take him toward our end of Divisadero, but back the other way, toward the Financial District.

The streets of the Financial District are flat because they rest on landfill. Beneath all these businesses that keep San Francisco's economy afloat, the skeletons of abandoned ships lie buried. Mrs. O'Leary, my former landlady, had told me about this—how during the Gold Rush so many people had left their wooden ships in the harbor to rot while they pursued their dreams of gold that the ships became a nuisance, and a health hazard as well. So someone had the bright idea of pushing them up against one another and filling the area between with rubble, then paving the whole thing over. Thus the City obtained this flat "made land" and a new shoreline, and the Embarcadero itself.

For my purposes this afternoon, the flat streets were a boon. Michael left the Embarcadero on Front Street, and so did I. He walked down to Pine, and then up to Sansome; for a moment I thought we were on our way to the Monkey Block—which is really the Montgomery Block, but nobody calls it that. But no, there on the corner he went into a tobacco shop, and I recalled he'd said he needed some for his pipe.

I crossed the street and busied myself among the sweet-scented and colorful wares of a flower vendor's cart. I longed for some of the purple irises, though I knew I should not buy them. Their long stems in a paper cone would be unwieldy, and the bright color would call attention to me. On the other hand, I reasoned—or rationalized—if need be I could also use them to hide my face. So I bought the flowers and had just paid when Michael exited the shop. I made a mental note of its exact location and the approximate time. Then we were off again, up Sansome this time, to California, where Michael took his place in the queue waiting for the cable car.

There were enough people milling about that I didn't think he would pay attention to me, but nevertheless I strolled on by. I went into one of those corner markets that are ubiquitous in San Francisco—helpful for those who want to do their shopping on their way home, or to lurk about and spy on people, as the case may be. Such markets always seem to keep their fruits and vegetables near the window, and this one was no different, so I stood sorting through the apples and potatoes until I heard the clang of the cable car bell and the ratcheting sound of its arrival. Through the window I watched, waiting, waiting . . .

My heart was beating rapidly to the thrill of the chase. I waited until the last minute, my eyes scanning the passengers as they boarded, but I did not see Michael. Surely he hadn't given me the slip? There was no time, the cable car had already begun to move, and I must get on or let it go. I ran, jumped, grabbed hold, and was on—irises, walking stick, and all. Quite a feat; in a skirt I could not have accomplished it.

A pretty girl, no more than fifteen or sixteen, I guessed, smiled at me; I had to pretend I hadn't seen, but I was pleased nonetheless. Her smile gave me confidence that my disguise was as good as I thought it was. My end of the car was so crowded that only the women were sitting, the men were all standing, and I had an awkward moment of juggling my stick and the flowers while reaching into my pockets for the carfare, but I managed.

At last, I caught sight of Michael's silver-shot dark head and could breathe more easily, knowing I had not lost my quarry. Ever the aristocrat, he had somehow obtained a seat in the middle section of the car, which has glass windows and a sliding door, and is sheltered from the wind. I was in the back, in the open. I didn't mind the wind, I liked it, as long as it didn't blow off my fedora. And as the cable car climbed Nob Hill, the view behind us, out over the Bay, became increasingly glorious.

There was still a great deal of rebuilding going on in this section of the City, even two years after the Great Quake. One presumed that was because the homes here were large and expensive, and thus took more time to complete. I wondered who would live in them. The great palatial homes of Stanford and Hopkins and their ilk were, alas, no more. All around us, the noise of pounding and sawing, and workmen calling back and forth, was so great it could be heard even over the screeching of the cable car's brakes as it ground to a halt at every corner.

In my preoccupied exhilaration I'd forgotten to count streets, but we had gone past the crest of Nob Hill when I saw Michael rise and turn. He intended to get off by the back, my end, of the cable car. *Bad luck.* I tugged down the brim of my fedora while I wondered what to do. Getting off right behind him would be far too obvious. I should just have to go on to the next stop, and hope I could come back and pick up his trail.

Thankfully, I was able to do both. Michael was easily spotted, about a block and a half ahead of me going downhill on Larkin. He was walking more slowly than usual, and looking up at the house numbers. These streets had also been destroyed during the earthquake, and had been rebuilt in a combination of apartment houses and office buildings, much as before. It was easier here to follow him without fear of detection because of the stoops and doorways, which made good hiding places. In the block between Bush and Sutter, Michael stopped, looked up at the house in front of him, down at something in his hand, put that something back into his pocket, and began to climb the steps.

I judged the time, at this point, to be between four-thirty and four forty-five. Quite likely this would be Michael's last stop before heading back to Divisadero Street. When he had gone into the house and did not reappear, I quickened my steps until I came to the house he had entered. At least I thought this was the one, but as it was almost identical to those on both sides . . .

Oh, botheration! I thought. *I shall never get the hang of this!* I should have looked for some sort of identifying object in the vicinity of where Michael had been standing before he went in. Well, I hadn't, and it was too late now. All I could do was hope I'd gotten it right. It would be too bad if I were to ruin my delicious surprise when I had come this far.

These houses all had steps leading up to an entry beneath a small portico—the exact number of steps for each being related to the downslope. Thus each house also had a basement level, with access through a lower door in a well beneath the steps. I could wait, sheltered there, until Michael came out—that would be the safest course, particularly if I'd judged wrong and he came instead out of one of the houses next door. But that was not what I wanted to do. I wanted desperately to surprise him, and had planned it all out; for my surprise to work, I would have to arrive back at Divisadero Street before him. I decided I would rather risk being wrong than give up my cherished plan.

I climbed the steps—in this case, five—and paused beneath the portico. The place had more the look of apartments than offices, and I found myself reluctant to trespass. There was a glass in the door, in a large diamond-shaped pattern, but it was pebbled and when I looked through it the effect was much the same as opening one's eyes underwater. Everything looked blurred and a bit murky. The door itself was oak with a golden sheen, and the doorknob was brass. No knocker—that seemed odd. I turned the doorknob, the door was unlocked, and I entered.

I was standing in a small foyer, perhaps nine feet square. Directly opposite the door by which I'd entered, a console table had been placed against the wall. Behind the table, where ordinarily one would have hung a mirror, there hung instead a dark blue velvet curtain. That seemed in questionable taste, a tad theatrical; of course I wanted immediately to look behind it, but I did not. To my left and right there were doors, now closed. From the right rear corner of the foyer a staircase curved upward and disappeared through an opening in the high ceiling. In the other direction, beneath my feet, the hardwood floor showed a high polish. The whole place smelt faintly, pleasantly, of wax.

Uncertain how to proceed, I stood listening intently. I could hear nothing—the doors were too thick. I walked carefully, so as not to make noise on the bare floor, over to the console table.

Aha! Here was something useful.

In the center of the table sat a decorative bowl, but it was being used for more than decoration. I gathered this bowl served in lieu of a guest book and that one was supposed to leave one's card: it contained several, of both the personal and the business kind. I did not add mine. I did not need to in any case, because Michael had already left a J&K card right on top. Better yet, flat upon the table right in front of the bowl—one could not see it at all from a distance—lay a plaque with intaglio carving: WILLIAM VAN ZANT, DOCTOR OF PHENOMENOLOGY AND HYPNOTISM, SUITE 4, SECOND FLOOR.

Quickly I set down the paper cone of flowers and tucked my walking stick under my arm so as to free up my hands. Though I trust my memory for most things, I wanted to be sure I got this absolutely right. I copied the details about Dr. Van Zant in the small notebook I carried for that purpose, then put it away, and in a state of combined curiosity and jubilation, I left. Luck held—I was able to hail an auto-taxi on Sutter Street, and very shortly I was back at home, which is to say, at the office of the J&K Agency.

The little bell on the front door jingled. I swiftly assumed my planned position: feet up, leaning back in the chair. I wished I had a cigar; even though they are nasty, smelly things they do create a certain effect.

"I beg your pardon!" Michael said, in a tone that did not sound as if he were doing any such thing.

I pushed up the brim of the fedora in back, so that it slid down my forehead toward the bridge of my nose, and said in the deepest voice I could muster: "Sez who?"

"I don't know who you are, and I don't care, but if you know what's good for you, young man"—Michael advanced as he spoke—"you'll take your feet off that desk and get out of here this instant. Otherwise I'm calling the police. I suppose you're some friend of Wish Stephenson's, is that it? Well, you can tell him—no, I'll tell him—that we don't appreciate cheeky fellows putting their feet up on our desks. Where's Miss Jones?"

I had to suck in my cheeks to keep from laughing out loud. With my feet still on the desk, I took up the notepad and began to read in my normal voice—quickly, because from the tone of Michael's voice, another few seconds was all he would tolerate the cheeky fellow who was really me. "At 3:55 P.M. the subject, Michael Kossoff, came out of the Red Line offices on the Embarcadero. He walked south, leaving the Embarcadero at Front Street . . ." and so on.

He came right up to my desk. I could feel his eyes moving back and forth over me, examining this new creature he had never seen before. I continued my reading without missing a beat, until finally I concluded: "For follow-up—obtain more information about Dr. Van Zant and subject's connection to the doctor."

Now I looked up and said, straight to Michael, "Submitted for your consideration by this investigator, Fremont Jones."

His smile began as a twitch at the corners of his mouth and spread from lips to cheeks, to a dawn breaking in his eyes. It was worth waiting for, worth risking almost anything for: that smile.

"I don't believe it," he whooped, "I simply cannot believe it!"

I swung my feet down off the desk, pushed back in the chair, and made a little bow from the waist while still seated.

"The fellow with the flowers, on the cable car, that was *my* Fremont?"

"I wouldn't put it quite like that," I said, stroking my false mustache with my index finger like a dandy, "but quibbles aside regarding your use of the word 'my,' then yes. The fellow with the flowers was me. I mean I."

"Oh, well done! Stand up, please, turn around . . ." Michael went on like that for a while. Then we locked the door and went upstairs, where nothing would do but that Michael himself should remove my costume piece by piece. He wanted to be sure I was really under there—or so he said.

I may have played the man, but I was not above using woman's wiles when necessary to obtain information. We'd had our supper and were back in bed again, supposedly to fall asleep, when I remarked in an offhand manner: "I wonder what a doctor of phenomenology does. The hypnotism part I understand, or at least I think I do. Hypnotism is the same as mesmerism, isn't it?" I raised up on my elbow. "I thought mesmerism went out of vogue long ago."

Michael, who had been lying on his side, rolled over onto his back with a little snort and said to the shadows on the ceiling, "I suppose you are following up now, is that it? Let's see, it's been five or six hours since I agreed you have all the necessary skills to do investigations on your own, and you've decided to start with me. Am I right?"

"Something like that." It was a clear night. Moonlight drifted through the window, illuminating parts of Michael's bedroom and throwing others into shadow. I traced the line of his profile with my fingertip. Such a noble brow; such a fine, straight nose; such a shapely mouth, which remained so stubbornly closed. "Please, Michael," I pleaded, withdrawing my hand, "I'm dying of curiosity."

Still he said nothing, so I went on, "Besides, I can't help thinking you might have gone to see someone like that because of me. And Frances, and all. Maybe this morning at her house, when you came whistling so considerately toward the morning room, it wasn't the first time you'd been down that hall. Maybe you were listening outside the door all along."

"Why, Fremont, I'm offended to think you believe me capable of such a thing!"

"Hah! Not likely."

"Actually . . ." His voice trailed off, and softened, and he opened one arm for me to snuggle beneath. I put my cheek in the soft hollow of his shoulder, where I could feel the faintest of vibrations as he spoke. "I had hoped not to have to tell you this until later, if at all. You're perverse, do you know that, Fremont Jones?" He gave me a little squeeze. "That you should pick this afternoon, of all times, to follow me . . ."

Michael sighed, a heavy sigh, and I said, "You don't have to tell me if you'd rather not. We agreed we would not necessarily tell each other everything. If this is a private matter, I won't pry."

"No, it's all right. This does concern you, but not in the way you think. I went to see Dr. Van Zant for reasons that have nothing to do with anything you and Frances may be involved in. I've avoided it for as long as I can. A certain group of Russian nobles who are very influential with the Tsar have proposed that I perform a, um, disagreeable task. If I do undertake it with success, I've been promised they will persuade Nicholas to let me go for good."

"And this task is?"

"To force Rasputin from the court, by whatever means necessary, before he has gained further control over the Empress."

I rose up. This was not something one could lie still for. "B-but—you're here and they're there! It's so far away. It's another world. How could you possibly—"

"Ssh, my love." He pulled me back down. "That's precisely the point. I can study and organize from a great distance. When the time comes to strike, I will dart in and out like a snake, no one will even know I was there. However . . ."

After a minute, when he did not continue, I said, "However what?"

"However, I have to be certain Efimovich—that is, Rasputin— is the fake I believe him to be. The people who contacted me could be using him for a scapegoat. So, right now I'm studying the situation, gathering information, learning about mesmerism and psychic healing. That's why I went to meet Dr. Van Zant."

"Oh," I said, somewhat mollified. I snuggled again, feeling a welcome heaviness steal across my eyelids. Sleepily, as if asking for a bedtime story, I said, "Tell me more about Rasputin."

"He claims to be a healer. It is said that his body carries a sort of magnetic aura that has healing properties. Simply being in close proximity to him is supposed to impart a salutary effect. Something that is not widely known about the imperial family is that the Tsarevich Alexei is not a healthy child. The Empress is said to feel comforted by having Rasputin near the boy; indeed she believes the man is holy, and a healer."

I stifled a yawn. "Where's the harm in that? It's not as if there aren't lots of other people around all the time. I mean an imperial court sounds busy, crowded. So what's one more person?"

"Rasputin does not stop with simply imparting the beneficence of his presence, or whatever he calls it. He dabbles in mysticism, in reading minds and predicting the future. It is feared that he will begin to give advice, and to insist that his advice be followed, on threat of his withdrawal from Alexei. I'm no authority, Fremont, but I suspect Rasputin achieves his effects through the use of hypnotism. And that's why I went to see Dr. Van Zant. He has an interesting philosophy."

"Ummmm," I murmured.

Michael finished as if talking to himself. But I do think I heard everything he said before I fell asleep: "Van Zant believes that hypnotism is a legitimate tool in the hands, and eyes, of a trained practitioner. He calls this science, not magic. He is a debunker of the Spiritual, the mystic, and the clairvoyant. A very interesting man."

TEN

Approaching the Unknown

THE MOST DELICIOUS SMELL came wafting into the office, along with the tall figure of Wish Stephenson, who carried a paper bag in his hand. It was a little past noon, and I did not have to be an investigator—dared one say "detective"?—to guess what was in it.

"Lunch?" I inquired with a smile. "I didn't expect you back in these parts so soon. I thought your investigation at the Red Line was supposed to take weeks."

"I've brought us lunch to share, in a sort of celebration," he said. "Michael didn't tell you?"

"No." I came out from behind the desk and followed Wish through the office and back toward the kitchen, thankful to be walking behind him because I felt myself blush as I explained: "We became involved in something else when he came back from his meeting with you yesterday, and I suppose he forgot. So, you may have the singular pleasure of telling me yourself."

"He's not here, then?" Wish nodded toward the open door of Michael's small study as we passed.

"No, he's out again. I believe he's working on one of his own projects, nothing to do with J&K."

Wish put the bag on the kitchen table, sat down, and began removing paper cartons from the bag. "All the more for us then, Fremont." He grinned.

"Italian?" I inquired, sniffing—I hoped delicately—as I collected plates and forks and spoons. "Shall we have a glass of red wine alongside? I believe there is a bottle already opened in the cabinet."

"No, thanks. Water for me. I've got spaghetti here and three kinds of sauce: mushrooms with tomato, marinara with shrimp, and Bolognese with those tiny little meatballs. All from Vitelli's— I came back through North Beach and I couldn't resist."

"Mmmm," I murmured appreciatively, "Michael will be desolated to learn what he has missed!"

As we ate, Wish explained that he had caught the Red Line's miscreant. The proof had been in the papers he'd shown Michael in their meeting yesterday, and Michael had agreed it was sufficient. So this very morning Wish had told the head of the company, and produced the proof. "I'm to get a bonus," he concluded, twinkling, "for my quick work."

"Good for you!" I reached over and squeezed his hand. "Now I have news of my own, though not nearly so profitable as yet."

I went on to tell Wish how I had successfully tailed Michael, wearing my masculine disguise. First Wish looked a bit shocked, then his lips began to twitch, and finally he was laughing out loud as I related how irate Michael had been to find a young man—or so he thought—with his feet up on my desk.

"Oh," Wish said, "I would've liked to be a fly on the wall, to see that!"

"Yes," I agreed, laughing too, "but I couldn't prolong the ruse for as long as I wanted, because I do believe Michael would have snatched me up and booted me out onto the street in another half a minute!"

After a little while, when we had laughed ourselves out, Wish said, "I suppose now you'll be getting all the best cases. The clients will come in the door, take one look at you, and they won't be wanting a beanpole like myself to do their investigating."

"Hah!" I said. We both knew he was only being kind. I would be extremely lucky to have one case to four of his; and if Michael ever decided to become an active rather than only an advisory member of the staff, I doubted there would be work enough in San Francisco for all three of us. Especially considering we already had a branch of Pinkerton's in the City—stiff competition, indeed.

After we had done very well by the Italian dishes, and I'd stored the leftovers in the cooler, Wish and I settled down at our respective desks. He to write his report for Red Line, and I to write a letter to my friend Meiling, as I was all caught up on paperwork. A peaceful silence came over us. There is something so pleasant about working quietly in shared space, in perfect trust and camaraderie.

A few minutes before two o'clock it was up to me to break that silence. "I have an appointment soon," I said. "What are your plans for the afternoon?"

Wish looked over his shoulder at me. "Maybe I'll type up this report, using my foolproof two-finger method. How long will you be?"

"An hour, perhaps two. I'm not sure. This is not business, it's . . . well, personal."

"The plot thickens. You have your personal project, Michael has his . . . Well, I'll have you know, Fremont, that I also have a personal project. But it doesn't require my attention until after you return, at whatever time that may be.''

"Thank you. That is most kind.''

"Doesn't look like I'll be too busy, in any case. The phone hasn't rung all afternoon,'' Wish said. Being on the police force had conditioned him to expect that something would be happening every minute. But Michael had told me that in the investigatory business there would be many times when we could expect to be idle, especially while the business gained its reputation. So I was not unduly concerned.

"We'll be fine, all of us, you'll see,'' I said, and gave him a pat on the arm before going upstairs to change before walking to the McFaddens' house.

Frances always dressed so fashionably; I reckoned that I myself should go to see her looking more like her guest than a servant, even if I did plan to enter by the back stairs. So I took the time to change into a navy-blue dress Michael had given me, made in a simple style but of elegant heavy silk—the sort of dress that is dear to the heart of every Boston matron because it will never go out of style. There was still enough of the Bostonian in me to appreciate that. Around my shoulders I draped yet another gift: the fringed amethyst shawl from Mrs. O'Leary, the same one I'd let Frances wear a few days ago. Probably, I thought as I took one last critical glance in the mirror, I should put my hair up—but I wasn't going to. I was going to wear it in the same unfashionable way I've preferred for years: pulled back and fastened at the nape of the neck in a tortoiseshell clasp.

A small involuntary sigh escaped me as I tossed one end of the shawl over my shoulder, and an involuntary thought came with it: How nice it would be to have enough money of my own, so that I could buy something nice and new, and not have to rely on gifts from people like Mrs. O and Michael. But that made me feel bad, as being ungrateful, so I put it out of my mind.

* * *

Having committed to memory the diagram Frances had drawn for me, I found the seldom-used side door to the McFadden house with no difficulty. The black slicker, with its now familiar musty smell, hung just inside. Because I was already a bit late, I wasted no time in crossing the small room and exiting; the back stairs were straight ahead, everything as Frances had described, right down to the sound of voices coming from the kitchen. There was baking going on, and suddenly, for only an instant, I was a child again in my father's house on bread-making day. Now I knew he was coming, and in not too many more days, it seemed every place and everything was providing me with some memory of Father.

I resisted the urge to run up the stairs and climbed them instead stealthily, quietly, slowly. The steps themselves were narrow, the risers high; I should not have liked to be a servant going up and down these steps countless times a day, especially with my hands so full I could not see my feet. In the way of most sets of back stairs, they were spartan; but when I reached the second landing and passed into the corridor, the décor was quite something else again. I doubted Frances had had a hand in it, for the hand that had accomplished this effect had been a heavy one.

The corridor was wide, the ceiling high, the ambience oppressively rich and dark. The colors in the carpet might have glowed, the handsome wood of the wall paneling might have found a luster, but for the panes of a large stained-glass window that filtered all brightness from what light it allowed to pass through. As that window was at the other end of the corridor, I couldn't readily see what it depicted, nor was I to have the chance to examine it further at the moment because Frances had apparently been listening and watching for me. The second door on my right opened out and suddenly she was there, like a pale apparition.

I hastened to her, apologizing briefly for my lateness.

"You're not really so late," she said kindly. "We should get on with it though. There is no time to waste."

Her room was both as impressive and oppressive as the corridor outside it, though there was a good deal more light. It was neither feminine nor masculine, but rather had almost the look of one's best guest bedroom.

"Through here," Frances said. After giving the corridor outside one last swift check and closing and locking her bedroom door, she indicated that I should follow her. I did, and we passed through an inner dressing room—where indeed there were wardrobes (two) and chests (I did not count them) with shiny new brass locks—into a small sitting room with windows on two sides. This was more pleasant, with the little touches that make a room feel lived in, such as a fashion magazine lying open on an ottoman, a graceful little writing table with paper and pens out, and a small gas fire burning within a fireplace surround.

"So this is where you spend a good deal of your time," I said.

"Yes, as much as possible," Frances replied; and in the awkward pause that followed I reflected that I was glad there was at least one space in this vast unwelcoming house that she could call her own. A hint of anxiety stirred deep in her eyes but was quickly banished; she put her hand on the back of a straight chair pulled up to the writing table and said, "Please take a seat, Fremont. I'll be here, so I can write, of course. . . . Shall we begin?"

"By all means," I agreed.

I took one of a pair of wing chairs by the fire and shed my shawl. This was almost too much to watch, I felt like a voyeur . . . but not for long, for it was soon abundantly clear that my friend had gone into some special place where only she could go.

Like me, she had not put her hair up. But as I have said, Frances had hair that was nothing like mine; hers tumbled and curled and, when she bent her head, made a curtain to hide her face. She placed her hands, palms up, on either side of the pad of blank writing paper in some sort of invocation. The only sounds were

the faint exhalations of her ever deeper breaths and the tiny tick-
ing of a jewellike little clock upon the mantel. As for myself, I lost
track of time.

I did not know, could not tell, how long had passed before she
picked up the pen. She wrote rapidly without cease or pause, page
after page, pushing each sheet impatiently off the table to the
floor as space ran out. And when at last she was done, she
dropped the pen, slumped back in the chair with her arms hanging at her sides, the palms open again in supplication. Her eyes
were closed. Her breath was labored.

After a moment, without moving or opening her eyes she said,
"Fremont, you brought me luck. I have never felt his presence so
strongly, but I'm exhausted. Will you read the pages to me?"

I said of course I would, and bent down to gather them up,
carefully, in reverse of the order she'd written them. As the pages
were not numbered I took care not to disarrange them, all the
while watching Frances from the corner of my eye. She appeared
absolutely depleted. Surely this could not be good? But I did not
know what else to do, and the papers were in my hands, and so I
began to read.

" 'I, Norton I, Emperor of the United States and Protector of
Mexico, am here. Hello, pretty lady!' "

"He always starts like that," Frances murmured, so unexpectedly she almost startled me out of my skin. I waited in case she
had more to say, but she didn't, so I went on.

Norton had a lot to say. He was concerned about the state of
our nation and the state of the world. He was in particular unhappy about the way President Theodore Roosevelt had been gov-
erning the country. Norton delivered a diatribe against democ-
racy, then, in a striking example of illogical thinking—especially
since the spirits are supposed to be in a position to know so much
more than we do—inveighed for a while against what he called
the inbreeding of the European monarchies, which, according to

him, was turning them all into feeble-minded fools unfit to govern even their own bathroom habits.

As the pages went on, Norton's language grew coarser, though never vulgar outright; and the more I read the more I wondered: *Can Frances have written this herself? Is there really a spirit named Norton that has guided her hand?*

The clock on the mantel struck four; the sweet sound of its chimes hung like shimmering jewels in the air. I paused, not having realized it had grown so late. There was one page yet remaining to be read.

"Jeremy will be home soon," Frances whispered. She had been quiet for so long I had almost forgotten she was there. "Please finish, Fremont," she said without looking my way. She had propped her chin on her hand and was staring out the window. "There is more, I know it, I still have this lingering feeling of terrible urgency and anticipation. I must know what it's about, and I expect you would like to know too. Then you'll have to leave in a hurry."

I read the last page, which began with another salutation to Frances herself: " 'Fair lady, you could do us both a favor if you would be so kind. See, this old reprobate and miscreant—meaning myself—can't quite get back there or I'd do it alone—

" 'Hey!' " (This was apparently an aside within the narrative of the automatic writing, set off from the rest by scrawling dashes.) " 'Hey you, Bummer! Damn dog. Always nippin' at the heels of people passin' by, can't understand they don't have heels to nip no more! Still I was mighty glad to find him again Over Here, I certainly was, and Lazarus too. Who'd have thought. Good dogs, yes, that's right, you both lie down right there. . . . Now lessee, where was I?

" 'Oh yes, I was about to ask for the favor. See, I had this whatchamacallit, that's part of the trouble, I can't remember what it was. It won't come clear, on account of all them years my mind was in such a fog. Heh heh, mind in a fog, that's a good 'un for an old fella like me who loved to roam the streets of San Francisco more'n anything. Still and all, it's better when the fog stays on the outside and doesn't get in your head, know what I'm sayin'? This whatchamacallit, it was valuable. It meant a lot to me, only when I was alive and in the flesh, what with the fog in my mind, I forgot where I put it. Now I'm Gone Over to the Other Side, I know *where* it is but I can't remember *what* it is. Ain't that just the damnedest—oops, not such a good idea to say that word Over Here, never can tell who you might be givin' ideas to—just the most downright frustratin' thing you ever heard tell? So if you'd care to, you could help me, pretty lady—' "

"Stop!" Frances shot up from her chair like an arrow. "I heard Jeremy's auto outside. He's home."

I hadn't heard anything, but I obeyed. "Let me just scan this quickly, I can't leave it just yet!" Even as I was saying the words my eyes went flying across the rest of the page. I had barely finished when Frances snatched it from me.

"Go out the way you came in. Thank you, Fremont, thank you so much. I'll call you, or come by, or, or . . . I'll see you somehow!" As she was saying all this she was also bustling me out through the dressing room.

"Wait," I said, trying to turn around and feeling like a recalcitrant sheep at the mercy of a particularly adhesive Border collie, "I forgot my shawl."

"Oh, bother!" Frances herself ran back for it, tossed it to me, and pushed me out the door, whispering, "Really, I'll be in touch with you soon. Be careful, Fremont. I don't know what he'll do if he finds you here." And with that, her door was closed in my face.

I found myself in that oppressive corridor with only a sickly hue of greenish light falling through a section of the stained glass to keep me company. Yet the air now seemed somehow charged. Maybe this was a house in tune with its master, maybe it only came really alive when he crossed the threshold. . . .

"Really, Fremont, you are too fanciful," I muttered as I moved quickly toward the back stairs.

But I did not quite make it. There were footsteps coming, suddenly, from both directions. A servant approaching from one; the master, one assumed, from the other. And there I was in the middle, with no place to hide.

ELEVEN

Bargains Are Struck

BEING TRAPPED between two undesirable alternatives, I chose to confront the servant rather than the master—even though I had a sneaking suspicion that the servants in this house told the master everything. Thus I passed rapidly by Cora at the top of the back stairs, holding my index finger up to my lips for silence, while at the same time giving her as fierce a stare as I could manage. She seemed surprised but said nothing, and I was down the stairs in a trice, and gone.

The next morning I told Michael I needed to go shopping in preparation for my father's visit. I expected that the ever restless Wish Stephenson would be out on his own looking for something to do, some trouble to resolve or to get into as the case might be, and that Michael would therefore have to tend the office or else leave it unattended. This didn't seem like such a bad idea, as it could only contribute to his understanding of why we needed to have a receptionist.

"When will you be back?" he asked, looking up from his task of the moment, which was putting on his socks. His feet were unbelievably white, tender as a babe's, and there was that one spot inside the arch—

He interrupted my thoughts with more questions, when I had not figured out the answer to the first one yet. "What will you buy? A dress? Shall I come with you?"

Oh Lord! There was a wrinkle I hadn't thought of. This being half a couple was enjoyable, but complicating when one had things to do. Certainly I couldn't have him coming with me, yet he did have excellent taste in clothes, and as a matter of fact I did intend to buy a dress. In addition to the other thing I wanted to do.

I said: "I'm just . . . shopping. What I really need to do is sort out my thoughts about Father's visit, and I can do that better by myself. I may buy a dress in the process, if I see something I like." I turned around to face the mirror and began to arrange my hair on top of my head, since I was going downtown. I had already dressed, and over my own shoulder I could see, in reflection, Michael sitting on the edge of the bed.

He put on the other sock. He said, rather gruffly, without looking at me, "Would you like me to leave for a few days? While your father is here, I mean?"

I was so surprised by this offer that I let go the heavy twist of my hair before I'd gotten the pin in, and it came tumbling right down. I spun around. I could not think what to say, for although I certainly didn't want him to leave, it would be the solution to a very large problem. Yet tears pricked at my eyes, and so I went and sat next to Michael and said softly, "It's so very unfair."

"What, my love?"

"Oh, I don't know! I was going to say the rules of society, but maybe it's me, maybe I'm the one who's unfair—" and suddenly I was crying, the tears were trailing down my cheeks and I couldn't stop them, and Michael was kissing them away while shushing me, as if I were a child.

In that moment I wanted him so much, so very, very much, that I reached out and touched him, felt his hardness, and knew he wanted me too.

"Oh, sweet!" he said, or something like that, I am never quite sure at such times.

I cried all the while he was making love to me, not great sobs but tears leaking from my eyes; even in the building of that unbearable, delicious tension, and the release of it, I could not let go this strange mixture of joy and anguish.

He stayed above me, stroked my cheeks, kissed them, and whispered, "Tell me, Fremont. Whatever it is, for God's sake please tell me."

I was too physically spent to do more than murmur, yet the words did not come easily. "I love you so much, Michael, sometimes it frightens me. I don't want to be without you, and it used to be . . . it used to be . . ."

This was something I had not yet told him, and hadn't thought I ever would. My mother had taught me a couple of things before she died, even though I was only fourteen, because she knew the day would come when I'd need to know, and she would not be there to tell me. One (for which I've blessed her oh, so often!) was that a woman may desire a man as much as he desires her; there is nothing wrong in it, and the sex act itself is not a duty but a great pleasure. The other was that there are some few things a woman may keep to herself, even from her husband, for it does him no good to know, and indeed might harm them both. In other words there are some burdens a woman must carry alone. The tricky part, which she also told me—it had been beyond my comprehension then, and very nearly was still—is that there are no hard and fast rules about what to keep and what to tell, you simply have to do the best you can. I based my decision now on the need I saw in Michael's searching eyes.

"It used to be," I admitted, "that you would go away, as was your habit, with very little warning, and I was always afraid—that is, I never knew when you were coming back. You haven't been away since we've been together as we are now, but I know the time will come when you'll have to go, and I won't like it any better than I used to, in fact I shall like it far, far worse, b—"

He stopped my mouth with a kiss, one of those sweet, prolonged, languorous kisses that come only after, and then he rolled over, taking me with him, still locked to him, lying in his arms. He said, "The great 'but' that was hanging in the air between us just now goes like this. Correct me if I'm wrong. *But* even though most women would assume it to be far more likely that I, or any man, would come back simply because they were married, this is not sufficient reason for you to marry me."

"Yes," I said, somewhat miserably. How I could feel at once so resplendent in body yet so miserable in mind was indeed a wonder.

"Fremont, I will always come back to you. Always. Death is the only thing that could prevent me. Whether or not we are married has nothing to do with it. I will always come back for the same reasons I've come back before: Because after a certain time passes, no matter what else I may be doing, I want to see you. I want to hear your voice, to know what you have been up to, what kinds of mischief you have caused or cleared up. My darling Fremont, I've heard you say more than once that your father is besotted with What's-her-name—"

"Augusta," I supplied, beginning to feel much better.

"Augusta. Well, I am even more besotted with you."

I smiled at him, at that fine, bearded face so near to mine, and I said, "You know, Michael, I do believe you are telling the truth."

And that was how we decided that this time Michael would go

away, not for himself but for me, so that my father would not have to be suspicious of our domestic arrangements. It was not an ideal solution, but in the circumstances I felt much relieved.

Mr. Patrick Rule was not hard to find, as it turned out. When I rang the bell at the house Mrs. Locke had occupied on Octavia Street, he opened the door. By the puzzled look on his face, I could see he did not immediately remember me, and I thought I should play upon this advantage as long as possible.

"Mr. Rule, how good to see you!" I deliberately did not supply my name, but advanced as if I had every right to be invited across the threshold and indeed expected it. He stepped back to let me in.

Quickly, so as to keep him off balance, I said, "I was distressed, of course, to see the awful news about Mrs. Locke's death in the newspaper. But she always did tell me, if ever I were in need of guidance in matters otherworldly, and she were not available, I should come to you."

At this he smiled a little, his facial lineaments relaxed, and I had cause to silently remark what a classic face—of its type—he had. Its hawklike qualities remained, but at close hand his visage was interestingly able to be both sinister and ascetic, depending how the light struck his features. A mere tip of the head and one's impression could alter entirely. My Michael had such a face, and so of course Patrick Rule fascinated me. His hair, whose color I hadn't been able to discern on the night of that fateful séance, was dark auburn, an attractive and unusual color. His eyes were gray, not changeable in the blue-to-gray range like Michael's, but a pale, clear gray that was curiously flat. I wondered whether those eyes had had depth when he gazed on Abigail Locke, whom he'd seemed to so adore.

"And do you find yourself now in need of such advice, Miss, or Mrs.—?"

"Miss," I said, and no more, as I moved into the parlor, in spite of the fact that the room looked as if it had not been in use for a very long time. I chose one of the side chairs pulled up to the oval tea table in the window. Following my lead, Patrick joined me and leaned over to turn on the lamp, which was made of glass in the old style but fitted with an electrical cord right up through the middle.

I lowered my voice and leaned forward confidingly when the lamp was lit: "It is not for myself that I've come, but for a friend. She cannot come herself, you see."

He tilted his head. A raised eyebrow and a certain set to his mouth indicated his skepticism, but those flat eyes did not change at all. How strange.

I continued, "She has some talent as a medium, and had been told that your Mrs. Locke could be trusted, that she was honest. My friend requires guidance, a teacher, preferably another medium, and with dear Abigail gone . . . Well, you do see the problem."

"And the name of your friend is?" Now the other eyebrow joined the first.

"I am not at liberty to say."

"I believe you must be inquiring for yourself then, miss. You are familiar to me, you seem to expect me to know who you are by some previous tie of . . . friendship?" I nodded, thinking so far so good. He was being careful not to offend me. This was all going very much better than I'd thought it might. Patrick went on, "So I must apologize for being unable to recall your name, and I assure you that in the transaction of spiritual matters, anything we say to each other is confidential. You don't need to hide behind that old, transparent ruse of seeking advice for a friend."

As I bestowed the smile he expected for his cleverness, I wondered if I dared omit my name once more. No, better not. "My name is Fremont Jones, Mr. Rule, and I really am asking for a friend, whose name I may not reveal. I will of course be willing to pay a consultation fee, if necessary."

"That will not be necessary. I've heard that name before, it's unusual, but I can't quite place—"

"Do you yourself have clairvoyant powers, Mr. Rule?"

He preened a little; my question had diverted him, which had been my intent. "I'm a sensitive, I can sense when the spirits are near. With Mrs. Locke I had a close bond, and sometimes felt I was able to receive thought messages from her. However, my contribution to the advancement of Spiritualism has been more in the way of serving those whose talents and abilities rank far above mine."

Getting comfortable, he leaned back in his chair and crossed one leg over the other. "Now, how exactly may I help you, Miss—it is Miss?"

I nodded.

"Miss . . . Jones?"

"By giving me the name of another medium who can be trusted, whom I may approach with the object of asking if she will guide and teach my friend."

This request met with pursed lips, a wrinkled brow, and silence.

I plunged on in what I hoped was my most persuasive manner, putting a note of desperation into my voice. Indeed, when I thought of Frances furiously scribbling at her automatic writing, that was not hard to do. "I know about Ingrid Swann, of course, everyone in these circles does, but from all I know of her she would be far too busy. If there is no one else, perhaps I should go to her. Is she honest, do you think?"

He crossed his arms and looked more like a hawk than ever. What was going on behind those flat gray eyes?

Making the greatest effort, I summoned a smile and cocked my head a bit to one side. "What is it, Mr. Rule? What is holding you back?"

"I've remembered who you are. The woman you were with that night is known to me: Frances McFadden, the wife of Jeremy McFadden. She is the friend to whom you refer. Yes?"

Ah well, no ruse is likely to last forever. I nodded. "Yes."

Patrick Rule rose, and when he had unfolded to his full height and I was looking up at him, he suddenly appeared ten feet tall to me. Yet I would not get up myself, because to do so would have indicated a willingness to leave. I was determined to stand—or sit—my ground. He glared along the sharp planes of that handsome nose. "What is she up to, this Frances McFadden? Tell me and I may help you. But I'll give you no further information unless you do."

For some inexplicable reason, I hadn't anticipated this question. I wasn't prepared, and stumbled a bit. He did notice of course; I was sure he noticed everything. "S-she has been taken by surprise in this," I said, feeling my way along, "and doesn't know herself what is happening."

"You'll have to be more direct than that, Miss Jones."

"The, ah, terminology doesn't come easily to me."

"That's surprising, isn't it, since you presented yourself as such a dear friend of Abigail's. You were not her friend, of course. You breezed your way in here on false pretenses. And if you were not quite so"—the gray eyes swept over me, and now I understood his full attraction, and his power, because as his gaze touched my face, my breasts, sped down the folds of my skirt like lightning, to rest on my barely visible ankles, the gray eyes flashed silver—"so obviously a respectable woman, I would send you on your way."

Now I did stand. "Perhaps I should be going, at any rate."

"No. Sit down. I'll help you."

I expected him to say, *for a price,* and was prepared for the price named to be in something other than money, but he did not. So I sat. Patrick Rule remained standing, and crossed his arms, which made him all the more formidable.

"Now," he said, "you will tell me everything you know about what is going on with your friend, and when you have done so I'll decide how best to proceed. We should work together on this, Miss Jones."

"I don't understand."

"Simply this: Danger came into that séance where Mrs. McFadden was present and went into a trance of her own. I believe she was the conduit, the open door, to the kind of malevolent energy that resulted in my dear Abigail's murder. If it had happened only the one time, I might not consider this avenue worth pursuing. But you tell me Mrs. McFadden continues to have . . . visitations?"

"Yes, she does."

"From the same spirit who came through that night?"

I shook my head. "I don't know. I can't be sure. Nor can Frances." I had my suspicions that this was the case, but I certainly wasn't going to tell him that—though in truth I could not have said exactly why.

Now Patrick Rule slid back into his chair, leaning urgently toward me. "An untrained medium who has made contact is like a door standing open, with no lock and no hand to close it."

"But what can that have to do with the . . . the murder?"

"More than you know. You must believe me, that's all. I'm determined to find Abigail's killer. The police will never do it, you know. A dead medium is of hardly any interest to them. Whereas I . . . I have lost my life as surely as if the unknown perpetrator had killed me too. Bring Mrs. McFadden to me, Miss Jones, or take me to her. I was a valued assistant to Abigail Locke, I know how to draw the spirits out when they show, and how to command them to leave. I cannot teach anyone to make contact—that part is still a mystery to so many of us—but once the contact has been made, I'm expert at eliciting information. In this case, I believe it would be valuable information. Certainly to me."

Wheels, big wheels, began turning in my mind. "That may produce something helpful to you, and certainly I'd like to see Mrs. Locke's killer brought to justice. But all the questioning in the world will not help Frances to learn to control whatever has begun to happen in her life. As her friend, that's my primary concern."

"It's a bargain. Tit for tat. She does this for me; I provide a teacher for her."

Those wheels gave one last turn and came to rest in a most satisfactory place. I reached into my pocket and drew out a business card for the J&K Agency. I put this card on the table between us, face up. "Mr. Rule, I am a private detective. As Frances's friend, I cannot advise her to do as you ask, because her husband could take her to task for it. But if you were to hire me . . ."

He picked up on it right away, with enthusiasm. His face lit up and once again he was a handsome man. "Yes! I can see it! Together we may move through the shadowy world of San Francisco Spiritualism in search of the despicable person who stabbed my Abigail through the heart. Along the way you may, of course, wish to interview certain people—shall we say 'in my presence?' "

I inclined my head in acquiescence.

"And Mrs. McFadden would be one of them."

I inclined my head again.

"Oh, you were sent by the angels, Fremont Jones."

Well, I supposed that was a little better than having been sent by God, which had been said of me (with little evidence) in the past, and so I remarked. This elicited the first smile I'd seen from Patrick. "Part of the payment for my services as private detective"—I narrowed my eyes—"will be your delivery of the kind of help Frances needs, and that part will be due at the outset. Is that understood?"

"Perfectly."

"Come to my office now, Mr. Rule, and we'll draw up the contract." I stood decisively. In business I have found it is always best to continue to move briskly ahead, whether or not one knows precisely where one is going. The impression of forward motion is wonderfully effective. "Now, we'll need a letter of agreement first thing, to specify exactly what I am to do so that there will be no misunderstanding."

"Yes, of course. If you will allow me to get my hat? Oh, and Miss Jones. What are your fees for this service?"

"I have a fee schedule back at the office. I don't carry about that information in my head."

In truth, I hadn't the slightest idea what to charge. This was my first real, unsupervised case and I was delighted beyond all proportion.

In fact, it did occur to me, as Patrick Rule and I descended the steps of the house on Octavia Street, that I must have a ghoulish streak, to be so looking forward to my descent (as it were) into the netherworld of Spiritualism in search of a murderer.

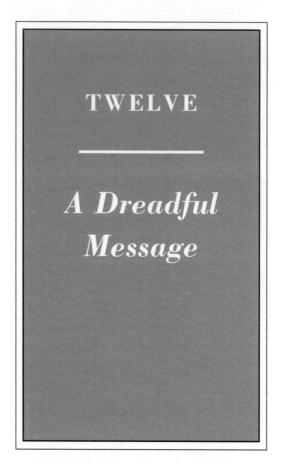

TWELVE

A Dreadful Message

PATRICK RULE and I signed a contract late that afternoon. When we arrived (I had driven him in the Maxwell, as he did not have an auto, and he intended to go on somewhere else afterward) at J&K's offices in the double house on Divisadero, I had to use my key to let us in. Michael had apparently grown tired of minding the store alone, so to speak, and owing to one of my more perverse streaks this pleased me well. I could choose my own time to tell Michael and Wish of this coup. My first case, and I had landed one that could make headlines in the newspapers! To think what the publicity would do for our agency, not to mention my own reputation as an investigator, a detective if you will.

Of course, it was always possible that I wouldn't solve the case, and nothing would come of it but a bit of money (though of course I had no such thing as a schedule of fees, I had lied about that, and not being sure what to charge, I may have made it too little; besides, I was in a way also being paid by Patrick's taking care of Frances), but even so . . .

So it was that I managed to keep my good news from Michael all night, and to make my announcement to both him and to Wish around the kitchen table during a morning coffee break. They expressed their individual degrees of surprise and amazement (and on Wish's part, a bit of envy, I thought), which I accepted as graciously as if I had been the queen instead of just a penniless private detective on her first case.

That was in the morning; by noon everything had changed because another medium was dead: Ingrid Swann.

Frances was our messenger; she delivered this dreadful message in a hurried, breathless telephone call: "Fremont, Jeremy is in the—the necessary facility. I must hurry and get out of his study before he gets back. But I overheard him talking just now on this very telephone instrument. I was out in the hall—listening on purpose actually—he has seemed so intense lately, I just can't help but wonder what is going on, so I eavesdrop."

"Frances," I interrupted her babbling, "you must get to the point, particularly if time is of the essence."

"Yes, yes, of course. Jeremy said on the phone that Ingrid Swann is dead, it is to be in the afternoon's *Examiner.* Can you imagine?"

"Good heavens!" I said. "Another medium. How very . . . odd. And terrible, of course, it's terrible." As if, I thought with a chill, someone had decided to murder all the mediums in San Francisco, one by one. Oh, surely not!

This new development put a different light upon my investigation on behalf of Patrick Rule, I saw that right away.

"Who can be doing this, Fremont?" Frances cried, "Who would

be so monstrous as to do such a thing? Right on the heels of Abigail!"

"I haven't a clue, but I expect I may come closer to finding out than you can believe, Frances, before this business all plays out." Then I told her how I'd been hired by Patrick Rule to investigate Abigail Locke's death.

"We want to interview you," I added, in as offhand and casually nonthreatening a manner as possible. "I could bring him to your house, by the route I came in the other day. Or if you prefer, you may come here."

I did not tell Frances what else I intended. She would be hostile, I was sure, to anything that might affect her free and easy fantasies about the ghost of this Emperor Norton.

"Not today, tomorrow— Oh, he's coming! Noon tomorrow, I'll come to you!"

In a stunned state I'd hung up the telephone and conveyed Frances's information to Michael and Wish. We were still all seated around the kitchen table, where we'd spent the morning in a kind of staff meeting. Our lighthearted mood had been broken. Very shortly I excused myself and went to my desk, Wish went out somewhere, and Michael retired to his office.

I got out paper and pencil to make a list. The first order of business must be to obtain a copy of the *Examiner*, to confirm what Frances had overheard. I wrote that down, and then I wrote: *Jeremy M.—How did he know before it made the papers?*

The most obvious way, of course, would be if he had done the murders himself. Or caused them to be done. But that was *too* obvious. Wasn't it?

I pondered this possibility. Could Jeremy McFadden be so jealous of his wife's time, attention, and affections that he would commit murder in order to . . . to what? To keep Frances from attending any more séances? To scare Frances off such activities?

"Oh, pshaw!" I muttered. Surely that couldn't be, it was too outlandish, no one could possibly be that possessive. Or, being that possessive, go to the extreme of murder. Twice.

And yet, having had the idea, I could not let it go no matter how outlandish. Maybe it was just that simple, and the police didn't know to look at Jeremy as a suspect because I hadn't wanted to get Frances in trouble by reporting Abigail's body.

Oh Lord. I was seized by a horrid, creeping sense of guilt. If that did prove to be the case, if Jeremy McFadden turned out to be the murderer of both these dead mediums, then I myself could be held responsible—morally, anyway—for the death of the second one, Ingrid Swann. Because the police didn't know, they had no idea, that Frances McFadden had been in any way involved. If I hadn't decided not to report Abigail Locke's murder to the police . . . I couldn't even bear to finish the thought.

I felt as if my career in detection had been the briefest on record, and now must be over before it began. How could I carry on in the business if I had no more sense than to conduct myself in such a way as to get people killed? I was supposed to be solving crimes and puzzles and conundrums, not making them!

For I don't know how long I sat still as a stone, my mind a complete blank. I just could not deal with this. I didn't know how. And then, suddenly, I did.

I pushed back from my desk and went back to Michael's office, intending to confide in him, to tell him what I'd done, to ask what I should do now. His door was open and he sat bent over a book, reading with the absolute concentration he has that shuts everything else out. Even me. I stood there for a heartbeat or two, and then stealthily I went away. Back to my desk, to make my list, to answer the telephone, to watch the hours of the clock creep around to two, when the afternoon edition of the *Examiner* would begin to hit the streets.

I was sure my situation now was not one my mother could ever have visualized, but I applied her lesson nonetheless: This was a burden I had to carry alone. My first case. I had to do it right, at least from this point onward, and I had to make it on my own.

"You have heard, I presume," I said to Patrick Rule late the next morning. We sat at the long table in the conference room, preparing for Frances's arrival at noon.

He nodded gravely. "You mean about Ingrid." His face seemed drawn and was pale, hollow-eyed, as if he had been for far too long without sleep.

"Yes," I said.

The *Examiner* article had been terse and to the point: The body of Ingrid Swann, world-renowned medium now based in San Francisco, had been found by her brother, Ngaio, early the previous morning. She had died from stab wounds to the chest. Whether or not the wounds themselves resembled those in the chest of Abigail Locke, the newspaper article hadn't said. This morning's more sensational press had had less compunction, they'd come right out with banner headlines proclaiming MURDERER OF MEDIUMS ON THE LOOSE IN CITY BY THE BAY! Michael, ever helpful, had brought all the morning editions home with him from his breakfast bakery run, and the papers lay now fanned out on the conference table.

"Perhaps the police will work harder now to catch the killer," I said, hoping to allay Patrick's misery.

He nodded again but said nothing further, and as I did not know what to say myself, we sat in silence. I could hear Michael as he turned the page of a book in his office, it was that still; I could hear the tick of the hands and the tock of the swinging pendulum of the old wall clock out in the kitchen. It was a sunny day, with light pouring through the lace curtains (perhaps not all that appropriate for an office, but this had been a dining room before and they'd come with the house) to make intricate shadow patterns on the rug. In the next room, Michael turned another page. From the kitchen, the clock struck in rapid little pings, twelve of them: high noon.

Still no Frances.

Patrick Rule bestirred himself, adjusted his necktie, fiddled with his collar, and aimed his curiously empty eyes toward the front door.

Ready and waiting, I thought. Then suddenly I recalled how he had looked not at me but through me to the door beyond at the séance, and had announced Mrs. Locke's arrival before that door behind me opened. What curious ability did he have, to perceive someone's coming before they came?

Whatever it might be called, he certainly possessed it, for in that very instant the door opened, its bell rang, and I hurriedly said, "I need to prepare her. She isn't expecting you. I was able to leave her only the briefest message. Stay here, please. We'll be right in." Raising my voice, I called out, "Frances! Wait right there if you please. I'm coming out."

The Emperor Norton, ghost or no ghost, was doing well by this young matron. I had never seen Frances McFadden so glowing, nor more attractively dressed. Her day dress was a rich, deep shade of blue, of some simple material like chambray, but far from simple in design. The collar and neck insert were of sheer white cotton, embroidered with little blue flowers, and so were the cuffs on the long sleeves. Her modishly short skirt just grazed her ankle tops and showed enticing flashes of a similarly embroidered petticoat when she moved.

I tendered the usual greeting, then drew her aside, speaking rapidly and low: "Frances, I must brief you about this meeting before it begins. Mr. Patrick Rule is in the other room. He has hired me to augment the police investigation into the murder of Abigail Locke."

Frances's eyes widened enormously, her lips parted, but I covered them with my own fingertips before she could say anything. "Part of the bargain I've made with him concerns you. In return for my help, Patrick Rule is to find you a good teacher and mentor for your mediumship."

"My . . . mediumship?"

"You do want to develop that talent, don't you?" *So that you can get away from a husband who mistreats you,* I thought but did not say.

Too surprised to argue, she merely nodded. I'd been counting on that.

"Just one thing," I said. "No matter what happens, you must say nothing about our having been the first to find Mrs. Locke's body. I wish now that I'd acted differently, but I didn't and that is that. Do you agree?"

"Yes, of course. Whatever you say, Fremont."

"Good. Well then, are you ready?"

"Oh yes. Where is he? In the next room?"

Before I could answer, Frances began to move toward the dining room like a woman in a dream, like a woman being reeled in on an invisible line. How extraordinary!

Some minutes later, watching them together, I had a new and altogether unexpected thought: Mr. Rule has found his next medium. The instant rapport between those two astounded me.

Either Patrick and Frances had been made for each other, and only just now found their chance to come together, or the things he'd told me about himself the previous day had been a lie. This was not a performance by some mere "sensitive" man who could sometimes receive thought messages in a passive way from a woman, one woman only, and she now dead. In fact, this man was not passive at all. He had somehow, instantly, established such sway over this particular woman, Frances, that she was focused on him like a hypnotized snake. Yet he had not hypnotized her, I knew that because I'd watched and listened every minute. Still she swayed, as it were, to the curl of his fingers, the curves of his voice.

Theoretically, Patrick Rule was only here to test the range of

Frances's natural abilities, something I was far from qualified to do myself. He was only asking her questions, and she answering them; questions of a routine sort, such as, *When did you first become attracted to Spiritualism? Was it idle curiosity or had you had some experience?* But I sensed there was more going on, and it made me uneasy.

"Do you wish to make contact with anyone now," Patrick was saying, "or is there a spirit already in contact with you who wants to come through?"

Frances closed her eyes. She leaned a little from side to side, as the weeping willow will bend to a wind so slight it can scarcely be felt. My own skin broke out in goose bumps all over. I leaned forward.

Patrick Rule, without taking his eyes from Frances, placed his left hand on the table, palm up. I knew somehow he meant me to take it, and I did; I placed my own right hand in his left and his fingers closed over mine. His touch was hot and electric, producing a shock of a most embarrassingly sexual kind. I felt it in that part of my body that I have come to think of as the seat of pleasure—but only for an instant, then it was gone, and my attention back on Frances. Patrick's own attention had never left her.

Have I mentioned that Patrick had an exceptional voice? A smooth, rich baritone that he could manipulate to good effect. He spoke now as if bringing up that voice from deep in his chest: "If there is any spirit present who wishes to come through this woman, Frances McFadden, I invite that spirit to make itself known."

Eyes closed, Frances frowned; she bent forward, as if straining . . . straining . . . In sympathetic tension, I felt Patrick's fingers tighten over mine. Indeed, his grip became almost painful.

Frances exhaled a long breath from her mouth, incredibly long, it seemed to me. I wondered how she could have any breath left in her body after that. Then rather noisily she drew in an equally great breath through her nose, her bosom rose . . . and just when I had the absurd, not to mention irreverent, thought that she might burst like a balloon, her eyes opened. Her shoulders settled into their usual fashionable slope, and she looked at us with quite her normal, pleasant expression.

"The dogs were there," she said, as if it were the most reasonable thing in the world, describing some tea party she'd been to, or a sporting event, "and they will not let him cross."

"Were you in contact with the spirit?" Patrick asked.

"No, not in the sense that he was speaking to me, or putting thoughts in my head, but I knew he was there. I could tell. And I could—well, it's hard to describe."

"Do the best you can. I shall be able to follow you."

"I could feel the presence of the dogs, guarding him. They were like—like a barrier, an invisible wall."

"Ah. Dogs."

"Yes. The same as barked through Mrs. Locke that day, you remember, when I went into trance so unexpectedly at the séance. Mr. Rule, it is not I who first made this happen, it was she. She was the one who gave voice to the dogs, or one of them. Lazarus, it was. I only happened to be there in the room, and receptive, so that he could come through me. And then he was able to find me again."

"He? Who is it that you speak of?"

"The Emperor."

"Ah, the Emperor. Frances, let us return to the dog or dogs. Tell me more about them. They sound like familiar spirits, and familiar spirits can be either benign or malign. One must be careful in making contact with spirits that come across on the ethereal plane as being other than human."

Frances flicked her eyes at me. Patrick Rule still held my hand. I could see no need of it, because the part of the interview that might have turned into a séance was clearly over now, but I did not want to disturb this process by reclaiming my hand. In the overall context of things, it would have seemed unnecessarily disruptive at that moment. I gave Frances the slightest nod, and immediately she continued:

"They're just dogs. You know, curs, mongrels. They've passed on too. Lazarus was the first to go, and then Bummer—he's the more playful of the two. They're the Emperor's dogs, that's all."

But Patrick was skeptical. "We can't be certain. You should not be so accepting of that; more investigation will be required. Now tell me more about the Emperor himself."

"His full title is Norton I, Emperor of the United States and Protector of Mexico. Of course he knows he isn't, not really, but that's what he thought when he was alive. He's a good fellow. Mr. Rule, Fremont, I don't understand why you're asking me all these questions."

Now seemed the perfect time for me to take my hand back, which I did, and put both in my lap. I chose to answer her myself. "Mr. Rule believes some kind of negative influence—is that fair to say?" I waited for his nod of assent before continuing. "Some kind of negative influence may have come through that day you and I attended the séance. It was the last séance Abigail Locke ever gave, after all, and something peculiar did happen."

Rule gave an emphatic nod, a quick, hard down-pull of his head.

"But I myself"—I sat a little taller, as if that could establish some authority on my part, which I felt had been sadly lacking in this interview process so far—"cannot believe spirits have anything to do with murder. In my opinion, the murder weapon in both these cases had to have been wielded by a human hand."

"Yes, a human hand," Rule said, looking at me sidewise, "but yet a malign spiritual influence may have been at work. Abigail had protected herself from such influences for a long time, with certain spells and wardings, yet something broke through. And it must have happened in roughly the same time period when you came to see her."

Frances shrugged, handling the gesture in a way that was so

ladylike it became almost elegant, as if to say, *What could things of this nature possibly have to do with a refined female like me?*

I took up her cause again, as I had been doing perhaps far too often—but at the moment I was unaware of that. I said, "It is my own belief—and please recall, Mr. Rule, you're paying me to look into these matters in a professional way—that Frances's Spiritual-istic abilities have nothing whatever to do with the deaths of the two mediums. That part is simply coincidence. However, you've seen—and may I say participated in?—a clear demonstration of her natural abilities in this area and must therefore be able to understand that she needs a teacher."

Rule didn't want to let it go, to allow me (a woman, after all) free reign in the case. He wanted to hover over me, pulling strings. I wasn't going to have that, couldn't have it; to give in would have established a pattern that would then become the norm for future cases. So we had a silent battle of wits and wills and eyes, his eyes having become that flat, clear gray so curiously devoid of content. He really had the strangest eyes I had ever seen.

At last he said, "Very well. You take care of the investigation, Miss Jones, and I will work with Mrs. McFadden to see she receives guidance. Toward that end"—he turned slightly, addressing himself to Frances alone now—"I'll need to know more about the automatic writing I understand you've already done."

I sensed I was no longer needed, and left them to it.

They departed together half an hour later, walking with match-ing strides like lovers, her head tipped up to him and his bent down to her, still talking, talking, in murmurs intelligible I sup-posed only to themselves. I watched them out the door, then moved to the window and watched them down the street. *They belong together:* impossible not to have that thought. It proclaimed itself so loudly in my mind that I almost uttered the words aloud. Yet I knew, somehow I knew, that this was not a match made in heaven but in hell.

"Fremont Jones, you are losing your mind!" I muttered, a bit louder than was quite necessary. How could I possibly know something like that? He was going to help her, he'd be good for her, and besides, the man she was married to acted like such a brute—

A low chuckle from behind startled and interrupted me, sending a chill through my bones.

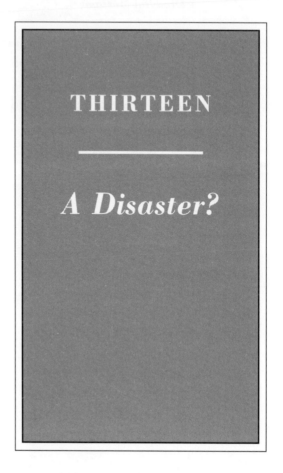

THIRTEEN

A Disaster?

YOU ARE DOING IT again," I said without turning around, "sneaking around, and this time scaring me half to death. Wherever did you get that evil chuckle, Michael?"

He came all the way up behind me. As no one was about, he indeed moved entirely too close, and as we stood there front to back looking out the window he became aroused. Even through skirt and petticoat I could feel him pressed against me.

"They make a handsome couple, I'll grant you that," Michael conceded, and then took it back in his next breath, "if appearances were all one had to go by."

I slipped to one side and left the window, for a moment wondering what had ever possessed me to think I could work in the same space as this man, the two of us self-professed partners in love and work. When Michael was in one of his amorous moods it was terribly hard to get anything done.

"Who are we to be judgmental, Michael?" I asked from the relative safety of my desk. "He has lost his working partner, who may have been more than that to him—I mean of course Mrs. Locke—and she, Frances, is in a loveless marriage that is more like a lifetime prison sentence than anything else. If they find pleasure in one another's company, who are we to deny it to them? Or to make unkind remarks about them?"

Perhaps I had expressed myself a little too strongly; I know I do that at times. At any rate, Michael froze. His entire manner changed, and he became more like the Michael I had first known at Mrs. O'Leary's house some years ago, remote and mysterious. He can do that instantly, tuck his personality so deep inside himself that even I cannot find it, not even through the windows of his eyes.

I was in no mood to soften or to placate. He was on the verge of stepping into my case, I knew that as surely as I knew my first name was Caroline—and I liked the idea of his doing that about as much as I liked my first name, in other words, not much at all.

A moment later he confirmed it by saying in a leading tone of voice, "Of course, you must run your investigation in the manner you choose. I'm here for consultation, only if you wish it."

"I appreciate your confidence in me," I said both formally and firmly, "however I do not wish to consult at the present time."

He shot me an impenetrable look and turned back toward his own little office; then changed his mind and spun on his heel, heading instead for the front door. Which meant he was going to go out on his own, for a walk, or to do whatever he did when he was out of sorts with me.

One hand on the doorknob, he looked back at me over his shoulder. "You can be cold. Do you know that, Fremont Jones?" he asked, then opened the door and was gone.

Michael did not come to me that night, nor did I go to him; and the next morning when I came down there was a note on my desk. *It is seldom wise to take a case on impulse. A judicious background check on one's potential client is often in order. MAK.*

I sat down abruptly, as if all the wind had fled my sails. I am never at my best first thing in the morning, and I had not yet even had my coffee. I was vulnerable, my defenses down, and somehow the use of all his initials—MAK, for Mikhail Arkady Kossoff— made me recall in a rush all that I had been through with this man, not to mention how embarrassingly well he knew me. Or how good he had been to me. Most of the time. Of course there had been some times . . .

Well, the main thing was, he was right. I tucked the note into my pocket and went to tell him so. But when I got to his side of the house Michael was not there. In his bedroom the wardrobe stood open, clothes obviously having been snatched out and packed in haste, in the leather case that was also missing. He had gone. Apparently he had decided to take his trip, the one meant to save me from having to explain our relationship to my father, a week early.

I felt bereft and shaky, though this was what I had wanted: A free rein, the autonomy to conduct my first case my way, on my own.

Wish Stephenson used his old police department contacts to do a check for me on Mr. Patrick Rule. It was still not an easy thing to do much by way of looking into the backgrounds of people in San Francisco, or in California, or in the whole of the American West for that matter. If the West was the land of opportunity, that was true in part because here people tended to be taken at face value. You didn't get introduced to someone new, and then in the next five minutes find yourself answering questions like, *What was your mother's family?* and *Where did you go to school, my dear?* True enough, a stratified society of sorts had grown up in San Francisco during the fifty-something years since the Gold Rush, but it was a society based on wealth, not on family; therefore, anyone could get in.

This was not at all like Boston, where it has been said the Cabots talk only to the Lowells and the Lowells talk only to God. (Which was untrue, by the way; the Lowells talked to my mother and father on quite a regular basis when I was growing up.) For my immediate purposes the important point was that in Boston, in all of Massachusetts and the New England states—indeed throughout the East—records were kept of everything. But here in the West that was far from the case; and in San Francisco particularly, most of the records we'd ever had were burned up in the fire after the earthquake. That fire had destroyed City Hall, and a huge percentage of all the places of business in the City.

Criminals and opportunists were of course having a field day. I did sincerely hope Patrick Rule was not one of them. On the other hand, we San Franciscans have a rather loose definition of what constitutes a criminal; some crimes are worse than others. . . . With my thoughts running along those lines, it really was just as well that Michael was not here.

"Can't find much on Patrick Rule," Wish announced on the afternoon of the day of Michael's departure.

That was not exactly bad news; it was, in fact, a relief. I said, "Well, are you going to tell me what you did find?"

"It's more what I *didn't* find: no criminal record, for instance. Owns no real property—that's as in real estate—has no visible means of support. That is, no job."

"His job would have been looking after Abigail Locke."

"But, Fremont, that was a personal relationship. Or so you said. Didn't you?"

"I don't recall." I fell to musing over this, just talking aloud as I mused—something Wish himself did, as a matter of fact—and I knew that if he picked up on anything valuable in my musings he would point it out to me, as I would have to him. "She must have paid him, because apparently he maintained his own household. At the very least he had a room he lived in somewhere, he didn't live at the house on Octavia Street."

I was silent for a few minutes, mulling things over. Then went on: "But he lives there now. According to the newspapers, Patrick Rule was the principal beneficiary of Abigail Locke's estate. He was the only person to benefit financially from her death."

Wish inserted, "The estate wasn't large at all, if the newspapers are to be believed. If she was paying him, he'd probably have done better to continue working for her. What are you thinking, Fremont? That your client has hired you to throw the scent off himself?"

I studied Wish, who leaned with his elbows on his knees, big hands dangling down. He had such an earnest, puzzled expression on his face it was almost comical. I smiled, and in the process became aware it was the first time I'd smiled since Michael's leaving. "Wish, I do believe you're even more ready than I am—make that than I used to be—to take people at their word."

He blushed, but only a little. Not long ago he would have blushed a lot. After hanging his head for a moment, in what might have been self-deprecation, he looked up grinning. "I guess that's true. Always think the best until somebody does something to prove otherwise."

"That's not a particularly useful philosophy in our profession. I'm surprised you've been able to stick to it."

"Useful professionally, no. You're right, from that point of view it's kind of . . . dumb. But personally, it makes me a whole lot happier. I've gotten pretty good at sorting out the bad apples, Fremont. You want me to interview this Patrick Rule on some pretext? Tell you how he comes off to me?"

If Michael had made the same offer, I would have rejected it instantly. But coming from Wish, I considered it. Why? Why should I be so prickly only with Michael, whom after all I knew far, far better than I knew Wish Stephenson? It did not stand to reason.

"Fremont?" Wish prompted.

I widened my eyes, mentally shaking myself. "I'm here. I was just thinking. . . . Wish, let me think upon it overnight. I'll speak to you again on that tomorrow. Oh, and Wish? Do you know anyone, man or woman, who might like a job answering the telephone here for the next two weeks? And permanently after that if we can get something worked out?" I had decided to take matters into my own hands. I would pay out of my own case fees, if necessary, but I simply could not be tied to that desk any more.

Wish chuckled. "When the cat's away, eh, Fremont?"

"I suppose you could look at it like that. But really, Wish, one cannot conduct an investigatory business by staying in the office. Nor can I ask you every time I want to go out. Oh, I can hardly wait, there is so much to do."

Opening his central desk drawer, Wish (who was very neat) started putting things away as he did every night before leaving. He poked at the inside of his cheek with his tongue. "Well," he said, "about someone to answer the telephone . . . I do have an idea. A couple of them, actually. Leave it to me, Fremont. I'll have someone here for your consideration tomorrow morning."

Late afternoon, just after four o'clock. Wish had left, saying on his way out that he was going to do a bit on his own special project on his way home. I was curious, of course, to know what his special project was; nevertheless I did not ask. I had a strong hunch it had something to do with those graves, which I had not liked at all, and if that were the case I did not want to know.

I roamed through my side of the house, at first idly and then with the dawning realization that I was looking at my space through my father's eyes—or as near to that as possible. His visit, coinciding with my birthday, was just a little more than a week off.

The entire downstairs, the office suite, Father could not help but approve. He would not expect the mahogany-paneled solemnity of his own offices at the bank. Nor even, I daresay, the elegance of his library and study in our own Boston house. Our three rooms here, including Michael's minuscule study, were tastefully furnished and as filled with light as any space can be in this city of ever changing moods and fogs. The kitchen he would ignore as not being his domain, therefore not a place about which he felt entitled to render an opinion.

With an increasingly heavy heart and a sheen of apprehension appearing on my skin, I climbed the stairs to my private rooms on the second and third floors. The wall along the stair needed pictures—paintings, or at least photographs. But art takes both time and money to acquire; one cannot (if one has any sense of taste at all) just put up any old thing, buy old paintings out of the barrel at the junk shop, which was about all I could afford for now, and in the foreseeable future.

My own sitting room had a nice Chinese rug on the floor, a sort of house-warming gift from my friend Meiling Li, who is Chinese and a special student at Stanford. This rug had a border pattern in a subdued apricot shade, a central sort of mandala predominantly of the same shade, and a background field of ivory with tiny apricot, brown, and green flowers woven into it. Father would like the rug—even Augusta would have to like that rug, as it was very fine—but he would look around and think, if not say, "And where is the rest of your furniture, Fremont?" No, he wouldn't, he'd say, "And where is the rest of your furniture, *Caroline?*"

I found myself resenting that mightily, though he was not even here yet, and even though I knew I could hardly be certain what he'd think.

"Oh yes, I can!" I said softly but intensely, leaning in the sitting-room doorway, heartsick. I loved my father dearly, and he would never understand, never appreciate how long it had taken me to trust that the J&K Agency could provide me with income-producing work, work which would enable me to support myself as I'd done with my typewriting service that first glorious and strange year in San Francisco. He couldn't know that only recently had I dared spend a substantial portion of my little remaining hoard of money for the two chairs the room did hold. These were a pair of velvet-upholstered wing-back chairs in a rich butterscotch shade, one with a matching footstool. I had been so proud of purchasing those two chairs, yet now I saw that to Father they would look like nothing. Perhaps even worse than nothing.

"It's not much, by damn, but it's mine!" I yelled the words out into the room, knowing that when Father was present I should have to swallow them, and I heard the echoes of my voice bounce off the walls, break into fragments, and quiver at last to rest in the invisible air. Then step by step I forced myself through the rest of the apartment, noting with a merciless eye how shabby the remainder of my furniture was, looking like castoffs because for the most part that is what they were. The maids in our Boston house had had better-looking bedrooms than mine—at least if you considered only the furniture.

Palm of my hand flat against the silken coolness of the spread on my bed, I smoothed it, caressed it, and let my eyes roam over the mementos that made the room special: the postcards tucked around the edge of the mirror over my dresser; a tastefully mounted collection of casual photos taken by Michael in Carmel of all our zany friends there, who were in some sort of costume often as not; tied round one of the bedposts, a shining teal-blue ribbon with a single golden thread running through it, which had been wrapped about the stems of the first bouquet of flowers Michael—then Archer—ever gave me. Then I sat on the bed, pushed back against the headboard, and let it all wash over me: How much happiness I had felt in this bedroom with its shabby furniture (but, admittedly, a good mattress), and quite soon I didn't give a fig about what Father thought any more.

I did miss Michael though, a great deal. The house seemed so empty. And to think I'd be without him for two whole weeks, such an awfully long time.

A brisk walk before supper, I decided, would be just the thing. And if I should just happen to walk by Frances's house, I might be able to see if anything were going on. Her house was, after all, right on the way to several other places, such as the little branch library . . . well, to be perfectly honest it wasn't on the way to the library at all, but if one were fond of loops as a walking pattern . . . and I really should go to the library before it closed for the night, as that librarian was keeping her eye out for me for materials having to do with Ingrid Swann.

So it was that I found myself, at an hour when most people are sitting ensconced in their homes with their children crawling all over them, walking briskly down the hill toward Broadway. The McFadden mansion, when I sighted it, was blazing with electric lights; and when I passed it, I felt as if every window were an eye looking at me, watching me suspiciously, curiously, and with a good deal of caution. "Go away!" the house said. "Don't bother me! Be gone, Fremont Joo-o-o-nes. . . ."

I, however, am stubborn and pigheaded, and do not take it lightly that a house may be ordering me about. So I stood my ground and became rooted in place on the sidewalk looking up at it. Something was going on in that house that was not the usual sort of thing. I was absolutely sure of it, yet I could not for the life of me see or hear anything beyond those great, thick walls.

Leaving the sidewalk, I walked around to the side where Frances's favorite door was indeed open. It stood ajar by one or two inches. I feared Patrick Rule would be inside, up those stairs, and I was in an agony of wanting to know. I leaned toward the opening, my already keen hearing sharpened to its highest pitch, and listened: a humming, buzzing of conversation, probably in the kitchen, was all I heard. Not a single individual word had been discernible. Nor any one voice recognizable.

Should I go in? Go up those stairs, burst in on them in Frances's rooms, warn them? Say something like, *Patrick and Frances, be lovers if you must, pupil and teacher if you will* (after all, hadn't I done the same with Michael?), *but for heaven's sake, Not So Near the Dinner Hour!* And not in her own house where her husband could come in at any moment.

I placed one foot on the threshold. I told myself I had my own key to this door still; Frances wouldn't have given it to me if she didn't want me to use it. I smelled the loamy odors of the garden room, or flower room, or whatever it was that Frances had called it . . . and then, Crash! Someone had dropped something in the kitchen, a load of crockery by the sound of it.

Whatever had I been thinking of? I came to my senses and fled.

I had collected every newspaper article to appear so far in connection with Ingrid Swann's death, and the following morning sat reading them at my desk. Wish was late; I didn't mind. As far as I knew he didn't have a case, so it didn't really matter; and it had been days and days since a single client had come to our door. We were still in that stage of having to go out and drum up business for ourselves.

With a thrill I realized, just looking at all this publicity for the famous Ingrid Swann, that the investigation I was conducting on behalf of Patrick Rule could make the reputation of the J&K Agency. If I could find the killer when the police couldn't, and somehow let the press in on it . . . Oh, I could just see the headlines! For here, every photograph of Ingrid was accompanied by a banner two inches high. And of course every paper had a photograph, because Ingrid Swann had been a beautiful woman. Extraordinarily beautiful. Even the harshness of newsprint could not dim the effect of that face.

She had a neck like her name, like a swan, made to appear all the more delicate by the bouffant Gibson-girl style of her hair, which apparently had been palest blond in shade. As each newspaper had a slightly different photo, it was possible to regard this dead woman from straight on, in three-quarter profile, and in one demure complete profile with head and eyes cast down at an angle. The nose, the cheeks, the perfect rosebud of her mouth all seemed as perfect in proportion and line as those of a Greek statue.

No, I thought with a frown, that was not a good comparison, for the Greeks made statues of heroic size, whereas Ingrid's features were delicate. More like an Italian Renaissance statue, a little Donatello perhaps—though if I remembered my art from Wellesley, Donatello had mostly sculpted boys. That looked like girls.

I mentally shook myself to stop my mind wandering, got up from my desk, and let my body wander back to the kitchen for another cup of coffee. I got this way in the mornings with no one to keep me focused. I had become dependent on Michael, I realized, to talk to me until I was well awake, to help me ease into the day . . . and now he was not here.

"Ridiculous!" I scoffed aloud. I hadn't needed anybody to get me going in the mornings before, I had always done it by myself just fine, thank you, for years. Yet I stood staring out the small window over the kitchen sink while the coffee warmed—it would be bitter, too strong, I'd cooked it too long—and thought of nothing except how hard it was for me to think of anything or anyone except Michael. How I wished I'd acted more wisely, listened to his counsel! How I wished I had not driven him away.

That was what I'd done, wasn't it? My vaunted independence had driven him away many days before the time we'd agreed he should be gone. I wanted him back, wanted to say I was sorry . . . but it was too late. The damage had been done.

Just then the coffee flared up and boiled over. Before I could snatch it off the fire, the hot black liquid had filled the room with the acrid stench of burned brew. "Botheration!" I said, and set about cleaning it up.

I never did get that cup of coffee drunk, for when I returned with it to my desk, the little bell let out its silvery peal along with the opening of the front door. And A Disaster walked into the office on Divisadero Street.

FOURTEEN

Dead Space

"FREMONT, may I introduce my mother, Edna Stephenson? Mom, this is Fremont Jones, one of the owners of the J&K Agency."

"Howd'ja do," Edna said, while I said simultaneously: "How do you do, Mrs. Stephenson."

Then she said, "Best start out calling me Edna." This rather unusual request was punctuated by one sharp nod of her head, more like a jerk, setting asway the one forlorn flower that hung from her bonnet rim. She was a short, almost round woman whose physical appearance could not possibly have contrasted more with her son's. Either Wish must resemble his father, or

151

they had found him under a bush, where he had been abandoned by some tall, thin person.

With a sinking feeling that only increased as Edna toddled into the room, I soon realized why she had phrased her request that way. I raised my eyebrows at Wish in mute supplication, but he just smiled. A benevolent, almost beatific, typically Wish smile that was completely maddening in the circumstances.

"This is your office?" Edna said, going from one desk to the other. She had a pattery sort of walk, with an occasional lurch to one side or the other, like a toddler uncertain on its feet.

Assuming the question to be rhetorical, I did not reply. Instead I folded my arms, tapped my foot beneath my skirt where no one could see, and waited for an explanation.

Wish walked around behind me without a word, took his mother by the elbow, and gently steered her to his own desk. "This is my desk, where I work, Mama."

"Nize," Edna said, touching the desk. Then, looking Wish up and down as if to establish the connection between son and desk, she touched it again. The seating arrangement appeared to have been given her blessing.

"Fremont, Mama would like to try the receptionist job for a few days."

I said noncommittally, "I see."

The woman's eyes lit up, and she nodded so vigorously I thought the forlorn flower might fly completely off. "I'd get to talk on the telephone, that's what my boy Aloysius said. I'm real good at that," she insisted. "I'm a modern woman, I am, not afraid of newfangled machinery. Why, I took to the telephone just like a duck to water!"

"That's right, she did," Wish confirmed, still beaming.

Yes, I thought. I remembered how Wish used to tell me about his mother calling the precinct house where he'd been working as a rookie policeman, and how unless you stopped her she'd keep you on the telephone for hours. . . .

152

"Where's your phone?" So, Edna Stephenson was on such familiar terms with that instrument that she had already adopted the shortened form of its appellation, as more and more people seemed to be doing these days.

"Oh," she crowed, "there it is!" and then she pounced. Quite a feat that was, since she had to get all the way across the room from her son's desk to mine on those tiny little feet before pouncing. But she managed it in record time.

I scooted back out of her way and watched, a little stunned, as Edna seized the telephone, removed the ear trumpet portion and held it to her ear, jiggled the hook a couple of times, and then said into the mouthpiece on the base, "Hello, Central?"

Central apparently said hello back, because Edna was quiet for a moment, while her little round, brown eyes danced in pleasure. "No, thank you," she rather abruptly sang out, "I do not wish to make a call. I just wanted to be sure my telephone is in working order. Ta-ta!"

"It's working," she announced. "Now let's see the rest of the place."

I couldn't help but smile, even as I shook my head slowly, in amazement. Edna was already pattering her erratic way toward the conference room, so I said, "Wish, why don't you help your mother off with her coat and bonnet, and show her the rest of our office space. When you're in the kitchen, you may want to make a new pot of coffee. Meanwhile I'll clear my stuff out of the front desk so I won't have to bother her later to get my things."

Wish winked, and the beatific smile became more of an elf's grin. He'd pulled off a coup, and he knew it. "Mama!" He reached one long arm out after her. "Hold up. Let's hang up your coat and hat first, like Fremont says."

Edna was in that three-foot-deep arched passageway between the office and the conference room, rapping on the walls and asking with impatient curiosity, "What's this, then? What's back there behind this wall? Is there a door? Is it a closet? Well, son, speak up, I can't hear you!''

"I'm trying, Mama, if you'll just be quiet long enough for me to tell you."

"So I'm quiet. Like a mouze." "Nize" for nice, "Mouze" for mouse . . . I wondered how many more of these charming little eccentricities of speech Edna had.

"We don't think there's anything back there," Wish explained. "Certainly there's no door or anything. Architect probably just made a mistake in the proportion of the downstairs rooms compared to the upper ones, and to balance it out created a dead space."

"Oh?" Edna cackled. "Ha-ha, hee-hee, that's a good un, dead space, for a detectives agency. Dead space! Ha-ha, hee-hee . . .'' And she was off again.

I smiled, shook my head again in answer to Wish's mute shrug, and began the job of removing my files and so on from the desk. Of course I had no idea where I was going to go; I hadn't thought that far ahead, had assumed there would be candidates for the receptionist position to be interviewed before things got so far as my needing to relinquish my desk.

Perhaps Michael's study, since he wasn't here? Only as a temporary measure, of course. I approached the small room with my arms full and, in the doorway, stopped, waited a moment, then abruptly turned away.

Michael's study smelled like him, a subtle masculine scent that I could not possibly describe, somewhere between soap and leather and . . . skin. I couldn't work in there, it would drive me mad.

So I camped out at the end of the conference-room table, stacking and arranging things that had been in drawers—and when I was done, I preferred the table to any desk I had ever owned. Everything so easily to hand, plenty of room to spread out. The coffee was perking; its delicious smell wafted from the kitchen, and I let my nose ("noze," Edna would probably say) lead me back there. Soon the three of us were laughing and talking, and Edna was telling stories on Wish as a boy; then she asked me how I'd liked coming West on the train . . . and then the telephone rang.

Edna Stephenson was up like a shot, those short legs and tiny feet pumping along with far greater reliability than one would have thought possible. I heard her pick up the instrument and say into it clearly, "The J&K Agency. This is Mrs. Stephenson, the receptionist, speaking. May I help you?"

"You taught her what to say?" I asked Wish, quietly.

"Yep. Made her repeat it to me about a million times."

"She did it very well," I acknowledged.

"Fremont, give her a chance. She needs something else to do besides whist at the church and her women's sodality. We won't have to pay her much, and if we hit a bad patch and can't pay, well, she's well enough off it wouldn't hurt her once in a while. My dad left her pretty well fixed for money."

"Hey, Fremont!" yelled a big voice out of a little round woman, all the way from the front room. "This call's for you!"

Three days later I had to admit that Edna Stephenson was not turning out to be at all the disaster I had feared. Wish had done us a favor, probably at some expense to himself—because she did treat him more like a son, like a boy, than like the man he had long ago become. But he bore it with good grace, and Edna, true to her word, had no fear of modern machines whatsoever, so she was soon teaching herself the typewriter. To coin a phrase from school report days, she "showed initiative," and was forever plucking papers, or whatever, out of my hands, saying, "Here, let me have that, I can do it for you on the phone."

She could, too. Edna would do things on the telephone that never would have occurred to me. Library research, for example. She would call a reference librarian who was a personal friend of hers and say: "Listen, dearie, I'm at me job—What, you din't know? I got me a nize little job now. Days, working for a detective agency. That's right, a detective agency, like for investigatin' things, same as the police do only better. My son works here, Aloysius, you know. Now, dearie, here's the thing. We need to know. . . ."

Whatever we needed to know, if it was in a book, Edna's friend would find it—and usually pretty quickly, too. (Probably because Edna wouldn't leave her alone until she'd done it, but no matter.) Edna also had a very neat handwriting, much easier to read in truth than her typing—at least so far—and she produced copious, meticulous notes on whatever subject she had been asked to tackle, plus a few she decided to tackle just because they interested her.

Edna's favorite subject at the moment was Ingrid Swann. She had, by relentless telephoning around town, uncovered something that had not been in any of the newspapers: Ingrid Swann had had a husband, from whom she was not divorced. Nor had she lived with the man for years and years, but he was right here in San Francisco. On the south side, in Bernal Heights. His name was Conrad Higgins. Ingrid Swann's real name had been Myra Higgins—not a bad name at all, but not nearly so exotic, nor as descriptive of the woman's beauty, as Ingrid Swann. I decided that I would go to see Conrad Higgins, because if the police had located him they hadn't told the newspapers. And I badly wanted an edge if not an outright coup.

But first I had to leave some instructions with Edna. I rather dreaded it, for although she was great at taking initiative, she was not so good at following orders. Quite frankly I worried about leaving her alone.

"Edna," I said in a forthright manner, "I have to be out for a while, but there are some things I want to tell you before I leave."

"Sure, okay, Fremont." She leaned back in her chair—her feet didn't touch the floor, so she looked a little like an old child—and laced her fingers together over her round middle. "What do you need? Don't look so serious on me. Has someone died?"

"No, quite the contrary. But I'm just a little concerned . . . Um, it's about these people who are coming here to the offices this afternoon. One is the principal client in this case you've helped me with so much, by gathering all that information on Ingrid Swann."

"Ooh, that's the double murder! And the client's coming here? How exciting."

"It wasn't exactly a double murder," I said patiently, "there was one murder and then another. Some weeks and some days lapsed between the two. First Abigail Locke and then Ingrid Swann."

"Yes, I know," Edna said, nodding wisely, "and they were both your so-called mediums, though your first one hasn't been nearly so effective as the second one, meaning Ingrid, used to be. Dunno what to think of that."

I didn't know what to think of that either. In fact, I hadn't understood a word after "mediums." I said, "I beg your pardon?"

"Oh, you don't have to do that, Fremont, though it's very *nize* of you all the same. You didn't do nothing to be pardoned for, far as I know."

I suppressed a smile. "What I intended to say was, I don't take your meaning, about the first and second mediums—you know, what you said just now."

"Oh, now I see! Fremont, for a nize girl, sometimes you do talk funny."

"Probably because I'm from Boston." Conversations with Edna did have a way of getting out of hand. If she didn't explain herself in the next sentence, I intended to press on with my own agenda.

"Boston!" She winked. "Well, la-dee-dah. I better be on me peaze and queuz. Anyways, about those two mediums: The first one, that Abigail Locke? She was never as great as Ingrid was in her best times. Mrs. Locke, she didn't have style. She just sat there and talked up a storm. Could maybe contact a few dead loved ones, that was all. Nothing exciting. Soze I heard tell, you unnerstand."

I nodded, to keep her talking. So she did know something after all. I wondered if she, being a widow with some money and time on her hands, had ever availed herself of a medium's services— particularly the services of the two in question.

"Now Ingrid Swann, she was something else. Beautiful woman, that. Kind of woman even other women, as well as all the men of course, could admire the looks of. And oh, she had talent. She didn't just talk. Ingrid weren't no trance channeler, no sireee, she could do all the fancy stuff: Psychokinesis, apports, remote views, ectoplasmic extrusion . . ."

"I've heard about the ectoplasmic extrusion. She worked in a cabinet, yes? You wouldn't happen to have seen any of that, would you, Edna?"

Edna beamed, and tipped forward in the chair so that her tip-pytoes reached the floor. To keep from slipping right down, she had to hold on to the chair arms with both hands. "Me and a couple thousand others!" she announced with glee.

"Thousand? Edna, that sounds hardly possible. There's no place in all of San Francisco to hold such a large audience."

"Well, it wasn't all on the same night, Fremont. She did seven performances, seven nights in a row, back about five years ago, I think it was, in one of the bigger the-ay-ters. I fergit which one. Nearly killed her, so they said. The effort, you know. But it made her famous all in one fell swoop."

"And you saw one of the performances. Would you describe it to me?" I had been standing near a corner of my former desk, which was Edna's now. But I took a chair, the one designated for prospective clients, from against the wall and sat down at an angle.

Edna scooted back in the chair, refolded hands over tummy, and told the tale with a glittering eye: "It was like thiz, now. The stage was all hung in black drapes, black as night they were. Nize material, looked like, probably black velvet. Anyways"—she closed her eyes for a moment and screwed up her features a bit as if that might help her remember—"right in the middle of the stage was this black box—the cabinet, that was—inside a big huge box made all of glass. Like a little room of glass built right there on the stage—walls, ceiling, and everything. Had a door, too. Only thing wasn't glass was the frame of the thing, to hold it up, you know."

Fascinating! I thought, but did not interrupt.

"So out comes thiz man what works with Ingrid Swann, her consurge or whatever he was—"

I doubted "concierge" was the word she'd been looking for, but accepted it without breaking into giggles, which took some effort.

"And he does his introduction: 'Ladeez and gentlemens,' and all that. Dee dum dee dum dee dum. Then here comes Ingrid Swann, and that whole audience gasps, everybody all at once, like some huge animal taking a breath. Oh, you shoulda seen her, she looked like a bride in a silvery dress, silver threads sewed right in. No, not a bride, more like an angel, or a fairy. You know, a good fairy like in one of them fairy tales. 'Ceptin' no wings."

"It must have been very exciting," I contributed.

"Oh, it was," she nodded, "it was that. Exciting, and she hadn't never even done a thing yet. So she goes right up to thiz glass box and the consurge, he makes a coupla fancy passes at the door of the thing, like a magician, and then he opens it. And in she goes. In he goes, too. They both go right up to that other box, which is black and looks like a steam cabinet, you know with the head poking out and all the rest of the person inside."

I nodded. Steam cabinets were a fairly common phenomenon, though I had certainly never tried one myself, nor did I intend to.

"Then the consurge, he opens that black cabinet up wide and calls two men out of the audience to come take a look-see, that there's nothing inside it but only a stool for Ingrid to sit on. No false panels, no light switches, no levers nor strings to push and pull. Which there wasn't. Then the men leave and Ingrid, she sits down on that stool and the consurge, he locks that cabinet up around her tight as a drum, with only her pretty head sticking out."

Edna's voice dropped a notch. "Then he leaves by the glass door, locks that too. In her glass cage, Ingrid Swann, she closes her eyes while the consurge steps over to the edge of the stage—he has a real big voice, y'know—and says in a kinda confidential tone but not so soft as you can't hear: 'And now we must ask for complete silence and ab-so-loot stillness from the audience. Anyone who is easily frightened should be warned, you're about to witness an eerie experience that is not for the faint of heart to see. If you think it might upset you, you should leave now, because any noise or other disruption during Mrs. Swann's direct link of her body with the spirit world could cause her serious physical harm.' "

"You seem to remember it word for word," I observed. Having such an ability myself, I recognize it in another, though I was frankly amazed to find such ability in the person of Edna Stephenson.

She simply nodded her head, as if she did this kind of thing so often that it was not worth remarking, and indeed she probably did. She went on: "You know what that blessed angel Ingrid Swann did right there on that stage in front of all those people, Fremont? She let the departed spirits, which is bodiless, use her own body for to make themselves hands and arms and feet and the like. Ectoplasm, that's what they make it out of, and it come out of her. Out of Ingrid Swann. I seen it with me own eyes."

"I can't imagine!" I said, which was true.

"Well then, lemme tell ya." She scooted forward again and told the rest of her tale with breathtaking urgency: "The the-ay-ter went almost all dark, just only a few little glimmers of reflected light from somewhere off her silvery dress, and off the frame of that glass house. Which you could see the inside of through the glass, of course."

Her head nodded vigorously, and so did I.

"Such a silence that was, of waiting. All eyes on the woman. Then, little by little it starts. First like a wisp of white smoke curling out of her mouth. She breathes the stuff out, y'see, out of her nose and her mouth."

Charming, I thought but did not say.

"So this white stuff keeps coming, and coming, till pretty soon it's coming out of her in such a steady stream she has to open her mouth, and out it pours, and swirls around and begins to climb the glass walls of that box—that's why the glass is there, y'see, so's it won't drift out over the audience. And my goodness me, did it ever get colder'n a witch's titty in that the-ay-ter while Ingrid was a-doin' her ectoplasmic extrusion."

Now, I did not believe in the least that Ingrid Swann was somehow using her own body to give shape to spirits, nor did I think that anything like ectoplasm actually existed. What I really thought was that the phenomenon of having discovered and harnessed an invisible substance—electricity—to do our bidding in such recent years had given rise to the thought that there might be many other invisible things that can be made to work for us . . . and this idea has sometimes been taken to ridiculous limits. As far as I was concerned, the concept of ectoplasm was right up there with the most ridiculous.

Yet, as I listened to Edna tell about Ingrid Swann alone on a darkened stage, inside her black cabinet, inside a glass box, with this substance—whatever it was—streaming out of her mouth, wreathing around her, I found myself more than half believing. Certainly I wanted to believe. And so I asked:

"Did the ectoplasm then form itself into a body? Any recognizable shape?"

"Hands." Ha-a-ands, she said. "Fingers, long skinny fingers reaching out, feeling the glass of that box. It was just a demonstration, see, that she could do it. Not like a real séance where there might have been something happening."

"And in a real séance, what would have happened?"

"Why, the ectoplasm would have formed itself into the recognizable shape of someone what's passed on. Or the person in control—that's the consurge—he'd ask it questions or tell it to do things, like hold a trumpet and blow it, ring a bell, rap on the table once for yes, twice for no, stuff like that. Which she didn't do none of."

"How long did it last?" I asked, unable even in my wildest dreams to imagine ever having such an experience.

Edna shook her head wonderingly, again looking like an old but credulous child. "Dunno. Long time, it seemed. Afterward, that's when I got to go up."

"Got to go up?"

"Uh-huh. From the audience, we could go up inside the glass box if we wanted. See the residue of the ectoplasm."

In spite of myself, I felt a chill creeping along my skin.

"Like slime, it was," Edna said.

FIFTEEN

The Spirits Are Moving

WHEREVER MICHAEL had gone, he had not taken Max; which was a good thing, because of Bernal Heights being some distance away and not easy to get to by streetcar. In fact, since I did have the use of the auto, I had not bothered to ascertain whether there was or was not a streetcar to that part of town.

Mr. Conrad Higgins lived on Precita Avenue, a short street of Victorian houses clinging to a hillside with a spectacular view of the City of San Francisco in the distance, and the Bay with its boats and islands. I stood looking at that view for quite some time, because it refreshed me and gave me hope. I had found Edna Stephenson's story of Ingrid Swann's ectoplasmic extrusion to be both affecting and depressing, and in fact had felt, during the longish drive out from our house on the north end of Divisadero to Bernal Heights, as if a residue of the story itself were somehow clinging to me like that cold slime.

"Poor Ingrid," I murmured. The logical part of my brain told me I should not feel sorry for her, because she must have been a charlatan of a very high order indeed to produce such an illusion; but some other part of my inner self, the part that is commonly called in sentimental parlance the heart, simply understood how hard Ingrid had worked, and how desperate she must have been, to produce this illusion. Finally, in spite of myself, in spite of my very best efforts, there was an even deeper, darker part of me that asked the question: *What if it really happend?* What if Ingrid Swann, at risk to her own health and certainly great expenditure of energy, had really produced the substance called ectoplasm out of her own body, so that spirits might have substance for even the shortest and most futile of explorations in that glass box?

"How lonely she must have been," I murmured. In my mind I had such a vivid vision of her sitting enclosed, trapped, in that glass box. And now the poor woman was dead. All because some vicious, cruel person was murdering the mediums of my beloved City. Well, it just wouldn't do.

I pulled myself together, marched up some very steep steps to a front door, and rang the bell. I was quite prepared for no one to be at home, as it was only the middle of the afternoon; but somehow I didn't have the feeling that Mr. Conrad Higgins would prove to be a nose-to-the-grindstone type of man. Else why would a woman like Myra, also known as Ingrid, decide to leave him and earn her own way in the world in the manner she had, which ultimately had gotten her killed?

My surmises, or hunches, proved correct. I had to ring a second time, and stand waiting for a while longer but then the door opened inward to reveal one of the ugliest-looking men I had ever seen in my entire life. I instinctively moved back half a step, which on those narrow steps put me in danger of overbalancing and going right down the whole steep flight. But I was able to stop myself from that happening, and so cleared my throat and said, "Good day. Mr. Higgins?"

"Who wants to know?" That voice might have come up from a gravel pit. It suited his face, which was pitted, as if from the smallpox, and in addition looked as if it might have been pounded out of shape more than once. He had what I believe is called a cauliflower ear, and his nose had been broken so many times it lay like a squashed mass in the middle of his face. He was a good two inches shorter than I, but perhaps three times as broad. A nasty customer.

"My name is Fremont Jones." I produced a card from J&K and handed it to this troll masquerading as a human. "I am a private investigator working on a case that has direct bearing on your wife's murder. I'd like to talk to you. May I come in?"

"Wife?" He tilted his head back and to the side, as if that would help his eyes to emerge from the loose folds of flesh that draped from his eyelids down below the orbits. "Don't have a wife. Haven't had for years now. But come on in." His eyes swept over me from head to foot as he stepped back to allow me entry. "You'll see I'm telling the truth about there being no wife. Never realized till she was gone how much the woman must have done to keep things going around here."

He did not exaggerate. Conrad Higgins lived like a pig. He acted worse, scratching himself with a dirty hand as he preceded me down the hallway, saying, "The kitchen I do manage to keep pretty clean. Also keep a pot of coffee going in there these days. Never know when a pretty lady will drop by. Heh-heh-heh."

This last was accompanied by what he may have considered a coy look over his shoulder. *Disgusting!* It was really all I could do not to run away. "The kitchen will be fine," I said.

I did not, however, accept a cup of coffee but asked my questions in a rapid-fire and efficient manner. I imagine I must have come off like a severe schoolmarm, because he gave me no more of those disgusting looks, nor did he seem anything but relieved when I decided I had learned enough and rose to take my leave.

Out in the fresh air once more, I took a deep breath and prayed (to the God I don't quite believe in) that I should never, ever fall so low as this man had allowed himself to go.

On the drive back into the City, I mentally reviewed what I had learned from Conrad Higgins: First, Myra had been an orphan destined for "the fate worse than death, for a woman, if you know what I mean" when he had "rescued" her by marrying her; second, only two years later, he had tossed Myra out on her rear end (his inelegant words) for being an unfit wife when she had month after month demonstrated her inability to conceive a child; third, Conrad himself was a famous prize fighter, deserving of the best in wives, since he could "whup anything that stands on two legs and some that stands on four in the state of California"; and fourth, since it had been *her* fault he'd had to throw her out, and it certainly wasn't *his* fault that his last fight three years ago had left him unable to continue in the ring on account of he'd lost his sense of balance, *then* it was only right she should now be supporting him. Finally (he'd roared in that gravelly voice), what the hell was he supposed to do for money now she was dead?

Not wanting to put ideas into the head of this gross individual— the thought of Ingrid Swann's delicate beauty in those hands being truly repulsive beyond belief—I had not asked about a will, or who would inherit whatever estate had been left. I assumed, since she had reputedly been so successful, there would be a will. Of course I must look into it. I was operating on the assumption that she would have legally changed her name. I should have to go to the Court House, the Hall of Records or some such. I wondered about the so-called brother, Ngaio Swann.

"He will have changed his name from something more ordinary too," I mumbled. "Nobody has as interesting a name as Ngaio Swann unless he has made it up himself."

At any rate, the gross personage known as Conrad Higgins was extremely unlikely to have had anything to do with the death of his wife by either name, Myra or Ingrid. Because Myra Higgins had been his meal ticket, his only means of support.

As I proceeded into the City on Mission Street, I mused over something that had not occurred to me before: Why had Myra/Ingrid been so willing to support this despicable man? Was Ngaio maybe not her brother, and did the despicable husband know about that and use it to blackmail her?

"Hmm," I said aloud.

I had a lot to look into. How much of it would have to be done before I dared leak the information about Conrad's existence to the press, I did not yet know.

It was, I thought, a good beginning for Ingrid Swann's side of my case. As for Abigail Locke's side, the best entry I had there was probably still back in the office at Divisadero Street. Patrick Rule and Frances McFadden were all too likely, whenever they got together, to lose track of time.

"They're in the kitchen," said Edna as soon as I walked through the door. No hello, no "How was your afternoon," no nothing, just "They're in the kitchen." It was really quite unlike the gregarious, not to mention garrulous Edna, so I nodded and proceeded on the assumption that "they" were Frances and Patrick, and that there was something going on that Edna did not particularly like. Actually her facial expression told me as much: Her lips, which were usually so busy flapping that I could not have told you the shape of her mouth to save myself, were compressed into a tight line.

"I gather you wish me to, um, go and speak with them? With Patrick and Frances?" I removed the black sweater I'd worn in the auto and hung it on the clothes tree. "Is anything wrong, Edna? Anything you want to tell me first?"

She crooked her finger at me, a come-hither motion, and raised her face toward mine as I bent down. "He's got her hypnotized,"

Edna said softly, her voice tight with disapproval, "only he don't call it that. Calls it something else. She's in his power, poor woman. I may not know much but I know that when I see it, and I know it's dangerous for a woman to be in somebody's power. So I didn't let them use that little office you said they could use, where he could shut the door and do . . . things as shouldn't be done! I put them in the kitchen and that's that." One emphatic nod of the head punctuated her statement.

"Quite wise of you," I said, and patted her shoulder as I passed. I was growing as fond of Edna as I was of her son, and that was saying a good deal. "I'll go on back there with them and see what they're doing. I have some questions for both of them anyway. Oh, and Edna?"

"Yes, Fremont?"

"Did anything come up while I was gone that needs my attention before five o'clock?" I estimated it was probably about four-thirty, and even as I did so, the chiming clock in the hall landing gave the one chime with which it marks the half hour. I had become quite good at telling time without a watch.

"No, not a thing. You folks need more work, and that's a fact. My Aloysius, he's out doing something of his own for no pay, he says. Course, it's not as if he's likely to starve without—what's that you call them, cases—but still when he was in the PD they always did have something to do."

"I know, believe me." I also took that mild criticism like a blow to the heart. I cared far too much whether the J&K Agency succeeded or not, and so—probably unwisely—instead of just putting what Edna had said away in some mental filing cabinet, I explained: "Michael Kossoff, the other partner, is away at the moment. I don't believe you've ever met him?"

Edna folded her arms and rocked back and forth a little in her chair. "Can't say as I have, no. But Aloysius has told me about him plenty of times. Admires him. Wants to be like him, to e-moo-late him. Hah!"

"He could do worse," I said rather grimly . . . because I knew all too well that, with his particular temperament, Wish Stephenson could also do better. Wish is basically a sunny person while Michael has moods, and a black streak a mile wide.

I got lost in amorphous thoughts of my complex life-and-work partner for a moment, but soon recalled myself. "At any rate, one of Michael's contributions to the business, aside from bankrolling it single-handedly and volunteering his time as consultant, is that he goes out and recruits business through his personal contacts. When he returns from his current trip, I'm sure he'll bring some new work with him."

I wasn't sure of any such thing but felt a need to appease Edna. To prepare the way for her to like Michael, since I didn't want to lose her.

"Oh, and Edna—" I began but then I stopped myself. I had been about to tell her of my plan to use my current case to get us some newspaper publicity, but I thought better of it. I wasn't ready yet to have anyone else know that but me. So I changed in midstream, rapidly, and went on: "Please feel free to lock up the front door and go home a bit early. I'll look after Mr. Rule and Mrs. McFadden now. We'll be fine."

Edna Stephenson cocked her head to one side and regarded me skeptically, those round brown eyes of hers full of questions. But then to my relief her expression cleared, she smiled and regained her more habitual bounciness. Edna could bounce while remaining attached to the seat of a chair better than any human being I had ever known.

"That'd be nize," she said, "on account of I could stop in me favorite market on the way home, get there a bit early, before the crowd, maybe they'll have some fine lamb chops. Aloysius does love a good lamb chop, and so do I, but you haveta get there early."

"By all means," I agreed. It did sound good; my own stomach rumbled at the thought of lamb chops, and I realized that I hadn't given thought to my own dinner at all. More evidence of missing Michael, and how quickly all the patterns of one's life can become entwined with another's.

Well, never mind. What was waiting in my kitchen had nothing to do with lamb chops. I said a final good night to Edna and went on back.

Halfway through the conference room I heard them, a low murmuring exchange of voices, male and female, so soothing it was like the ebb and flow of a quiet sea. The peacefulness, the quiet tone, caused me to slow my steps, to listen all the harder, and to proceed with care.

Whatever Edna Stephenson may have feared, it was not what I found in my kitchen. I found a man and a woman so remarkably in accord with one another that they seemed almost to be functioning as two halves of one person.

Neither was aware of me. They were off in a land of their own, whose boundaries, I imagined, might be fragile. So I hung back just beyond the door. From there, I could see both Frances and Patrick in profile; without turning their heads, they could not see me.

Patrick Rule seemed to be burning with quiet intensity—I could almost feel it myself, as if it were through riding on his energy that Frances was able to do whatever it was she was doing. Though he stared raptly at her face, her eyes were closed, and her face was . . . incandescent.

He murmured, but by listening intently now I could just make out the words: "Tell me, describe for me, dear Frances, the place where you are now."

Long exhalation of breath, like an endless sigh, then Frances said, "I am walking down a street, it's very flat. The street is broad, and there are trees on both sides, huge old trees—are they oaks?—whatever they are, their branches meet overhead and turn this street into a kind of leafy tunnel."

Another long sigh.

"Continue, my dear," said Patrick, positively yearning toward her. "And tell me, if you can, why you are on this street, and if you know it, the name of the city you are in."

A single faint frown line appeared between Frances's brows. "There is someone here who needs . . . diagnosis. A woman who is ill, in one of these houses."

"Tell me about the houses."

"They're old. They have long porches, all the way across the front." A silence ensued, as if Frances were walking past one house and then another. "Some of them have columns . . . others are not quite so grand . . . but they all have the porches."

"A warm climate then. Southern perhaps?" Patrick suggested.

Frances, off in her own dream now, or whatever peculiar state she was in, ignored this comment to continue her perusal of the landscape: "All the houses have these fences made of wrought iron, very nicely done, with spikes on top. This is . . . this is . . . New Orleans." The line between her brows passed away.

I folded my arms and leaned against the wall. They had been at this for at least an hour and a half, maybe longer, because I had no way of knowing exactly when they'd arrived. I supposed Patrick Rule was only continuing to do what he'd said he would do— determining the nature and extent of Frances's psychic ability—so how could I complain? Yet how walking around the streets of New Orleans in one's mind, especially considering that it seemed to take a considerable expenditure of energy on both their parts to get and keep her there, could be of any help to anyone was beyond me.

Benefit of the doubt, I told myself, benefit of the doubt.

Frances had now found the house wherein the person needed her to diagnose something. As far as I knew, Frances had never diagnosed anything more than an overcooked egg in her entire life. So I nearly fell through the carpet when she exhaled another of her long sighs and then said:

"The patient is here, a woman named . . . Jean."

I leaned away from the wall and looked again through the door. Frances had spread wide the fingers of both hands and was holding them palms down about six inches above the surface of the table. Patrick had pulled back to give her room. With her eyes still closed, Frances moved her hands back and forth in small circular motions made with agonizing slowness.

She said, "Jean has a tumor in her abdominal cavity." More slow motion of hands and fingers. "It is located in the lower right quadrant. The appendix is absent in this person." Small frown. She turned her head just slightly, as if she were listening to something or someone she could hear a little better that way. "The appendix was removed when Jean was sixteen years old. She is thirty now. If this tumor is not surgically removed, Jean will die because it will grow so large as to obstruct bowel function. In itself, the tumor is not life-threatening, in other words it is not cancerous. But due to its size the tumor must be removed because it is functionally dangerous. That is the end of the information available for Jean."

"Good!" Patrick declared, in much more his normal tone of voice. "Remarkably good, Frances. You've done extraordinarily well."

Frances opened her eyes and smiled at him, but she did not really return to anything like normal consciousness. She was herself, and not herself. It was exceedingly strange, and now I knew why Edna had been so upset.

Patrick turned his head and saw me. Rather than be startled, or resent the interruption, he seemed genuinely pleased. "Fremont, do come in. Sit down with us at the table and let me tell you all that Frances and I have done this afternoon, building on some work we began a couple of days ago. Frances, say hello to Fremont."

I joined them at the table, on the side opposite the door; and as I sat down I remembered another round table where Frances and Patrick and I had all sat; at the head of that table, although properly speaking a round table cannot have a head, had sat a medium now dead: Abigail Locke. And Abigail's faithful servant Patrick had found himself a new . . . what?

"Hello, Fremont," Frances said. She smiled, but the smile was vacant, without warmth. Yet she seemed so serene, so peaceful. Her eyes did not connect with mine, though she turned them on me for a moment. They did connect with Patrick Rule; as soon as her roving eye had found him again, her face lit up (again) like a Christmas tree.

I looked a question at Patrick, not knowing how to ask it in Frances's presence.

He understood the question I hadn't asked, and he answered: "We have discovered that Frances McFadden is a natural somnambulist. I have become her mesmerist. We work together; this type of work requires the combined energies of both. This afternoon we have done some remarkable things together."

I'm sure, I thought. But I asked, "Such as . . . ?"

"Traveling clairvoyance—in this case, the diagnosis of illness and prescribing of treatment by seeing at a distance. Also simple clairvoyance, and some telepathy. The telepathy works extremely well, extremely; I can't thank you enough, Fremont Jones, for bringing Frances McFadden into my life."

"Yes, thank you, Fremont," Frances said, with that eerie, disconnected smile.

"We're going to work together, it's perfect," Patrick declared enthusiastically.

"I beg your pardon?" I said. "I don't think Jeremy McFadden is very likely to allow that. He wouldn't have two weeks ago, I can say that for certain."

"Oh, I'm not worried about that," Patrick said dismissively. "With a talent as big as hers, the spirits themselves will find a way. Doors will open, you'll see."

"No doubt," I said dryly. I expected him to say next something

173

about money being required to open doors. He did not disappoint me. He said:

"Of course, there will be expenses in getting her set up. Therefore I'll be dispensing with your detective services, Fremont Jones. Effective immediately."

I was stunned. This could not be happening. My first big case, for which I had done so much extra work, and which could get J&K the publicity we so much needed . . . *No!*

I did the only thing I could think of to do. It was a drastic remedy, but I was desperate. I focused on Frances, until she turned and focused equally on me. Then I said, "Frances, what does Emperor Norton think about all this? About your becoming a somnambulist?"

There came Frances's little frown again, and this time it deepened. Patrick Rule looked at me with wide eyes, his whole face having, it seemed, turned into a question mark. Frances's eyes began to clear, and she looked at me as if she recognized me, as if she were herself again. She blinked a couple of times, sat up a little straighter, and said in her usual tone of voice: "Emperor Norton? I forgot all about him! Imagine that."

SIXTEEN

The Emperor Rules

YOU HAVE to let her go," I said quietly, so that only Patrick Rule could hear. My right hand on his shoulder restrained him from following Frances. I could feel the tension in his body, longing to follow as surely as a dog must follow its master. I was wondering which one of these two people held the other in thrall.

Frances ran lightly down J&K's front steps to Divisadero Street, and when she had reached the bottom she turned and waved. "Patrick," she said, "you know how to get in touch with me. I just need time to contact the Emperor, that's all. My first loyalty must be to him, surely you can understand that? Why, without his help

I could not have come this far. I wouldn't have known where to begin."

"And he did give her a task to do," I murmured, again to Patrick alone.

He raised his hand in a halfhearted wave and, to give him credit, gave a small smile that no doubt was at odds with his feelings. "Whatever you think is best, Frances. The gift, the talent, are yours. I am only your connection, the link that would otherwise be missing."

She smiled then, fleetingly, and set off at a brisk pace. She had not far to walk, she would be at home within a few minutes, and then I would rest more easily.

As soon as she turned the corner and passed out of sight, I said in my normal tone: "Now, Patrick, we must talk. Because your case is one thing, and Frances McFadden is quite another. She was first my friend, and I won't have her put into danger."

As he followed me back into the office, he said, "I would not place that woman in danger for all the world."

I looked back skeptically over my shoulder at him, wondering if he was speaking that way because she represented his next meal ticket, or if he genuinely cared. Having once seen them linked as mesmerist and somnabulist, I could not forget the eerie power they had in those roles. It made me uneasy about them in a way I had not been before.

Though it would not be dark for a couple of hours yet, the fog was coming in and causing an early waning of the light. From the north windows you could see the thick, burgeoning, insubstantial bulk of it pour through the strait of the Golden Gate. I began turning on electric lights, first the desk lamps, then the overhead chandelier in the dining room.

"Take a seat at the conference table," I directed Patrick, indicating the chairs grouped around the end of the table nearest the main office space. The other end, near Michael's office and the passage to the kitchen, I was now using for a desk. I added, "I'll just see to the doors. J&K's office is officially closed for the day, but you and I still have some work to do."

He did not like being ordered about, of course. That proud face with its hawklike nose lifted, and he glared momentarily at me. I did not stay to see any further reaction, but went on doing as I'd said, locking first the back and then the front doors. Both had heavy new locks, installed at Michael's direction, with bolts one throws from the inside. The latest thing for security.

Of course it did occur to me that I might be locking myself in with a murderer. Nevertheless I went back into the conference room and took my place opposite him at the table. I folded my hands in front of me. "Now," I said, "suppose you explain to me just what is going on with you and my friend."

Patrick stared at me for a moment without speaking.

Eyes of a mesmerist, I thought. *Be careful, Fremont Jones!*

But his eyes, hypnotic though they might be under certain circumstances, were also tired. So dark-circled they had a hollow look. And his face was more gaunt now than it had been a week ago. He looked like a man who has either been working too hard or not sleeping much, or both.

Finally he said, "Frances McFadden has psychic ability, but it is of a passive, not an active kind. She fell naturally into the state that you saw earlier, during my second time of working with her. Miss Jones—"

"Fremont."

"—Fremont, I have been looking all my life . . . well, at least for all the part of it since I discovered the excitement of psychic phenomena for myself, and my own small talents . . . for someone like Frances. There is literally no end to the good we might do together; and who knows to what heights of celebrity we might rise!"

"You aren't going to rise very far if Jeremy McFadden beats his wife to death. And he could, you know. My partner, Michael Kossoff, was right. I should have listened to him."

"I don't know what you're talking about. Jeremy beats his wife? A man like that, who is known in this, of all cities, as a fair-dealing businessman?"

I inclined my head gravely. "The very same."

Patrick could not, apparently, sit still for this. He popped up out of his chair and began to pace back and forth like a long-legged, lithe animal trapped in a cage. 'I can't believe that," he muttered. "No, it can't be!"

"I've seen the evidence with my own eyes, Patrick. She has admitted it to me. There are times when he keeps her a virtual prisoner in the house. That is why she has devised this means of coming and going by a seldom-used door. The one you yourself have used. You may be sure Jeremy will find out eventually—about you and about the door."

"How do you know about that?" The hawklike nose went up in the air, and he looked at me from the corners of his eyes. It was effective, intimidating.

"I just do. I'm a detective," I said with more than a little satisfaction. I leaned forward and patted the table in front of the chair where he'd been sitting. "Sit down again, please, and I'll tell you why I think it's entirely possible Jeremy McFadden killed Abigail Locke—or had her killed. About Ingrid Swann, I'm not yet sure. However, if you want Frances free to work with you, the best and fastest way is to let me continue to work this case and hope I can find evidence enough on Jeremy McFadden to have him arrested. If money is a concern—"

"Of course it's a concern," he snapped as he resumed his seat, "money is always a concern. But more than that, I'm appalled by this theory you're putting forth. Whatever makes you think such a thing?"

"Jeremy found out that Frances was leaving the house to go to Mrs. Locke's séances. He was so unhappy about it that he . . . became violent with her, then kept her locked in the house a virtual prisoner for days."

"Nonsense! She has her own way out. We have seen that."

"Why are you defending him? Because he's a man, a husband, is that it?"

"Because . . . because, it's just so damn unreasonable. And she does have her own way out, you can't argue that."

"He locked up her clothes, Patrick. Frances came to me one morning in her dressing gown, under a thoroughly disreputable rain slicker. I'm telling you, if you aren't careful you're going to get her in a lot of trouble."

I could see credulity growing, though slowly, on his face. "And you think her husband would . . . kill Abigail, just to keep his wife from going to her séances ever again? That sounds so . . . bizarre."

"Yes, I grant you that. But he's powerful enough to do almost anything he wants. I don't think McFadden did the actual killing himself, I think he paid someone else to do it." Maybe even you? I wondered, even as the other words were coming out of my mouth. "And more as a lesson to Frances than to the medium herself. Sort of a warning, in the manner of suggesting that if anyone or anything came before himself in his wife's affections he would see that it was taken from her."

Patrick's eyes opened wide, as if to capture the maximum light; then he let his head fall loosely on his neck, slowly, gravely shaking it back and forth. When finally his voice rolled out, it sounded sepulchral. "I didn't know. I had no idea. If you had any idea how special Frances is, how potentially great her talent . . . that was all I could think of."

I was reminded that he seemed to have forgotten Abigail Locke and *her* talent pretty quickly, but I did not say so aloud. What I said was: "So you see why I must continue the investigation. But about the money, tomorrow I'll make up a bill for what you owe so far, and we'll go over it together. Any time I put in from now on, I'll work at half the rate I quoted you. Does that sound fair?"

"Yes. The money is coming from Abigail's estate anyway. I've barely two pennies to rub together on my own. And it's true Abigail may not like my spending her hard-earned dollars to set myself up with another medium."

"Medium? I thought you said Frances was a natural somnambulist."

"She is, but a somnambulist is a particular kind of medium."

"One who requires a partner," I said somewhat acerbically.

"That is true," he acknowledged.

"Mrs. Locke could have worked without a partner?"

"Indeed, yes. She had no need of anyone except her spirit guide. I simply made things more convenient for her, established some order in her life. And I"—he put his hand over his eyes for a moment—"loved her."

When Patrick Rule removed his hand, that emotion blazed from his face. Only briefly, like the last bright flash of a guttering candle, and then it was gone. But I did not doubt that I had seen it, or that I had understood what I'd seen. From that moment on, Patrick Rule was off my list of suspects.

"Thank you for telling me that," I said softly.

He merely nodded, then passed his hand over his eyes again. In that position, with his eyes closed, he said, "Now perhaps you'll tell me what you meant by invoking Emperor Norton."

"I meant only to buy us time," I said, "to give Frances something to do while I try to get solid evidence that her husband is Abigail's murderer. And besides, Patrick, if you are going to believe in Spiritualism, then you certainly wouldn't want to slight the Emperor. Frances truly believes he is a kind of, well, avuncular figure of the spirit world for her."

He removed his hand and looked at me resignedly. "I've read her automatic writing. It's an ability of a far lower order and will only drain her energy to no purpose should she go back to it. On the other hand, the Emperor is not a harmful spirit, as I had at first feared. I am at least satisfied on that point. I do believe now that Abigail Locke was killed by some human hand, without the influence of the spirits. And you may be right, Fremont Jones, her husband may be responsible. I can't say you yea or nay." He unfolded himself and stood up.

"Now, I'll say good night. I believe I could sleep for a week," he said, and murmuring assurances that this was a good idea, I accompanied him to the front door. Then breathed a sigh of relief when he had gone and I had locked it behind him. I was safe, and my case was safe as well.

Within twenty-four hours it became obvious that Frances did not want a breathing space during which to commune with her Emperor—or any other kind of space. Having tasted . . . what? Danger? Excitement? The power of being linked hypnotically with Patrick Rule? Having tasted these things, it seemed Frances could no longer be still. All traces of timidity and docility had been erased from her character; and while I was naturally enough glad to see this—for I am entirely in agreement with Susan B. Anthony on the subject of the subjugation of wives to their husbands, i.e., that there should not be any—nevertheless I did worry about Frances.

Greatly daring, she had called me from her husband's study the very next morning. "Jeremy isn't here, Fremont," she explained when I asked how she'd managed it. "I made Cora open the door so that I could use the telephone. She has a key. Keys. Cora has all the keys."

I heard from Frances a little gasp, as of indrawn breath, and then a slightly hysterical laugh. She said, "I should have them, you know. I'm the wife. But no, not in this house. The housekeeper has all the keys. I could just make her give them to me, couldn't I? I could just do that. I wonder why I never thought of it before?"

"Frances," I put in quickly, "do get hold of yourself. Just now, it's very important you not do anything unusual at all. Promise me."

"Oh, all right, I promise. I do see your point."

"I am very glad to hear it. What were you calling me about?"

"Oh, about Emperor Norton. I talked to him last night. Everything is fine, really. But he does want me to do that, that *thing* for him. You know? That I wrote in the automatic writing?"

I knew. I found myself nodding as though she could see me. "I remember," I said.

"Fremont, I just can't . . . I mean, I've got to work with Patrick. I've simply got to. You don't know what this could mean to me."

"I think I do," I said cautiously. "But if you could see your way clear to waiting just a few days, I think you'd be safer."

"I'll leave him! Jeremy, I mean," Frances hissed into the telephone in a heavy whisper. "We'll just go away. Run away. Patrick and I can make money together, he told me we could."

This was serious. I had to dissuade her. "Don't do anything, go back up to your room, wait for me. I'm coming over."

"But—"

"Don't argue, Frances. I'm coming over! I'll be there shortly."

By the time Wish Stephenson and his mother arrived, I was ready to leave. "I could be out all day," I said to them both. "Something important has come up."

"A break in the case?" Wish inquired.

"No, not exactly. More like the possibility of something really bad happening, and I have to do what I can to prevent it." I turned away from Wish to his mother. She had removed her hat and coat and was hanging them on the clothes tree near the door.

"Edna," I said, "I have a job I think you're going to love."

"Well now, dearie," she said brightly, "that's a fine way to start the day."

That was how the news of Ingrid Swann's, shall we say highly colorful, husband came to the attention of San Francisco's press. Edna immediately got on the phone, told a friend, who told a friend, who told a friend, who *was* a reporter for the afternoon paper, the *Examiner*. And a photo of the charming fellow subsequently appeared, along with a speculative article, that very afternoon.

To think they must have held the presses for such a visage! It was a bit much. But the J&K Agency, which figured prominently in the article, came out sounding every bit as sharp and promising as I'd hoped we would.

Midafternoon: I was wandering the streets and hills of San Francisco, bent on an impossible task that had been set for me by a ghost. The ghost of a madman, Emperor Norton. Actually the task had been set for Frances, but she had hired me to do it. Not that I would actually accept pay from a friend, but we could work that out later.

That she should hire me did make a certain amount of sense, I suppose. The Emperor's instructions were so bizarre, she would never have been able to follow them herself; even in the unlikely event that her husband would trust her out of his house long enough to accomplish anything.

Having come downtown on the Powell Street cable car, I got off at Union Square, entered right into the square itself, and walked up to the Dewey Monument, which featured a woman poised on one foot on top of a column. I looked up at her, knowing that the model for that statue had been none other than society matron Alma Spreckels (known as Big Alma to distinguish her from her daughter, Little Alma) in her extremely handsome youth. This statue had not been here when Emperor Norton died in 1880. Nevertheless, his instructions said: "Start at the statue in Union Square . . ."

"This is mad," I muttered, "utterly and insanely mad." Well, of course it was; the Emperor himself had died insane, so why should his instructions from the grave be any different?

I looked at the instructions again, scribed in the loopy hand that constituted Frances's automatic writing. "Walk northwest two blocks."

That was more easily said, or read, than done. There were no streets moving in a northwesterly direction, only due west or due north. I was getting a headache. I decided to take a midafternoon break in that delightful little restaurant in the City of Paris, which just happened to be diagonally across from Union Square.

I folded Frances's papers and stuck them deep down inside the unfashionably large leather bag I carry in lieu of purse or reticule, and after looking both ways (what with the proliferation of automobiles, one cannot be too careful) I crossed the street to that august, not to mention extremely large, department store.

It was a pleasant place to be, buzzing with conversation, brisk with myriad transactions, full of color to delight the eye and fragrance to tease the nose. I will have to bring Father here, I thought, as I took an elevator made of brass mesh down to the basement floor where the restaurant was located.

Each section of the store had its own distinct wares and the odor that went with them, like a series of miniature bazaars all under one roof. After leaving the elevator I passed by a tobacconist (pipe tobacco, a kind Father used—or so I thought, but then he was much on my mind—with a faint whiff of cherry to it); a candy shop (chocolate—it made my mouth water); cut flowers, much fancier, longer-stemmed than those carried by the flower vendors in their carts out on the street; and so on. Finally I reached the restaurant. Having arrived at an odd hour (which I could identify no further than that it must be midafternoon—it had been a confusing day so far), I had not long to wait before being seated.

I ordered a pot of tea and a plate of cookies and settled back to appraise my situation. I had struck a bargain with Frances: I would do the Emperor's task on her behalf, provided I could sandwich in the work between the other things I was doing for the far more important murder investigation, and I would daily report to her my progress, which she would then relay to Emperor Norton. I forbore to ask how, if she was communicating with him through automatic writing, she got her messages to him. Presumably his to her came out of the pen onto the paper in the Emperor's own handwriting, thought it was Frances's small hand that held the real pen; but who was taking care of the process the other way round? It was true that the loopy script she produced when in the trance state was not at all the way Frances usually wrote; it was also true that the loopy script she produced resembled more a style of penmanship that had been popular in the previous century.

Hmm, I thought; if he was as popular as I've heard, some public institution around here will have a copy of something he wrote, one of his edicts perhaps, and then I could compare that to what Frances has done . . . It would be interesting. Trivial as it seemed, my curiosity was definitely engaged.

Even though the task itself was ill-defined.

SEVENTEEN

The Hands of Time

APENNY for your thoughts."

The familiar words, uttered in a warm, masculine voice, startled me near out of my wits. It was what Michael might have said if he had come across me here at the City of Paris, musing and staring idly into space, with my tea growing cold and my plate of cookies untouched.

But of course it was not Michael who had spoken. It was my coworker, Wish Stephenson. And actually his voice was nothing like Michael's—aside from his being also a man. Michael has a deep, rich voice, whereas Wish's is lighter, shades more gentle.

"I wasn't really thinking," I said, looking up—way, way up. Always tall, he seemed even taller to me from my vantage point behind a decidedly small tea table. "What brings you, Wish, into a place like this?"

He grinned, shrugged, and stuck his hands in his pockets. Every now and then it struck me anew how much better he looked out of his police uniform; and in fact it struck me now. He was wearing a style of clothing considerably less buttoned-up, more casual than those dark suits men usually wear from one day to the next; indeed his outfit reminded me of the way the men had dressed in Carmel—those men who were considered, and considered themselves, Bohemians (whether or not they were actual members of the Bohemian Club—though in fact most of them were).

"Surveillance," Wish said, still grinning, "undercover. May I join you, Fremont?"

"Of course. So that's the reason for the, er, more casual style of dress than you were wearing this morning." He did look quite nice, in trousers that shade of beige the English call fawn (which I have never quite understood because fawns in my experience have spots, but who can argue with fashion?) and a tweed jacket in some appropriately tweedy brown, beige, and black mix, plus a chocolate-brown sweater vest.

"In a word," Wish said, "yes." He then addressed himself to the plate of cookies, and I bade it a silent, fond farewell. In fact I would not have been much surprised if, when he had worked his way to the bottom of the cookies, he started crunching on the plate as well.

In the meantime the waitress came and brought another pot of tea, and Wish explained as he ate and drank that he was tracking a woman's husband's movements, and had happened to see me crossing the street from Union Square. His new client, the woman, was looking to catch the husband in an illicit affair, perhaps of business, but most probably of the heart.

"How did she hear about us? I mean J&K? Or about you?" I asked, always curious now to know how to increase business.

"She knows someone who knows Michael."

"Ah. I see," I said, inevitably wondering if she might know Michael herself . . . but I put that thought right out of my mind.

"He knows a lot of people," Wish said.

"Um-hm. But now I think on it, I can't see what good it will do her for you to catch her husband out," I said, lifting my teacup and then putting it back down. I had poured from the new pot, and the cup was too hot to put to my lips. "I mean, it isn't as if an affair is against the law or anything. It's just . . . immoral."

Wish shrugged, simultaneously licking his fingers. Poor manners or not, I did not find the gesture offensive at all. It was more something a boy would do, and there was so much of the boy still in Wish that his finger-licking was rather endearing.

"Perhaps she will use it to blackmail him," I mused, still wondering.

"Perhaps," said Wish, now applying napkin to fingers, "but even so, that's not the reason I took the case. It's a boring sort of case in itself. However, this fellow belongs to all the top clubs, Fremont, all of them. And the wife—she's from one of those society families—has arranged—don't ask me how she did it, I don't want to know—guest status for me at the clubs. I'm supposed to be a cousin or something, visiting for two weeks from out of town. Don't you see?"

I frowned. "No. I'm afraid I do not see."

"I can contribute something to your case. See what I can hear about Jeremy McFadden. See if there's anything to that rumor about Ngaio Swann. Get myself placed on the inside, that's what we've been wanting to do, isn't it? And all while I'm still working my own case."

Oh yes. That was what we'd been wanting to do, and it was the one thing that I as a woman could never, ever do, because the clubs were for men only. I tried to keep my pea-green envy out of my voice: "That's . . . good, Wish. I'd appreciate it, especially as I've taken on something extra for Frances. I can use the help. But tell me, what rumor about Ngaio Swann?"

"Oh, hey, that's right, you haven't heard it yet. Something my mom picked up today. On the telephone of course. She'll have written you a note about it."

"So what's the rumor?"

"It's pretty wicked, really."

"Wish!"

"Okay, okay," Wish chuckled, "okay. The rumor is, Ngaio Swann is really a woman."

"No!" I had spoken too loudly; several startled patrons looked my way and I smiled sheepishly to let them know that I, a proper lady, was aware of my gaffe.

"It may not be true," Wish conceded.

I leaned forward eagerly, tea forgotten. "I'll bet it is. It just feels right. It would make such a lot of sense. After that brute of a husband terrorized her, she couldn't bear to be voluntarily in the company of men. She and this woman masquerading as a brother don't necessarily have to have had a sexual relationship."

Wish's face darkened. If the lights had been on at a greater intensity, I knew his face would show bright red. "Fremont!" he said in a scandalized whisper.

"Well, for heaven's sake, it's only a word," I whispered back.

"If you can say it, you'll do it, that's what my mother always told me."

"I'll just bet she did." I was dying to ask him if he was a twenty-five-year-old virgin male, but that would have been just too wicked of me, and I already had another idea that was equally wicked. In fact, it was so completely delicious that I could hardly bear not to act on it right away.

Instead, I played the good investigatory partner. I suggested that Wish and I finish our tea as quickly as possible and then go back across to Union Square where he might help me with something.

"That is," I said, "If you have the time."

"All the time in the world, Fremont. All the time in the world.

Mom can lock up on her own. And speaking of Mom: she's doing pretty well, don't you think?"

"Indeed I do. I'm hard put to remember what we did without her."

Thus with various tits and tats of small talk, Wish and I paid our check and wandered a bit among all the bounteous offerings on display as we made our way out of the City of Paris and back to Union Square. As we wandered, I explained about Frances and Emperor Norton and the automatic writing.

Standing once more at the base of the Dewey monument, I showed Wish the Emperor's first set of instructions: *Walk northwest two blocks*. With hand gestures for punctuation (maybe even substituting for the occasional word) I declared: "But this is as insane as the Emperor himself was. There are no streets running northwest."

"Not exactly, but let us start out anyway. I have an idea or two," Wish said, starting off. By the time we had crossed Post Street he'd realized that with his long legs he was bound to outwalk me and had courteously moderated his pace so that I could keep up.

"There's just one thing you haven't quite gotten to, Fremont," Wish said, "and I have to wonder why."

"Oh, my goodness!" I exclaimed suddenly, ignoring his remark. "I didn't know this was here."

It was a narrow little street not on the map, more an alleyway than a street. San Francisco is full of such little passages, especially in the downtown area, and I saw that if we took this one we would be making a kind of jog in a northwesterly direction.

"How clever you are, Wish," I said as we set off. Then I took up what he'd previously said, taking for granted Wish's ability to follow my sometimes convoluted mental processes: "I know what you mean, I'm not deliberately being obtuse, it's just that I'm not in the least sure what I'm looking for myself. The Emperor hasn't exactly said. He said that since he passed over to the other side his mind has gradually been growing clear, and he can remember now where he hid some valuables of his before he went away on the two-year journey from which he returned insane.''

"Fascinating," said Wish. "You know, there have been rumors ever since he died that he had assets stashed away somewhere, and in his, er, incapacity he just forgot where he'd put them. So it makes sense, in a kind of weird way."

"Yes. What he specifically says is 'my most valuable possession.' That could be anything. Unfortunately he himself—that is, if this automatic writing of Frances's is really a communication from the ghost of Emperor Norton—"

"Do you think it is?"

"I don't know. Well, of course I don't *really* think so. How can one think that? It's just that Frances is so convinced, and I did see her that one time when she was definitely in a trance. . . . Wish, I don't honestly know what to think about any of these things. I only know there will be answers if one keeps on going, and that's what I've decided to do."

"Makes good enough sense to me. All right, we're about to cross Grant Street. Now watch this—" Wish strode along a few steps ahead of me, peering between buildings. We were getting into the edge of Chinatown, and so the buildings seemed to huddle closer together, to take on a different character, somehow less imposing yet more secretive about whatever might be going on behind their facades.

And then, all of a sudden, Wish Stephenson disappeared. I was left standing on the sidewalk with the sounds of the City around me: The street traffic; the pattering of feet, most of them Chinese in their soft shoes; the sounds of music, the distinctively different harmonies of the East and the West, filtered through the cracks around closed windows and doors.

A moment later, barely more than time to get my breath back after it had unexpectedly caught in my throat, Wish popped out again.

"Don't do things like that to me!" I exclaimed, for although I'd known he was likely to show back up immediately, there are times when what you think is most likely to happen is not what happens at all.

Wish held out his hand. "Come on!"

I took it and he pulled me into the narrowest alley I had ever seen. But it did go through, all the way through to Kearney. By making a kind of zigzag through the two narrow streets, we had traversed the Emperor's two blocks in a northwesterly direction.

"This is quite amazing," I said, as I had that realization.

"Now what?" Wish asked when we came out onto Kearney.

I reached into my bag for Frances's papers, but paused before drawing them out. Wish and I had stayed longer in the City of Paris than either of us had realized. Time had gotten away from us somehow, for night was falling. One of those rare, clear nights when the sky turns a deep blue violet that steadily darkens to deep purple and then to black. On the second and third levels of the buildings around us, where people lived over their businesses, lights were coming on. Some were electric, but many had the softer glow of candles inside the pleated white paper lanterns that the Chinese use when they want light primarily to see, rather than to be decorative or festive.

There is something about that hour of the night, when you can look through the windows of people's homes and find them for a little while unguarded, before they realize the dark has come and they should close the shutters, draw the drapes, pull down the shades . . . something about it that is both beautiful and sad. Why sad, I could never say, I only knew that was how I often felt, and I had never tried to express it to anyone, not even to Michael.

So I said to Wish Stephenson, "It's too late to continue this now. It's time to go home. I'll make a note of where we came out, and return here another day."

"Yes, I suppose that's wise." Wish sounded a bit disappointed. He took my elbow lightly in his hand and tried his best to tame his long stride to match mine. He talked of inconsequential things, and I paid him little heed. My melancholy mood had taken over, and he sensed it. He did not try to josh me out of it, for which I was grateful. And even though it took him far out of his way, he accompanied me on the streetcar home to Divisadero Street, on account of its being dark outside. And I, who am so independent, unaccountably allowed him to do it.

Half that night, I sat by my window in the dark, looking out over the City, gripped by melancholy and also severely chastened. Not that Wish had chastened me, oh no, he was far too good a creature for that; I had chastened myself. Wish had merely said, as he stood on the top step outside the door to my half of the house, "Fremont, there was something I took it upon myself to do after you left this morning, because I knew it had to be done, and I hope you aren't going to mind. I don't want to give the impression I'm trying to interfere with your case."

At those words a knot had formed in my stomach, and it hardened as Wish went on to explain that, while his mother was making her phone calls, he had quietly slipped down to the SFPD and put out the word on Ingrid Swann's husband. "Otherwise," he had concluded, "we'd make enemies of the police and they'd never cooperate with us. I know you don't like them, Fremont, because of the way you were treated when your friend Alice was murdered, but still, private investigators and the police department have to get along. We are, after all, trying to do the same things, and we can do it better if we work together."

He was right, of course, and I'd told him so. Not only that, I'd thanked him profusely for saving me from a blunder that could have been bad indeed. In my eagerness to garner publicity and praise for J&K, I had overlooked the very point on which Wish had been so sensitive.

As I sat by the window in the dark, a part of me argued: Of course Wish was sensitive to things like our relationship with the police, because he used to be one of them, he'd been trained to

think like that. Which didn't necessarily make that kind of thinking right. . . .

For even deeper down inside of me, in another, darker place
entirely, there was a stubborn, usually hidden woman who did not
agree with Wish at all. This was my most dangerous self; this was
some wildness in me that did not believe justice was necessarily
accomplished within the so-called law. And I knew, oh yes, I
knew, that when the wild part of me rose up she would not be
denied.

So I sat through the dark hours and struggled with myself, because although I had some skills and some training, and according
to Michael, my mentor, excellent instincts, still it was perfectly
true that I did not know what I was doing. I was wandering in this
strange world of ghostly emperors, mesmerists and somnambu-
lists, mediums and murder. And I felt as if I were wandering in
circles, getting nowhere at all.

It was a long time before I slept, and when I awoke I did not feel
refreshed.

Several cups of coffee, combined with general good health and
comparative youth, soon had me functioning as if my night had
not been such an unmitigated sinkhole of worry and indecision.
By the time the Stephensons, mother and son, had arrived at J&K,
I was ensconced at my table/desk and deep into planning, with
calendar at hand.

Today's date was April 6. My father would arrive on the ninth,
in three days, staying over my birthday, the tenth and returning to
Boston by train on the eleventh. I rather wished, as he was coming
so far, that he could stay longer, but gathered from the tone of his
correspondence that this was not possible—I supposed, because of
Augusta. I stared into the distance, lost for a moment in amorphous thought, only vaguely aware of Edna's scurrying about the
kitchen to set a fresh pot of coffee on to perk, and the soothing
drone of her son's voice on the telephone out in the office. I could

not seem to make my mind grapple with the essential question: Why, after all this time, was Father coming here for this particular birthday? Why now and not last year, my first birthday post-earthquake (we San Franciscans tend to mark everything now by whether it happened before or after the Great Quake in 1906), when I had wanted so much to see him that I had practically begged him to bring Augusta and meet me at the Hotel Del Monte in Monterey for just a few days. His flat refusal had been such a bitter disappointment at the time that I had tucked away my longing to see him deep in one of those back closets of the mind whence it would be difficult, if not impossible, to retrieve. And now, all unbidden and unexpected, he was coming. Alone. It was rather strange. Wonderful, but strange.

Edna reeled through the conference room on her way back to the office, patting me on the arm in passing with a cheery, "Working hard already, eh, dearie?" that broke my reverie. It was just as well, for I'd been getting nowhere.

"Hard enough, Edna," I called after her, missing the beat by not very much. And then Wish came in to tell me his schedule, and the telephone rang again—new clients, I hoped—and so the day got off to a start.

I had to see Frances. I had tried calling, on the off chance that one of the servants might pick up the telephone in Jeremy's study and I could persuade him or her to bring the lady of the house to the phone. That had not worked; the study must have been sitting locked, and the telephone in it, because it rang and rang. That left me no choice but to pay her a call, which in turn did set up the choice of whether I should go in by the front door as a guest or surreptitiously by the side with my own key.

I walked over to the McFadden mansion. The day was as fine, for weather, as the previous night had been. Such perfect days are rare in my foggy city, and we who live here treasure them. Of course the sun could be shining brightly in one neighborhood while another could be shrouded in fog; or it could be raining on one of the City's hills but not on any other; and so it went. One accepted good weather as the gift that it was, and enjoyed it while one could, which, as I thought about it, seemed not too bad a way to go about living one's life in general.

When I sighted the large house that was my destination, I slowed my pace but did continue walking. As I approached, I wanted to be sensitive to the place itself . . . not that I believed myself to have psychic powers, but rather that I thought a finely tuned instinct to be one of the private investigator's best weapons. And as I've said, during my training Michael had confirmed something I'd already suspected: I did have good instincts. I just had never paid much attention to them before, and now I tried to—at least, whenever I thought of it.

Sometimes there are houses, or certain well-defined outdoor spaces, that one can read rather like a book. They have a certain mood to them, as if at some indelible point in time something had happened there so momentous that the event and its lingering echoes of energy had become embedded in the place forever.

What was it I felt from the McFadden house?

I drew closer. It was as if a kind of aura surrounded the house itself, a field within whose bounds the house could grab you and draw you inevitably in; but if you stayed beyond that invisible perimeter you were safe and could pass by unscathed. I let the house have me. I would indeed enter in, but on my own terms; and so I used my key and went in by the side door.

Disturbance. That was the aura this house exuded. Not violence so much as simple turmoil. Things moving, nothing ever truly quiet, nothing ever really still. No peace, no love, no . . . quietude. A favorite word of my mother's, that had been: "quietude." And it had been she who engendered that atmosphere in our Boston home.

Having crossed the garden room, braved that hall space near the kitchen, and entered the back stairs, I paused, still sharpening all my observational senses. There had been bacon here for breakfast.

The smell of it lingering in the air made my mouth water—though since I'd learned bacon was sliced pork belly (Michael told me; I hadn't particularly wanted to know) some of the pleasure of eating it had been ruined. Whatever midmorning routines the housekeeper and the maid—and the gardener if he should happen to be about—maintained, they were apparently at them. There was no talking and carrying on, but there was a sense of general busyness in the air. And of course that ever present *dis*quietude. Ah! Yes, that was the word that described the atmosphere of Frances McFadden's house to a T: "disquietude."

I silently thanked my dead mother for her powers of description and went on up the stairs as quickly and soundlessly as possible, holding my skirts up close to my body, so that I would not trip or brush against anything that might be knocked down and thus cause an alarm. I passed through the stairwell and out into the second-floor hallway uneventfully. The door to Frances's little suite of rooms stood open and I headed straight to it. Rapped lightly with my knuckles once, and then again. If she was inside, she took no heed.

So I went on in.

Frances was there. She was not alone.

EIGHTEEN

The Mesmerist and the Somnambulist

THE MESMERIST and the somnambulist were deeply engaged with one another. In point of fact, if I were any judge (and by now I should be, Michael being not at any disadvantage in this department), they were engaged in one of the deepest kisses I had ever had the luck—bad or good, it depended how one looked at it—to intrude upon.

The kiss went on while I observed that they had at least made some pretense, perhaps even a sincere effort, to get down to their peculiar work before becoming, shall we say, distracted. Both Frances and Patrick were fully dressed, Frances in a demure frock that looked about as designed for seduction as Little Miss Muffet's tuffet had been for comfortable seating. Her hair was down; but then, I had learned myself that her hair was often down in the mornings. Patrick was buttoned up to his earlobes in a stiff white collar, along with the usual shirt and dark suit. They were each sitting in a straight-backed chair, facing one another, with a small round tea table between them. On the tea table were a small round crystal ball that looked suspiciously like a paperweight to me, and a deck of cards, face down. Cheap cards, the kind with bicycles on the backs, which suggested that Patrick had brought the cards and the paperweight. Er, crystal ball.

So they must have started out to work, and then . . . Yes.

If they had leaned any harder toward one another over that little table, some architectural or engineering law having to do with pressure points or irresistible forces would have been broken, I was sure of it.

I turned my head away, burning in the place one might think one would burn if one happened to be watching a kiss such as theirs. It was shameful . . . and yet, not.

"Tell me when you're done," I said in a clear voice.

I couldn't help smiling as my remark brought a little stifled yelp from Frances, followed immediately by much rustling and settling into place, and finally Patrick clearing his throat preparatory to saying, "Good morning, Fremont!" in his most stentorian tone of voice.

"Good morning," I said pleasantly, turning around.

"Were you expected?" Patrick inquired, as if this were his home, and blissful Frances just sat there with a wide, foolish smile on her slightly swollen lips.

"In a way, yes, and in a way, no," I replied cryptically.

"I don't see how it can be both," said Patrick, each word uttered distinctly, as if he must be extremely careful of whatever he might say to me. I supposed he might feel that way, that he must be careful, particularly if he had something to hide.

And here not more than two or three days ago I had mentally

removed this man from my list of murder suspects because he'd said so convincingly that he'd been in love with Abigail Locke.

"I wonder . . ." I mused aloud, then caught myself. What I was wondering was whether Patrick could have been sincere when he'd said that—he'd certainly looked sincere—and then so soon fallen for Frances, with what appeared to be equal intensity. Could such a thing happen, if the man were not a bounder or a cad? I really didn't know. I should have to ask Michael. Maybe.

I shook my head a little, then started over. They were both gazing at me in a kind of stupor. "Never mind. What I really must say is, although what you do when you're together is none of my business, I do have a considerable interest in both of you as my clients. As long as you're my clients, I feel honor bound to try my utmost to keep you out of harm's way."

They nodded in unison. Really it was rather sweet.

"And if ever there was a place where doing what you were just doing could put you—as my mother, who came from Virginia, used to say—*right smack dab* in harm's way, this would be it!"

"Oh!" said Frances, the light of understanding finally gathering in her eyes. So she wasn't hypnotized, or mesmerized, whatever they were calling it. I chose to believe that was good. Frances went on, "We didn't mean to. We meant to work. Patrick brought some new materials for me to work with, to psychically read for him. We just—"

"It was my fault entirely," Patrick said. Suddenly realizing that he was sitting while there was a lady (myself) in the room standing, he popped up out of his chair, then with a sweep of his hand offered the chair to me.

I took it, though there were other places I could have sat. I did it to establish authority. I was the one who would set the rules here, and make these two comply, or we should all be in a great deal of trouble.

"You couldn't help yourselves?" I inquired brightly.

Frances nodded, taking me with perfect seriousness. "That's right. We couldn't."

Oh my! It was all I could do not to roll my eyes.

Frances rushed on: "It's safe, really. Jeremy has gone to work. Cora is my friend, she won't interrupt; and besides, I've bribed her, so even if she isn't really my friend—I mean sometimes, not often, I make mistakes about who my friends are. Anyhow, I know at least that she'll keep quiet as long as I pay her."

"Frances," I said, "I have reason to believe Cora spies on you for Jeremy. She is probably working both sides of the street."

"Fremont!" Frances appeared scandalized. "Have you no shame? How can you use such a figure of speech! And about Cora, too."

Ignoring this, I turned to Patrick. "What was so important as to bring you over here this morning? I mean, considering that we've just had a talk about how you could get Frances in some serious trouble if her husband finds out that you're even working with her. Much less . . . doing what you were doing with her." For a moment I wished I'd simply said "kissing" because the other sounded somehow dirty, which was hardly fair—what I'd witnessed could only have been termed dirty by someone who knew little about the real meaning of love. I felt like a mother with two unruly children whose behavior was going to get us all in trouble.

"Frances called me," he replied, with a finality in his voice that said more clearly than words: That explains everything, she calls, I come, nature of this beast. End of story.

"And you called," I said to Frances, "because . . . ?"

Frances flushed delicately along her cheekbones. Nowhere else, just the cheekbones. It was exceedingly becoming. "I wanted to get started on this new technique Patrick is going to teach me. It's called, um, Patrick?"

"Extrasensory perception. ESP for short. The experiment is for the mesmerizer to be the sender and the somnambulist the receiver. I will choose a card at random, hold it up before my own

201

eyes, and concentrate. Frances will see the card through my eyes and tell me what she sees. This test yields scientifically quantifiable results. It was devised in England many years ago, and recently brought to this country by the American Society for Psychical Research."

"It is a way of establishing credentials," Frances said eagerly.

"Yes!" said Patrick, unconsciously (or so it seemed) reaching his hand out across the table and opening his palm, into which Frances placed her own hand with equally unconscious and natural grace.

Egad! I thought. The star-crossed lovers.

I sighed. "All right, you two, repeat after me: We will find another place to work."

"We will," they began, then broke off, looked at each other, then back at me; whereupon Frances said reasonably, "What could be more open and aboveboard? If we meet at my house, is it not a guarantee that we are . . . that our intentions are . . ."

"Yes, well, you already see the flaw in that argument, no doubt." I nodded in an exaggerated manner. Frances nodded with me, and Patrick turned his head away. He was beginning to reason again, to see the light, to get the point. I proceeded to drive it further home: "If Cora had witnessed what I just witnessed, I should be very much afraid she would report it to Jeremy. And then, Frances, you know the least that could happen. As for the worst . . ."

"I get in more trouble when I go out," Frances argued. "No one knows Patrick is here, any more than I daresay they know you are here. He came in by the back, and he will leave by the back, and in between, if necessary, he can hide in the wardrobe."

I moved my head back and forth, slowly. "Noooo. When the two of you get involved in anything, whether your mesmerist/somnambulist routine or that other kind of thing, you lose all sense of what's going on around you. I've seen you, I know what I'm talking about. And if we're to solve these cases it's got to stop.

Otherwise, you're going to get caught, and Jeremy McFadden will do something drastic. You know he will. Let's have no more argument on that point. Agreed?"

"Agreed," they said sullenly—but only after quite a long pause.

"All right," I said. "Point number two: Frances, I have a report for you concerning that other matter you wanted me to take care of. And Patrick, if you can bear it, why don't you go downstairs and wait outside for me. I have some questions to ask you, and I can do it while walking with you in the direction of your home, because I have an errand to run over that way when I'm done with Frances here."

They looked at each other. Frances sighed; Patrick said to her, "She's probably right. Don't worry, Frances, we'll work something out. Meanwhile, keep the crystal ball and practice with it. Write down what you see, and we can discuss it the next time we're together."

"When will that be?" Frances asked in a breathless voice. I wondered if he had already made love to her, in the fullest sense that is. My guess was that he had, and that she could not wait to do it again, which I could understand myself, all too well.

"Soon," Patrick promised. He was already standing, and could not resist bending down to kiss her cheek. He scooped the deck of cards off the table and dropped them in his jacket pocket. And then he left the room.

Immediately I felt as if a load of bricks had been removed from my shoulders. Before Frances could do or say anything to put the load back on, I said quickly, "I have a report for you on our Emperor Norton search. It's encouraging."

Then I went on to explain how Wish Stephenson had helped me find a way to thread through the streets near Union Square so that we ended up in a northwesterly direction, as instructed. I said I had no doubt that if I patiently followed his other instructions as they were given we should find the Emperor's most valued possession. I ended: "But that means you must keep in touch with him and continue to do the automatic writing, Frances. The City is not now what it was when Norton was alive, and I think he must be made to see that his instructions have to make a kind of present-day sense. Do you think you can convey that to him?"

She nodded thoughtfully. "I think so. He doesn't come through so clearly now, though. I mean, it's as if . . . as if there's too much noise in my brain. Too many other things going on."

"Do you suppose you could concentrate on just doing the automatic writing with the Emperor for, oh, say—the next four days? Stay away from Patrick. Don't give Jeremy any reason to be jealous. And above all, don't trust Cora. Now"—I reached down into my leather bag and brought out a pad and pencil—"what is Cora's full name?"

"Why do you want to know?"

"I'm going to investigate her. If I can give you reason to dismiss her, I think you'll be safer, at least for a while. Now don't argue, Frances, just give me her whole name."

"Freeman. If she has a middle name I don't know it. Just Cora Freeman. I don't want to dismiss her, she knows the jobs here, I'll be lost without her."

This was too much. My patience was gone. So I put my elbows on that little round table and stared hard at Frances, being purposefully intimidating. "You'd best get one thing straight, Frances McFadden. You cannot have it both ways. You cannot continue to have the luxuries Jeremy McFadden can buy you while at the same time preparing yourself to go off seeking fame and glory, not to mention true love, if that's what you think it is" (there, the blush along the cheekbones again) "with Patrick Rule. So which is it to be?"

"Patrick," she said without hesitation, "and my new work. I'm good at it, Fremont. It's the first time in my life I've really had something all my own, something nobody can take away from me. A talent, I mean, part of me, the way who you are is part of you. Do you understand?"

"Oh yes, certainly I do. Now please listen to me, Frances. This is important, and I don't want to keep Patrick waiting down there too long. Do you think you can find out from the servants whether or not your husband was here at home the entire evening and early morning of that day when we found Abigail Locke's body? I can't question them myself. As I've told you, I believe Cora at least would report anything and everything back to him."

France's eyes widened. "Fremont! You don't think—"

"Yes, I do think it's possible. A man who would do to his wife what Jeremy has done to you has no love of women, either his wife or any other."

"I resent that. Jeremy does love me, he has often said so. Of course, his love is of the very possessive type, that is why he, he . . ."

As she faltered, I stepped in: "Why he punishes you? Because he can't bear the thought that you might leave him?"

"Yes, that is more or less what he says."

"He regards you as his personal possession, Frances, and that is not love. Would he kill to keep you close to him? What do you think?"

"Y-you mean would he kill Abigail just so, so . . ."

"To teach you a lesson. Which apparently you haven't learned, if that indeed was what he did. And if he figures that out through finding you with Patrick, he may kill again. We mustn't let that happen. You must stay away from Patrick for a while, concentrate on your doings with the Emperor, see if you can get that information for me. The next three or four days must show some progress for us, because after that my father will be in San Francisco and I'll be too occupied with him to work on our case."

Poor Frances. She had gone pale, and seemed shaken. Well, there was no help for it. Anything short of severity would never have obtained her agreement to stay away from Patrick. I hugged her and kissed her cheek, assuring her that I would be talking with her daily one way or another.

And then I went downstairs, where Patrick Rule waited outside not far from the rear door, which I closed and locked behind me.

There was no point beating around the bush with him. I'd already tried both courtesy and reason, and neither had done any good. Therefore, without greeting or other verbal pleasantry, I said, "You will get that woman killed too, if you don't stay away from her. Is that what you want?"

If looks alone could kill, I myself would have been dead that very minute.

Nevertheless, I did walk Patrick to the house he now occupied on Octavia Street, the former home of the murdered medium Abigail Locke, and as we walked I wondered again about him. He was the only person who had benefited materially from Mrs. Locke's death. What if his vaunted love for Abigail had been only a pose, the flash of it I'd seen in his eyes a mesmerist's trick?

I watched him from the corner of my eye as we walked along, and I kept him talking about the uses of crystal balls. For scrying, he said, either into the future or at a remote distance; this latter being now called by psychical researchers by a new term, remote viewing—something that, according to Patrick, Frances was particularly good at. But all the while he was talking I was paying attention not really to that topic but rather to my own internal monologue, which went like this: The newspapers reported that the police did not consider Patrick Rule a suspect. Wish Stephenson had found out from his source in the SFPD that Patrick had an alibi, a witness who placed him at a séance in a private home. The unnamed source did not say who had been the medium at that séance. And I wondered. I wondered if I dared ask.

But in the end, as my last chance approached with Octavia Street and his house, I lost my nerve and did not ask. Perhaps it was because of his height, which impressed upon me that I would be no match unless I had a weapon—and foolishly, I had come out without my walking stick. I vowed never to do that again, at least not when I was working a case. Or perhaps it was because I was reluctant even to hear the name of another medium right then, for fear that person would also become jinxed and fall in harm's way. Some other things, no doubt, it also could have been.

But it was none of these. In the end, I simply did not think the killer had been Patrick Rule because he reminded me so much of Michael.

Of course, Michael in his spy persona no doubt could kill, had killed, and at this very moment might be planning to kill again.

After making a perfunctory stop at the little library on Green Street, only to peruse the new books and find none I wanted to check out, I returned to the house on Divisadero Street. I felt I had spent a profitable morning even if I hadn't learned anything new, because I was certain I'd made Frances McFadden and Patrick Rule see the error of their ways—at least for now. Frances was going to get information on her husband for me, which I'd been unable to obtain any other way. It was so peculiar, really, how the harder one looked into Jeremy McFadden's affairs, the cleaner the man seemed to become. Aside from beating his wife—which I happened to think was a rather large aside—he was, as they say, clean as a whistle.

I did not really believe that. I believed that Jeremy had surrounded himself with layers and layers of protection, in the form of paid people (no doubt well paid) who insulated, covered for, and defended him. Lied for him, in other words. Maybe even did very dirty deeds for him—whatever dirty deeds might be required for a particular occasion. Of course, that was what I wanted to believe. I did not like Jeremy McFadden. Certainly the only happy ending I could think of to our drama involved Jeremy's being put away and Frances's obtaining her freedom, preferably with at least some of his money to get her a start.

I was heavily preoccupied as I pushed open J&K's door and heard the little bell ring sweetly.

"Guess what, Fremont!" Edna Stephenson called out as soon as I'd put my foot in the door.

"I can't possibly, Edna, I've been thinking much too hard on the way home. So please tell me."

"I got us a coupla things you wanted, while you was out. Copies of Ingrid Swann's and Abigail Locke's last wills and testaments."

"How in the world did you do that?" This was good news indeed.

"Just gotta know who to ask," Edna beamed.

NINETEEN

A Cruel Turning

MORE FRIENDS in low places, is that it?" I asked with a chuckle, reaching for the papers Edna handed to me before I had even shed my shawl.

"Could be, could be," she nodded. She had taken to wearing her hair in corkscrew curls, a style I had seen nowhere else, uniquely her own. It could have been more attractive if she had not screwed up the curls so tightly that her scalp showed through in between—but then, Edna was Edna, one made allowances.

"Come on," I cajoled, "who among your army of cleaning persons, secretaries, nurses and/or nursemaids, file clerks, and so on, was it this time?"

"Certain file clerk in the Board of Supervisors' office. Has access to all county records." Edna rocked her round body back and forth in the chair, hands clasped over tummy, the picture of satisfaction.

"Um-hm," I said, now lost in perusal as I perched on the corner of her desk.

By these presents be it known that on this day in the City and County of San Francisco in the State of California, and in the company of two witnesses signed here below . . .

Uh-huh, uh-huh, uh-huh. Reading as rapidly as possible through the dense legal language, I concluded that the two last wills and testaments held no great surprises but, unfortunately for Patrick Rule, some rather damning evidence. I could not understand why the police were not interested in him as a suspect. Patrick had inherited all of Abigail Locke's estate, down to the last penny. She had named no other heir and had excluded certain specific relatives by name, for *causing me pain and suffering due to their having shunned me and having cast vile aspersions on the nature and value of my true calling.*

Unfortunately, the documents themselves did not include information as to the extent of the dead women's individual assets. Well, I was not a banker's daughter for nothing; perhaps I could find that out myself.

Ingrid Swann had left nothing to her husband, but she had not excluded him by name, either—which could present a problem at some time down the road for her principal heir, Ngaio, the supposed brother.

I sighed, told Edna I'd be taking the papers back to my desk, and accepted several little note slips with her telephone messages. In a rather unhappy daze I went into the conference room. I was thinking that by finding Conrad Higgins I might have caused a significant problem for Ngaio, whom I had not yet met (he or she seemed to have disappeared off the face of the earth or at any rate off the streets of San Francisco), but was predisposed to like. I found myself quite partial to the idea of Ngaio Swann as a woman. The problem was, since Ingrid aka Myra Higgins had never divorced Conrad, as husband and therefore legal next of kin, he had an excellent case for breaking the will, particularly if Ngaio were not only not really a brother but not even a male. And even if Conrad was in too drunken a stupor himself to do it, he could always hire someone, some sharp lawyer probably, to accomplish that very thing for him. Which would put poor Ngaio out in the cold.

Of course, he—Conrad—would have to think of it first, and to tell the truth, the thinking department had not seemed to be his forte.

How to track down Ngaio Swann? What would he or she know? Was it a good idea to try? Or would I be going down yet another false trail, taking precious time, getting nowhere?

"Fremont!" Edna yelled out.

I did not reply; I had asked her many times not to yell between the rooms, but to no avail. I knew my lack of reply would not deter her as long as her son was not at his desk. If Wish were in the room, all he had to do was look at his mother with the tiniest of frowns and she would stop whatever it was that she happened to be doing that bothered him. Then as soon as his back was turned, or he had left the house, she would be back at it. Edna Stephenson was quite incorrigible.

"Wish is coming back here at noon, said he'd bring lunch. Should be here any minute," she said at the top of her big voice. "Thought you'd want to know."

"Thank you!" I called back. I did indeed want to know that.

There was something I had been thinking about ever since Wish told me about his guest status at the various men's clubs around town and, by God, I was going to do it.

"Strike while the iron is hot," I muttered; then winced as it came out sounding such a bland platitude. However at the moment I couldn't think of one more original that was also apt.

And then, because Edna was such a champion overreactor that

I never, ever wanted to take her by surprise, I went and told her what I intended to do.

I'd felt uncertain how Edna would react. She was, after all, an older woman and somebody's mother. But I needn't have worried. As she had declared on her very first day at J&K, Edna Stephenson was a modern woman—with the added fillip of a delightful sense of mischief.

"Oooh, Fremont, I think that's just dandy. I can't wait to see the look on my son's face. You run along upstairs and change. He could show up at any minute, so you go on now, you scoot, and we'll see you after a little while back in the kitchen for our noon meal."

"You're a dear," I said, bending down and giving her a quick hug.

Then I went upstairs and began the process of turning myself, once again, into a young man: Trousers, shirt, stiff high collar, suspenders, vest, socks and shoes. And then, a new addition to the outfit: a wig, bought at the same theatrical shop where I'd obtained the mustache, because after all a man cannot keep his hat on at all times.

"Thank heavens I thought of that," I said to my reflection in the mirror as I began to wind my long hair around and around the crown of my head, pinning it down tightly as I'd been shown. The wig was a good one, of human hair (one did not like to think whence it might have come, but at least it did look natural) in a reddish brown quite close to the shade of my own. Rather than attempt to approximate today's predominantly sleek male hairstyle, the shop's makeup artist (whom I had taken into my confidence, explaining that I was in the private investigation business) had suggested that I play up the impression of myself as a youth, with the wig's hair being a little longer, slightly unruly, to more readily accommodate the bulk of my own hair underneath.

It did take a bit of pulling and tugging, and was none too comfortable, especially considering I did not even like to wear hats;

but eventually I had the wig in place and was sufficiently pleased with the results that I decided I could forgo the mustache. And that would be a blessing, because the latter was far less comfortable than the wig; also probably more likely to be detectable should anyone subject me to serious scrutiny.

As I was tying my tie, from downstairs I heard the front door open. Wish called out a tentative "Ma?" and Edna returned an effusive, cackling greeting. True to her word, by the time I was donning shoes and socks I heard the sound of their footsteps as she shepherded her son back to the kitchen. Minutes later I joined them there.

Wish's face underwent several transmogrifications in succession, before his voice at last issued from the round, gaping hole that had previously been his mouth: "It can't be! But it is. It *is* you, isn't it, Fremont?"

"The very same," I allowed with a small bow. Then I took my place at the table and calmly began to fill my plate. The food was Chinese today, but it could have come from anywhere for all I tasted of it. With the donning of my disguise, a more fundamental change had come over me: I was out to catch a killer, and I wanted to do it in the worst possible way—with a vengeance.

Wish's guest passes carried the name Aloysius Bell. I became Timothy Bell, another cousin. I gathered that the man Wish had been paid to track must be yet another Bell . . . and if so, then so must be the wife. All these Bells. I wanted to make a joke of it, whisper *Ding-dong* in Wish's ear or some such, but I refrained.

"You'll do just fine," Wish reassured me as we boarded the California Street cable car. "The disguise is good enough. Just watch how you walk, and try not to talk. Leave the talking to me. You can be a country cousin, a young man just at that awkward stage of leaving adolescence. Boys that age always act goofy and gawk, so do a little of both. And at that age there isn't necessarily much facial hair. All right?"

"I shall make every effort," I assured him acerbically, rolling my eyes. I had no intention whatever of acting goofy or gawky; I should not be any good at it, I would just have to be a quiet, polite young man. With somewhat unruly hair.

We went to three clubs in succession that afternoon: the Pacific Union, the Parnassus, and the Native Sons. This last turned out to have nothing whatever to do with natives that I could see, being unaccountably the stuffiest of them all; whereas I had thought the Pacific Union, from its august reputation, would fill that bill.

Our game plan in each club was simple. Wish presented his credentials; he was recognized and quietly welcomed, on account of his patron having called ahead; he in turn introduced me as his guest, and we proceeded inside. Now of course I had long been exceedingly curious as to what really went on in such places, as they do not allow women except on the occasional ladies' night, when one assumes the members are on their best behavior. (Father had assured me this was not so when I had pestered him into taking me to his club on several occasions; only I'd discovered to my disappointment that it was all rather boring, and the food was nowhere near as good as Locke-Ober's.)

What really went on in San Francisco's bastions of masculinity turned out to be about what one would expect: A lot of smoking, some drinking, much reading of newspapers and magazines, and as we surmised, in some rooms where Wish and I were not invited to go, some gentlemanly gambling at cards.

I did look the part of the country cousin in my secondhand suit, whereas Wish played the debonair with a flair I hadn't known he possessed. And indeed, I did not think he had possessed it two years earlier.

He has learned a lot from Michael, I thought, watching and listening to Wish at the Pacific Union Club from behind the pages of an open issue of *San Francisco* magazine. There was in this magazine an article so fascinating I was hard put to keep my mind on my job; it told of plans on the part of the city fathers to have

San Francisco designated a host city for one of the World's Fairs sometime in the next decade. This would, the article claimed, bring more money flowing into the City's rebuilding coffers. And, not coincidentally, would encourage visitors to come to our fairest of cities again by showing how thoroughly we had recovered from the earthquake and that we had no fear—no siree—of another coming along to demolish us again. At least, not any time soon.

That had been, as I said, at the Pacific Union Club. Wish had obtained there some information about the Bell he was ringing, er, tracking; but I had overheard nothing about Jeremy McFadden, nor had Wish been able to elicit any conversation on the topic of McFadden even when he had specifically asked. Wish's story was that he had money to invest in some scheme McFadden was backing anonymously.

"They stick together," said Wish with some discomfort as we were walking to our second stop, the Parnassus Club—McFadden's own club, where we were much more likely to have the kind of results I wanted.

At the door, as we were being admitted in the usual routine, Wish quietly inquired if Mr. Jeremy McFadden might happen to be in and was told that he was, indeed, having a late lunch with another member in the dining room. "Shall I announce you, sir?" the employee on the door asked Wish, who shook his head.

"No need, I don't want to interrupt them. I'll catch him later. Come on, Tim," he then said to me, giving me a comradely shove between the shoulder blades. "First time in the City," he confided to the man at the door in a stage whisper as I staggered on in.

"Thanks a lot, cousin," I muttered. Glancing at him out of the corner of my eye, I decided that Wish Stephenson was having the time of his life.

The interior of the Parnassus Club was more opulent than the Pacific Union. As it, too, was located on Nob Hill, the building was new and managed to smell that way even through the ubiquitous cigar, cigarette, and pipe smoke. I rather liked the place, especially the plush carpet in a shade of deep forest green. I even gawked a little at the windows of stained glass all across the back wall of the large, high-ceilinged main clubroom.

"Go on, lad," Wish said, poking me in the ribs playfully when he saw where I was focused, "take a closer look. Bet they don't have anything like that back where you come from."

I was too fascinated even to give my colleague the evil look that his remark required. I walked on over to those windows and stood up close, staring. I had of course removed my fedora, but declined to turn it over at the door, and so I carried the hat in one hand politely up against my chest. And a good thing, too, for a few moments later I was able to raise the brim up to my face to hide an unavoidable blush.

The stained-glass windows, which from across the room appeared to be simply lovely patterns and colors in the sort of style they are calling in England now pre-Raphaelite, actually depicted nude women twined about with various vines and flowers, though not in the strategic places one is accustomed to seeing such flowers. Women of quite voluptuous proportions. Nipples in stained glass, who would've thought; oh my. I screwed up my mouth and, sticking tongue in cheek as I imagined an awkward adolescent male might do to deal with some embarrassment, turned my back on those windows and strolled with an exaggeratedly long, slow gait back to where Wish had taken an overstuffed leather chair on one side of a drum table, leaving its identical twin on the other side of the table for me. Amusement danced in his eyes and played about his lips, but he did not tease me, for which I was grateful.

Instead, Wish leaned across the table and said in a tone clearly meant for me alone to hear, "We should have something to drink. The Parnassus is a hard-drinking club where men are expected to imbibe and to hold their liquor—or so I've been told—and I think it will look better if we at least have drinks in front of us."

I nodded. Heads turned our way, one at a time; one man in my peripheral vision had summoned the discreetly circulating waiter and whispered something, glancing once in our direction as he did so, and then the waiter disappeared.

"What do you think you can handle, Timothy?" Wish asked in a slightly louder tone of voice.

"Whiskey, with seltzer," I replied, dropping my voice into the huskiest register I could manage. I had, of course, practiced this; and as my natural voice is more in the alto register than the soprano—that is, if language were sung instead of spoken—I did passably well in sounding like a young man.

Wish appeared pleasantly surprised. "Say something more," he urged, whispering.

I said crossly, and loudly enough to be overheard, "I don't see why we couldn't have gone to the races, cuz."

"Your mother would have my head," he replied, laughing.

The waiter discreetly circled himself around our way, we ordered our drinks, which came with gratifying rapidity, and I sat sipping mine while Wish began to circulate and do the male version of gossiping, whatever that might consist of. I watched him closely, having decided that it would not be out of character for a beardless young man to hero-worship his older cousin.

He was good, no two ways about that. He had done his homework, learned things about the Bell family, and began every conversation by introducing himself as one of them. Of course his ruse would soon be known, because it would get back to the miscreant Mr. Bell that his young cousin had seemed a fine young man, or some such, and Mr. Bell would ask, *What cousin?* and that would be that. But we needed only today and tomorrow, by then we would have found out all there was to be found out, and of course we would go to each club only once. This was working. Finally, because of Wish Stephenson, I felt we were doing something constructive about the case against Jeremy McFadden.

Then the man himself walked into my line of vision even as I'd thought his name. He proceeded in that ponderous way of his across the vast expanse of deep green carpet from a direction in which, I presume, lay the dining room. I picked up the nearest magazine from the drum table and buried my face in it. Unfortunately this magazine turned out to have photographs of women in various stages of removing their underwear; nevertheless I made a good show of devoting myself to its perusal with eyes and mouth gaping—the latter not being at all difficult to arrange.

Keeping one eye, as it were, on Jeremy, and the other on this disgusting yet oddly fascinating reading material, I suddenly realized that I had done something awful. Something absolutely appalling, without ever meaning to do it. And to top it all off, just as if he knew what I had done, here was McFadden headed right at me.

TWENTY

Blind Justice

HOW COULD I have done that? I wondered, feeling slightly panicky. Indeed, it was so unlike me that I could not help feeling a little disoriented, as if I'd lost a piece of my own identity, and with it my equilibrium.

What was this awful thing I'd done? Why, I had set out to prove Jeremy McFadden's guilt, which was going about the process entirely backward, for in our legal system people (even persons who beat their wives, more's the pity) are presumed innocent until proven guilty. This was very bad of me, but as I watched from the corner of my downcast eye his heavy, graceless feet in their incongruously well-made leather shoes stop not two feet from where I sat bent over the magazine; and as I felt his probing, rude, staring eyes move over my hunched form; and finally as I could hear perfectly well in my mind what he was in all likelihood thinking: *What is this ill-clad probably ill-bred person doing in my club?* I could not help but reflect that, although Justice might be blind, I myself was not. Not blind at all to Jeremy McFadden's defects, though he apparently hid them so well from most of the world.

At least, that was the case if the reports Wish Stephenson and I had been hearing from most of his clubmates continued along the lines they had so far.

Speaking of Wish—he had seen McFadden bearing down on me and now came to the rescue. "Say, aren't you Jeremy McFadden?" Wish asked in a most persuasive tone, one indeed that I had never heard from him, that of the disingenuous young businessman. He continued speaking, while in my line of vision I could see his feet (in old policeman's shoes, the heavy leather soles rendering footgear of that sort not the thing to throw away) and McFadden's elegantly clad ones almost toe to toe: "I ask because if you are he, sir," Wish said, "then I have some information you absolutely cannot afford to miss. Got it straight off the Chicago Stock Exchange day before yesterday. Been traveling, you see."

Oh certainly! I thought, hunching harder. I also looked harder at that magazine open on my knees. Really, the pictures of these women were enough to make one stop wearing underwear altogether, as anyway the underwear did not seem to be able to contain the parts assigned without bits of flesh spilling over or popping out here and there.

"And you'd be who, exactly?" That was McFadden's gruff voice.

"Aloysius Bell, distant cousin of your illustrious Mr. Bell here. Somewhat a favorite of his charming wife, you know her, of course?"

"I believe so," McFadden acknowledged. "Stock tip, you say? In the market, are you?"

Wish had hooked his fish already. I turned a page in the magazine; fortunately what was on the next one was not very racy by comparison—I was able to read word for word the liquor advertisements and thus appear well occupied. In a minute, though, Wish was probing my shinbone with the toe of his clodhoppers and saying, "Hey, you stay put. Me and Mr. McFadden are headed into the bar for a couple drinks. Business talk, nothing you'd be interested in."

"Sure." I shrugged in my best postadolescent fashion, as I turned another page and bit my tongue. A piece of fiction resided on the new page, illustrated most tastefully, not to say graphically: Europa and the Bull. Yes, certainly a bull.

I felt greatly relieved when Wish and Jeremy had gone out of my line of vision, and then out of the room, for I could at last put that magazine aside. I felt as if I should wash my hands, and indeed I did wipe my palms on my trousers.

I had no intention of staying put, no matter what I'd said to Wish. I was restless, eager to learn something concrete, do something significant, on my own. So I got up, retrieved the fedora, and started to stroll around, playing not the gawky boy but just a young man in a new place, looking around.

I had some conversations, cautiously at first, and then more confidently as I seemed to be accepted in my country-cousin persona. The men would talk to me, but only perfunctorily; my cheap suit and celluloid collar labeled me beneath their notice and so they did not even look me in the eye. But I did learn two things that were useful. First, Jeremy McFadden was not liked, but he was respected—his support in this, his own club, was rock-solid. Second, the men of the Parnassus cared not a whit that two women mediums were dead. These men were not interested in the occult, the supernatural, or the Spiritualist, and they thought women who were involved in such things were uppity, in some ways worse than whores, who at least knew their place.

I suppose I could have gotten away with asking, wide-eyed, "And what place would that be, sir?" I was tempted, just to hear them say it, but as I already knew the answer I did not. It would have served no purpose except to further rile me.

Finally I roamed toward the bar, where I assumed Wish was still conversing with Jeremy McFadden, as I had not seen either of them since they'd headed in that direction. I spotted them standing right up at the bar, where I couldn't handily eavesdrop on their conversation. That was a disappointment.

I moseyed on over in that direction anyhow, keeping to the periphery of the room, which was square, not so large as the main room but not small either, and sparsely populated. Most of the men were seated in little clusters of two or three around small tables, muttering low. I kept glancing up at the paintings hung on the walls. I was beginning to see the reasoning behind the Parnassus Club's décor: It was all mythologically based, what with Parnassus being the Greek version of Mount Olympus, home of the gods; and Greek gods giving artists an excuse for depicting an astounding variety of mostly naked males and females engaged in various activities.

Then there were the animals and the women, for instance a truly astonishing painting depicting Leda and the Swan—which had me thinking odd thoughts about feathers.

At last I had worked my way around the room to where I could sit partially concealed by a potted palm and overhear parts of two conversations: Between two men at the nearest table and, in the lulls between their words, snatches of whatever topic Jeremy Mc-Fadden and Wish Stephenson were so ardently engaged in.

From Jeremy I heard: "My wife (mumble mumble) serious waste of time. Tried to get her (mumble mumble mumble)."

And Wish said, "Oh, certainly, I couldn't agree more. But about that investment, where did you say—"

It went on in that fashion for a couple of minutes, until the pair at the nearby table drowned out the other pair in the octogenarian enthusiasm of their leave-taking. I used this bit of a fuss to approach Wish directly, and came up alongside him at the bar, using his own body to screen me from McFadden.

"Hey, cuz," I said in a stage whisper, tugging on his sleeve, "time to go."

I could see from the way the back of his neck tensed up that I'd startled him, but he hid it well. Wish turned his head toward me slowly, without moving his body at all, and said, "Hey yourself, brat. But you know, for once in your life, you're right." And in nothing flat, he'd extricated himself from McFadden, stuck him with the bill, and was shepherding me down that long green-carpeted hallway and out the door.

From the Parnassus we went on to have our stultifying experience with the Native Sons, which owing to that club's being quite nearby, did not allow us much time for talking in between. Nor did the stuffiness of the latter allow me as a reckless (or perhaps feckless might have been a better word) youth the opportunity to do much more than sit stiffly in the clubroom under the watchful eye of a major-domo, who appeared to be about a hundred and ten years of age. I couldn't even trail after Wish, which I figured was no great loss, as the men looked about as fossilized as the collections in glass cases spread around the room.

At last, late in the afternoon, we caught the cable car and then the streetcar that would take us back to Divisadero Street. Again all talk had to wait because both were too crowded for private conversation. Finally, after we'd dismounted and begun to walk the half block uphill to the double house, I said: "One gathers the Native Sons were not at all helpful about anything."

"Too right!"

"But what about at the Parnassus? We were there such a long time. You must have learned something valuable." It was impossible to keep the eagerness from my voice.

Wish tugged at his earlobe, a mannerism as characteristic of him as Michael's rubbing his hair the wrong way was of Michael himself, and serving approximately the same purpose. "Sometimes," Wish said carefully, "what you don't learn can be as important as what you do."

"And sometimes you just haven't learned anything," I snapped, not in the mood to be coddled. "So which is it this time?"

Wish looked down at me. Though I am tall, he was much taller, and his warm hazel eyes appeared a bit turbulent in their depths. "Jeremy McFadden is every bit as powerful as your partner Michael Archer—excuse me, Kossoff—was trying to tell us a while back. Nobody is going to cross that man. It would be too dangerous."

I stopped walking. The house was only a few yards away, and I wanted to finish this conversation without the assistance of Edna Stephenson. "If he's that powerful, he could have arranged the murders," I said. "He'd know how. It would be no problem at all for a man like that to set something up."

Wish nodded unhappily. "That's true. But what is equally true is that we'll probably never know. If he did it, Fremont, his tracks are so well hidden that they're damn near impossible to discover. No one I talked to would say anything more definite about the night when we assume Abigail Locke was murdered than that they believed Jeremy McFadden had been at the Parnassus Club all evening as he generally was, but without his wife, who had asked to be excused. It had apparently been Ladies' Night that night."

"Go on."

Wish shook his head and shoved his hands deep into his pockets, a sign of resignation, or so it seemed. "I've seen men like him get away with murder before. Not to say he necessarily did it, you understand, we don't really know that."

"I realize that," I said, wanting to be fair and to erase my lingering sense of guilt for having in my head convicted a man who only stood accused—and that by very few.

"Nobody will be able to shake McFadden. His friends and those who depend on him for their business—and the numbers of people in those two categories are many, by the way—will not let him down. We'll never be able to prove anything against McFadden himself, Fremont. That just isn't going to happen. We'd stand a much better chance trying to find out who he hired to do it, if he did indeed hire someone. And that's really not a job for the likes of us, it's more for the police."

I knew what he said was true; I just hadn't wanted to admit it. Still didn't, even if the most incontrovertible piece of evidence to that effect should happen to appear right in front of my face. I didn't say anything, didn't respond at all to Wish's earnest words, but turned on my heel and set off to walk briskly the few remaining steps up to the house. I could not speak for disappointment. We had seemed to be doing so well, and yet we'd learned nothing.

"Fremont!" Wish sprinted after me. A few long strides brought him to my side. "Don't be so discouraged. This is early stages yet." His voice dropped a note or two in the register. "And you must really allow me to give you a compliment." His hand on my arm stayed my progress.

I looked silently at him. It was late in the day. We had been long at our work, and the softness of the air with twilight coming on seemed to soften his features and to blur the edges of his body.

"You were . . . you are . . . wonderful," he said.

Then he paused, while I thought, Oh dear. Such a lovely young man, and while I had often sensed he might be rather more, shall we say, interested in me than was a good idea, I had never really seen it in him. Or felt it, as in the faint trembling of his fingers now lightly touching my arm. I did not know what to do, so I did nothing. Said nothing.

Wish rallied, gathered himself together, and went on in more of a comradely tone of voice: "Your disguise, I meant. It's very good, really." His eyes swept over me quickly and returned to rest on mine. "Of course I prefer you as a woman, but you make a very convincing, and handsome, man. Even that voice you used was passable. You must have had to practice a long time."

I grinned, giving him an A for effort. "I certainly did," I said. "And now, before it gets any later, let's go tell your mother what we did this afternoon. She's always an appreciative audience, and will make me feel better, since we didn't get what we set out after."

"Oh, I dunno," Wish said cryptically as we climbed the steps to J&K's side of the double house, "I got some pretty good stuff there, even if it wasn't what I thought I was looking for."

I assumed he was talking about the Bell case. It wasn't until much later I found out I was wrong about that.

I couldn't sleep. I missed Michael so much it was like—like what? Like nothing I had ever known. I only knew I could not stay one more minute in the bed alone.

I got up and went to the window, the one from which I can in daylight see the Golden Gate, that narrow entrance to San Francisco Bay; it was my distant relation, John C. Fremont, who named that strait the Golden Gate—or so the story goes. Always a controversial figure was Cousin Fremont, and his wife Jessie even more so, and so there were some people who would, out of envy, take away all his honors, including the naming of the Golden Gate. But I had adored Cousin Fremont—or at least the idea of him—for almost my whole life. For the most part in secret, because even my mother had not approved.

Of course at night I could see nothing but a few stars and some wispy high clouds. No fog, because the day had been both clear and cool. It is on warmer days when the sun heats the land in California's great valleys that the heat in turn pulls the fog in off the water. I shivered, went and got my green wool robe and put it on, then returned to the window as if I had nowhere else to go. Nor did I.

My eyelids felt stretched tight and the eyeballs as if there were grit in them. Yet I could not close my eyes; if I did, they would pop back open all of their own accord.

So I stood by the window and thought about my father's visit to San Francisco, because that was what was really on my mind. Two more days, and on the third Father would arrive and check himself in at the Hotel St. Francis on Union Square. I was immensely glad he was coming alone. Yet why . . . why would he come without Augusta?

For my twenty-fifth birthday, he'd said. Something he wanted to give me, now and not later.

"Another watch?" I wondered aloud. He'd given me an elegant little lapel watch when I turned twenty-one, but it had been smashed in the Great Quake. But no—Father would hardly come all the way across the country to give me a watch that he could just as easily send through the mail.

No, it must be something important. *Very* important.

I liked thinking about this, liked the curiosity welling up from inside me and pushing out the other, more uncomfortable emotions. I nurtured it, making lists in my head of all the things I could think of that Father might want to give me in person: Something of my mother's that I didn't know about, something that had been precious between them. Something of Mother's that he'd kept secret from Augusta, which was why she could not come. Hmm. That certainly seemed possible, as well as plausible. But what could it be?

Some exotic, valuable piece of jewelry.

Love letters. *(What an interesting thought!)*

The deed to a piece of property that had been theirs alone, a place for secret trysts. Where would such a place be? In the mountains of New Hampshire? No, Mother had disliked mountains intensely, "all that up and down" she'd said she didn't care for. So, along the sea somewhere, perhaps an island. Yes . . .

With my thoughts running thus, I wandered back to bed and lay down to continue my hypothesizing. An island . . . where?

And so musing, I fell at last asleep.

* * *

My two days would have to be packed with activity if I were to make the most of them. Having awakened from my relatively brief sleep as entirely refreshed as if I'd been much longer abed, I dressed with somewhat more care than usual in a real dress rather than the skirt and blouse I usually wore. This dress, although bought, like most of my clothes, secondhand after the earthquake, was one of my best and I knew I looked handsome in it. It was cranberry wool, tissue-light yet warm, with a bit of ivory ruching at the high round collar and edging the cuffs. The color brought out the red in my reddish-brown hair, which for once I took the time to arrange in a pouf on top of my head.

All this care with my appearance was in part practice for when Father would be here, and in part it was for the benefit of Dr. William Van Zant, the hypnotist and debunker of Spiritualist fraud. I had decided to pay him a visit at his earliest convenience—this morning, if possible. Some instinct told me that he might hold a piece of the puzzle; but then, I might just be grasping at straws.

TWENTY-ONE

Cries in the Night

DR. WILLIAM VAN ZANT was a type of man I remembered all too well, though I had not recently encountered one: a self-assured intellectual, as well groomed as he was undoubtedly well read. He would have seemed at home on any of the great university campuses back East, but out here in the West he appeared somewhat at a loss, as if he might have forgotten the directions for how to get home to his ivory tower.

"Miss Jones," he said when I arrived promptly for our one o'clock appointment, "I recall your, er . . . um, *partner* Mr. Kossoff. Charming fellow, interesting as well. Russian extraction, I think he said?"

"Yes," I acknowledged, inclining my head and moving to take

possession of a chair to one side of the huge desk that dominated the room, "but I am here on an entirely separate matter. As you were so helpful to my partner, I hoped you might prove to be equally so for me."

Van Zant, who was a man of average height and weight but excessive neatness—from his carefully waxed mustache down to the mirrorlike shine of his black shoes—leaned against his desk and crossed his ankles precisely. The pose appeared studied, affecting a casualness this man could never hope to achieve. He nodded his head up and down and made a sound that might have been "Um-hm," or any number of indistinct offerings of encouragement.

So I arranged the skirt of my cranberry-colored dress somewhat more prettily about my legs, crossed my own white silk-clad ankles, which I had taken care should be just visible, and said: "I understand that you are an authority in the field of—how should one say—the mesmeric arts?"

"Oh no! My dear woman, you have been sadly misinformed." This galvanized him into uprightness once more, and quickly, too. He raised his eyebrows and puckered his mouth in disapproval, which rounded up his cheeks and chin in an unattractive way. Van Zant was one of those unfortunate people whose faces are defined more by flesh than by bone. He raised his arm with index finger pointed upward pedantically. "I am a scientist, a practitioner of psychology in the new tradition being pioneered in Europe by the followers of Dr. Freud. Dr. Freud, you see, has proven the existence of the subconscious mind. My specialty is the scientific use of hypnotism to access the subconscious."

As this was exactly the direction I'd intended to lead him in, I was not distressed by either his words or his tone. Meekly I ventured, "I do beg your pardon. I'm afraid I haven't the slightest idea what the difference is between mesmerism and hypnotism. I had thought them to be identical processes."

Now Van Zant went behind the desk, sat, and folded his hands on top. He had short, stubby fingers with nails impeccably groomed. I glanced at him quickly, and then away. As one might have expected of a hypnotist, or a mesmerist, his eyes did have power once he had trained them on you in a certain manner. They were such a dark brown they were almost black, and had a curious intensity of focus that was compelling, although the orbs themselves were no handsomer than the man; they were rather too small and too close together.

So, as he talked, I did not look directly at him but rather in a subtle manner took in the various accouterments of his office: A fine carpet of silken wool in shades of muted red fading to rose, worked in an elaborate pattern with other colors too numerous to recount; mahogany glass-fronted bookshelves; the huge desk itself, also of gleaming mahogany; heavy curtains of ivory damask with an excellent drape that spoke of expensive material; a scent in the air of fine cigars—which, though I loathe the things, I had to allow was another indication of no expense spared by this man.

"A mesmerist," he was saying, or rather lecturing, "is not a follower of the scientific process. The mesmerist seeks to establish a link between himself and his subject, whom he deliberately makes dependent upon him. He reduces the subject's will to compliance with his own will, and while she is in that state—I say 'she,' you understand, because those with illnesses that respond to this type of treatment are virtually always females—he makes the suggestions that are designed to, upon their adaptation, return her to health.

"Whereas"—Van Zant leaned forward and I felt the intensity of his gaze sharpen, though still I did not meet it—"the hypnotist merely induces a trance state in which the subject, or patient, has access to the contents of his or her own subconscious mind. We believe, as does Dr. Freud, that once the contents of the subconscious are brought up into the light, as it were, of day, where they can be examined and interpreted by experts—that would be your psychologist and psychiatrist—a cure can be effected."

"I see." Now I looked at him. "And which are you, Dr. Van Zant?"

"Which . . . what?" He frowned.

"Psychologist or psychiatrist?"

"Oh. I am not a medical doctor. Therefore I am considered a psychologist."

A rather devious answer, I thought, but I let it pass. I was reminding myself that Michael, who was nobody's fool, had been impressed by this man. I could not help wondering why Van Zant was not creating a similarly favorable impression upon me. I pressed on: "So you would say that mesmerism is . . . what? An inferior form of hypnotism? A trick?"

"Or a fraud, or charlatanism. Mesmerism has gone the way of vaudeville, not the way of science, Miss Jones. If that is why you wished to consult me, because of some misguided interest in an outmoded, often deceptive practice, then I fear you have come to the wrong place."

"No, I do not think I have come to the wrong place at all," I said, summoning a smile, "because I desire to be educated and you are educating me. Michael, Mr. Kossoff, told me you have acquired something of a reputation for debunking fraudulent Spiritualist practices in the East. Have you been involved in any of those same activities since your arrival in San Francisco, Dr. Van Zant? And how long is it you've been here in the City?"

He smiled at that, a mere curving of the lips that did not reach his too intense eyes. "You San Franciscans say that, 'the City,' as if there were no other on earth. It is arrogant."

"There is no other quite like this one," I said, "and if we are arrogant about it, well, perhaps we are entitled. But that does not answer either of my questions."

"Touché. I can see you would make a formidable opponent, Miss Jones. Or partner—I think one would rather prefer to have you on one's side. Mr. Kossoff seems to have chosen unconventionally but well."

"Thank you. And my questions?"

"I have been here for a little over six months. I am not at liberty to discuss the particular, ah, project that brought me here. And as for exposing fraudulent Spiritualists: They are all frauds. There is no such thing as the spirit realm. If I were to spend my time that way . . . well, I should have time for nothing else." He opened out his hands in a helpless gesture, and again smiled the insincere, lips-only smile.

"I thought I had read an article in a newspaper or magazine, or perhaps I only heard it somewhere, that you were investigating Ingrid Swann?" I had in fact read no such thing, nor had I heard it; it was only a hunch, but a strong one. A stab in the dark.

A stab in the dark that drew blood. For the intensity went out of Van Zant's eyes and was replaced by watchfulness of a very different quality. I could actually feel the difference, sitting there across the desk from him. "That is true," he said, "but it was a . . . private matter. You cannot have read about it anywhere. So how do you come by this knowledge?"

"I'm an investigator. It's my business." *And I am good at what I do*, I wanted to add, but rather thought I had better not. I did want William Van Zant to continue to help me, so I had best go carefully from here on. He did not seem the type of man who would much appreciate strength in a woman, in spite of his flattery, so I finished in a deferential tone: "I had assumed you knew of my involvement with Ingrid Swann, as it was in the newspapers recently."

"I seldom read the papers."

"It was I who found Ingrid Swann's husband, along with her true name, Myra Higgins. And I was hoping, if you had indeed scrutinized Mrs. Swann's situation with your reputed thoroughness, that you might be able to give me a lead on the whereabouts of her supposed brother, Ngaio, who seems to have disappeared."

A laugh that was more of a guffaw burst from Van Zant's lips, whose thinness was mercifully camouflaged by the handsomely kept mustache. "Ngaio! Such ignorance, it is appalling."

"I beg your pardon?"

"Ngaio is a name for a woman, not a man."

"It is a very exotic name, sir, with which most of us are not familiar—but it does have the sound of a man's name."

"It is aboriginal in origin. From some far outpost, I believe, in the South Pacific."

"I did not know that," I admitted. I was beginning to feel as if I had indeed been transported back to Boston, and into one of those predinner conversations of the most disgusting intellectual kind.

"European colonists take it as a woman's name. Ingrid Swann's brother was no brother. They were two females, living in an immoral fashion."

"Oh." I felt a slight shock. This had not occurred to me, I had thought only . . . Well, I could not very well examine what I'd thought, at the moment. Only that morality, or the lack thereof, had had nothing to do with it. "This is something you know for a fact? And so you were able to investigate Mrs. Swann, I take it? Then why did you not publish your findings and expose her as a fraud? It would have made quite a splash, I should think, and I myself would like very much to know how she did the manifestation of extruding ectoplasm!" I leaned forward, hoping my enthusiasm did not sound as false to him as it did to my own ears.

Van Zant looked away, turning his profile to me. I observed that his nose was disproportionately short for his face, but rather daintily molded, like a girl's. On the surface of the desk, one of his fingers tap-tap-tapped very softly, making only the slightest sound. That was the only sign of his disturbance, which I sensed was much greater than he wished to acknowledge, perhaps even to himself.

When at last he spoke, he did not look back at me but rather seemed to address the corner of the room: "I regret I did not have the opportunity to proceed far enough to learn any of the tricks of

Mrs. Swann's trade. Someone, shall we say, 'got to her' first. It was most unfortunate, both for me and for my . . . for the sake of my project."

"And surely," I interjected, "for Ingrid Swann!"

"Yes." Now he looked full at me; severely, too. "Of course. I should have thought that went without saying."

I locked gazes with him. "In my business, Dr. Van Zant, nothing goes without saying."

For a few moments there was silence on both our parts. Then, as he began to stir in a manner that might have led to my dismissal, I quickly asked: "Can you suggest where I might find Ngaio Swann?"

To my surprise, he immediately recited an address out in the avenues of the newly forming Richmond District—in fact, he almost spat it out, as if the name of the street were distasteful to him. I wondered what that was about but did not ask, not wanting to press my luck. I was not quite done with him yet.

"And one final thing, if I may, Dr. Van Zant," I said. "Can you tell me anything at all about this practice called traveling clairvoyance?"

"Hah!" he said in an explosively sharp fashion. I was hard put not to jump in reaction, but I kept my composure. He continued, "You have some very strange tastes, Miss Jones. And you have not been very forthcoming. Why is it you want to know about these ridiculous practices? Answer me that and I may satisfy you."

"As I believe I said, I am looking into the deaths—the murders—of two prominent mediums. In order to understand why they were killed, I need to understand what it was they did, in case there is any connection."

Van Zant cocked his head to one side, as if a new idea had suddenly occurred to him. "I am not aware that either Mrs. Swann or Mrs. Locke—surely that is the other medium to whom you refer?"

I nodded.

"That either of them claimed to practice traveling clairvoy-ance."

"You were not?" I asked, injecting a note of the highest incre-dulity into my voice, as if I were completely astounded by this omission on his part. Of course, I had no evidence along these lines either; it was merely something I wished to know a great deal more about for Frances's sake. And after all, it had been she who'd gotten me so involved in all these things in the first place. I went on in similar vein, "But it is newly all the rage, or so I have been led to believe."

Van Zant calmed down and assumed his pedantic pose again, tucking fingers under both lapels of his jacket and leaning back in his chair. "Actually, traveling clairvoyance is quite an old practice, though it has been called by various names throughout the ages. It is merely a process by which the seer, the see-er, the one who sees, puts himself or herself into another place. Sometimes with the aid of a reflective surface, such as a calm pool of water, or a basin of the same, or a mirror, or a crystal ball. Though increas-ingly these days it is done—or claimed to be done—without any such aids, just by the power of the mind alone."

"And the purpose is . . . ?"

"It varies. But it is always suspect."

"Nevertheless . . . ?"

Van Zant sighed heavily. "Very well. In the previous century, the mesmerist and somnambulist most often used traveling clair-voyance to diagnose illnesses. This is still done occasionally. There is a fellow here in this country by the name of Edgar Cayce, who claims to be able to do it on his own, by putting himself into a hypnotic trance, and no doubt he will single-handedly make it into a craze again. Unless someone shuts him up. Discredits him. The medical profession should certainly be concerned; it is a mys-tery to me why they have not moved against him. I may just do it myself, when I return to the East Coast where he is located."

"How does traveling clairvoyance work?"

"It works, my dear young woman, by the simple power of suggestion. In the case of the mesmerist and the somnambulist, the latter reads the former's mind."

I made a mental note to ask him about that later, when it wouldn't interrupt his train of thought.

"In the case of Mr. Cayce," he continued, frowning severly, "I don't yet know how he does it. But I suspect the man has confederates who scout the territory and feed the relevant information to him."

"If you will be so kind," I urged, as sweetly as I knew how, "I really have very little idea just what you're talking about. I am at a loss to understand the process itself."

"The, shall we call him the clairvoyant, the one who sees clearly, goes by telepathic means to another place and observes and reports what he sees there. We are talking about a specific geographic place. And in the case of someone ill to be diagnosed, a person in this specific place, who then becomes the object of yet another level of study by the clairvoyant."

"It sounds so . . . fascinating," I commented honestly.

"Incredible is a better word." Van Zant's lips curved in an unpleasant fashion beneath his mustache.

"But tell me, because of what you said about it working in your first example through the somnambulist reading the mesmerist's mind: Do you then believe in telepathy? I thought you denied the existence of all of these things."

"Without a doubt one person can influence another. We all see this every day. Humans are sensitive to the nuances of one another's behavior, and it is this, not magic or spirits, that shapes us. I do not mean to say that one person reads another's mind, you understand, but maybe, through concentration of the mental faculty, those who have a close tie or bond can come to the same conclusions."

"But how would the mesmerist know what was going on in this

other place?" I persisted, though I could see Van Zant's tolerance for me had by now worn very thin indeed.

"Through fraud of some sort, of course. I told you, Miss Jones, these people are all crooked. None of them is honest. They are not to be trusted, and don't you forget that. Lovely young woman like you"—his eyes swept me up and down, once only—"should be doing other things. If I may say so. I fear if this is the level of investigation you are involved in, your partner is doing you a disservice after all."

I stood, taking that as my cue to go. "Of course you may say so, if you wish, Dr. Van Zant—but you must leave my partner out of it. This investigation is mine entirely. You have a right to your opinion, sir, and you have been very helpful to me this afternoon. If you will send a bill for your services—"

He interrupted by coming around the desk to take my hand warmly, smiling. With joy to see me leave, no doubt, he said, "Professional courtesy, Miss Jones, professional courtesy. I wouldn't dream of billing you. I may need to ask a favor of you in exchange someday."

I thanked him profusely and left, after pausing long enough in the rather odd vestibule of his building to write down that address in the Richmond District. I was not quite sure what I'd learned. Nothing was really very clear to me about anything at the moment. I could only keep going on, and hope for the best.

That night I was in the living room of my upstairs apartment on Divisadero Street, reading a rather lurid novel I had obtained from my favorite branch of the public library on Green Street, when the strangest feeling came over me. I went prickly all over, not outside but in, as if muscles and nerves were quivering beneath the surface of my skin. It was most unpleasant.

I shifted in my chair, thinking this must be yet another—though admittedly extreme—form of my basic apprehension over Father's impending visit. I tried to continue reading, as I was in an exciting part of the book. Ordinarily it would easily have held my complete attention. But not tonight. That inner quivering continued, and escalated, until I simply could not sit still, could not remain in my chair. I placed a bookmark at my page, closed the book with a deliberately slow movement—for I do not like to give in to irrationality—and arose. As is my wont in the evenings, I was not dressed but rather had taken a relaxing bath and afterward put on my robe and nightgown. I certainly did not expect to be going out of doors at that hour, which was nigh onto eleven o'clock, and in such garb . . . yet that was what I did.

The darkness outside seemed to call to me, to lure me on, first to the window to look out on a typical San Francisco night: swirls of fog, no stars. One of the two streetlamps I could see from where I stood had burned out. I narrowed my eyes and shielded them with cupped hands against the glare from the light behind me in the room, yet I could see no one abroad on either side of the street.

My extreme physical restlessness escalated. I left the window and went downstairs, forcing myself to move slowly, telling myself every step of the way that this was ridiculous, that I would only go to the door, open it, look out, and of course see nothing at all unusual. And that was what I did.

Yet I heard something. Very faint at first, so that I had to strain every nerve in order to be sure I'd heard it, and strain yet further to discern from what direction it came. And there! Again. From the bottom of the steps and to the right, where up against the house, because of the burned-out streetlamp, lay an area of deepest shadow, I heard it . . . the sound of someone crying.

TWENTY-TWO

Naked We Come Forth

I FOLLOWED the sounds, blindly at first; then as my eyes adjusted I managed to see a form huddled up against the house, behind a row of low-growing juniper bushes that screen the foundation. Its human shape was discernible only from its paleness, which reflected what precious little available light there was. And as I drew nigh I knew with a sinking certainty to whom that shape belonged.

"Frances," I whispered, "is that you?"

She whimpered once and recoiled. Crouching, she had wrapped herself into the smallest possible shape. Yet she did manage to say: "F-Fremont?"

"Of course it's Fremont. Who else, on these premises?" I said, intentionally a bit harshly, as I took a last sweeping glance around to be absolutely certain there was no one hanging about. There was not. So I went on in a no-nonsense manner, as my experience with traumatized people after the earthquake had taught me—for why would she be hiding in the bushes if she were not traumatized, and I had only too good an idea by whom: "What in the world are you doing back there in the bushes when we could be inside? Why ever didn't you just ring the doorbell, you silly ninny? Come on, then!"

Frances took the hand I extended and allowed me to pull her to her feet. Only then did I realize that she was entirely naked. I sucked in my breath but was able to prevent myself from saying a word, or indeed from making any sound, while I led her as quickly as possible up the steps and into the house.

Once inside I ordered her, again in that no-nonsense voice, "Go on up the stairs to my apartment. I'll just lock the door and then I'll be right along."

"I c-c-can't!" Frances said through chattering teeth. She had crossed her arms over her breasts, as I supposed I should have done in her place, but that did not hide the rather spectacular sight of her other red-gold hair.

"Don't be silly. Of course you can."

"C-c-close your eyes then, if I g-go up first."

"I promise I won't look," I said, making a fuss over locking the door, which was a mere matter of throwing a bolt. "And don't worry, the first thing I'll do when we get up there is provide you with one of my bathrobes, and then I'll run you a nice, hot, relaxing bath, and only after that will you have to tell me what has happened."

"Thank you, Fremont," Frances managed to say with some dignity. I did not look, and she did go on up the stairs.

Frances seemed to recover her spirits quickly. In body she had not suffered—Jeremy McFadden had spared her, for once, and although I was glad, I wondered why. She sat in the other wing chair, wearing my best bathrobe and sipping the tea I'd made for us both.

I thought it prudent not to ask questions. Surely she would tell me all I wanted to know, in time. I was right about that; it was not long before she started to talk.

"I suppose I must tell you everything, since I've thrown myself on your mercy this way," she began.

"Not necessarily. I'm curious, of course, but mainly I'm glad to see that you are all in once piece. You have escaped with your health, and your life, and considering how things have been going for some women lately . . ." I thought it best not to finish that sentence.

"It was . . . it *is* the oddest thing!" She paused, looking into the distance vaguely, with a tiny frown that creased the space between her brows in quite an attractive manner. I was perversely glad of Michael's absence, for my friend's hair flowed about her neck and shoulders and curled around her face in a way that I— with my dark, straight-as-a-stick locks—could not help but envy. Not to mention that she filled out my robe in a fashion I could never have done myself.

After an overlong pause, I prodded: "Odd?"

"Yes." She sipped her tea. How maddening that she would not continue!

I poured more tea, counseling myself to be patient. Eventually Frances began to speak again, this time gathering momentum and continuing on in earnest.

"Perhaps he didn't beat me because I stood up to him for the first time ever. I don't know how I managed, really. No, I *do* know—I thought of Patrick, and what a team we make. Oh, but I should begin at the beginning!" She flushed in a manner most becoming.

"It might be helpful."

"Of course. Well, this is what happened. You did persuade Patrick, Fremont, that we should not meet in my rooms anymore, for fear my husband would find out and misunderstand.''

I doubted there would be much misunderstanding, based on what I'd seen pass between Patrick and Frances, but I let that go by, and she continued.

''But I just couldn't allow our work, my own training, to stop. You see, there's a certain kind of momentum that builds up, it's rather difficult to describe. But it depends on us being together. Without Patrick I feel less than whole. It's as if the other half of myself is missing. You must know what I mean; you and your partner, Michael . . . ?''

''We don't have that kind of a relationship,'' I said quickly. Yet in truth I did know what she meant. I knew that feeling of missing an important part of oneself, and it bothered me a good deal, as I did not know if it was a good or a bad thing. I said, truthfully but vaguely: ''We are very independent, Michael and I.''

Frances leaned forward, as if the change in posture might help to win me over to her point of view. I was feeling a certain amount of resistance, and she may have sensed it.

She said, ''Well, all right, then I'll just say I didn't want to be without Patrick, I wanted my training to go on, and so we met instead at his house. You know, the house on Octavia Street—it's his now.''

''Um-hm.''

''I walked over, and as it is a long walk, I suppose my longer than usual absences were noted. I don't know if Cora told Jeremy, or if he just came home unexpectedly one afternoon and found me not at home, or what. All I know is that he had me followed. Or so he said—I never saw anyone following me, of course, or I would have come straight to you and asked what I should do about it. You know these things, Fremont. I don't.''

Some of the charm that worked on men she now turned on me. I felt it working, as I inclined my head in mute acknowledgment of her flattery.

She continued: "Jeremy assumed the worst—that I had done it, I mean. I couldn't bear that, just couldn't bear it, because that is not at all what Patrick Rule and I are about! And so"—her shapely chin rose—"I told Jeremy that he was entirely wrong, I was not doing anything sordid, rather I was developing a God-given talent in the hands of a master."

A rather large promotion for Patrick Rule, I thought. Not so long ago he had characterized himself as Abigail Locke's flunky. Which meant, didn't it, that my friend Frances had given him the means for a promotion? And I wondered when, at what point, he might have begun to realize that this might happen.

"Jeremy laughed," Frances said. "He said something horrible, obscene, about a—a talent for whoring. I couldn't have that, you see"—her eyes flashed—"and I said so. I said a gentleman does not speak to a lady in such a manner, and he himself had made me into a lady, therefore I required that he apologize."

"Good for you!" I exclaimed, truly proud of her. So proud that I forgot for a moment my dark train of thought, and where I had been going with it.

Frances's eyes flashed, and she had a slight smile on her lips. "He didn't apologize. Well, I never thought he would. But he didn't strike me either, though he raised his arm. I forced myself not to cower. After a minute he looked pretty silly standing there with his arm in the air and a face like the wrath of God. Or so I thought. Then he put his arm down, stuck his hands in his pockets, and got very, very quiet, which turned out to be in a strange way even more terrible."

"I can imagine."

"Can you? I was . . . I really wondered if he would kill me then. If he would suddenly let go of that iron control that kept his voice so low and his hands in his pockets, and come at me in a rush and strangle me. He didn't, obviously, since I am here. What he did was, he said sure as he had made me he could break me. That I had betrayed his trust and no longer deserved to be his wife, no longer deserved to be fed, clothed, and sheltered by him. He ordered me to take off all my clothes, and I did, without protest. Then he ordered me to leave the house, naked as the day I was born. With that, I did argue. But he was like—like a big dog herding sheep, relentless, and I was the lamb. All I could do was move in the direction he drove me, toward the front door, and out . . . out into the dark and the cold. I couldn't even get that slicker from the side room because the door was locked and I didn't have my keys. I don't have . . . anything."

"That's not true, you know," I said softly. "You have yourself, your life, your hopes, your talent, your abilities. And you have quite a lot of luck on your side, I think."

"L-l-luck?" Struggling to control herself, she daintily touched her nose with the heel of her hand.

"You made it here, naked, without being arrested." I smiled.

"That is so." She tried to return the smile, but instead, tears filled Frances's eyes. She didn't let them fall. She blinked them back, tossed her head, held out her cup, and asked brightly: "Is there more tea?"

I put Frances in Michael's bedroom, because it was the only other bed in the house. I gave her my spare key to his side of our dwelling, which meant unfortunately that I had none, and so could not go checking on her in the middle of the night if I should happen to become anxious. I could call her on the telephone, though, from the office downstairs. Michael, of course, had a phone number separate from the business. He kept it unlisted, but I knew the number by heart.

I was much troubled by what had happened to Frances, and for a reason so very odd that I felt rather guilty: For her to be simply turned out, even naked, did not make sense. Did not fit my notions (which I had been so intent on reinforcing of late) of who Jeremy McFadden was and what he had done—would do—to keep the exclusive affections and attentions of his lovely but quirky wife.

In the process of getting myself ready for bed I pondered: Why would McFadden have gone to the trouble of murdering the two mediums, or even just the first, Abigail Locke, yet then toss Frances out at the first real hint of infidelity? He wouldn't . . . would he? And yet, how could he not be the murderer when he was already guilty of physically abusing his wife? Were France's bruises not the proof, which I had seen with my own eyes, of the lengths to which the man would go to keep her all for himself? From physical abuse to murdering one's rivals—the rivals for her time and attention in this case being not lovers but the mediums— seemed like an orderly progression to me. Or it had until now, when he had broken the pattern.

I had reached the stage of brushing out, then braiding, my long hair before sleep. I was sitting on the side of the bed, my side, wishing Michael were here to brush my hair the way he loved to do—the way I loved him to do—when suddenly there came back to me the thought about Patrick Rule that I had pushed away days earlier: *What If Patrick had had some sort of squabble with Abigail Locke that no one knew about? What if he had, that night he'd helped me put the entranced Frances into the Maxwell, seen possibilities in Frances McFadden, and had decided to bide his time, to lay his plans carefully, maybe rid himself of Mrs. Locke and then . . .*

"Oh, surely not!" I muttered, brushing with renewed vigor. I hung my head down, flipped the hair over, and brushed it from underneath, which is supposed to be very good for circulation of the blood in the scalp, and stimulating to new hair growth. Perhaps it would stimulate new growth in my brain as well. I had so hoped to have this case wrapped up before Father's visit . . . but now that was only a day off. It wasn't going to happen. And how could I pay proper attention to both Frances and Father?

"Oh, botheration!" I said, somewhat too loudly, as I sat up and tossed my head, hard, so that the hair obediently fell back into place. Sleek as you please. No tumbling curls for Fremont Jones, alas.

God help me, I was in a quandary. For even as I fell asleep I found myself wondering if Frances and Patrick had known each other all along, if they had set this whole thing up just so that he could murder Mrs. Locke and end up with my friend. With a sinking feeling so profound it was almost as if the pit of my stomach had nailed me to the bed, I wondered: *And what if they killed Ingrid Swann, too, just so that when Patrick and Frances started out their tandem enterprise, there would be less competition?*

But I could not think about it for long, because I was very tired, and I fell asleep still wondering.

I do not sleepwalk. Absolutely do not, never have, never will walk in my sleep. So how in the world was it that I found myself outside my bedroom before I was truly awake? Or was I dreaming?

I have heard that the urge for self-preservation is very deep, and perhaps that was what had propelled me from my bed and into the corridor in my nightgown, where I stood trembling, coming awake to the rapid beating of my own heart. Coming awake quickly, too, for all in the same instant I remembered rolling out of bed and slithering out into the hall, along with the sounds that had caused me to do it.

If I got through this, I realized not much later, I would owe my survival to Michael twice over, although he was not even physically present: First, because he had given me the silk nightgown I was wearing—and this gown was not some pale bit of fluff, but rather oriental in style with a high neck, long sleeves, and side buttons, and most important of all it was dark in color, garnet red. Second, because I'd been sleeping alone, missing Michael, I had been curled around his two pillows as if they were him . . . and had left those two pillows like a lump under the bedclothes when I rolled out of bed.

Therefore, as the sound of stealthy footsteps came inexorably up the stairs, I faded farther and farther back along the hallway, keeping to the shadowy side of the wall. There was very little light anyhow, as the night outside had apparently clouded over and we were missing one of the two streetlamps. Quickly I undid my braid, shook my head, and let the hair fall over to obscure my white face. I might have gone down the back stairs and out of the house, and perhaps I should have—for I had no weapon, the gun being in the drawer of the bedside table, and my walking stick with its trusty hidden blade standing in its customary place in the corner of the bedroom. But I did not go so far as the back stairs. I wanted to see who had invaded my house.

A large person but light on his feet. A man, surely; dressed in dark, conventional clothes, including gloves; he seemed to have no face at all. An illusion, of course. He must be wearing a mask. There was no way on earth even to begin to guess at his identity. I held my breath, my mind a catalog that ran like lightning through every way conceivable—and some inconceivable—to surprise him into taking off that mask while not physically endangering myself.

It was hopeless. There was no way, and without a weapon there was nothing whatever I could do. If I'd had Michael's keys, if I'd kept them instead of giving them to Frances, I might go over to the other side of the house and lock myself in.

Frances! Yes! Big as he was, that masked figure (which had just now entered my bedroom) was not Jeremy McFadden, but that meant nothing. McFadden had many people in his employ. And what if he had assumed she would logically come to me, or indeed if he had had someone already in place to follow her here, with instructions to wait until the house was dark and quiet, then go in and do the deed. What if I had dismissed my earlier suspicions of McFadden entirely too easily?

I shuddered, as from within the bedroom came a muffled, whompish kind of sound, followed by an equally muffled excla-mation, and then some ferocious slashing. I surmised what my truder had done in Michael's pillows. Later examination of the bed's carnage—or I suppose one should say rather "featherage"— proved me correct in this surmise. But at the moment the time had clearly come to flee, and so I did, down the back stairs, which was the logical way to go.

All the way down, my mind continued to run rapidly through the various possibilities—there had to be, *must* be, a way to catch this dastardly fellow, take him into custody, and force him to Tell All. But there was not, for without a weapon I was helpless. I could not hope to overpower someone so much bigger than I.

When I reached the first floor I hesitated, listening hard, and bristling with questions: *Why had I never taken the time to learn jujitsu, like my friend Meiling Li? Might I have time to call the police from the office? Even if I did, could they possibly get here in time to get this intruder?*

The footsteps, which were the only sounds this fellow made, other than stabbing and slashing, came to the top of the back stairs and started down. I held my place there at the bottom, not at all sure what I would do.

TWENTY-THREE

A Paterfamilias in the Midst of Everything

THE BACK STAIRS ascend from—and therefore descend to—an enclosed area off the kitchen that the previous owner of the house had used as a pantry. To one side is the back door, and to the other, the door into the kitchen. I noted now that the back door stood ajar, though I was certain I had locked it earlier, at the end of the workday, as was my habit.

I assumed the intruder had gained entry that way—in spite of Michael's installation of the new, heavy bolts on all outside doors. A swift glance at the door to the kitchen confirmed that it was still shut, as I had left it; or perhaps this intruder was a neat sort of person who had closed the door behind himself on entering the house proper, while leaving the outer door ajar for a quick getaway. For he *had* gone through the house; with my own eyes I had seen him come up the main stairs.

I did not so much *decide* what to do as just wait until the moment came when I *knew*, and then I did it. The intruder was descending the stairs slowly, carefully, probably on the lookout for whomever he had thought he'd find in my bed—i.e., myself or Frances McFadden. (I still hadn't a clue which one of us he was after, but Frances did seem the more likely.) There was no place for me to hide except beneath the stairs themselves, so that was what I did. I tried not to breathe at all, which of course was impossible, and so I took only the shallowest sips of air. The footsteps sounded directly over my head, then passed as it were down my shoulder, and all the while I listened with every bit of accuracy I could wring from my normally keen hearing. Would he leave the house by that open back door, or would he go through the kitchen, to search further?

Suddenly it was absolutely clear to me what had to happen: He must be made to leave the house, in a way that would convince him returning, or proceeding to the other side, would be a poor idea indeed. I had but one weapon: the element of surprise.

And I used it. When I heard his footsteps reach the bottom of the stairs, I filled my lungs, and as those steps paused, the way we all do in moments of deciding where to go next, I burst out from my hiding place screaming at the top of my voice. My hair streamed down in front of my eyes, I could scarcely see what I was doing. I must have looked like a Fury as I charged at the intruder full tilt with my arms braced out stiff in front of me, screaming all the while. I knocked him off balance, jerked the door open with one hand, and while he was still off balance, with all my strength I kicked him through, slammed the door after him, flipped the bolt, and realized first that I had ripped my nightgown up one side with that forceful kick, and second, that the intruder must have picked the lock or had some sort of master key, because the lock was intact, bolt and all. I should have to take Michael or Wish Stephenson to task about that, because hadn't they both said the new locks were virtually foolproof?

After a moment of euphoria, I knew I was not necessarily safe yet. Protecting myself came first. I went upstairs and got the gun I so hated to use, the Marlin that looks and sounds like a small rifle. I levered a cartridge into the chamber, making the distinctive ratcheting that fell like music upon my ears. Perhaps guns are not so bad when one truly has need of them. Then I snatched up both the leather pouch containing additional cartridges and my walking stick for good measure.

This time I went down by the main stairs, half expecting to see, silhouetted against the etched glass of the front door, a man's dark shape—the shape of an intruder, perhaps a murderer, identity as yet unknown.

Yet he was not there. I telephoned Frances, and it was only then I realized, with a sudden, sickening sinking of my stomach: He could have gone to the other side of the house first! What if she did not answer? How could I bear it? The telephone rang, and rang, and rang. . . .

At last, after a delay interminable and intolerable, when I was about to give up and had begun to mentally prepare myself for the worst, I heard a click . . . and then Frances's sleepy voice said, "Oh, hello? Did you ring?" She sounded so vague, she might have been making inquiry of the instrument itself.

All my protective instincts, which for some reason she could always evoke, came rushing to the fore and I heard myself lie to her: "Frances, it's Fremont. I'm sorry to wake you, but I've had a bad dream, a nightmare, and now I'm afraid to be alone."

"Oh, well then . . ." she said, still vague, still more than half asleep.

I interrupted: "I'm coming over to spend the rest of the night on Michael's couch. If you don't mind, give me about five minutes, then go to the front door. I'll knock three times—then you let me in."

She agreed. I used my five minutes to call Wish and explain everything. He said he would come right down to the office and bring the police with him. He would handle it, he promised; and knowing my aversion to his former colleagues in blue, he said he would manage it in such a way that I would not even have to talk to them if I didn't want to. Of course I assured him that I did not want to!

It rather quickly developed that I wanted only to escape back into sleep. So, obviously, did Frances, who was yawning and rubbing her eyes as she let me in.

Shakespeare, I reflected as I curled up beneath the afghan on Michael's couch, had said something about sleep knitting up the raveled sleeve of care. *Macbeth*, was it? Regardless of the play, it did seem to me a good idea, as at the moment I felt considerably raveled. With the gun behind the cushions and my walking stick to hand, I managed to go off into the Land of Nod, where I hoped the Hand of Morpheus would reassemble me.

At ten o'clock the next morning we held a conference around the kitchen table: Wish, Edna, Frances, and I.

Looking rather grim, Wish said, "It would take a master locksmith to open that particular type of deadbolt lock without leaving a trace. This is someone highly skilled we're up against, very clever, and I'm inclined to think—begging your pardon, Fremont—that his slashing the mattress and pillows may just have been the work of a professional burglar venting his frustrations when he found you had nothing worth stealing."

"And what do the police think?" I asked, stiffening my backbone. It was a little insulting, though a better solution to the problem of the intruder than any I had thought of.

"They think the same. With some encouragement from me, of course," Wish said.

"Then why, I ask you," Edna chimed in with a note of incredulity in her voice, "didn't the bur-gu-ler, when he saw how it was an office here, go straight to the other side of the house where there's nize stuff, an-tee-kees and all? And why didn't he open up desk drawers down here looking for money? He could've took the typewriter, too, that's worth a lot."

"She has a point," I said.

Frances stifled a yawn politely with the back of her hand. She looked pale and strained, an appearance which was not helped by the fact that my plain skirt and blouse appeared, on her, excessively severe. Especially as the blouse did not quite meet over her ample breasts, and so she had taken my old black shawl and crossed it, like a fichu, over the offending appendages, then anchored the shawl's ends beneath a belt that emphasized a slender waist upon that otherwise curving body.

I did not think there was much point to asking her, other than to keep her alert, but I asked anyway: "Frances, last night on your way here, did you ever at any point suspect that you were being followed?"

She frowned, not in perplexity but in displeasure at the question. "No, in fact I am quite sure I wasn't. I didn't exactly go walking right out on the sidewalk, Fremont. I slouched from house to house, keeping to cover as much as I could—along fences, behind bushes and things of that nature. And of course I was continually looking around, checking, because I didn't want anyone to see me. I'm telling you, nobody followed me!"

"As far as you know," I said evenly, bowing my head as if to acquiesce, though my words themselves implied otherwise.

Two deep rose spots bloomed suddenly on her cheeks. "You want me to take the blame for what happened to your mattress and your pillows, is that it? You want me to replace them? Well, by all means let us go to the City of Paris"—she leapt up from the table—"without further delay. If we get there soon enough perhaps Jeremy will not yet have removed my name from the account and I will be able to buy not only mattress and pillows but also clothing for myself. The bill can be his final remembrance of me!" Her chin came up defiantly—quivering, to be sure, but defiant all the same.

"I meant nothing of the kind, no offense was intended," I said, my voice gently insistent. But I did not try to tug her back down into her seat. A weird sort of energy had started to build in the kitchen. It flashed through my mind that this could be what Frances felt at automatic-writing time. I felt as if some spirit were hovering nearby, uninvited but not necessarily unwanted.

Indeed, the feeling was so strong upon me that I almost reached across the table for the writing tablet that Edna had brought to the meeting, as was her habit, in case one of us decided that notes should be made. I stayed my hand, though, watching Frances from the corner of my eye, for she was nothing if not skittish. But the moment passed, the feeling subsided, and so did the high color in my friend's cheeks. Edna, as alert as always—a keen woman our Edna—flashed me a questioning glance, to which I gave a barely perceptible shake of my head. Wish cleared his throat, scratched at his ear in an overly casual way, and said, "Well. Where were we?"

At that, Frances sat down again and normality appeared restored.

"I think Frances had an excellent idea," I said with enthusiasm. "She and I will go to the City of Paris to shop for some things we must have, and if she can put them on her husband's account, well, why not? Edna, if you would be so good as to call the St. Francis Hotel and inquire as to exactly when my father is expected, I should be most grateful. His name is Leonard Pembroke Jones. And Wish, as much as I've benefited from your help the past few days, you really must talk to your mother about the client who came in when we were both out yesterday. Now, what have I forgotten?"

"Do you have any idea when Michael is coming back?" Wish asked. He alone, of us four around the table, was still dissatisfied about something. I could tell by the expression on his face.

Normally I would have taken time to deal with his dissatisfaction, to draw him out if need be as to its source and possible solution. But nothing seemed normal now, and I was possessed—one might even say consumed—with a sense of time running out. Therefore I gave him the short yet truthful reply: "I don't know. He never said." Then, with an artificial smile on my lips, I cast a rapid glance around the table and rose. "Now, if there's nothing else, we should get on with our day."

The ferry bearing the passengers from the cross-country train trip, which ended at the Southern Pacific station in Oakland, crossed the Bay in late afternoon. My father arrived at his hotel approximately on time, that is to say at 5:45 P.M.; the hotel desk notified me at his request; and I presented myself at the door to his room on the third floor at seven-fifteen. I knocked. While waiting for the door to be answered, I reflected that if I had not gotten turned around in the corridors, this would be a corner suite overlooking Union Square.

I had butterflies in my stomach. A thousand of them.

The door opened inward.

"Father?"

He opened his arms, tried to smile, and his eyes glinted with a sudden sheen of tears withheld. With the smile I knew him—for otherwise my father was much changed. "My dear Caroline," he said.

I rushed into his arms.

Since my adolescence my father has not been much taller than I, and this was so still; yet he had always been a substantial man, not only in a business sense but physically. Broad-shouldered and equally broad of chest, with thick arms and legs, and a tendency, as he aged, to a paunch. Now as his arms closed around me I could feel his bones beneath the skin, even through his clothes. It was beyond shocking.

"Oh, Father," I said, my voice muffled as I buried my head, like a child, against his shoulder. I could not look full on him again until I had better control of myself. I trembled uncontrollably.

"There, there, child," he said, not awkwardly but warmly. He patted my back, my arm, and finally my head. "I see you still don't like hats," he commented, with some of the old verve in his voice.

I shook my head, which had the effect of rubbing my face against his shoulder, which in turn had the effect of wetting the fine but slightly prickly wool of his suit coat. I was crying, most unexpectedly, and had no more ability to stop the tears from falling than I'd had of controlling the earlier tremors. Those, at least, had stopped.

Father stepped back from the doorway, his arms still around me, and somehow—perhaps with the nudge of a toe, I didn't raise my head to look—closed the door behind us. I heard it click shut. "My little girl," he said, a bit thickly. "Come now, Fremont—if I may call you Fremont? That is what others call you now, isn't it?"

"Um-hm," I sniveled, nodding this time, smearing more tears but up and down.

"Let me look at you. It's been a long time." He took my shoulders in his hands then, and with more strength than I would have thought his newly frail frame could muster, moved me back at arms' length.

I sniffed, tossed my head, lifted my chin . . . and finally managed a smile. "I expect I've changed quite a bit," I acknowledged.

"Yes, you have," Father agreed, his eyes twinkling. Then in the blink of an eye, his face grew grave. He said, "But then, so have I."

In Father's hotel room we talked and drank some excellent dry sherry until the encroaching fog had absorbed the last pale rays of daylight, and Union Square, though it was just directly across Powell Street (Father did indeed have a corner room), had disappeared from view. For the most part I answered his questions, and did so truthfully. I did not like to ask him questions myself, because the ones I most wanted answered would be considered rude, even from so outspoken a daughter as I. For example: *How are you really getting along with Augusta? Has she made many changes in our house? If I were to come home for a visit tomorrow, would there be any little touches of my mother left at all?* And most importantly: *Father, have you been ill, that your face and form can have altered so much in only three years? And if so, are you still?*

When I had satisfied the minimum of Father's curiosity, we went down to the sumptuous dining room on the mezzanine, which overlooks the lobby with its tall marble columns, some replaced and some repaired since the earthquake. A string trio was playing quietly near one end of the balcony. Father had requested a table against the wall, far back in the room, as he is somewhat afraid of heights. A fault he does not admit to, of course; my mother told me long ago.

"This is quite elegant," I remarked, after the waiter had taken our order.

"You have not been here before?" Father raised one white eyebrow. His eyes nestled now in folds of crinkly skin, the whites of them faded, without luster; yet the green of his irises was bright as my own. Those eyes sparkled with an intelligence undimmed by whatever beset him physically.

"No, I haven't," I replied. "Before the earthquake I had been only to the Fairmont, and since the earthquake I haven't been able to afford to dine in a hotel like this."

"Oh?" Up went the eyebrow again. Now that I was getting used to his appearance, I saw that the thinness was in its own way rather becoming. Leonard Pembroke Jones had broad but prominent cheekbones I never remembered seeing before. His mouth, though—that had not changed. And why had I not realized until this very moment how much Michael's mouth resembled my father's?

Even as I thought of Michael my father said, "I would have thought your, hum, partner might have brought you on occasion to a place like this."

"My partner," I repeated dully.

The waiter arrived with bowls of soup, the first course, a crab bisque that smelled delicious. The string trio was playing something haunting, with a plaintive, moaning cello line. This was a moment I had both feared and anticipated with great excitement—for there was a part of me that wanted to tell my father everything. A part of me that craved his approval, and had once been so certain of his love that never would I have dreamed of holding anything back. But that part of me had either died or gone into hiding when he married Augusta.

Behind the waiter came the sommelier, with the silver apparatus for dealing with the long-necked wine bottle around his own long neck. This was done to Father's approval, and as it all took awhile, I had time to frame my answer.

"You mean, of course, Michael Kossoff. My business partner."

"Yes indeed. And is he not somewhat of a benefactor also? An older man, you said in one of your letters?"

The soup was delicious, even in such strained circumstances. "In the sense that it is Michael's money that has set us up in business, then yes, you could say he is my benefactor. But not in the sense that the business would function as well without me—in fact, it might not function at all." (This was true: I was the inspiration behind J&K. If inspiration could be the right word. Michael had told me many times that he hoped our business would enable me to use my God-given talents and at the same time keep me out of trouble. Of course, Father did not have to know any of that.)

I interrupted myself to say, "Father, please eat your soup before it gets cold. It's really very good."

Father obligingly dragged his spoon through the creamy pinkish liquid, sniffed, smiled slightly, and sampled it. I could never in my whole life recall his approaching food with such delicacy. He had always enjoyed his meals so much that, if anything, he'd leapt into them with a gusto that bordered on bad manners. Now he raised the spoon to his mouth, paused, and looked me in the eye.

"Caroline—Fremont—you have never told me the nature of the J&K Agency's business."

"We are an investigatory agency. We do confidential inquiries. Into whatever our clients want and need." I met Father's steady gaze, my green eyes and his locked. Father and daughter.

"You do not use that infernal machine, the typewriter, in your business? I thought you did. I thought you had thrown away all that education I invested in for you, as if you were a boy . . ."

"Not quite," I said grimly. This was an old, touchy subject for us.

"I beg your pardon?"

"I mean, Wellesley was a good school, but I did not get the same education I would have had at Harvard or Yale. But I did not throw my education away, Father. What I learned will remain forever in my head, in my brain, to inform and transform everything I say or do. Once one is educated, that education becomes a part of who one is. As mine is a part of me. Whether I sit at a typewriter or not."

"Nevertheless"—Father had become interested in his soup, and paused to indulge that interest—"if you are no longer tied to the typewriter, I am glad. And I'm grateful to this Michael Kossoff. You have a high opinion of the man, do you not?"

I blushed. I could not help myself. The flush began on my chest, where I felt it as a great, spreading warmth proceeding outward from my heart, and traveled then up into my neck and into my cheeks until I felt on fire. I did manage to find my voice, but had to swallow hard before I could make it work reliably: "I do indeed have a high opinion of him. He has worked for government agencies and knows what he's doing. In addition he's a very learned man. His library alone reveals the liveliness of his mind."

I realized I was about to say too much and stopped myself.

Father smiled. His face and his voice softened. "Ah, daughter, who could resist you when you look like that? I have just one question: When do I get to meet this man?"

TWENTY-FOUR

Not Quite Happy Birthday

I FELT MY EYES go wide, then reached for the wine, which was white, cool, crisp, and very faintly sweet on my tongue. I savored it even as I wondered what my father thought he knew, and how he could know that, what should I say, and last but far from least, what must *he* think of me?

At last I said, "Michael is out of town on business, Father. I do not believe he will return until after you've left again for Boston. You did say you could be here only a couple of days."

"That, lamentably, is true." He hung his head and briefly looked forlorn indeed. I wanted immensely to comfort him, and yet I did not know how. It was precisely the same aching feeling I'd had long ago, after Mother died, and I wanted so much to

262

bring her back not only for myself (although I was sorrowing too) but for him . . . because she was always the only one who could reach him when he was at his most solemn, his most bereft. With her gone, there was—there had been—no one. . . .

And so, because there was no one, and I could not do it alone, I merely waited.

In time he raised his head.

"Caroline—Fremont—daughter, I must be honest enough with you to tell you that I've come across the country against my wife's wishes."

All my muscles stiffened at the word "wife" on my father's lips, as it applied now to one who was, in my extremely biased opinion, unworthy of the title. "That must be difficult for you," I said.

Father nodded. Rather miserably, I thought. And in the lengthy pause that followed, the waiter came and replaced soup with a salad, which my father moved to the side with a request that the entree be brought: "Expeditiously as possible," Father said. The waiter, an ancient man with yellowed white hair, merely stood there. "Quickly!" Father translated, with a wave of his hand for emphasis, and the waiter nodded, this time speeding away.

When he'd gone I said quietly, "You seem to me to have been ill, perhaps for some time. Is this true? And if it is, why didn't you, or even Augusta, tell me?"

"I didn't like to worry you. And I thought I would recover, in time—especially with Augusta to nurture me. She's good at things like that, you'll find out, I'm sure."

I was much less sure, but forbore to say so. Instead I said, "You are fully recovered now, I take it?"

"Fully, no. Enough to get along, yes. But still Augusta would never have agreed to my making the long train trip. I thought it best, therefore, to spare her the worry of knowing that I was coming here."

"Father, if you don't mind my asking—what was the nature of your illness?"

His eyes left mine and seemed to stare, unfocused, into some middle distance that only he could see. After a pause in which, for a moment, his mouth worked without producing a sound, as if he were an ancient no longer capable of speech, he said: "It's in the nature of a severe digestive complaint. That is all I can tell you. The doctors themselves don't seem quite to know. It comes and goes, sometimes better, sometimes worse, but since it set in about a year ago it has never been completely cured."

"I see," I said; and because he seemed so uncomfortable I returned to the topic he himself had broached. "Since you are obviously out of town, where does Augusta suppose you to be?"

"In Chicago at a professional meeting," he replied, with a sudden, impish smile.

Impulsively I reached across the table and put my hand on Father's, where it rested just to the left of his plate, politely, as if ready and willing to dive back into his lap at any moment. "Yet," I said, all the warmth I could muster, which was considerable, in my voice, "you did come, all the way here, just to see me. Thank you, Father. I can never thank you enough."

"You don't need to thank me. In the morning, on your birthday, you'll understand exactly why I came. In the meantime, if you could continue to put up with me tonight just for the sake of companionship, I'd be honored to hear the story of your life before and since the earthquake. Every single minute you can remember."

So I launched myself into the story of my life over the past three years. I omitted only the strange subject of Edgar Allan Partridge, who had also been known by his real name, Peregrine Crowe—because there are some stories that, while true, are so incredible as to invite disbelief.

Thus was the rest of the dinner passed, and I left after agreeing to return at nine o'clock the following morning. My father still kept to his banker's hours—that about him had not changed. And that was almost the only thing that had not.

*   *   *

My bed had a fine new mattress, which Frances and I had bought on her husband's account, yet lying upon it I seemed unable to sleep at all. There was far too much going on in my mind. What a jumble it was, a maddening kaleidoscope of thoughts. I may have dozed; there were times when I could not tell the difference between those half-awake thoughts that take us on one or the other edge of sleep, and dreams themselves.

One thing I did remember clearly, when with the first certain light of dawn I left my bed and gave up even the pretense of sleep: Emperor Norton. He had appeared to me in the outlandish military-style costume he wore in the one photograph of him that I'd seen in the old newspaper archives at the library. Perhaps, like the previous night's intruder, the Emperor had mistaken me for Frances?

I did not really think that was so. Rather, I must have seen the Emperor in an ordinary dream, as I have no psychic ability whatever, nor do I wish to. Yet as I splashed cold water on my face in a vain attempt to feel alert and halfway human, I had the oddest feeling that the Emperor had been in my dreams for a reason. As if he were trying to draw my attention to him . . . and perhaps through him, elsewhere . . . as if he might help me to solve some problem, or, more likely, as if my attention to Frances's problems would help her solve them.

"Well," I said somewhat huffily to the mirror, not looking at my own face but rather over my shoulder into the depths of the room that was actually behind me (an odd sensation, to be sure), "if I am to help her solve her problems she will at the very least have to cooperate with me!" Then for no reason I could think of, I heard myself mutter as I turned away, "And your cooperation would also be greatly appreciated, Your Sovereign Majesty!"

Honestly, I thought, shaking my head and commencing dressing, *what nonsense will I be into next?*

The previous night I had worn my good dark blue silk. For

today, my twenty-fifth birthday (something of a milestone, a quarter of a century), I had a new dress. It was only cotton, but of a fine hand, polished like satin, in an amber color that brought out the red in my hair rather nicely. Michael would like that, I knew. *And Father would like Michael,* I thought. *If only* . . . but then I nipped that train of thought in the bud, as being unprofitable.

My amber dress had a round collar of heavy ecru lace. To wear with it I had earrings of real amber in a teardrop shape; one of them had a tiny spider trapped inside. You could only see that it was a spider beneath a magnifying glass. I rather liked the idea of wearing a spider dangling from my earlobe.

I ate a solitary breakfast, for Frances did not appear, and I was not in the mood to call and wake her. I wanted only for the time to pass so that I could be with my father again. I had the oddest feeling. . . . Another unprofitable thought, which I likewise pushed away. I went into the office, sat at my old desk, and wrote a note of detailed instructions for Edna Stephenson. Included was an alert: I expected to bring Father back here before the day was over. He would not want to go back to Boston, I was sure, without having seen where I live and work.

The lavender shawl was the best I owned, and so I wore it when I left the house, although it would not have been my first choice to go over an amber dress. I should much have preferred a darker color, but the black shawl was entirely too disreputable, and I had not had a coat or a cape for ever so long. Would Father notice that I was without certain, shall we say, wardrobe essentials? Probably not. He had never been too interested in the subject of women's clothing, though he shared my dislike for those elaborate concoctions most women like to put on their heads.

I walked uphill to Broadway, and then down Broadway toward Van Ness, a bit of a hike but it felt good. The sunlight fell thin and thready through the fog; the more I walked the more the golden threads burst through, until, by the time I had obtained a cable car for the ride down Powell Street, the sun was shining in earnest.

So, I thought, smiling as I descended gracefully from the cable car directly in front of the Hotel St. Francis, *my birthday will be a sunny one after all. It is a good omen.*

It all went by entirely too fast, and seemed to be over almost before it began. Success, whirlwind, both: that was my twenty-fifth birthday. Father gave me another watch, this one lavaliere-style on a chain, for which I thanked him profusely. He hung the watch about my neck, right there in his hotel room, as he was finishing up a breakfast brought him by room service. On the tray I noted the remains of dry toast, coffee with cream and sugar, and half a grapefruit all nicely segmented, with a cherry in the center, which remained untouched.

Then we left the hotel and went to the Bank of San Francisco. I thought at first this was only a courtesy call, as my father is himself a banker and knows others all over not only this country but the world; but I soon learned I was wrong.

They had known we were coming. Heads turned as Father announced himself in a voice with just the right edge and hint of command to make it carry. Deference was shown through a certain modicum of bowing and scraping.

And when we left half an hour later, the bowing and the scraping were being done for me, Fremont Jones, holder of a new account in this establishment—a new account containing more money than I had ever in my wildest dreams thought would be mine. Certainly I had not known, nor would it ever have occurred to me to inquire, the extent of my father's wealth. When I was living at home, I'd taken all that for granted. With some amazement, as I signed paper after paper acknowledging the transfer of funds, I realized that being largely without money for the past couple of years had taught me its true value.

"This represents a little less than half your inheritance," Father had said, taking my hand and tucking it into the crook of his arm as we left the bank, "the discrepancy having been caused by the fact that I had to sell some stock in order to come up with the cash amount, and the price of that stock fluctuated downward that particular day. The other half of the inheritance is to be yours upon my death."

"But what of Augusta?" I'd blurted out the question, when I should—had I thought about it—have restrained myself.

"She is also to be provided for. But nothing is to go to her many relatives, including that son, who is a ne'er-do-well if ever I saw one."

"Son?" This was the first I'd heard of a son.

"Yes," Father said with a hint of bitterness. "I didn't find out about him until near the end of that first idyllic year with Augusta. He has been like a plague upon us ever since. But let us talk no more of him, as I have only this one day with you."

So the day had gone on, its highlight a visit to the double house at Divisadero Street, Wish and his mother a great hit—Edna thankfully on her best behavior, and Frances nowhere in sight. Father's only comment that could be construed as negative was: "Well, Fremont, now that you have some of your inheritance, you will be able to complete the furnishing of your apartment." To which I'd merely nodded. But then that night, once again unable to really sleep, I'd wandered around half fantasizing, half planning what I should buy. After, of course, buying my half of the house outright from Michael. How good that would feel!

Now, at seven o'clock in the morning on April 11, I stood on the dock at the Embarcadero with Leonard Pembroke Jones, waiting for the ferry that would take him to Oakland and the train back to Boston . . . and a part of me was filled with sorrow and gloom and a horrible foreboding that I would never see him again.

Of course I could not tell him that.

"You're awfully quiet, daughter," he said, looking over at me.

Since we are nearly the same height, our eyes met on the level. "It's not like you," he added.

I smiled. "No, it isn't."

"The life here suits you, it would seem."

"Yes. I do love San Francisco. But I didn't realize until seeing you again how much I've missed you, Father. I'm sorry you have to go so soon."

"So am I, dear heart. So am I." My father could be affectionate on occasion, but never demonstrative in public, and so I was surprised when he reached out, put his arm around my shoulders, and drew me close.

"There was only one thing missing from our visit," he said, very quietly.

"And what was that, Father?"

"Your friend Michael. Your partner. I'm truly sorry I was not able to meet him. I suspect he is more than just a friend and business partner to you."

"Why, what makes you say that?"

"Any number of little things that have come to my attention over the past few years. If nothing else, the persistence with which he remains in your life. How many years older than you is this man?"

"Roughly, um, twenty," I answered truthfully.

"You're my daughter, I know you. I watched you grow up, don't forget. I've seen how the older men were the ones who interested you most, and you them, while you treated the boys your own age like brothers. Finally, my dear, there is the expression on your face whenever his name is mentioned, and the unusual blush that overcame your composure that first night when I asked after him. So tell me now, for I'll be leaving soon; has he asked you to marry him?"

As he asked that so touchy question, Father's grip on my shoulder tightened. I was going to have to deal with this, I could not escape it, and so Michael's leaving, all the days and nights alone, had been for nought. I bit my lip briefly, drew in my breath, and answered: "Yes. He has. But I have refused. I do not wish to marry, Father. You know that. I do not wish it now any more than I did when I was living at home with you. Though of course my home is here now."

"Yes, I have seen that it is, and a clever arrangement it is, too. One must assume that you and Michael get along well, to live and work in such proximity."

I nodded, and turned a bit toward Father so that I could better see his face. What was he getting at?

"You are in love with him, and apparently he is with you, or he would not be asking you to marry. Yet you will not do it. Why, Caroline?"

I ignored Father's inadvertent use of my first name; under the circumstances that was the most unimportant thing he'd said. "I don't believe in marriage. I told you that long ago, and it hasn't changed. J-just because I've found the man I love, who loves me, doesn't mean my beliefs have changed a bit." My chin went up reflexively, defensively.

Father's eyes went soft; he removed his arm from around me and with the back of that hand he stroked my cheek. "My little girl," he said, almost in a whisper, "I would like to see you married before I die."

My voice stuck in my throat. Something very painful, and inevitable, something that had been growing there since I'd first seen how much Father had physically changed, cracked my heart.

"Think about it. That's all I ask," Father said.

A sudden gust of wind off the Bay stirred my skirts and tugged at his bowler hat. The thrum-thrum of the approaching ferry's motor filled my ears, and tears filled my eyes. Wordlessly I reached for my father and embraced him, he with one arm around me and one hand removing the wayward hat from his head, then that arm around me too, and both my arms about his neck.

"Daddy," I said, the childhood name I had given up with a

certain scorn in adolescence, "Daddy!" I did not want ever to let him go, couldn't think how I'd been able to bring myself to leave him all those years ago.

"Caroline, my only child."

I pulled away. Though tears streamed uncontrollably down my face, there was something I had to ask. I knew by the bustle all around us that the ferry had pulled into the dock but my focus was only on Father. I asked the question: "Am I a great disappointment to you?"

"Ah, no. You're unique. You are yourself, Fremont, as you've always been. I wouldn't want you to be any different. Closer, perhaps, not so many miles away—but not different." He managed a smile, though it was as difficult for him as it was for me.

But I smiled too, even through my tears.

"I will come and see you," I said, "in a few months, in Boston. Now that I have the means there is no reason why I should not travel. I'm grateful for what you've done, Father."

He tucked my hand into his arm once more and we joined the end of the queue for the ferry. "It's my very great pleasure to see you set up now as a woman of means in your own right. I know you will use the money wisely. And I hope you'll think on what I said."

"About Michael?"

"Yes."

"Father, I will."

I stood waving at that ferry until long after the people on deck, Father included, were no longer discernible to me. I still had the most awful feeling that I would never see him again.

TWENTY-FIVE

Will-o'-the-Wisp

"OO LA-LA!" said Edna Stephenson, waving her hand in front of her face like a fan, "your father is handsome, Fremont. And he seems like such a nize man. Pity he couldn't stay longer. Your mother's passed on, you said?"

I could see the wheels turning behind Edna's bright little eyes, and it didn't take much deduction or imagination to know which way her thoughts were headed. "That's right, Edna, but Father married again the same year I came out to San Francisco. Which is why he couldn't stay longer. His wife needs him at home." *Wants* him at home was more like it, but I didn't like to imply that Augusta's every wish had to be my father's command. Sometimes I wondered, though.

I changed the subject by asking: "Where are the others?"

Edna rocked back and forth in her desk chair, swinging her feet, which as usual did not quite reach the floor. "Let's see," she said contentedly, "Aloysius has gone off to work on that special project of his, whatever it is, he never will say. So mysterious he is, sometimes. Oh well, but what's a mother to do when he's a good boy otherwise? And your friend Miss Frances—well, I know she's Mrs. McFadden, but the way she's acting, sure as I'm born you never could tell she was a married woman—well, she's gone out somewheres. Just breezed right on by without a word, she did." Edna stopped rocking, leaned back in the chair, raised her eyebrows, and gave me a wise-old-owl look. "She looked mighty sharp in her new clothes. Mighty sharp. Peach-colored, her dress was today. Lotsa lace. Nize. Too bad her manners isn't."

"Um-hm," I nodded. I went over and sat at Wish's desk, thinking. I remembered that peach-colored dress, which had indeed been remarkably becoming to Frances's skin and hair coloring. "We shall have to do something about Frances," I said, "but exactly what, I do not know. I'm not sure she's safe here in the City. If I had relatives in the country, or even just an acquaintance with whom she could stay, I swear I'd send her out of town."

"Dunno as she'd go."

Good point, I thought. The telephone rang, and Edna pounced on it, answering in her usual efficient fashion. When it came to business, she was all business. I did hope Michael would be pleased with her. And then, with a glow of pleasure, I realized that if he were not it would scarcely matter. I could pay Edna myself now! Of course, one would prefer to pay her out of profits, but if lean times persisted . . .

"Oh my, yes," said Edna into the telephone, "I'm sure Miss Jones would like to speak with you, but she's in conference with a client at the moment. Will you give me the number where she can ring you back?"

I frowned mightily, shook my head, and started to get up and cross the room to take the telephone, but Edna motioned me back down with a firmness that would not be brooked. What was going on?

"Oh, well now, dear, that is a problem, isn't it? Because I just can't interrupt her, it wouldn't be fair to the client who's already here and paying for her time. You can see that, now can't you? So why don't you just make an appointment yourself and come on down to our office on Divisadero Street? You know where it is? No? Well, I can give you direc—" She broke off and turned to me, beaming. "He rung off. Thought he would."

"I don't know why you're so proud of yourself. Sounds like you just lost us a customer." But a smile was tugging at the corners of my mouth. When Edna looked that pleased with something she'd done, it was always with good reason.

"That customer, dearie, is one you don't want to have to deal with. He was in-ee-bree-ayted, oh my, yes, he was! Let him sleep it off or work it off and then call back. That's for the best, I'm sure." She scooted her chair up to the desk in rapid, efficient little motions that I could not have duplicated no matter how hard I tried. "Now if there's nothing else, dearie, I've got some of your letters to type."

"Just one thing." I stood up, though I was myself uncertain as to what I should do next. "Who was that inebriated person on the phone?"

"Just that nazty man Higgins. Conrad or something. Ingrid Swann's husband that was. And a real mess he sounds like, too."

"Oh, Edna!" No longer amused, I could cheerfully have throttled her. "He might have had something important to tell me. I'm all at a loss on this case, it's simply impossible, and I had so much hoped to have it all nicely wrapped up by the time Michael came back!"

"Michael?" She snapped her head up and tossed me a very curious glance over her small shoulder. "Coming back? Any time soon? You've heard from him?"

"No, I haven't, but I know he was planning to come back after Father's visit." *And he will have found out how long Father stayed, I know he will, he has his ways, he's probably right here in the City even now. . . .* It gave me an odd feeling to think that my friend and lover might be somewhere nearby without my knowing. But then, I'd often had odd feelings about him in the past. The constancy and trust between us now was of much shorter duration than my former suspicions.

That was not a good direction for my thoughts to be running. I shook my head a little and said rather severely, "Edna, don't change the subject. I would have liked to speak to Conrad Higgins. You really should not have put him off like that!"

"Dearie, don't be annoyed with old Edna. Believe you me, you don't want to talk to anybody in the condition that body was in, and that's a fact. Can't trust anything they say when they're like that. Besides, he sounded like one of them as could be dangerous when they get likkered up, if you know what I mean."

"I suppose I do," I said reluctantly, "but in the future, I'd prefer that you let me decide these things for myself." I wandered slowly through the deep alcove and into the conference room; but then turned around and went back. "Did Mr. Higgins say what he wanted to talk to me about?"

Edna cast me an exasperated look. "He said he saw something would interest you. Hinted he wanted money before he'd tell. Likely it's nothing, Fremont. Just him wanting money. Nothing good a-tall."

She was probably right about that; still, I was feeling desperate enough that I'd have been willing to grasp at straws. I made some noncommittal sounds, for I didn't want her to think I had or had not forgiven her, and went on into the conference room. There I sat at the table that was now my desk, thinking, for much too long a time. I wasn't getting anywhere with this case I'd counted on to put us on the map, I was harboring a woman who had made someone angry enough that he'd tried to kill either me or her, my father was dying (or so I suspected), and I felt as if Michael had been away far too long . . . even though I really would have preferred to prove myself by solving the case before he returned, so I supposed I couldn't complain about that. I wanted to complain, though; I wanted to complain about everything.

Instead, I went upstairs and changed from the blue silk dress into my working costume of skirt and blouse—dark green and white respectively—and then I set out in search of Frances. I took the Maxwell, as I had a good idea where to find her and was inclined to waste no time about it.

Patrick Rule came to the door of the house that was now his, on Octavia Street. He appeared relaxed, well rested, without that haunted and haunting hollowness to his eyes.

"Good morning," I said, somewhat mollified by his undeniable handsomeness. "Is Frances here? If she is, kindly do not deny it, because I need to talk to you both."

He smiled, quite genuinely, one might say almost incandescently. "Yes, she's here. Do come in, Fremont. Did you know she's left her husband? They are to be divorced. Isn't that splendid?"

"I suppose that depends on how one looks at it," I replied, pausing in the vestibule while he closed the door behind me, "but I will say I'm glad she's not with Jeremy any longer. No matter what kind of reputation the man may have around town, I know he was harsh with her, and that sort of thing is never good."

"Certainly not. She and I are in my dear departed Abigail's private drawing room. It's toward the back of the house, if you'll follow me."

"Still," I persisted while I followed him down a short hall, "she is in a precarious position. She has no money, no means of any sort, which will be difficult for her. Jeremy has taken complete care of her since she was quite young, I believe."

Patrick turned around and stood blocking my way, looking

down at me, and said with quiet intensity, "She does not have to worry. I'll take her away from here, to the East. I'll work with Abigail's former contacts there, set up some private bookings for us. Frances is an excellent somnambulist, and beautiful besides—when working with the public that never hurts, you know—and we will do well. I'll take care of her now. She will want for nothing. You aren't going to stand in our way, are you, Fremont Jones?"

Like lightning the thought flashed through my mind: *But what if he is the one who killed Abigail, and Ingrid too?* Could a man look so relaxed and happy, and yet be guilty of such a heinous crime? Perhaps. Particularly if he had now gotten what he wanted, and so was enjoying himself.

"I won't stand in your way as you are now standing in mine," I said pointedly, poking him in the chest with my walking stick—I was not going anywhere these days without it—"but as for the rest, we shall see. As I said, there is something I need to discuss with you both. Shall we join Frances?"

"As you wish." He stood back and motioned me ahead of him with a bit of a flourish. "To your left."

I entered the room, which was something like a library but without so many books. There were shelves on one wall with only a few; but the room's main feature was a large round table in the very center, and at the table sat Frances McFadden with a map open before her, and something like a locket on a chain dangling from her hand.

"Oh, hello, Fremont!" She looked up at my approach. Though the inside of this house was gloomier than most, owing to the heavy curtains at seemingly every window (one supposed a medium like Abigail Locke would have wanted the means to shut out the light whenever she preferred), there was plenty of light from an electric chandelier overhead. In her peach dress, with her red-gold hair, Frances McFadden positively glowed in that light.

"I'm surprised to see you. I thought you'd be with your father again all day."

"He left this morning. I saw him off on the ferry. Whatever are you doing with that locket, Frances?"

"It's not a locket, it's a pendulum. I'm letting it choose the places I will visit clairvoyantly. It's great fun, and good practice, Patrick says. What are *you* doing here?"

Though I hadn't been invited, I sat down at the table, choosing a place near the windows from which I could see the door into the room. Patrick had not come in with me, he had disappeared into the bowels of the house somewhere, and that worried me. Not much, but a little. I said, "I was concerned about you when I found you weren't at home. At my house, that is. I seem to recall we had an agreement about your keeping out of sight. Someone may have tried to kill you, you know."

"Me? That's nonsense. It was your bed that got slashed. And besides, you weren't even worried that much yourself. You didn't even tell me until the next day. Anyhow, Wish says it wasn't anything personal to either of us. Most likely it was just a burglar who was angry that you didn't have any jewels or anything good to take."

I frowned. It is one thing to be charming and lighthearted, quite another to be irresponsible. "Wish and I were both trying to protect you, because we thought you had already been traumatized enough. The truth is, even though the intruder is not likely to return to Divisadero Street, he could conceivably follow you if you leave the house, Frances, and now you have led him here—"

"Where Patrick will take care of me!" She beamed, then turned her head to the door a fraction of a second before the man himself appeared there.

Egad! I thought. *She is so attuned to him she knows when he is about to enter a room.* Criminals or not, whether or not they had lied to me about not knowing each other previously, Frances and Patrick were most certainly in love now. Not only that, but he had already begun taking care of her, because he looked quite domestic, carrying a tray bearing cups, saucers, and a steaming pot of coffee.

"I really do not require refreshment," I protested, but quickly gave it up as a lost cause. Being forceful would get me nowhere with these two. I should have to be devious instead, and I might as well sit and drink coffee while planning exactly how to do that.

"Fremont, truly," Frances said while pouring out prettily, "Jeremy doesn't want me anymore. He won't waste any time on me now. He thinks I'm soiled. He'll just wash his hands of me, cast me off, get his divorce, and that will be an end of it where I'm concerned. I won't fight him, I don't want any of his dirty old tainted money. I want to be like you—I want to earn my own!"

Accepting a cup, I tried not to grimace. Frances was not exactly prepared to earn a living in the same way I had been prepared, but I couldn't tell her that. "You're sure about Jeremy? It strikes me that a man who was so possessive of you that he would physically hurt you, and lock up your clothes and so on—"

"That was before he thought I'd been with Patrick"—heightened color came up in her already rosy cheeks—"when he thought he was the only one who had ever, well, you know, touched me in that particular way. He said so, specifically. You remember. I told you that word he called me. It's as if I'm dirty to him now."

"Don't talk about yourself that way, dearest," Patrick said, reaching out and taking her hand. "You could never be *dirty*. Only the worst sort of mind would think so."

"You're so sweet," Frances said.

For the moment, I might as well not have been in the room, and that was fine with me. I had some thinking to do.

Suddenly I had it, an inspiration! Oh yes, a real, true, bonafide inspiration . . . and it came in the form of none other than the Emperor Norton himself. Just as I had seen him so recently in my dreams.

I got the lovers' attention by rapping on the table with my knuckles, and then I explained to them in some detail what I had in mind. Briefly, it was this: That they should give Frances's spirit mentor, the Emperor, his due. For if they did not, he might become angry, and then things would not go well. What the Emperor wanted (or so I said, and indeed I was convinced of it myself by the time I'd finished) was that Frances should take on the pursuit of his lost treasure. She herself, with Patrick along if she preferred, must follow the instructions he had set out in the automatic writing.

While they were doing that, I boldly stated (although I had no idea whatever how I would accomplish it), I should bring the investigation into the murders of the mediums to a successful close. After which both Patrick and Frances could leave San Francisco and go East with impunity.

Patrick took up my cause with alacrity. Apparently it made sense to him that the spirit of the Emperor, who was very real to Frances, might not otherwise take kindly to Patrick's whisking her away from him—as it were.

And so it happened that some twenty minutes later I, waiting just around the corner in the Maxwell, saw Frances and Patrick set off up Octavia Street and turn on the next corner up onto Green Street, walking toward Van Ness. Off on Emperor Norton's quest, no doubt, which might or might not be a wild goose chase.

While they were gone, I intended to be on a quest of my own. As soon as they were well out of sight, I left the auto, rummaging inside my leather bag for a hairpin as I walked back to the house they had just left.

I was not the least bit certain that the lock would yield to my amateurish ministrations, and reminded myself to talk to Michael again about getting a set of lock picks. Wish Stephenson had qualms about private investigators having tools not available to the police—and the police are not supposed to pick locks. Though why they do not do that, when they do any number of far worse things they are not supposed to do either, I could not imagine, nor did I waste my time trying. Still, Wish had a few of these pruderies that were truly annoying and restricting.

"Oh!" An involuntary, soft little cry escaped me when the hairpin suddenly engaged the tumblers in exactly the right sort of way and the lock clicked open as if by magic. Such a sweet, gratifying little sound. How nicely the door swung open.

I do love being in places where I am not really supposed to be, I admitted to myself as I entered the hall, taking care to close the door behind me. I wondered if Father would find that shocking or amusing.

Now, the question was, where to go first? I intended to search the house for Abigail Locke's belongings, looking for anything that might give a clue as to who had killed her. Of course, if Patrick had done it, he would have destroyed anything incriminating by now. But maybe not, one never knows.

Not having the slightest clue what I was looking for, it was hard even to begin to know where to look. I decided to search the downstairs first, as there are always more places to hide in bedrooms if one is about to be caught. There are wardrobes, cupboards, large chests, and in dire circumstances (as I had actually been once, in Michael's bedroom, of all places) if there is no time to find a better place, one can hide under the bed. Starting in the formal parlor, I looked everywhere that might provide a hiding place, or even just a container, for something else; and I found nothing of note. I did find a cache of money, in twenty-dollar gold pieces, inside a hideous ceramic vase on the top of an *étagère*. I wondered if Patrick knew it was there, if in fact he had put it there himself? Somehow I rather doubted that, and made a mental note to tell him before he and Frances set off—if they ever in fact did get to set off together. They could use that money.

Here I was thinking of helping them, while I was also looking for evidence to incriminate them. How disgusting! It just went to show the state of my confusion.

In the kitchen the most remarkable thing I found was a whole drawer full of mousetraps, which smelled of both mice and old cheese—*eeuw!* And in a funny, deep little drawer set into the clothes tree in the hall there was a cache of odd buttons, some of them quite beautiful and some of them odd indeed (such as three silver ones shaped like ducks). But nothing that had anything to do, even remotely, with anyone murdering anyone.

I was not really concerned about Patrick and Frances returning to the house any time soon, so I took my time upstairs. Patrick was not sleeping in the bedroom where Frances and I had found Abigail Locke's body, that was evident. In fact, he had kept it intact—if not exactly like a shrine, then certainly in pristine condition. Perhaps he simply didn't like to come into the room, which did have an eerie feel—or was that just my imagination, building upon the fact that I'd discovered the body there? Whatever it was, a shiver of the most unpleasant proportions raced down my spine as I crossed at the foot of that bed. I opened the wardrobe to find Abigail Locke's dresses—all in either white or cream, not a single bright or dark color among them—hanging there like little ghosts themselves.

At one point in searching that bedroom, I could have sworn I heard someone moaning: "Oooooooh!" Followed by the even worse sound of a long, outrushing sigh, as if that were their last breath on this earth. But I ignored it. At that point I was meticulously searching through a massive chest of drawers.

In a pale pink silk satin lingerie carrier, one of those that folds like a large flat envelope, tied with a braided silken coil, I found the letters. Not many, perhaps ten, and obviously treasured. I sat down on the bed, opened the first one, and read until I got to the signature: *Willie.*

Willie who?

TWENTY-SIX

Someone's Sleeping in My Bed

WISH STEPHENSON still had not returned to Divisadero Street when I got back myself in midafternoon. His mother was worried about him, but she clothed her worry in annoyance:

"I'd just like to know what he's thinking," Edna said, "off doing his own thing, not even a job that pays, when we've got all these calls coming in all of a sudden. It's irresponsible, that's what it is, and that's not like my boy at all, not a-tall!"

That perked my ears right up. "All these calls, Edna?"

"Oh yes, you just take a look at these messages, if you please. There's at least a dozen. I thought maybe if you'd sort through them, I could call back and start making appointments for you.

For Aloysius, too, if he'd just get on back here. You put 'em in order, Fremont, from the most important down to the least important. That way I'll know who to call first.''

"I'll be more than happy to do that," I agreed. I took the notes to my table-desk in the conference room and began to read and evaluate, which took longer than I had expected—especially when Edna began to return calls and set up the appointments. It was certainly a stimulating way to spend the last couple of hours of the workday.

Wish never did return. Unlike his mother, I did not think that was particularly remarkable; if anything, I saw his prolonged absence as a sign that things were finally moving on this mysterious private concern of his. I told his mother so, in an attempt to placate her that seemed to work. She did mumble, though, as she was getting ready to leave at the end of the day, about the likelihood of Wish showing up at home just in time for supper. Apparently this was something he had managed with a great deal of regularity when he was on the police force—even when he was working the four-to-midnight shift.

I had no sooner waved goodbye to Edna than Frances returned, and nothing would do but we must sit down and she must tell me every detail of the afternoon's wild goose chase on behalf of Emperor Norton. He had led the two of them on a lengthy trek indeed with his cryptic clues, taking them from downtown into the Western Addition, and finally out into the avenues. But at that point Frances and Patrick had decided to call it quits for the day. The avenues would have to wait for another time.

After that, it was too late to think of shopping and preparing dinner, so Frances and I went out to a little family-run Italian restaurant in North Beach where I'd been several times before, with Michael. I was able to persuade the owner to seat us at an inconspicuous table—not so much because I cared what anyone would think of two young women dining alone, but because I was concerned about either or both of us being recognized. I wasn't entirely convinced that the intruder with the knife had given up on us. I wasn't unduly worried, just cautious, carrying my walking stick with its concealed blade just in case.

All the way back home after dinner I kept feeling as if I'd forgotten something, yet I didn't know what it was. Frances chattered on about her plans with Patrick, and I replied by rote, only half listening; my role with her at the moment appeared to be to advise her to wait, wait, wait. Otherwise she would run off with Patrick tomorrow, begin living with him without benefit of matrimony, and so on. I did think she should have her own lawyer for the divorce proceedings, but I kept this opinion to myself, because I knew Frances did not have money of her own to pay a lawyer. And I was not prepared to pay one for her, because I really had begun to mistrust her a bit.

On arriving back at Divisadero Street, Frances went straight to what she was now calling "my room" though it was, of course, Michael's, and after cautioning her to lock all the doors and windows and keep them that way, I went straight to mine. I still had that waiting-for-the-other-shoe-to-drop feeling, without any idea what it might mean.

I was tired, so tired that I washed my face and brushed out my hair and got into my nightgown without even thinking of the long hot bath that was my usual way of unwinding at the end of the day. Before I knew it, I had fallen into a deep, dreamless sleep.

It was as I imagine coming back from the dead would be: Fighting one's way back to consciousness; swimming up as it were from the lower depths through water thick and cold as marble; splitting the surface finally, only to find not light and air but perpetual night.

Had I died? Was this the Abyss of Hell?

"Ssshhh!" a voice whispered. And in that moment a hand came over my mouth to stop the scream that had begun to climb into my throat.

He was behind me. In the bed, on my new mattress, the man

had tucked himself up right behind me, and I couldn't see a thing. I could only hear his breathing. And the terrified pounding of my own heart.

I felt an obscene softness, the moistness of lips grazing the nape of my neck, and I tried again to scream; tried to twist my own lips against his restraining palm so that I could bite the hand that stopped my voice. It was then I heard the chuckle. . . .

And recognized it. Or thought I did. Michael chuckled like that, with a hint of irony that could sometimes sound a bit wicked, or evil. Surely this *was* Michael, and not the intruder returned? I stopped struggling, went quite still, but not yet limp, listening with all my might. Inside my bedroom it was pitch-black; I myself had closed the blinds although the room was on the second floor and there was no way for anyone to see in—at least not well. I had done this because the intruder had seriously spooked me, but now I wished I had the light.

At last the man behind me in my bed did something, touched me in a special way, by which I knew that, without a doubt, he was Michael. He let go of me then, too, and I turned over and opened my arms to him.

Instantly I was caught up in a rush of joy and desire, and I put all of that into saying his name: "Michael!"

He kissed me, very thoroughly, before saying anything at all. Then he said, "Dearest, I know you missed me, but you didn't have to provide me with such a magnificent gift on my return."

"What are you talking about?" I asked contentedly, not really expecting an answer or caring if I got one. I was far too happy. I was almost purring.

"There's a woman in my bed," Michael said, "a gorgeous woman—who isn't you. I'm sure of it. I checked. This is you, Fremont, right . . . here!"

I giggled, but not for long, because passion overcame me; and it was a long, long time later that I thought to ask what Michael had meant by saying he'd checked on Frances. He assured me then that she was a sound sleeper, and that he'd done nothing more than look. I believed him, of course.

"Fremont," Michael said as we had our breakfast not in the usual place when we were together, his dining room, but in the office kitchen, "why does the house require watching? And further, if it must be watched, don't you think it would make more sense to hire someone than to saddle one of our own investigators with such a duty?"

"Hmm?" I was busy licking strawberry jam off my fingers. "I'm not sure what you're talking about. We did have a break-in a few nights ago. Didn't you notice the mattress on my bed is new? It's very comfortable, don't you think?"

A huge grin claimed Michael's face and made him look, momentarily, like a mischievous boy—in spite of his handsome beard. "Any bed with you in it is supremely comfortable, my dear," he said, "but that has nothing to do with the mattress." The grin disappeared. "Tell me about this break-in."

I gave him the official police version, that it had likely been a burglar who vented his frustration at the lack of things to burgle on my pillows and mattress stuffing. "I was never in any danger," I assured him; and then I went on to tell about how I'd screamed like a Fury and booted the intruder out the door, which soon had Michael laughing again.

"All right," he said when finally the laughter subsided, "but what about poor Wish? He can't work all day and watch the house all night."

"I didn't know he was watching the house. I assure you, Michael, I never asked him to do such a thing. That's ridiculous! Do you suppose he's out there now? Let's bring him in and talk to him. Where can he have gotten such an idea? It's crazy!"

Michael went outside to get Wish . . . and returned without him. "I suppose," he said, rubbing the silver streaks at the side of his beard, as he does when he's deep in thought, "with the dawn his vigil was over."

"Well," I said, looking up from the section of *The Chronicle* I was reading, "when he comes in today I'll have a talk with him about his self-appointed vigil. It's unnecessary, and I don't particularly appreciate it even though I'm sure he meant well, and I'll tell him so."

In the quiet time we had left, I told Michael about my father's visit. I told him everything, except Father's expressed wish to see me married. Perhaps I would also tell him that in time. For the present I submitted with good grace to being teased about my new status as an heiress.

"You'll be out on your own," Michael said. "You won't need this old man anymore for anything."

"I will always need this old man for certain things," I replied, putting my hand into Michael's lap beneath the table, "because there are certain things a woman just can't do for herself."

However, they can be done while sitting in a chair, particularly if one's skirts are wide enough . . . which was something I had never thought of before. It is always inspirational to learn new things.

Wish Stephenson came in with his mother at the usual time. Edna was as bouncy as ever, but her son looked awful. In fact, to me he looked even more awful than the loss of a night's sleep could possibly account for.

"Michael is back," I announced to them both as we assembled around the very same kitchen table that had seen some interesting doings not too long before. "He had some business at the bank and wanted to get to it first thing, but he'll be here soon. You'll finally get to meet him, Edna. Wish, I guess you've seen him already?"

Wish nodded slowly. His eyes were bloodshot, and he moved his head as if it had become a burden to his neck. I soon realized he didn't intend to comment, the nod was all we were going to get.

That earnest face looked ten years older than the last time I'd seen him. I shot a quick glance at Edna, who was already looking straight at me, and as our eyes met she raised her eyebrows as if to say, *Who knows?* and shrugged. Of course she had noticed the difference in him, how could a mother not notice something like that?

I decided to talk to him about it right then and there, in front of her. Perhaps if he would not open up to me, he would for his own mother; at any rate, I needed to know what was going on. So I asked, I probed, he evaded and denied . . . until finally I thought to say: "It must be something to do with that special project of yours, though how that can have gotten tied up in your mind with the necessity to watch this house is beyond me."

Wish looked at me with a suddenly keener comprehension, as if a bit of fog had lifted from inside his tired brain. "It's all part of the same picture, don't you see, Fremont? Life and death. That's what we deal in after all, that's our stock in trade."

"Aloysius, I declare, sometimes you give me the willies! Lemme out of here. I'm going back to my desk with the nize telephone and talk to somebody sane for a change."

"Willies!" I exclaimed, jumping up: "Willie! That's what I forgot! You must excuse me, please, I'll be right back. . . ."

When I jumped up, Wish stood immediately. "Where are you going? I'll go with you."

"Don't be silly. I'm going upstairs to my apartment, and you're not invited. Stay here with your mother, help her make some appointments for you. We had a dozen calls yesterday—think of it, Wish, a dozen all in one day! It never rains but it pours." Even as I said this I was on my way toward the back stairs, as from the kitchen they were so much closer.

With one long arm, still seated, Wish barred my way. "I think I should stay with you. It might not be safe. The . . . the intruder might have come back."

"In daylight? Inside my house where I haven't even been alone since Michael's return? I don't think so." Gently I removed Wish's arm, pushing it away, but he resisted with surprising strength.

"I should stay with you," he repeated.

I gazed down at him, exasperated, yet touched in spite of myself by this doglike devotion. "I will only be upstairs," I said softly, and because I was feeling kind and we were alone, I bent and lightly kissed the top of his head, adding: "I won't go anywhere. I'll be back down presently, and I think you should stay in the office with your mother. What if Michael returns before I'm back down? I haven't yet told him about your mother—she'll need you to do the honors, make the introduction."

Wish frowned, and for a moment seemed confused in a rather childlike way, but then he touched the top of his head where I'd kissed it and smiled, like his usual self. "You're right, I should do that. My mother's so in awe of Michael Kossoff, she would probably faint dead away if one of us weren't there to back her up when he comes through the door for the first time."

I laughed, greatly relieved, said, "Get on with you then," and ran lightly up the back stairs. I had not felt so lighthearted in weeks. Not only was Michael back, and Wish's aberration seemed to have been cured with one tiny kiss on the head (maybe he'd been bewitched, like the prince who was a frog, or vice versa?), but also I had a clear and welcome premonition: I was going to solve the case of the murdered mediums, and I was going to do it this very day! I could feel the excitement flowing right along with the blood through my veins and arteries, like a mighty river. I wouldn't tell Michael, I'd take Wish with me—that would please Wish since he wanted to stay close anyway—and my resolution of this case before the day was ended would be the best welcome-home present I could possibly give my partner, the other half of the J&K Agency. The other half of my heart.

I knew, oh yes, I knew with a certainty, even before I'd read the rest of those letters, even before I could piece together all the wheres and hows and whys, who Willie was. Willie, the signer of those letters hidden in Abigail Locke's lingerie case, which had lain folded at the bottom of my leather bag, forgotten . . . until now.

"You gotta admit," Edna sighed, with her hands clasped over her round middle, "those two will get around you, will get around most anything, after a while."

She referred to Patrick and Frances, who had just left together, determined to pick up Emperor Norton's trail where they had left it off the day before, out in the Richmond District. "We want his blessing," Frances had explained, her face aglow, "and if together we find what the Emperor has lost, he will give it, I know he will. I can feel it."

"Yes," Patrick had nodded, "it would be unlucky for us to proceed with our arrangements otherwise. We have you to thank for recognizing that, Fremont, and insisting on our doing this."

"It was nothing." I'd shrugged modestly. Indeed, on my part it had only been an urge to get rid of them both so I could search Mrs. Locke's house that had motivated me. If, however, the mesmerist and the somnambulist wanted to assign to my actions a higher place in the cosmic order of things, who was I to disagree?

And so off they'd gone, Frances wearing another of the new dresses we'd put on her husband's account—this one a thin, light wool in a delicious shade of mauve, with a matching waist-length jacket of slightly heavier material—and Patrick long and lean and handsome in spite of his rather threadbare suit. I had a feeling, watching them through the window as they proceeded up the sidewalk, that Patrick would not be threadbare much longer. Perhaps today they would discover a real treasure left by Emperor Norton. There were those, both in the Emperor's lifetime and since, who thought he had not lost his millions by squandering them on all that rice, but rather that he had cannily hidden the money and then, in his madness, had been unable to recall where it was.

Wouldn't it be something if I caught a murderer and Frances and Patrick found a treasure, both on the same day?

I shook off that thought just as the two star-crossed lovers turned the corner and went out of sight. Then I turned my own attention toward Edna Stephenson and proceeded to give her detailed instructions on how to introduce herself to Michael when he arrived. She was intimidated; she said she couldn't possibly do it.

"Nonsense!" I upbraided her. "Of course you can. He won't bite. And besides, you have to. Wish and I are going to catch a killer, and we aren't telling you where, because if we do, Michael will get it out of you, and we don't want him to know. We want this to be a great, wonderful surprise for him."

"Well, I like that!" said Edna huffily. "A body'd think she wasn't appreciated around here. I'll have you to know I've done my share, and kept things confidential, and proved I can be trusted. Aloysius, I don't like you going anywhere your mama doesn't know where you are. Fremont, I'm surprised at you."

"Mama, you don't understand. Fremont's right, she knows what's best. We don't want Michael coming after us," Wish said, with a firmness I'd seldom heard him use to his mother.

"We'll be perfectly safe. The killer has no idea we know anything about him, he will be alone and probably unarmed, whereas both Wish and I have our weapons with us. Not to mention that your son is police-trained to handle just exactly this kind of situation. Really, we'll be fine." I had my walking stick, and Wish had his Colt revolver—I had made sure of that.

"That's right, Mama. Perfectly safe," Wish said like an echo. He was being entirely agreeable. I had not yet told him any details, he had no idea yet where we were going, but none of that seemed to bother him in the least, as long as we went together.

"Michael won't eat you, he's not an ogre. Just tell him he'll have to deal with me if he's not nice to you, and I said so," I teased.

"Humph!" said Edna, with her little nose in the air, but her eyes twinkled. She might protest, whine, and carry on, but she'd do fine.

I gave her a hug while her son stood by fidgeting, and by ten o'clock in the morning he and I were off on what I was sure would be an extremely profitable errand.

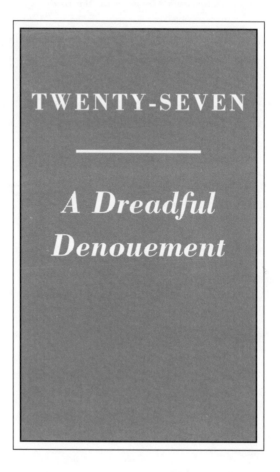

TWENTY-SEVEN

A Dreadful
Denouement

BRIEFED WISH along the way. It was a bright day, not clear
but with a high overcast of white cloud cover that gave a
pearly sheen to the cityscape; and nearly windless, on the warm
side. We could have walked down Van Ness and across to catch
the cable car, but I was in a hurry. I had no patience for peripatet-
ics this morning. So on Van Ness we hailed an auto-taxi, and I
gave the driver the Larkin Street address of Dr. William Van Zant.

Wish stared at me whenever he thought I wasn't looking; otherwise he pretended to gaze out the car window. I couldn't understand his lack of animation; he seemed most unlike himself, except for the way he watched me. Really, this excessive
attentiveness had gone too far. I must not tease Wish anymore, or

play with him, or encourage him further. Doglike devotion is a bit much for me. If I wanted that, I should get a dog. From my friends I want only simple friendship.

When the taxi pulled up in front of those steps I remembered well from my other visits, I reached deep into my leather bag, came out with a couple of bills for the fare, and automatically steeled myself to have the usual argument with Wish about a woman paying her own business expenses.

This time, though, he did not argue. He simply exited the door on his own side, went around and opened mine, and stood there waiting for me to get out. He continued to stand there as I mounted the first two steps, then turned and looked back at him. Wish was so tall that standing two steps up brought me just slightly above his height.

"What are you waiting for?" I asked, slightly exasperated. "This is where I need your assistance, you know. Van Zant is much bigger than I am, and if I'm right about what he's done—"

"I don't think you should go in there, Fremont!" The words burst from Wish's lips explosively, and almost in the same instant he clapped his hand over his mouth, as if horrified that he'd uttered them. Well, of course he would be; he knew how I felt about anyone, even Michael, giving me orders. Especially in the last stages of solving a case.

"Nonsense," I replied, "come on in, if you please. And keep that Colt of yours within easy reach at all times. You may need to draw on Van Zant before this morning is out. In fact, I expect you will."

Such foot-dragging I had never seen from Wish. He came up the steps one at a time; and even then I had to open the front door myself, for the both of us. I practically had to drag him by the hand to the door of Van Zant's apartment.

The self-styled psychologist was a long time in answering his door. I rang three times; then put my ear to the solid wood and listened. I couldn't hear a sound from within, but that could have been because the door was of good-quality, thick wood.

I glanced back over my shoulder at Wish. "Do you think we might pick this lock? I suppose we could find some evidence inside. It's possible. Of course it isn't exactly legal, but it would give us something to do until the doctor returns."

Wish rubbed at his ear. He appeared distressed. "N-no. I, uh, I think I know where he is. I-I-I'll take us there. We should have kept the taxi. Now we'll have to find another, or else it will take too long, and it's likely to be too late. . . ."

"Too late for what?" I asked, baffled, as Wish grabbed my hand and hustled me out into the blue-draped vestibule, out the door, down the steps.

"I'll take you to him. That will be best. The best thing. The right thing to do," Wish said again. He walked fast, and as his legs were long I had difficulty keeping up with him. We went up Larkin to California Street, where there was more traffic, and a couple of hotels that drew taxis to them like flies. We had no difficulty finding another auto-taxi then.

Wish gave the address this time, and I recognized it. I suppose I might not have, if it had not been that my mind was in that state of heightened clarity that I have learned comes with a certain amount of perceived danger. The address was a piece of unfinished, and temporarily forgotten, business that related directly to Dr. William Van Zant. It was indeed the very address the doctor himself had given me for Ngaio Swann, Ingrid's supposed brother.

"How do you know that address?" I asked Wish.

"It's in the Richmond," he said.

"So? Do you know who lives there?"

"No, not really, at least I don't think so. But it's in the Richmond, that's—well, that's how I, I guess I just . . . found it."

"Honestly, Wish, you say that as if the house were just sitting there, lost, out on the street, and you happened to stumble across it. Really! You're not being at all clear, you know."

He shot me a quick, worried glance and then returned to looking avidly out the taxi window. At least he'd regained some animation. He said: "I've gotten to know the Richmond in the past few weeks. Spent a lot of time there, seen and heard a lot of things. Things I haven't been able to tell anybody yet. And now I—" Wish passed his hand across his forehead, in a gesture that gave me a chill, because it was so reminiscent of one I'd seen Patrick use on Frances when he was putting her into her somnambulistic trance. "—I want to tell you . . . but at the same time . . . I think I'd better not. Not . . . yet."

"That must create a dilemma," I remarked acerbically.

"Yes, I guess it does," Wish said in his old agreeable way.

His dilemma seemed to have put him in charge, though; for without hesitation he reached into the pocket of his trousers and paid the driver when we reached our destination.

This area had been countryside until not too many years ago, and its development was still uneven. We left the taxi in front of a row of attached townhouses that looked fairly new, modern, and in good condition though painted a boring beige; yet just a block or so away there were houses that looked like little more than tumbledown shacks.

I was unpleasantly reminded of the day we had come out here to look for the graves that were not there. The very air felt the same; there was the same sense of desolation and dislocation. I wanted to ask how far we were from that cemetery, but the question most likely would have set Wish off into the obsession that had deranged his mind—or so I privately thought—in the first place.

"It happened here, too, you know," Wish volunteered, looking down earnestly at me. "And she saw it, she knew, she came and told me."

"She . . . ?"

"In—uh, Indigo. The woman who lives there. Dr. Van Zant's friend."

"Not Indigo, Wish, that's not what you mean. Her name is Ngaio."

"No," he shook his head vigorously, "Indigo. Like the color. It means blue. She told me herself. That other name, it was a stage name. She was supposed to be a man, it was supposed to look better that way. You know, because a woman is supposed to be escorted, there were places she couldn't go without a man and so Indigo became a man. She's very tall. She told me all about it."

We were standing out on an expanse of packed dirt that I presumed would one day become a sidewalk, having this bizarrely significant conversation, yet all I could think was that Wish's mind was not working right. Something was wrong with him, and I didn't know quite what it was, or how to get at it, or how much help he was going to be to me now. If the answer to the last question were, as I began to fear, not much—well, I was in trouble.

On the other hand, I was learning a lot, and we hadn't even found Van Zant yet. I decided to stop worrying, take my time, and go fishing in Wish Stephenson's mind.

"Who?" I asked forcefully. "Who was Indigo taking care of in this unusual fashion?"

"Her sister. But her sister's gone away now. Indigo is waiting for her to come back."

"The name, Wish, the sister's name!"

"I don't know. She never told me. She just . . . ." To my great surprise my seemingly innocent young policeman friend's face flushed a mottled red, but only briefly, as if by an act of will he could turn it on and off. "She was lonely. But she couldn't leave in case her sister came back, and she walked the neighborhood all the time for something to do, so she knew what was going on. She's my source, Fremont. Only now *he's* got her."

"He got both of them, didn't he?" I muttered under my breath. I did not mean Ngaio and Ingrid, I meant both mediums. Van Zant's connection with Abigail Locke was in those letters: "Willie" was none other than William Van Zant. I was sure of it, and I intended to make him admit it. He had fallen in love with Abigail, courted her up and down the Eastern seaboard some five and six years ago, only to have her ultimately reject him. I surmised William Van Zant's debunking activities, his presumed so pure interest in science had begun then, in reaction to his ego's having been dealt the blow of rejection by this tiny girl-woman in white. Abigail had kept those letters as evidence, or perhaps she had tried to use them to insure that he would leave her alone. Those letters were at first amorous but later they turned ugly, threatening. Had he killed her to get them back, and simply been unable to find them? Or had it been a crime of passion, a once lost love rediscovered, only to experience rejection again, and he'd snapped? Could I make him tell?

How the man had connected with Ingrid Swann was harder to say, though he had admitted that he'd come west precisely in order to do his own kind of debunking on her. But why kill her? What had she done? Did she reject him too?

Wish and I had stood there in front of that house for perhaps five whole minutes, each of us quiet, preoccupied for different reasons. Just as I was about to suggest we leave and return with police backup, my friend and colleague drew his Colt revolver.

"Good!" I said approvingly but in a low voice. "We may have need of that, but not yet, I think. I propose we get out of here and come back with some of your friends from the police. Some of the more honest ones, not open to, shall we say, influence."

To my absolute horror, my friend and colleague, Mr. Straight Arrow, the only innocent policeman in a morass of corruption (or such had been his reputation), turned his gun on *me!*

"Hey!" I protested. "Wish? That's not funny."

"Not meant to be," he said grimly. "We're not going anywhere. You're coming inside that house with me, right now. You wanted to see Dr. Van Zant, and he told me to watch you, not to let you out of my sight, and to shoot you if I had to, to keep you from doing anything foolish."

Wish had walked right up to me as he spoke, and now we stood only about a foot apart, with the long barrel of that Colt grazing my breasts. I looked him in the eyes. "My friend, what has he done to you? Did he hypnotize you, is that it? Against your will? But I heard that can't be done, you can't hypnotize someone against their will."

A cultured voice came from somewhere in the vicinity of my right shoulder, saying, "That is not so. I can hypnotize anybody. Even you, Fremont Jones."

Turning my head, I saw Van Zant at the top of the porch steps before one of the beige houses. Wish had a desperate, trapped expression on his face. "Indigo?" he said in a pathetic voice.

Van Zant sniggered. "Your precious Indigo is in here. Bring Miss Jones with you and come on inside. We must offer her the same hospitality we have given Indigo, mustn't we?"

"Go, Fremont, move. He means it," Wish said under his breath, and for a moment I thought he was only pretending to be under the influence of William Van Zant. I fancied that Wish would suddenly gather himself together and become a hero of legendary proportions. This was because I couldn't quite see what I was going to do, how I was going to get out of this alone.

But then I got a good look at Wish Stephenson's eyes, and it was like looking in at somebody else, a non-Wish, looking out from inside his head. Decidedly an eerie sensation. "I'm going, I'm going," I croaked, my voice breaking with strain.

"Where is she?" Wish demanded as soon as we'd crossed the threshold into the modest house. "I must see her!"

"In a moment," said Van Zant. "First we should talk to your friend Fremont and find out what she knows."

"I know a good deal more than you probably think I do," I said, on the theory that the best defense is a good offense. One learns these things playing field hockey at Wellesley; field hockey is much more of a blood sport than one might think, especially as played by women when there are no men around to interfere. But I digress. Returning to the point, I went on: "For example, I suggest that you not consider doing anything rash to my person, because I have in my possession—though not *on* my aforementioned person—certain letters you wrote to Abigail Locke."

"You have them? I don't believe it. Move, go on down the hall, back that way, to the kitchen. Mr. Stephenson, for God's sake do try not to be so clumsy!"

Wish had tripped over a clothes tree and sent it crashing to the floor. He did not, however, lose control of his gun—not even for a minute; and the gun was still trained on me, not on William Van Zant. I had no choice but to keep moving in the direction of the kitchen.

"Yes, indeed, I do have your letters," I said, deliberately provocative. "You must not have looked very hard. You gave up too soon. What happened, was killing Abigail more difficult than you'd thought it would be? Did you lose heart? Or is it just that your physical condition is poor and so you ran out of energy? Which is it, Dr. Van Zant?"

"There is nothing wrong with my physical condition," he said defensively, "and furthermore I think you're lying. There was nothing resembling a packet of letters in that whole house. I looked, I virtually combed through every inch of it, and I didn't have to rush. She was dead, she couldn't bother me, could she? And that dandy of hers, that hanger-on, Mr. Charming and Debonair Rule—well, he was off somewhere, wasn't he?"

"So," I said, pausing in the doorway to the kitchen and turning around, "you admit you killed Abigail Locke."

"Of course I admit it. She was a fraud, a charlatan, and a whore, who didn't deserve to live."

"Ah," I said, as if in agreement. And then I went into the kitchen, which was a mistake. A big mistake. A little cry escaped me when I saw what must once have been Indigo Swann, and that cry brought Wish Stephenson, and then all hell broke loose.

He had tortured her. She was indeed a female, tall, apparently accustomed to wear men's clothes. That she was female was evident from her bare and mutilated breasts, and the clothes she partially wore were trousers, undone; a shirt hanging open, with the buttons all ripped off; a jacket that matched the trousers . . . except for the patches that were soaked in blood. He had tortured her. She was seated in a contraption like a very high-backed chair, with a vise arrangement to hold one's head in place. I quickly surmised that this was so that the person in the chair would be forced to look into Van Zant's eyes.

Poor Indigo Swann had no eyes anymore. They had been burnt out. And her nipples had been burnt off, and her navel; and then she had been strangled with a four-in-hand tie, probably the very tie she had been wearing with that very nicely cut man's suit. As I looked at her I knew I would never, myself, dress as a man again. I'd never be able to, because from now ever after, when I saw a woman dressed in male clothing, I would think of Indigo.

"She had to be punished," Van Zant said to Wish Stephenson. "She would not tell me what I wanted to know, even under hypnosis. She was stubborn, wicked, disobedient."

Poor Wish had turned white as a ghost. His eyes, which, as I previously mentioned, were bloodshot, burned hot as the real coals that had put out the eyes of Indigo Swann.

"So," Van Zant said, in that ever so superior voice of his, "you, Mr. Stephenson, will have to tell me everything she knew. Because she did tell *you* everything, I know she did. You will cooperate because you were a much better hypnotic subject than she was. You will go into trance, deeper and deeper, until you tell me everything I need to know."

As Van Zant said this, Wish began to sway on his feet. In spite of his anger, which I could feel from many feet away, Wish's eyelids drooped until they were half closed.

302

"Deeper and deeper," Van Zant said. "Now, you will give me the gun. That's right. . . ."

But Wish did not give Van Zant the gun. He was not in deep trance, as anyone who knew him well could have told you. He was instead almost paralyzed by grief and rage, unable to move and scarcely able to speak.

Van Zant had no weapon; I still had my walking stick in my right hand. Like many a man of science and intellect, William Van Zant was arrogant—and I intended to exploit that weakness to my advantage. In one quick, practiced motion I unsheathed my blade, and I used it to keep the villain at a distance while I walked over to Wish and simply said quietly, "Wish, give me the gun." He did.

I ordered Van Zant, "Sit down at this table and stay there, or I'll blow your sleek, mean little head off with this revolver, and when I've done that I'll slash you to ribbons to make up for what you did to my mattress and pillows. That *was* you, I presume?"

Van Zant, obediently taking a chair, nodded yes. Like all persons of his type, if you took away his cherished but superficial trappings of power, he crumpled. Such men are not built to stand and fight, they are essentially cowards.

I asked Wish if he were up to going after the police and he said he was, that the shock of seeing what Van Zant had done to Indigo had broken through the hypnotic suggestions the psychologist had planted in his mind. "I'm sorry, Fremont," he said miserably.

"Don't be sorry, just go for help," I said.

"Let me cover her first," Wish said miserably, nodding toward the mutilated body of Indigo.

"Were you very fond of her, Wish?" I whispered.

He nodded. "I loved her. I never loved a woman until Indigo, not really. I only knew her for"—he hung his head abjectly—"less than three weeks."

I made a decision. "Cover her, then, even though the police won't like it. I'll say I told you to, I'll take the blame."

Wish covered Indigo, or Ngaio, I never did know which was her real name, with a bedspread he brought from upstairs. Then he left, and while he was bringing back the police, I got to ask my own questions of William Van Zant.

"You were in love with Abigail Locke, and she rejected you," I began.

Van Zant just sneered and preened a bit. He could see his image in the glass of the back door.

"You vowed to have revenge on her. But why kill her?"

"Because, as I keep telling you, she deserved to die. All those women do. Eventually I'd have killed them all. Next question."

"And you don't mind if everybody knows you killed Abigail Locke and Ingrid Swann."

"I'll deny it in court, mind you."

I ignored that. "But poor Indigo—what did she ever do to you?"

"She knew about my business dealings, which your friend and colleague Mr. Stephenson also found out. A very persistent fellow, Mr. Stephenson. He dogged me for weeks, always just a step behind me, before I was able to find out who he was. All these little intertwined relationships—ha-ha"—he laughed in a most unpleasant manner—"it's positively incestuous! You work with Stephenson, Indigo is the sister of another medium who had to die, and the two of them—Stephenson and Indigo—between them could destroy everything I've done to make myself a wealthy man so that I could leave this psychologist sham behind me forever."

"These things you've done to make yourself wealthy—they'd be illegal, one presumes."

"One presumes correctly. Haven't you guessed? Hasn't your colleague hinted? Don't you have any imagination, Fremont Jones?"

"Oh, I can guess, all right. It's a wonder you can sleep at night."

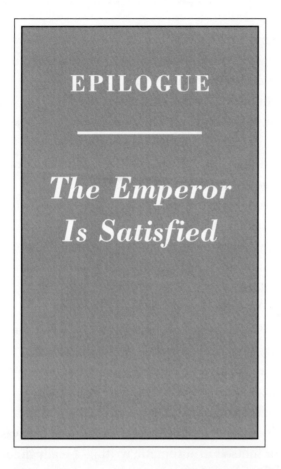

EPILOGUE

The Emperor Is Satisfied

AS DIFFICULT as it was to believe, by lunchtime the police had arrested William Van Zant, who was no more a doctor than I am, and Wish and Michael and Edna—who in the space of a couple of hours had become a great favorite of Michael's, and vice versa—and I were having a late lunch around the kitchen table. There was more interest in talk than in food.

Wish had explained to us how for weeks he had followed the progress of someone who was opening and emptying graves in forgotten little graveyards that dotted the Richmond District, then claiming the plots as newly cleared land and selling it for development. That someone turned out to be William Van Zant, and the person who had first identified him had been none other than Indigo Swann—who either had or had not been Ingrid's real sister. Now we would never know; I certainly didn't intend to make any effort to find out, because Wish had been in love with Indigo. It would do him no kindness to find out the truth, if that truth (say, that the two were lesbian lovers, or worse, incestuous sisters) were damaging to the image of his love.

"Your testimony and Wish's will put Van Zant in prison and maybe will hang him for murder," Michael said.

"And what is more important, the J&K Agency will get a lot of favorable publicity!" I said.

"Yes, you've done well, Fremont." Michael's compliment, his approval, was what I had been waiting for. "And so have you, Wish," he added.

"Maybe," Wish said. He was sunk in gloom.

I was about to suggest that he go home and rest for the remainder of the day when the little bell on the front door rang out and a woman's clear, high voice called out, "We're back! We found it!"

We all looked at each other around the table.

"Emperor Norton's treasure," I explained. "I sent Patrick and Frances to look for it, following instructions she'd received from the Emperor himself in automatic writing. I really did it just to get them out of my hair, I never expected them to *find* anything."

They came into the kitchen hand in hand, Patrick and Frances, both a bit disheveled, with smudges of dirt here and there, and smiles so incandescent they could have lit a goodly portion of San Francisco through the night.

Frances had obviously declared herself permanent spokesman of this pair, for she burbled on, "We saw you, Fremont, you and Wish, we were only a couple of blocks away, but then you went and disappeared into some house."

"Where were you?" I asked.

Frances shrugged, "Who cares?" She looked at Patrick.

He said, "We were in some cemetery, where half the graves had been opened and robbed. It was really, really unpleasant and spooky."

"We weren't there for the graves though, we were there because of this one particular old tree—"

Patrick had caught her enthusiasm now and took over, "—which was easy to find. It's a live oak and there aren't too many as big and as old as that one."

"And you'll never guess what!" Frances said, beaming.

I said my line: "What?"

"It was where he said it was," Frances said, her eyes open wide in amazement.

"Buried under the tree!" This they both said simultaneously, and again: "Look!"

The Emperor's treasure was wrapped in burlap that smelled to high heaven—and I do mean high; and it shed little bits and pieces of dirt as it was unrolled on the table. Patrick Rule did the unrolling honors, and then Frances lifted out a shining object: A ceremonial sword with a gold hilt, as untarnished as if it had been placed in the ground only yesterday!

"A fine piece," Michael murmured appreciatively.

"It's to be given to the City," Frances explained, "those are the Emperor's wishes. And it should sit in a glass case in a museum with a card that says: *Gift to the People of This Fair City with kindest regards from Norton I, Emperor of the United States of America and Protector of Mexico.*"

"But this," said Patrick, picking up a second, larger object from that burlap nest, "is for us to keep, and for all of us to remember, courtesy of the Emperor."

The object was a wooden sign, hand-carved, possibly by the Emperor himself. It had once been painted with red paint highlighting a surface of natural wood. And the sign said:

FOLLOW YOUR HEART.